For my mother, whose imperfectly perfect
self is an inspiration to so many.

While it may take a village to raise a child, it takes boundless creativity and buckets of intestinal fortitude to write a good fantasy novel. And although I had no village, I would like to express my gratitude to some exceptional folks who provided me support along the way.

Thanks to Sharon, my wife, and Jon, my friend, for walking the Path of the Reliquary and providing feedback and encouragement.

Thank you to Vincent Dominguez for designing the Horsemen Chronicles' road signs and rest stops along the information super-highway.

CHAPTER 1

It was a cool Italian morning, too early for most people. Marcello Rizzo, dressed in beige pleated slacks, white shirt, and black Armani jacket, stood on the yellow line and stared at the watchful faces inside the belly of the green-painted beast. Some showed angst, others concern, but most were just annoyed. With a heavy sigh, the recently minted Vanguard agent stepped through the side of the metal car, knowing full well that the train was a means to accountability, a conduit to his subjugation, at least for the next seventy-two hours. As the train left the platform ten minutes behind schedule, Marcello pulled the black satchel from around his shoulder, nestling the leather tote into the overhead compartment and settled into the window-side wooden bench for the one and one-half hour trip from Torino to Cernusco sul Naviglio, a small town on the outskirts of Milan.

A ninety-eight minute ass-numbing ride later, Marcello collected his satchel from the alcove above his head, slung it back over his shoulder and stepped onto the platform, thankful to be off the train.

"*Dai!*" he said, rubbing his left ass cheek, coaxing his gait back to normalcy as he limped along into the empty train station.

After taming the growls emanating from the pit of his stomach with a cup of espresso and two chocolate-filled croissants at the depot bar, Marcello exited the train station and began the five-block trek to his impending servitude. Aside from a stray dog sniffing at a food container in the gutter, Marcello was alone in the early morning hours of the sleepy city.

With his Brutini loafers clicking on the sidewalk, Marcello made quick work of four blocks and turned the corner onto Via Garibaldi. Five meters ahead, the avenue gave way to an open expanse: a public garden specked with tall trees, ponds, romantic bridges, and rolling green hills scarred by a winding gravel walkway. A dark blue Enel utility truck, parked at the curb, and a vagrant sitting on a park bench were the only blemishes on the flawless boulevard countenance. In stark contrast to the open expanse, ran a wrought-iron fence some eight-feet high and spanning the length of the block. The area inside the metal enclosure was littered with newspaper, and the land looked as valuable as sand in the desert, but the entwined iron screamed "Move on—we don't want you here."

Marcello walked close to the black railing, as he had done over the past six months, sticking his fingers between the bars, and with each passing step watched his middle digit leap from one twisted rail to the next.

The tap, tap, tap of his finger stirred a memory: him sitting at his commencement from Politecnico di Torino, bored off his ass. He remembered how he tapped his knee to break up the energy-sucking monotony of the chancellor's address and to take his mind off of the Windsor noose cutting off the blood to his brain. Boredom was his greatest adversary. His greatest fear.

Graduating at the top of his class with a degree in computer engineering and computer science had been no great feat for Marcello: he had always had a way with numbers. His brain was just wired that way. The more analytical and technical the subject, the easier it was and the more bored he'd soon become.

As graduation drew close, he was courted by leading hi-tech firms throughout Europe and was offered a position at Torino Piemonte Aerospace, which, when he thought about it, probably would have become boring...if, that is, he'd shown up on his first day, and if it hadn't been for the bald man wearing the wool Dolce & Gabbana three-piece suit sitting in the front row of the commencement ceremony.

Marcello recalled the words the bald man spouted as he passed by and how he fixed his eyes on the man, thinking that he was someone's demented grandfather off the leash. He also remembered how the man's words, *"La tua vita è noioso"*—"Your life is boring"—stopped him in his tracks. "Who is this man?" Marcello thought. "He doesn't know me."

But he did. He knew too well.

"*Che cosa?*" was the best response Marcello could muster. And the simple "What?" was all the opening the bald man needed.

"My name is Zachariah Prond," the bald man continued in English. "How'd you like a real challenge?"

It was a challenge believing the wild story of monsters, even more so believing the money they were throwing at him, but the triple-encrypted rotating algorithms with parallel hardware redundancy he had developed for the Vanguard, not so much. The code was simple for him. Marcello was bored still.

Marcello's memories dissolved into the present as his finger leapt from the last iron rail to a stone column. His middle finger traced the labyrinthine grout groove of the three-meter-high stone pillar until it reached a white intercom whose dark black camera eye stared back at him.

He punched in the five-digit code.

"Rizzo, would you mind not tripping the sensors along the whole fucking block," spouted the Cyclops.

Marcello winked at the lifeless eye and shrugged.

"Asshole," cracked the speaker.

Marcello held up a tired and blackened middle finger.

"Fuck you, too," the voice crowed, only to be drowned out by the loud buzzer.

Marcello pushed open the spiked gate barring the stone walkway, entered 6 Via Garibaldi, and headed up the long cobblestone path toward a two-level house. Marcello looked at his "office" and shook his head. To anyone looking the natural beige stone walls punctuated by wooden shutters and arched doorways cried country villa, and the vine-laden trellises completed the illusion. No one could have suspected this was a hi-tech Western European data communication and surveillance relay for a secret organization. Hell, he hadn't believed it until he'd seen the Vanguard technology hidden within.

From the shadows of the ivy-covered trellis came the sound of automatic weapons cocking as two Vanguard agents armed with Heckler & Koch MP5 submachine guns stepped into view, directing the baffled muzzles at Marcello.

"*Buon giorno,*" said one sentry.

"*Come vanno le cose?*" Marcello responded. His typical "How are things?" never failed to put the guard at ease, and Marcello unfastened his satchel, pulled out his authorization badge, and handed it to the guard.

"*Tedioso,*" the guard said, his eyes shifting from the badge to Marcello's face. "Okay," the sentry continued, handing the badge back, he lowered his weapon.

Marcello nodded. "*Ciao,*" he said stepping forward along the cobblestones. His lips turned up as he reflected that some lives were always going to be full of boredom.

Marcello stepped up onto the arched portico, opened the oak door, and entered the Vanguard surveillance center.

"Work, you piece of crap!" Abelia exclaimed.

With her hair in a bun and wearing cat-rimmed glasses, the middle-aged blond woman sitting behind the desk looked like a receptionist. The two Baretta .45 caliber pistols, one holstered under each arm adorning her white blouse, reaffirmed her role not as administrator but protector, one of six Vanguard sentries in and around the grounds. She was a trained killer.

In front of her sat seven closed-circuit TV monitors, and she, like a lion tamer in the circus, was master of them all and could shoot a piercing gaze at one or the group, spotting a warning or potential threat. Today, however, her cats were not behaving.

"Work!" she demanded.

"Good morning to you, too, Abelia," Marcello said with a touch of sarcasm.

"Not you," she said, slapping the top of one hissing monitor. "This piece of crap."

Marcello looked at the flickering snow on all seven screens. "December already?" he quipped.

"Smartass. The monitors haven't been working all day. One minute they're fine…" Her eyes flashed across the line of monitors, falling onto different black and white images of the surveillance center grounds. "See!" she said, pointing at the screens. "But the next, nothing but snow." As if on cue, static blanketed the screens. "Shit," she said, banging the top of the cubes like a drum set.

"What of the servers?" Marcello asked, his sarcasm replaced with seriousness.

"Your babies are fine. The problem is with the security system: the closed-circuit TV and the magnetic front gate."

«‹‹—»›»

Across the street, the vagrant's earth-crusted bare feet crunched the gravel beneath the park bench. He wore a long, dirty tunic that was ragged and threadbare in places. With a black goatee encircling a crooked smile, and long, stringy, dirty hair, the man looked like an escapee from a mental hospital. The sun stung his eyes, and he cursed the yellow ball above his head. He buried his dirty face in dirtier palms and struggled to find memories in the mist clouding his mind, concealing the answers to the questions pounding in his head. Where was he? Who released him? Where were the others?

Lifting his head, the vagrant looked from the corralled country villa in the background to the spiked gate in the foreground His answers were not at the end of a garden path. No, his answers must be inside the gated stronghold standing before him.

As the vagrant slid forward, grimy nails digging into the edge of the bench, pulse quickening, muscles tensing, his attention was diverted by a workman walking up the boulevard toward the gate. The man was wearing a yellow hard hat, a utility belt, and a dark blue jumpsuit with the letters *ENEL* in yellow on the back. He stepped in front of the spiked metal barrier, wrapped long, gloved fingers around the twisted iron, and pushed. With a click, the gate swung open. The Enel workman stepped inside 6 Via Garibaldi and trudged up the path.

The vagrant's dirt-smudged face exhaled, and he sat back, watching this new character play his part in the scene, content for the moment to simply observe.

«‹‹—»›»

Inside the converted villa, Marcello left the blond sentry to battle her gremlins and pushed open glass doors to exit the reception area. He walked down the hall and stopped and entered a small room where two espresso machines sat on a quartz countertop like Sirens beckoning passersby. Two pub tables positioned in the center of the space joined the chorus of distraction; one had already captured a traveler, Stefano Perugino, the only other computer engineer in the ten-person Vanguard facility.

"How was the pussy this weekend?" Stefano asked, scooping a spoonful of his wife's homemade frittata into his mouth.

Marcello pulled a porcelain espresso cup from the rack and positioned it on the drip tray. "You need to ask your wife to fuck you more often."

"Just wait until you're married, and we'll talk about who fucks more often," Stefano answered, smiling. "Well?"

As the espresso filled his cup, Marcello thought about the woman he had been with over the last two days: Camilla, her large, wide-set eyes, smooth skin, and full lips. She had kept his cock hard and ridden him until he was spent, wanting only sleep. He'd made it a point to make plans with her for next weekend, and he was looking forward to spending those days between her legs.

Marcello picked up his espresso, turned. "I will need to give this"—with his free hand, he grabbed his crotch—"three days to recover. She almost fucked me to death." He took a sip of the black brew. "Ah, her legs are ones I want to die between."

"There are worse ways to die, my friend," Stefano said, grinning, his mouth full of frittata.

Marcello finished his espresso and exited the room. He turned the corner and passed two doors labeled WC, pausing briefly to consider the effects of the latest espresso shot on his overdue morning constitution before continuing into the heart of the surveillance center, comprised of wall-to-wall glass-encased rack-mounted servers, switches, wires, and blinking lights.

Two female data analysts sat in the center of the room, their fingers skipping along keyboard consoles. Above them, a large LCD screen hung from the ceiling. On it, three blinking red dots flashed on a digital atlas. Next to each crimson spot, a picture: a raven-haired, gothic beauty in the United Kingdom, a young scientist in Hungary, and a tall blue-eyed soldier in the United States.

Marcello pulled off his Armani jacket and rolled up his sleeves, smiling at the two Vanguard sentries in the room. The guards, armed with automatic weapons, stood at attention, one by the entrance, the other by the bookcase of servers. They ignored the gesture, their seemingly lifeless expressions as cold as the computer hardware around them.

«««—»»»

Outside, the sun warmed the villa's brown stone. The sky's radiance reflected off the metal pliers, screwdrivers and wire strippers in the Enel workman's swaying tool pouch. The sun's rays did not touch a baffled barrel hanging covered at the back: a tool foreign to an electrician's tool belt.

"We have an electrician coming up," barked one guard into his shoulder mic.

Two other sentries stepped from around from the back of the country house to see the Enel workman walking up the pathway.

"Abelia must have finally had enough of the intermittent video feed," said one guard to the other, not seeing the workman as a threat and lowering his submachine gun.

A mistake the Vanguard sentry was to make once in his now-shortened life. The faux-electrician smiled and waved with his left hand while reaching behind his back with his right. He gripped the butt of the baffled tool and plucked it from the leather pouch. Each Vanguard sentry stared wide-eyed at the silenced Glock 18 as the *pfffft...pfffft...pfffft*...clipped the electrical circuits of each man's brain.

The Enel assassin stepped onto the arched portico and pointed the gun at the center of the oak door.

On the other side of the door, opposite the baffled barrel, Abelia sat at her console and continued to battle for a clear video feed.

"Come on!" she shouted, slapping the top of the front entrance monitor. The intermittent snow melted away, and the blond sentry saw the man in the dark jumpsuit and the gun pointed at the door.

The returning static on the screen heralded the sting in Abelia's chest. In front of her, three light beams spilled through holes in the brown door. She fought for a single breath where there was none and peered down at the red stain soaking into her white blouse. Darkness rushed in from all sides and swallowed her up.

Another shot blasted the door lock to pieces and the assassin crossed the threshold of the converted country house and, stepping through the hall, orchestrated a cacophony of death. Passing the bar, he shot Stefano. Two bullets parted the mouthful of frittata before cleaving the back of the engineer's throat. The Enel gunman pulled a fresh clip from his tool pouch, snapped it in, and flicked the Glock's selector switch; the weapon was fully automatic. The assassin rushed into the main surveillance center, grabbed the sentry nearest the entryway, buried the automatic pistol in his chest, and fired. The guard's heart was ripped to pieces.

High-pitched shrieks and screams filled the room to bursting.

Using the dead Vanguard as a shield, the assassin spun and unleashed a volley of bullets at the remaining Vanguard sentry. The spray of deadly shells peppered the guard, whose body shook and quaked, dancing to the muted serenade of death.

Marcello's body froze as bullets ripped through the room. His analytical mind shut down, adrenaline flooded his cells, and all rational thought was gone. He was lost to panic, paralyzed by fear, racked with pain. Marcello screamed and fell to the floor. He felt as if a hot poker had seared through his arm. He pulled up his shirt sleeve, and his eyes bulged at the sight of jagged bone sticking out of his arm like splintered wood.

Another burst from the Glock 18 quieted the women's screams.

Marcello screwed his eyes shut, trying to ride out the wave of nausea and pain. Tight lines creased his forehead. He clenched his teeth and held his breath, hoping to suffocate the agony pulsing up and down his shattered arm.

Frightening silence choked the room.

As shock rolled over Marcello, the biting torrent eased. He exhaled and panted heavily, gulping air as if it were an elixir.

Between his gasps, Marcello heard rapping metal on metal.

Tap! Tap! Tap! The assassin drummed the Glock barrel on the counter.

The tapping sparked images in Marcello's mind of commencement, thoughts of Zachariah Prond, his words *"La tua vita è noioso"* stuck in his brain. Was this the challenge the bald man wearing the Dolce & Gabbana suit had been referring to?

Marcello scooted his ass across the stone tile and behind a metal desk. A burning wave crashed over him, and he gritted his teeth, trying to stem the flood of pain. "Maybe a boring life is not so bad," he thought, his lips curling into a grimace-like smile.

As the tapping sound grew closer, Marcello held his breath. His mind spun like a ball on a roulette wheel of thoughts, finally coming to rest on the image of Camilla, her supple body straddling his….

Tap! Tap! Tap!

Marcello's thoughts returned to the here and now, and the pain. He stared up at the man in the dark blue jumpsuit with yellow Enel lettering straddling over him. He stared into the metal cylinder pointed at his head.

"These are not the legs I wanted to die between" was the last thought racing through Marcello's mind before the bullet spilled his analytical brain on the stone floor.

‹‹‹—›››

Outside, sitting on the park bench, the vagrant watched the Enel workman stride down the stone walkway and exit the gated compound, closing the gate behind him. Moments later, the silence of the garden was broken by the roar of a diesel engine. His unfathomable eyes watched as the dark blue Enel truck passed by and turned off Via Garibaldi.

The tramp's bearded lips curled upward. He rocked back and forth in his wooden seat and wriggled his dirty feet, burying them into the warm gravel like a child expending nervous energy. The vagrant stood up, kicking his blackened feet free from the gravel. He lumbered across the boulevard and stood in front of the wrought-iron gate. Mimicking the workman's actions, he wrapped a grimy hand around one twisted bar and pushed—the gate swung open.

The man placed one disheveled foot after another upon the warm cobblestone walkway and stepped slowly toward the Vanguard villa until his path was barred by the bodies of the fallen Vanguard sentries.

He knelt down over one body. With eyes full of wonder, he felt the texture of the cloth between his dirty fingers and brushed the microphone affixed to the dead shoulder, which sparked and popped, a swirl of smoke rising into the air. The vagrant pulled his hand away with a grunt. He reached over and stroked the gleaming tactical watch on the corpse's wrist; at his touch, the ticking second hand stopped cold.

From the corner of his eye, the vagrant spotted the Heckler & Koch MP5 submachine gun lying beside the dead sentry.

He stared at the gun with the innocence of a child. As the seconds drifted by, curiosity overwhelmed him: he reached out a dirty hand and touched the butt.

The weapon sprung to life as though an invisible finger had depressed the trigger. The machine gun cavorted on the ground as 9 mm shells rocketed from the baffled barrel, thirteen rounds per second, and buzzed through the air, cutting into the stone wall and wood shutters of the country house.

The vagrant jumped back, eyes wide, mouth agape.

With a final crack, the gun fell silent. The lines in the dirty man's face contorted into a confused road map. *"Kashurra,"* he said in an ancient tongue. "Amazing."

The filthy visitor continued up the walkway, stepped onto the arched portico, and entered the building.

He stared at the blond woman; her head tilted to one side, as if asleep on the job. The red stain soaked through the entire front of her blouse, blood dripping into a sanguine puddle on the floor beneath her. Turning his head, he listened to the buzz from the seven closed-circuit TV monitors on the counter. He reached out a dirty hand to the metal boxes, which sputtered and popped in unison, sending white wisps of smoke into the air.

The vagrant continued through the Vanguard building. Walking into the bar, he spotted the dead man on the floor and, more interesting to him, food on the table. The tramp picked up the plate of cold frittata, sniffed, turned up his nose, and tossed it on the floor.

In the next moment, the espresso maker sprang to life, grinding beans in a raucous roar. Steaming black liquid flowed from the spout. The man stuck his finger into the scalding stream. There was no reflexive escape from pain, no scream, as the boiling brew streamed over his dirty digit: the man felt nothing.

Wiping his finger on his stained and tattered tunic, the vagrant shuffled into the hallway, pushed open the glass doors and entered the main surveillance center.

His face was like that of a child staring at the jumbled pieces of a Picasso, a mask of confusion. His eyes rolled over rack after rack of glass-encased data servers. Red, yellow, and green lights winked at him. The whoosh of fans and power supplies filled his ears.

His gaze floated up to the LCD monitor. A spark of recognition shocked his senses. His gaze hardened and his brows narrowed and he stared at the images on the screen. *"Sananu,"* he said—"others" in his dead language—his jaw and fists clenched.

His body shook as he struggled to contain the anger burning inside him. The din from overworked fans and power supplies grew louder and louder, reaching a crescendo.

The vagrant screamed, *"Sananu!"* and he plowed his fist through the glass, tearing into the metal servers.

Sparks flew as the power surged around his balled hand. His fist was engulfed in a red brilliance that flowed into him like a transfusion. The overhead fluorescent lights popped. All three walls of racked electrical equipment blew up, and the transformers caught fire. In the shattered glass, the vagrant stared at his firelit reflection. In his face, clarity replaced confusion. Awareness displaced ignorance.

The vagrant pulled his hand back unscathed and touched his dirty face, stroked his stringy hair. In the spark-laden room, he peered down at Marcello Rizzo's corpse.

«« — »»

Later, outside, the Italian sun beat down on the country house as a man ambled down the path. His face and hands were clean, his hair was pulled back in a ponytail, and he sported borrowed beige and blood spotted pleated slacks, white shirt, and black Armani jacket. The vagrant smiled and walked with a swagger as his slightly used Brutini loafers clicked on the smooth cobblestone.

CHAPTER 2

The floral ballroom was a buzz of activity. The shy mountain laurels and wild columbine, dressed in a mosaic of yellow, red, white, and orange, mingled on the grassy dance floor. As the warbler's ringing chippy-chuppy, chippy-chuppy filled the Greenwich, Connecticut, countryside, the dancers rhythmically nodded on slender stems and swayed in the late afternoon breeze. A ruby-throated hummingbird glided from flower to flower, the avian Casanova cutting in on the flowered tangos, foxtrots and rumbas.

Faye Monroe sat on cool leather upholstery on the passenger side of a nondescript black sedan at the end of Round Ridge Road. The Pulitzer-Prize winning photojournalist was oblivious to the picturesque promenade around her. Her Leica camera with 300mm zoom lens sat idle next to her, as did her Vanguard partner, Julian Adeyemi.

Her wide eyes, with dark bags under them, stared down at the tablet in her lap and the image of a tall, handsome man in uniform shaking hands with dignitaries. Each swipe of her right index finger stabbed at the memory of Ben Sasson. She brushed another picture into view. Ben receiving a commendation from Mossad…he was brave. Another stroke of her finger, another picture of his past: a younger Ben Sasson wearing a baseball uniform…he was strong. Swipe: Ben in a Harvard University sweatshirt, with his roommates…he was smart. Swipe: Ben holding a woman, his late wife…he was committed.

Faye shifted her gaze to her left hand and to the gold band around her middle finger. She caresséd the wedding band and spun it around her finger. It was his, not hers, but it was her reminder.

Swipe: she looked down at Ben's chiseled chin, his lips curled up warmly, and those penetrating blue eyes. She twisted the ring, a reminder that he was kind, that he was a good man.

Swipe: Faye stared at the black-and-white photo, one she'd shot two weeks ago on one of her many unsanctioned surveillances. Ben leaning against a balcony railing, staring out, his face hard, creased, his jaw clenched. Where once there had been kindness now was hate, an almost palpable hostility. He was a man possessed.

Faye's lips curved down as she stared through the photo on her lap, her mind lost in the past.

It was eight months ago that she had been a photojournalist with the Tel Aviv *Times*, and a damn good one at that. Sure, she had seen her share of big news stories and bloody war zones, but nothing could have prepared her to witness the test of a deadly bioweapon, or the cruel arms dealer wielding it; the same bastard who murdered her parents, killed her friends.

The last year of her life had been a horror movie, and in it she was driving down Crap Alley en route to Hell's Diner.

Faye remembered the Vanguard assassin's words. "All folklore is based on some remnants of truth. The Bible is no exception. The Horsemen are very real. They are immortal, and their only goal is to enslave mankind."

The Four Horsemen of the Apocalypse. Even now, after all of the shit she'd been through, it was still hard for her to believe that the monsters were real. Harder still was the revelation that the architect of her fucked-up childhood, the arms dealer who had taken away every-thing near and dear to her, was the Warrior Horseman, an immortal warmongering S.O.B.

The horror movie called Faye Monroe then added a disturbing and nerve-fraying score, a mix of prog-rock and paranoiac orchestral music. Faye recalled how her body had frozen when she'd heard the assassin's insanity: You are marked for death.

Faye's memories flashed again to Ben Sasson, the Mossad agent who had saved her from the Vanguard hit squad. Her face flushed as she thought about him. The immediate attraction; how he was unlike any man she'd met: driven, broken, a little like her in a lot of ways.

Her thoughts soured as she remembered the night the Vanguard came for her and her question to the remaining gunman, "Why do the Vanguard want to kill me?"

And then it came, the coup de grace. The assassin regarded her solemnly. "You are the Host to the fourth Horseman." There it was, her "Oh Fuck" moment. She was possessed by Atra, the Spirit of Famine. Without knowing it, she had just been served Hell's Diner's specialty: a steaming pile of bile-laced vomit with a side order of shit.

Her pain and suffering didn't end there. Hell's Diner's second course: a stack of yellow-stained urinal cakes. In a cruel twist of fate with a bite of bitter irony, Ben sacrificed himself to free her from the Spirit of Famine, but in doing so was in turn possessed. He was now an immortal, one of the Horsemen of the Apocalypse. He was no longer just Ben Sasson, the man she had fallen in love with. He was also War, Horseman of the Apocalypse, a man…no, a monster that she despised with every fiber in her body.

Faye stared out the sedan's side window. She overlooked the last image reflecting up from the tablet in her lap: a self-portrait of melancholy.

Her eyes rolled over the green hills, the shimmering grass enthralling, transfixing her gaze; she couldn't pull her eyes away. Her mind wandered and found its way to memories of Zachariah Prond, the leader of the Vanguard.

"We don't fix Horsemen!" were his harsh words, his response to her plea: "We owe it to Ben to fix this!"

The Vanguard were the watchmen. Their charter: shield humanity from knowledge of the existence of the Horsemen, minimize their damage, and step in, as was the case with Faye, to prevent the return of Famine, the key to unlocking the full supernatural power of the Four Horsemen of the Apocalypse, which would mean the end of humanity.

At least the Vanguard's chorus to Faye's queries was consistent. "You're fucking kidding, right?" "What are you talking about?" "Get the hell out of here!" They thought she was crazy. The Vanguard weren't about to lift a finger to help free Ben from the spirit that possessed him, so she did all she could…alone. She spent hours, which led to days, which led to weeks and months pouring over the Vanguard archives. She read every scrap of paper and digital file with any reference to the Warrior Horseman.

She also sought out everyone she could, outside the Vanguard, without the Order's knowledge or approval, anyone who would listen: priests, monks, rabbis, carnival psychics, and gypsies, searching for a clue. In every case, she got the same response: laughter and then jeering, often followed by a call to the local authorities or psyche ward to come take her away.

The hum of the ruby-throated bird fluttering across her field of view broke the spell of the swaying grass. Faye's head snapped up.

"Faye?" Julian asked, staring at her from the driver's side, a French accent hiding beneath his English, "You okay?"

Her mind rebooted, pushing all of the past memories aside.

"Yeah, fine," she answered, thumbing the turquoise teardrop pendant around her neck. She reached over, grabbed her camera, and zoomed in on the 1931 Georgian Colonial. The stone monolith stood on a rise above a Civil War rock wall like a war-torn general overlooking his weary troops.

Julian Adeyemi raised the binoculars hanging from around his neck and peered at the rocky manor, his short-sleeve shirt straining to contain the biceps beneath.

"Still no sign of him," Julian announced. "I doubt the fucker is even in there."

One thing about Julian, Faye thought, he always spoke his mind, whether you wanted to hear it or not. It was just his way.

Nigerian-born, he'd been given away by his parents, who were working in France, when he was eight months old. He'd grown up in an orphanage staffed by nuns with no other African children, a climate chilly at best given repeated incidents of being physically attacked because of the color of his skin and his nickname: Julie. He took to fighting and was good at it. At seventeen, he was downright dangerous, almost killing two boys trying to steal his socks. The nuns at Petites Soeurs de la Charité pulled some strings and Julian was "invited" into the French military, and after 4 years, he was part of the French Army Special Forces, the 1st Marine Infantry Parachute Regiment, or the 1er RPIMa.

"He's in there," Faye responded, zooming in on the double French doors leading out onto a balcony, a location that had delivered results in the past.

"How do you know?" he said, lowering the binoculars. "No one has seen him for over two weeks. We're probably babysitting an empty house."

Faye lowered her camera and turned toward her partner. "The Vanguard says, 'Do surveillance,' then we do surveillance."

Faye targeted the balcony, panning her lens across the empty glass doors.

"You know," Julian said, clutching the binoculars in his lap, "I asked for this time off to be with my kids."

"Uh-huh," she mumbled with an absent nod, and then fell back into silence. Faye wished he would stop the chitchat, grow a pair, and shut the fuck up.

«««—»»»

On the rise above the black sedan, the dull blade of the afternoon light stabbed the glass doors of the Georgian Colonial but failed to pierce the shadows of the mansion study. Inside the dark wood and rough stone room, a Victorian oak desk, cluttered with papers, was pushed flat against the wall off to the right, next to a small table. A mounted stag with eight-point rack spanning forty inches across hung above, its glassy eyes ever watchful over the contents in the room: a telescope balanced on a tripod, a suit of armor from the Middle Ages, two cross-mounted blunderbusses, a standing Kentucky longrifle from the American Revolution, and a wall filled with medieval weaponry. Tall mahogany bookshelves partially lined two other walls. A lighted glass display case stood between the bookshelves.

In the center of the room, the Warrior Horseman sat slouched low in his large chair, elbow on the armrest, head to one side propped up on a clawed fist. From his throne, his cool blue eyes held a steady gaze forward into the large lighted cabinet. A saluki, a long-haired Persian Greyhound, lay at his side, uninterested. The illumination from the showcase cast a dim glow across the Horseman's creased and hardened features.

War's sharp eyes scanned across his treasures gathered over millennia, like a falcon spotting its prey. He first fixed his sight on a twelve-inch polished-steel dagger, the handle decorated with Roman eagles and griffins. Gold accents decorated the scabbard.

His eyes traced the etchings on the blade: *SPQR*.

The Horseman's lips curled up. "*Senatus Populus Que Romanus,*" he whispered: the Senate and the People of Rome. It was his dagger, and it was one of sixty that had stabbed and killed Julius Caesar. War

22

thought back to that late morning in the Theater of Pompey, when his power had enthralled the sixty Roman senators who, seething with the Horseman's anger, drew their daggers and killed the dictator on the Ides of March, 44BC.

War's gaze next set on a large circular shield. The one-meter, bronze-covered hoplon was pocked with a dozen holes where javelins and arrows had pierced. The red Greek letter lambda on the shield front was faded. The shield had belonged to King Leonidas I. War had taken it off the blood-soaked battlefield at Thermopylae.

His eyes rolled across the morning star cradled in its base. The silver spiked mace shimmered as it reflected the light. The medieval club was the last weapon held by King John of Bohemia. War remembered the bravery of the sightless fool as he rode into battle, he and all of his men's horses tied together, the king wildly swinging the morning star. John the Blind and his men had been slaughtered.

War stood up and stepped to the display case. His eyes focused on the jewel of his collection: a gold Ād tribal axe head with intricate etchings. A warm yellow luster reflected onto the Horseman's cold, hard face.

The Ād was one of the major pre-Islamic Arab tribes, from which the present ruling family of Oman was descended. The ceremonial axe was used by Ād kinsman to behead kings and queens alike. Long presumed lost during the Crusades and the countless battles between warring faiths, no one, save its headsman now standing before it, knew of its existence.

War tapped the glass, admiring his golden treasure. "You will be home soon, my old friend."

«««—»»»

Meanwhile, in the four-door cell on the road below the English mansion, Julian Adeyemi's rant continued to assault Faye's ears. The level of angst in the car had grown thick and uncomfortable as second-hand cigar smoke. She would have to talk to her Vanguard jailers about this cruel and unusual punishment.

Faye rolled her eyes as the barrage of bitching and moaning continued.

"Four weeks ago, I asked four weeks ago for time off, and they still denied it. Can you believe that shit? You'd figure they'd be able to find a replacement, with what, over twenty-thousand agents."

Faye ignored Julian's complaints. With her camera planted on her face, she swung her field of view from one side of the French doors to the other.

"Now I'm missing my son's jujitsu promotion," he continued, looking at Faye as if hoping to get a trace of sympathy from her otherwise frigid exterior.

"He's a badass, just like his dad, but those assholes in the Order, they could give a shit." He slammed his fist against the steering wheel. "Damn! You'd think the Vanguard would let me have just one day off, but no, they said it was important for me to be on surveillance. It's always important."

Faye lowered her camera and turned to the frustrated Vanguard. "Listen, Julian, I'm sure your boy will understand. We have a job to do...both of us."

The Nigerian was oblivious to her words.

Julian gripped the steering wheel tight, his brows furrowed, veins bulging like a roadmap on the back of his hands. He stared forward at the emptiness in front of him, captivated by the scenery of his mind's eye.

"Why do you to waste your time trying to save him?" he asked.

"What?" Faye questioned.

"You're a fool," he continued, his tone harsh.

"Julian?" Faye asked. Her hand started to move toward his arm.

"He is mine. He shall forever be mine," he said, his eyes locked forward.

The words rocked Faye to her core.

"The man you once knew is dead. His soul is buried in my rage." The words spilled out again from Julian's lips, words not his own.

Faye raised her camera and peered through her high-powered zoom lens. She could see the tall, dark-haired Horseman through the glass doorway of the study. What she saw chilled her.

War was smiling.

"There is nothing you can do." Faye heard the words from the man beside her at the same time she saw the Horseman mouth them.

He was toying with her, channeling himself through the man's anger.

She could see Ben's lips move as the words filled her ears. "It's not fair. You watch and watch."

War grinned. It was a wicked grin, the kind that made the blood in Faye's veins run fast.

Faye's mind and heart raced. She could feel her pounding heartbeat ringing in her ears. All this time, while she had been watching him, he had been watching her.

"But he'll never be free," the Nigerian puppet continued. "What is a weak and frail woman to do?"

Faye stared at the Warrior Horseman through her lens watching the words part his lips: "What will you do?"

"How's this for a start?" she said, sticking out her middle finger and flipping him off.

Ben's face dissolved into the shadows of the mansion study.

She lowered her camera and raised her eyebrows, a satisfying smirk crossing her face.

At that moment, Julian released his viselike grip from the steering wheel. His head snapped back as if he had been startled awake from a nap.

"Julian?" Faye said, touching his sleeve.

He turned and faced her. "I said, you'd think the Vanguard would let me have just one day off, but no, they said it was important for me to be on surveillance. It's always important," he repeated, unaware of his recent marionette performance.

Faye muttered, "Yeah."

Julian raised the binoculars hanging from around his neck. "Any sign of him?" he asked.

"I…I don't know," Faye lied. "A shadow maybe." She looked down at the black-and-white image of Ben on the tablet.

She felt a pang in her heart. It was fear, mixed with anger and sadness. It was uneasiness deep in the pit of her stomach, the feeling that the Vanguard was right, that no matter what she did, Ben, or at least the Ben she knew, was lost.

Faye pushed the vile thought out of her mind. She spun Ben's ring around her finger. He was a fighter. She looked up at the stone mansion. He was still in there, fighting that monster. She would not give up on him. There had to be a way to free him from the Horseman spirit imprisoning him in his own body.

Julian Adeyemi's voice crashed through Faye's reflective moment. "Why is the Vanguard worried about this new War anyway?" he said, panning the binoculars to the far side of the mansion. "He hasn't done any 'warring' for months."

"It has served the Vanguard well over the centuries to be suspicious of the Horsemen, active and inactive," Faye answered.

25

"All I'm saying is, what kind of War…doesn't war?" He lowered the glasses. "If you ask me, this new host, this former Mossad agent… he's a pussy," he said with a smirk.

"No one's asking you," Faye responded sternly.

Raising the binoculars and scanning the far side of the mansion, the Nigerian Vanguard continued his reproach. "I'd want one to go one round with him, just one, to see if he's so tough."

Faye looked up from the photo, ignoring her partner's boasts, and stared out the front windshield. She thought about simpler things. Sometimes simple things were all that was needed: long walks, movies, cooking dinner with friends. Simple things were the anchors of a normal life's humdrum reality. What Faye wouldn't give to have a normal life.

She imagined Ben, her Ben, beside her. She felt a wave of peace and contentment wash over her. The mere thought of him walking beside her on a sandy beach gave her a sense of inexplicable joy.

"Yeah, I bet it would take one punch, one good punch," Julian said, balling up one fist.

Faye let herself imagine a life free of Horsemen and Vanguard, a life about new beginnings, hope…babies. A little flush rose to her cheeks.

The ruby-throated hummingbird fluttered motionless over the hood. Faye thought again about "simple things."

Julian began again. "He's lost his edge if you ask m—"

Thump!

Faye watched as the hummer plummeted to the car's hood, flopping around on the hot metal like a crazed windup toy. As the bird wound down, its heart slowing from 1,260 beats per minute to 30, Faye's eyes grew wide as she understood the reason for the hummer's condition: its left wing had been clipped off.

"Julian, did you see that?" Faye asked, her attention focused on the dying bird. "That hummingbird just dropped from the sky with one wi—"

The sound of ice cracking stopped Faye midsentence, and she looked over to spot the driver's side spiderweb-cracked windshield and the narrow fissure crawling across the glass toward her.

Faye turned to Julian, who was leaning into the driver's side window.

"Julian?"

Faye tugged her partner's sleeve, intent on grabbing his attention.

The Nigerian Vanguard's head flopped to the right, blood oozing down his cheek. Faye looked into the sightless socket of her dead partner.

Shards of glass lay in Julian's lap, not from the windshield, but from the binocular lens that had been shattered.

Faye felt the blood drain from her face, her breath coming in short and shallow gasps. All of her energy leaked away like water through a sieve. She lowered her head and stared at the photo of Ben's hateful gaze, hoping that the man she loved was still somewhere within.

《《—》》

From the small opening in glass doorway of the study, War looked down the smoking barrel of his Kentucky longrifle. "Is that edge sharp enough?"

CHAPTER 3

B aggy-billed white pelicans soared effortlessly on the breeze. A bright yellow yolk frying all day in the amber sky dipped into the turquoise soup.

Under the tawny backdrop, the white Vanguard research yacht *Excalibur* was anchored in the still waters off the coast of Paphos, a sleepy fishing village on the southwest coast of Cyprus. An abandoned offshore oil rig, fifty meters away from the research vessel, stood out awkwardly in the coastal sea like a principal overlooking a one-person high-school dance.

Beneath the surface, Michael Cantal finished his survey of the bottom, snatched the bright fluorescent-yellow pony bottle with regulator nestled in the sand, and began his ascent up the coral shelf. Splashes of brilliant color reflected off of his dive mask. Red and white fan coral. Purple brain coral. Some of the living colonies were shaped like boulders, while others were flat. Still others, pillar coral, stuck up like fingers in a glove.

Among the natural formations, a manmade intrusion stabbed the ocean bottom. The steel girder was decorated with countless barnacles, starfish, and mussels: gift wrapping from the sea.

As he ascended, Michael stopped every five meters to decompress. He swept his head from side to side, spotting dozens of fish, from triggerfish and clownfish to large angelfish, swimming in and out of the coral recesses.

Michael kicked his fins and glided upward and around another steel girder.

On his next decompression stop, his eyes fixed on a huge coral outcropping growing from a long curved stone shaped like an upturned letter *C*.

He watched as a school of shimmering jacks raced along the coral shelf, a toothy barracuda hot on their trail. Just on the edge of what remained of his peripheral vision, he saw, or thought he saw, the coral move. Michael focused on the spot, and moments later, he was rewarded. "There you are," he thought and watched a few moments longer, the better to fix in his mind just where the octopus was hiding. Michael moved toward the camouflaged cephalopod. Realizing that it had been spotted, the eight-limbed illusionist broke cover and scrambled over the coral hills and valleys. As its tentacles slithered across one crevice, the spiked jaws of a moray eel jutted forward and grabbed the octopus, pulling it down into the crack in an inky cloud of death.

With his last decompression completed, Michael swam up through a curtain of white bubbles and surfaced next to the boat's diving platform. Michael slid the pony bottle onto the teak scaffold, doing the same with his mask, fins, and scuba tank, and then hauled himself out of the water.

"You pulled a late one this time," the twenty-year-old deckhand announced, pulling the dive gear on board.

"What can I tell you, Carl, I get immersed in my work," Michael quipped, the side of his mouth curling up.

"You were down there for almost an hour and that's the best you could come up with? I've got to start adjusting your mixture, maybe a bit more nitrous," the deckhand said, smirking.

"Well, I did have other things on my mind," the wet Vanguard said, stepping aboard and walking across the waxed deck to a table and chairs. Michael snatched up the towel that hung over the deck chair, dried off, and sat down in front of his laptop. He began typing, entering the findings from his latest dive.

"We're getting close to an artifact, Carl," Michael said.

"That's good, because after six weeks out here, I'm ready for a nice desk job, preferably with a desk that doesn't sway and spill my morning coffee."

A ghostly wail carried over the waves, stopping the conversation cold.

Carl fixed his gaze on the shore. "I'll be happy to hear sirens and car horns for a change."

"The Maiden's Cry?" Michael asked. "I thought you were more sentimental." The wail punctuated Michael's words.

Carl looked out over the waves. "Sentimental or not, that screaming bitch creeps me out."

Michael smiled, the sliver of truth resonating with him. The sound was disheartening to say the least, an unnerving melody one had to get used to, like the rumble of the D train passing next to your bedroom in the middle of the night.

"So, what's the great revelation?" Carl asked.

"Based on what we've deciphered from writings and drawings in the Horsemen Chronicles to date, the coral shelf below us was the coast of Turkey and Syria three thousand years ago."

Michael tapped on his computer. A digital map appeared on the screen.

Carl leaned over the table and stared at the ancient atlas. His eyes followed the dark tracings that formed a coastline. Inside the landmass was a drawing, and underneath a line of Sumerian text.

Michael's fingers danced across the keys.

"This is the coastline today," he said with a final tap. The men viewed both maps, side by side.

"Cyprus is missing," Carl declared.

"Exactly," Michael said. "A passage in the Chronicles describes a dark day. The Horseman raised the sea and cut the earth, killing thousands. Leagues of water blocked the passage to the light."

"And that?" Carl asked, pointing to the drawing on the ancient map: a man being eaten by a wolflike beast with six heads.

Michael translated the text beneath. "The Medusa and Bedouin guardian bar the paths."

Both men listen to the wail of the Maiden's Cry as it punctuated the dread in the passage.

"Forget I asked," the deckhand added.

«««—»»»

With each stride on the indoor track, Faye's legs burned and her arms pumped across her body. She looked out the large frameless window at a gloomy London day; much like the past two days, the sun was a dull ache behind a veil of gray. She was glad to be inside.

As she rounded the next turn, she glanced into the center of the oval and watched as a dozen men and women, dressed in black fatigues, sparred on foam mats.

Pushing the center-ring distraction from her mind, Faye focused on her next mile. Her mind was a maze, and she mentally traversed the happenings of the last three days. Yet Faye's cerebral labyrinth always led back to the same memory: "Your flight to Heathrow leaves in one hour. The Order demands an audience."

She quickened her pace. Her lungs burned, but her frustration burned hotter. "Shit," she grunted, sprinting the next one hundred meters. Even with running shorts and a tank top, she was sweating buckets and her cheeks were like two ripe tomatoes.

Faye slowed her pace, the words "disciplinary review and psychological evaluation" echoing in her mind. "What a load of crap," she thought.

She knew bullshit when she smelled it, and this bull wasn't a bull at all, but a scapegoat.

Julian's death was going to be blamed on someone, with a wife and two kids making a stink, no doubt. The Vanguard was going to throw money at the widow, a lot of money, and it would be, as was always the case, a quick remedy to her grief. While the Order was going to make it "go away," the Vanguard was going to take their pound of flesh and very likely chew a pound right out of Faye's ass.

Beep…beep. Faye's timer echoed from her wrist, and she sprinted the last twenty meters.

Slowing to a walk, hands on her hips, Faye's heart slammed in her chest as she sucked in air. The ten-mile run had helped with her frustration, but she was still pissed off.

Faye walked another lap around the track. Cheers from the center of the oval distracted her from her cooldown. Stepping off the track, she made a beeline for the commotion.

As she moved closer, she twisted up her lips, remembering her defense training eight months ago. At the center of the mat, surrounded by Vanguard spectators, Faye could make out a man and woman exchanging jabs, chops, and kicks. Accompanying the combatants inside the human arena was an instructor.

With each successful strike, cheers rang out for the conqueror.

Faye stepped up to the edge of the mats and inserted herself like a link into the Vanguard cage, standing next to a wiry redheaded trainee.

"Faye," she announced with a nod.

"Eric Stoneridge," the thin recruit replied. "And the bully in our Vanguard schoolyard, that's Graeme LaSalle."

Inside the human pen, a black mountain of a man sparred with an Asian woman half his height. Actually, he was beating the ever-loving crap out of her.

Faye's eyes shifted to the whistle-wearing Vanguard referee. She recognized the sadistic asshole from her training and knew that the son of a bitch wouldn't stop the fight, intent on letting the carnage continue regardless of the pain inflicted.

With his opponent bleeding and prone on the mat, the black Vanguard recruit raised his arms and pumped his fists in triumph.

Faye turned her eyes to the thin redhead.

She was surprised to see his eyes raised above the fight and locked onto a blond woman wearing glasses and a Fendi navy pant suit who stood on the elevated pathway on the outside of the track.

"Who's that?" Faye asked

"The Dragon Lady," he answered. "Diana Waterford."

A blank stare washed over Faye's face.

"She's number two behind Prond, with her sights set on numero uno, and the Dragon Lady always gets what she wants."

Faye examined the blond figure, her gaze caught by the intense expression on the woman's face: her mouth turned down at the corners, full lips pressed thin in a disapproving grimace.

"She's just waiting for us to fail," Eric announced, watching Ms. Waterford pompously stalk the path above. "I really hate that bitch," he added.

A chorus of groans diverted Faye's attention back to the mat as the man kicked his adversary, struggling to her knees, in the gut. The Asian woman rolled with the kick and sat upright as the black Vanguard lunged forward for another attack. Overconfident, the big man didn't notice the trap, but Faye did, and in the next instant, the battered woman drove the tip of her boot straight into the man's balls. While only a glancing blow, the big man's face twisted, his mouth agape, eyes wide, in an expression of surprise and pain.

Faye smiled, a small chuckle erupting from her pressed lips.

"What the fuck are you smiling at, bitch!" the black man steamed, staggering toward Faye.

"Leave her alone, Graeme!" Eric said. "You got your nuts cracked. Get over it."

"Shut the hell up!" the big Vanguard responded, wrapping a black claw on Eric's shirt. "Let her fight her own battles, pussy."

Faye glanced over at the Asian woman on the mat. The battered woman's face had already started to swell, her eyes mere slits.

"Yeah, I'll fight my own battles," Faye announced, stepping out onto the mat. "Let me show you how this pussy is going to kick your ass."

Two recruits cut through the Vanguard fence and dragged Graeme's punching bag off the mat.

Faye and Graeme circled each other. She worked her jab to find her distance and threw a quick body blow that the black Vanguard easily blocked.

"Is that all you got?" the big man questioned threateningly.

Faye shifted position. Her feet crossed, left in front of right. She spun on her left foot, and her right foot came up and out, catching the Vanguard in the jaw.

"Nope," she responded with a smirk.

The big man rubbed his chin and raced in, slamming his bulk into Faye. Outweighed by sixty kilos, Faye toppled backwards, crashing to the mat. Graeme followed up his attack, bashing his forearm across Faye's stomach.

Faye's wind disappeared like a deflating balloon.

"Too easy," Graeme declared.

«‹‹—››»

Above the track, Zachariah Prond, the head of the Vanguard, walked onto the carpeted pathway. He stopped and stood next to Diana Waterford, another observer to the clamor in the center ring. The bald man stared below and fixed his eyes on the woman flat on her back, the large Vanguard towering over her.

"Your agent is weak," Waterford declared.

Zachariah was silent.

«‹‹—››»

On the mat, Faye gasped, struggling to breathe.

The words "disciplinary review and psychological evaluation" crashed through Faye's wall of pain and exhaustion. Her renewed frustration electrified her. She kicked hard and swept Graeme's legs out from under him. She then brought her straight leg down on top of him, crashing her shoe into the man's balls.

The Vanguard cage moaned in sympathy.

Faye got to her feet, looking down at the man reduced to a fetal position, "You would have thought you'd have learned to protect those by now," she announced, winking at the Asian woman recruit at the side of the mat whose boot had first treaded on the mountain man's stones.

Turning her back on her vanquished opponent, Faye walked over and smiled at the wiry redheaded Vanguard. "Now there're two pussies on the mat," she proclaimed.

The recruits circling the mat broke out in laughter.

Graeme struggled to his feet.

The loud, high-pitched screech of a whistle silenced the chortling. "Okay, you pukes, training is over," the combat instructor yelled. "Get your asses to the showers!"

As the links of the Vanguard cage dispersed, Graeme's eyes sharpened to daggers under furrowed brows. He clenched his jaw so tight that the veins in his massive neck bulged.

In the next instant, the big man leapt at Faye.

Eric's eyes grew large as plates and his jaw dropped, but the warning would not sound.

Faye turned to face her attacker just as Graeme's hands clasped around her neck.

"This bitch is done!" Graeme screamed.

Faye clawed at the man's wrists and struggled against the choke hold. She kicked, but her foot bounced harmlessly off his massive thigh. The big man wouldn't be fooled a third time.

Faye gasped, unable to take a single breath. Her head was spinning, blackness closing in.

Eric leapt onto the mat to intervene, but a massive black fist crashed into his face and sent him reeling to the ground.

"Who's the pussy now, bitch?" Graeme spat.

With her remaining strength, Faye reached over the top of the big man's arms and stabbed two fingers as hard as she could into the soft spot in Graeme's neck just midline of the collar bone.

The big man released the vise from around her neck, stung by the blow to his trachea.

Faye gasped and sucked in as much air as she could. Knowing she had seconds to act, she followed up with a punch to the same spot and then, spinning on her left foot, delivered a roundhouse kick to the man's temple. The black mountain crumbled, unconscious, to the mat.

Faye helped Eric to his feet, and they both headed toward the Vanguard lockers.

«« —»»

From the high walkway above the track, Zachariah stared at Faye as she exited the oval below.

"What do you think of Faye Monroe, now?" he asked, turning to Diana Waterford.

"Her type doesn't belong in the Vanguard," the blonde replied.

"Her type?"

"She was one of them," Diana Waterford said, staring down onto the track. "She should have never been accepted into the Order."

"It's because she was one of the Horsemen, even for the briefest of moments, that she needs to be part of the Vanguard."

"I don't trust her. If I were leading the Order, she would be terminated."

"Then it's good that I'm leading the Vanguard."

A Vanguard messenger hurried along the path and approached Zachariah. "Excuse me, sir. Michael Cantal is on the line for you."

"Very good," Zachariah answered. "We'll take it in the boardroom. Oh, and will you please request that Ms. Monroe join us."

«« —»»

The boardroom was modest, by Vanguard standards. The red oak table in the center of the room was polished and matched the walls around it. Twelve black leather swivel chairs circled the table. The lighting in the room was bright, which offset the dreary gray English sky outside the wall of glass windows. A table, half the length of a wall decorated with two Louis Aston Knight paintings, was covered with silver trays full of pastries. At both ends of the table, next to a tray stacked with ceramic coffee cups, stood two silver pitchers.

Zachariah Prond and Diana Waterford sat at opposite sides of the boardroom table.

"Mr. Prond, shall I transfer Mr. Cantal to you?" asked a clear female voice over the wireless surround-sound intercom.

"Yes," Zachariah answered.

A chime affirmed the transfer.

"How are you, Michael?" Zachariah asked.

"I can't complain. Six weeks on the Mediterranean, it's almost like a vacation," Michael answered.

"Remind me to dock your pay when you get back."

"I said, almost like a vacation. How goes the cutting of that Vanguard bureaucratic tape?"

"I'm afraid the tape is as red and as thick as ever."

The informal banter between the two men was grounded in a friendship fostered over a five-year mentor-apprentice relationship. Both men enjoyed the exchange.

Diana Waterford tapped her finger on the red oak. She pressed her lips together, the scowl on her face a clear and unattractive message to dispense with the pleasantries.

The long pause was the signal to get back to business.

"We've made good progress and have put some of the Chronicle puzzle pieces in place," Michael began. "The location of one artifact is somewhere off the coast of Cyprus."

"I wish you would have taken a larger team."

"The fewer people who know about this, the better. There is too much at stake."

"The search would go faster with another set of hands."

"Are you looking to get your bald head burned out here in the Mediterranean?" Michael asked, falling back into informality.

"No, I'll leave the field assignments to younger agents."

"We're getting close, Zachariah. With a little luck, we may have an artifact soon."

"Well, I'll have to send some luck your way. Nice work, Michael."

The call ended, as it began, with a chime.

As if the sound of the bell were the beginning of a title fight, the large polished oak doors swung open and a featherweight champion, red marks around her neck fading, stepped into the boardroom.

Zachariah stood and greeted Faye with a firm handshake. His eyes were gentle but flashed a warning.

"Sit down, Ms. Monroe," barked Diana Waterford.

Faye looked across the table at the blond woman in the designer clothes, whose disposition hadn't improved since she had first set eyes on her from the center of the track, and then lowered herself into a black leather chair and waited. "Disciplinary review and psychological evaluation" crept back into her head.

"Make no mistake, Ms. Monroe, this is an inquiry into the death of your partner, Julian Adeyemi."

"Here we go. The shit is going to hit the fan," Faye mused, and the only question was whether she was the shit or the fan. Either way it wouldn't end well.

"So, Ms. Monroe, did you kill your partner, Julian Adeyemi?"

"Are you kidding me?" she replied, crossing her arms.

"Were you angry?"

"I am now," Faye answered, leaning back in her chair, venom lacing her words. She didn't like the blond woman's tone or formality.

"Do you deny unsanctioned surveillance on Round Ridge Road?"

"No."

"Or having a relationship with a Horseman of the Apocalypse?"

"What? That's insane!" Faye exclaimed, leaning forward, her hands slapping the polished oak. She glanced at the gold band on her finger and slid her hands from the table.

"I propose that you are in league with the Warrior Horseman, meeting with him to undermine the efforts of the Vanguard, and on the night in question killed your partner."

"This bitch will have her pound of flesh," Faye thought. As the accusation had surpassed ridiculous and become completely asinine, the words "asinine" and then "ass" sparking her imagination, Faye wondered how her ass would look with the pound removed. Would her clothes still fit? The sides of Faye's mouth curled up, the tomatoes on her face coming into season.

"Do you find this amusing, Ms. Monroe?"

"Let's see," Faye began, leaning back into her chair. "You're presuming I left the car, walked up to the house, somehow found a Revolutionary War rifle, and learned to load and shoot it well enough to clip the wing off a fucking hummingbird and with the same bullet pierce the lens of the binoculars that my partner was holding to his face? Are you fucking joking? Of course I find this amusing; I find it amusing as hell."

"Ms. Monr—" started the blonde.

The chime sounded through the room, ending the first round of the bout. Faye realized that it didn't matter what she said or did. The Vanguard would make their decision, and she'd have to live with it.

The chime sounded again. "Mr. Prond, we have an urgent message from European operations."

"Put it through," Zachariah ordered.

"Milan is down," stated the voice, trailing off. "All agents retired."

Zachariah stood up, the blood drained from his face. "Faye, this disciplinary meeting is over. You are free to leave."

"But I haven't—" started Diana Waterford.

"This meeting is over, Ms. Waterford. Ms. Monroe is free to go."

"Yes sir," the blonde acquiesced.

Faye stood up and exited the boardroom. Her memories again scampered about like a mouse through a maze. She thought about Julian, the black mountain of a man, and the wiry redhead named Eric. She thought about Ben and rubbed her thumb back and forth over the gold ring on her finger. Faye thought about the Dragon Lady and how good it felt to keep her pound of ass right where it belonged.

CHAPTER 4

Randolph Larcy sat on his porch, watching. He was one of the last residents here, an eighty-three-year-old man with milky eyes and slurred speech, but he remembered when his little New Jersey borough was a warm slice of Americana. Twenty years ago, the neighborhood could have been a scene from a Norman Rockwell painting. Today, with its abandoned lots one after another, rusty, burnt-out factories, and boarded up tenement houses, the place looked like a ghost town in a post-apocalyptic world.

Mr. Larcy and his wife of fifty-three years had resisted the scourge that claimed much of this city. He missed his old neighbors. But worse, he feared his new ones: the drug dealers, prostitutes, and hangers-out that had crept in. Last night, somebody broke into his shed and stole his shovel and snowblower, in July.

The city had promised restoration since the blight began, pledged to clean up the neighborhood. But until it did, Mr. Larcy planned to sit on his porch, listening to a transistor radio with a foil speaker, watching, watching the boys in white T-shirts take their posts on the corner and watching the occasional car stop. Never had he seen a shiny black limousine drive past, but he did today, right by his house. Maybe the city was finally getting around to its promise of restoration.

Sitting in the backseat of the black limousine, the man formerly known as Ben Sasson watched the New Jersey ghetto creep past his tinted window. There, reflected in the window glass, was a tired, hollow face. War had seen thousands of slums, created thousands more: decrepit old men sitting on porches surprised to see wealth come to visit, drug dealers and prostitutes hungrily eyeing a fleeting opportunity, the fear and desperation of humanity's depraved energizing him more with each block. The afternoon snack added only a paltry glow to his malnourished face.

Three minutes and two streets littered with the poor, corrupt, and homeless later, the limousine pulled into the entrance of an old, neglected four-story factory. The black car drove over the pothole-laden access road bordered on both sides by long brown weeds, past a dilapidated billboard, its face, Charley's Steak House, covered with graffiti tags, falling off. The limo stopped in front of the neglected building. The dirty orphan was adorned with crumbling red brick and dozens of second-story multi-pane windows, each of which looked like a crossword puzzle: dust-covered white windows and smashed panes, black. All of the tall roll-top steel loading-dock doors on the ground level were locked and chained shut except for one, and it was that one that rose up.

The limo crunched the gravel as it maneuvered its long form in front of the massive door, rolled down the cracked cement and then coasted inside. The metal door slid down behind. A white limousine and a fourteen-foot U-Haul moving truck sat motionless within. Two Mexicans from the Los Pagarones Cartel, one armed with an Uzi, stood waiting for their host to arrive.

From within the limousine, War's cold eyes scanned the warehouse like a sniper sighting his targets. Even with his powers weakened, he could still sense the fear and angst of other men, beyond the two in plain sight, in the building: the driver hiding behind tinted windows inside the pretentious white limousine, three, another three gunmen inside the metal box of the U-Haul, six, and the assassin at the top of the stairs, seven.

"So predictable," War murmured.

War tapped on the car's privacy divider, the chauffeur exited, automatic pistol slung over his shoulder, and opened the passenger-side door. The well-dressed Horseman stepped out.

The warehouse had tall ceilings, exposed pipes, and a flight of wooden stairs leading to an overlooking office on the second floor. The dirty windows let a dull and lifeless haze into the open room, accented by haphazard and piercing beams of light from shattered panes. Dust floated through the stale and stirred air that smelled of mold and urine.

The leader of the cartel, a fat drug lord dressed in white, stood at the center of the room and licked his lips, shifting his weight from one foot to the other. A shiny metal briefcase sat next to his pleated pants and polished black shoes. The drug dealer, flanked by his bodyguard, nervously glanced around the warehouse, inadvertently revealing each of his hidden men's positions.

"The man is a buffoon," War thought.

War nodded, and his driver positioned himself in front of the white limo.

The Horseman then took a deep breath. He could feel the anger, fear, and desperation from each man of the Mexican cartel in the building. The three men in the truck would be first. War's eyes shot to the moving truck, infusing murderous jealousy into the metal U-Haul coffin. *Bang...bang...bang.*

The drug dealer's bodyguard cocked his weapon, pointing the barrel toward the U-Haul.

War's concentration shifted upward. A red dot appeared and danced on his broad chest.

The leader of the cartel grinned wickedly.

"Jou are not the only one who is *muy inteligente,*" the fat man said.

The Horseman ignored the drug dealer's bravado, his concentration focused at the top of the staircase.

The laser site steadied on War's heart, yet no gunshot sounded. The left side of War's mouth curled up in a disarming smile, but his eyes were locked above.

The red dot crawled down War's leg and onto the concrete. It scurried over to a polished black shoe of the drug lord like a cockroach fleeing a bright room.

"*Basta, ya!* Juan!" the cartel leader commanded, his gaze fixed on War.

But the red dot did not stop.

The dot flashed across the chest of the drug lord.

"*Basta, ya!* Enough!" the fat man repeated, sweat beading down his face.

The cartel leader's bodyguard swung around and pointed his Uzi to the top of the stairs.

The laser trembled, and the red dot jumped across the gunman's face. But the Horseman steadied his puppet's hand, and the dot froze on the bodyguard's ear.

Bang!

The body fell to the ground with a thump.

War's driver, standing to the side of the white limo, cocked his automatic weapon and directed the lethal end toward the stretched white car. The drug lord's chauffer stepped out of the limo, hands raised in the air.

"Que chingados pasa aquí!" the panicked drug lord screamed, reached inside his pocket, and pulled a shiny 45 caliber handgun.

War's eyes narrowed into slits, his power over the cartel assassin above waning.

"What the fuck is going on?" the Horseman said mockingly.

War clenched his teeth, and the hidden assassin, fueled with the Horseman's infused rage, stood up and launched himself screaming over the wooden railing, executing a bloody head plant onto the concrete.

Blood spattered onto the white pleated pants and polished black shoes of the cartel leader.

Stupefied by the actions of his men, the drug lord dropped his handgun to the bloody concrete, his eyes wide with fear.

"What the fuck is going on?" War repeated. "You're a business man, are you not? Then let us conduct business."

The Horseman escorted the cartel leader and his chauffer through a warehouse side door. War's driver picked up the blood-spotted metal briefcase and followed behind.

Inside, five large wooden crates sat in the middle of the room. On top of the first: an AK-47 and belt-fed Browning machine gun. On the second: an RPG-7 launcher and antitank rounds. On the third: fragmentation grenades and military-grade body armor. The fourth and fifth crates were covered with bricks of C-4 explosives, boxes of shells, and antipersonnel mines.

"Enough weapons and ammunition to supply an army...or kill one," War announced.

"Impresionante," the drug lord said.

"You and your driver may leave...alive," the Horseman said, snatching the metal briefcase from his driver. He opened the case, admiring the bills. "If you are not out of the country in twelve hours, I will personally see to it that your children watch as your wife flays the skin from your body."

War turned to his henchman without giving the drug lord a chance to reply. "Load the U-Haul and see to it they're gone in ten minutes."

"Oh," War said, turning back to the drug lord. "Leave your limo. Consider it a payment for your disrespect."

"But…how am I to reach the airport?" asked the drug lord. "What about my cargo?"

"I suggest you find a cab with a trailer hitch," said War. "You're down to nine minutes."

War's gunman stepped in front of the drug lord, his automatic machine pistol pointed at the drug lord's chest.

"Nice doing business with you, amigo," the Warrior Horseman said as he sauntered across the room, briefcase in hand, and exited through another door.

«««—»»»

Faye Monroe rubbed her left shoulder. She rubbed her right leg. She'd had a hunch that three ibuprofen and a hot shower wouldn't stop the ache coursing through her body, but she'd had no idea that she'd feel like a steak that had just been tenderized. "Deal with it," she thought. "And next time, fight someone smaller."

She crossed her right leg over her left and exhaled, trying to relax and focus on the book in front of her. After a moment, she scooted her ass down in the overstuffed brown leather armchair. A moment more, she crossed her left leg over her right and wiggled some more, fighting to find a comfortable position in the chair. Faye turned her head to each side of the Vanguard reading room, hoping that no one else had noticed her excessive fidgeting. Finally succumbing to the nagging from her sore muscles, she stood up, book in hand, and started walking, hoping to work the lactic acid from her legs.

Trudging through the rows of floor-to-ceiling book stacks that had been her home for five months while surviving training in the UK, Faye was still amazed at the volumes of information chronicled by the Vanguard. This library, dedicated to the House of War and one of four in the building, each the size of a school gymnasium, was lined with bookshelves of Horsemen accounts over the past five centuries. Older resources were archived on the Vanguard database.

Faye stepped through the aisle and then turned into a row of bookshelves. She slid the book into its spot and then searched for another volume on the Warrior Horseman. Her finger bounced from spine to spine as she read the title on each binding. With all of the technological advances and digital resources available to the Vanguard, Faye often preferred a good book to an electronic file. There was something to the warm and textured feel of board and cloth, the gentle sound of pages flipping, and the musky scent of an old tome that was lacking in the sterility of a digital display.

Her eyes jumped from title to title, searching for something unfamiliar. She had been through most of these chronicles and recalled everything from their pages. Her newfound photographic memory was a side effect from her time as host to Famine, as was her ability to read and speak ancient Sumerian.

"You know they're talking about you," said a voice from behind.

Faye turned around to see the redhead standing in the shelved corridor.

"I can imagine," she replied, turning back and continuing her stroll through the stacks, the Vanguard recruit following behind.

"No, not about the fight, although that is making the rounds, too. No, about how you, you were the host of Famine."

Faye turned and faced the young redhead.

"Yeah, well…Eric, right?" she began. "It's probably chronicled somewhere around here. Go have yourself a good read."

"How did it feel? To be one with a Horseman?" the tone bordering on envious.

Faye felt the hairs on the back of her neck stand up. Eric's gaze covered Faye like a wet blanket; she felt smothered.

"I mean…to be the host to Famine and then freed from its embrace. It must have been—"

Faye drove her forearm into the chest of the thin man, forcing Eric against the bookcase. "My soul was in fucking prison!" she exclaimed. "What do you want?" Faye asked, her eyes fixed on the man's face, searching for any clue of deception or malice, a bead of sweat, a nervous blink, something.

"I'm sorry, I didn't—" he responded.

Faye lowered her arm. "I thought after all this time, I'd be okay talking about it. I guess I'm not."

The memories from eight months ago flooded into Faye's mind like a tsunami. The monster had seized control of her body, dampening her soul. She'd felt like a puppet on a string.

She stared at the Vanguard recruit.

"It was like being torn apart from the inside," she said coldly and continued walking through the stacks.

Eric quickened his pace, caught up with her, and matched Faye stride for stride.

Needing to change the topic and sensing that the recruit was not going to let her have any peace and quiet, Faye shot him a smile. "How did you end up here?" she asked. "The Vanguard, I mean."

Faye clenched a fist. She hated making idle chitchat.

Eric, on the other hand, jumped at the opportunity. "I was at the NSA, a data analyst. My mom was happy with that, but I wasn't."

"You don't strike me as a momma's boy," Faye joked.

"I'm not!" he snapped. "She'd been sick a long time, had no one but me, so I took care of her."

"Oh, I'm sorry," Faye remarked, feeling bad for her wisecrack. "So, the NSA—"

"Yeah, I wanted to be a field operative, passed all of the tests, scored the highest they'd seen on Field Strategy and Tactics, but failed the endurance challenge, my asthma, so the fuckers washed me out."

Faye stared at Eric, surprised at the intensity of his words. "I—"

"I guess it just wasn't meant to be, so I went back to analysis and then ran across some unusual data activity. One second the data was there on the servers and the next, it wasn't. Gone, totally cleansed from all databases. There wasn't even a ghost trail."

"Ghost trail?" Faye asked.

"Yeah, even data that's erased leaves a byte or two, some trace that it existed. This data didn't, not even an individual bit. So I started tracking every occurrence of the disappearing data. I sent it up the ladder, but the higher-ups didn't care, shelved it. The more I pushed the 'invisible data,' the more senior brass pushed back, and finally pushed me out. They said I had become obsessed. Developed conduct unsuitable, blah...blah...blah."

"You were kicked out."

Eric nodded. "But I didn't stop. Used my own systems and hacked the network. It took me three months, but I tracked the invisible data to one source in South America and then to another in Taiwan, a holding company."

Eric and Faye stepped out from the bookshelves.

"So I moved to Taiwan," Eric continued, "tracked the data to its source, found the man in charge, but in this case it was a woman, and started following her."

"Diana Waterford," Faye guessed.

"Yep, the Dragon Lady herself, and the bitch almost killed me. Took a shot at me. She thought I was a stalker or something. And then of all things, she offered me a job."

Faye's mind flashed to Zachariah Prond's words—"There is no going back"—his offer to her to join the Vanguard.

"I guess she figured better an asset than a liability," Eric continued. "So here I am. I transferred from the Taiwan office two months ago for training and reassignment. The food is better here, and that's not saying much, but I hate this crap English weather."

Faye and Eric stepped into the main reading room.

A set of brown eyes cast a toxic gaze at Faye. Graeme, clad in a gray tracksuit, hood pulled over his head, stood threateningly in the center of the room.

Faye saw the big Vanguard and glared back defiantly.

"Watch your back," Eric said and scurried away.

She stepped to the far side of the reading room toward one of the private glass alcoves. Keeping one eye on the black Vanguard, she pushed the door open and maneuvered her sore frame into a comfortable chair.

Opening the left armrest, Faye pushed a button on the hidden console, which raised a computer screen in the end table that swung in front of her. From the right armrest she pulled a keyboard.

She entered an encrypted password and then typed "Free host from War." The cursor flashed "Information not found."

This route had been a dead end for Faye the countless times she had tried to search the more ancient archives. Unless she specified the exact keywords to search for, she'd be better off in the book stacks.

Faye remembered the exact row and book she'd left off at before Eric interrupted her research. She thought about her exchange with the redheaded recruit. "Embrace," she said mockingly. "Give me a fucking break."

Her mind flashed to her acrid response and on a lark typed "Free from War's prison." One entry popped into view. Faye clicked on the file and read a brief passage: "The Lost One is abandoned, never to be free from War's prison."

Frustrated by the lack of progress on the Vanguard archive, Faye thought about returning to the bookshelves but reconsidered as she had

had enough of adoring Vanguard recruits and those giving her the stink-eye.

As Faye started typing another set of search terms into the computer, she heard the quiet whoosh as the door to her private room opened.

She first thought it was Eric, following after her like a homesick puppy, but was immediately filled with dread as she imagined Graeme entering the room for a bloody rematch.

Faye swung around, prepared to launch her boot into the black man's nether regions, and stopped, seeing the shiny bald head and welcoming gaze of Zachariah Prond.

"I hope that's not for me," the Vanguard leader said, seeing Faye's boot cocked and ready to fire. Zachariah's bodyguard, Kenji Watanabe, with ink-decorated arms and gel-messed hair, stood ready to block the kick.

"Sorry," she said, lowering her foot.

The guardian's gaze burrowed into Faye, its warning clear.

Zachariah turned to his escort. "Thank you, Kenji. I'll speak to Ms. Monroe now," and the bodyguard exited the glass room, but not before casting a final intimidating stare.

"He's not much for conversation," she quipped.

"He is more than what he appears. A master of netsuke," Zachariah said.

"Black belt?"

Zachariah's face reddened, the edges of his lips curled up. "Exquisite ivory carvings."

Faye's eyes flashed to the glass door. Her gaze fell on the body-guard's watchful stare, like a cat peering into a fishbowl.

"You seem a bit on edge."

"I thought you were someone else," Faye said.

"Yes, I've heard you've become quite popular with the recruits as well as the leaders of the Order."

"Diana Waterford?" she asked. "Sorry about that."

"Don't be. She was out of line today. Anyway, I've wanted to tell Diana Waterford off like that for years," he declared. "But it's best to put some distance between you, Diana—"

"I can be on the plane back to the US tomorr—"

"And the Warrior Horseman," he interjected, cutting her off.

"Ben?"

"Ben is gone, Faye. The sooner you realize that, the better off you and your next partner will be."

"I—"

"You're to join the Vanguard team on the research vessel *Excalibur* currently off the coast of Cyprus in the Mediterranean."

She looked at the Vanguard leader's face, hoping to find a hint of indecision and finding none.

"You leave tomorrow morning."

«« — »»

The inner office in the New Jersey warehouse was a contradiction to its outer façade; it was a secret beauty hidden within a diseased exterior. The lights were low, and wisps of white smoke danced in the air. The room was immaculate, paneled in dark wood throughout, with two grand crystal chandeliers hung low on each side of the space like giant earrings. Covering most of the front wall, and drawing all eyes, was a portrait of a general on horseback in the midst of a bloody battle. On the left hand side of the painting near the bottom was a cursive insignia, "Gebhard von Blücher, Waterloo, 1815."

The man sitting astride the white stallion looked different than the one sitting at the desk smoking a cigar, all except for the eyes: the cruel intensity of the eyes was exactly same as they stared down at the map spread across the mahogany top. War's eyes were glued to a narrow blue waterway, his thoughts thousands of miles away.

The ring of the cell phone was muffled in the breast coat pocket of the Armani jacket slung over the desk chair. The stocky bodyguard, neck as thick as his thigh, was in motion at the end of the first ring. He stepped to the chair and plucked the phone from the coat, setting it into an intercom docking station on the large desk. The henchman returned to his position behind his master. Two other gunmen stood at the doorway.

"I have news," echoed the hollow voice on the speaker phone.

The Horseman's eyes never shifted from the map. "Speak," he said, chewing on a stogie.

"The Vanguard search for artifacts, getting close to one in the Mediterranean. There is also a woman, Faye Monroe. She could be trouble."

War lifted his tired, bloodshot eyes from the atlas. "Do not touch the woman." He stabbed the speaker phone, and the call died. The Horseman cradled the side of his face in his hand and shut his eyes.

"You're making a big mistake." The deep voice resonated in the room.

War's head shot straight up. "Who dares?" he yelled, his fists balled. From the doorway, one of his henchmen stepped forward. War stood and clenched his teeth down on the cigar, his warring essence encircling the bodyguard. "Shoot yourself," the Horseman ordered. The big man stood at the front of the desk and twitched his nose as if to snub a sneeze.

War raised his eyebrows in disbelief and then furrowed them when the realization hit him like a slap on the cheek. He plopped into the leather chair. "Your new trick doesn't impress me, Kishar."

The human veneer melted away, and the thick henchman transformed into the beautiful black-haired gothic Horseman, Death.

"Leave us," War commanded, casting a pointed glance at the bodyguard to his side, and in the next moment, both henchmen exited the room.

"You've lost your touch, Seth." Death leaned in over the desk, her eyes scanning his face.

She pushed off the desk and paced in the center of the wooden room, her arms raised to her sides. "For me to be in the same room without your sensing my presence…That human soul makes you weak."

War pressed his lips together and sneered.

"It's a mistake to let the woman live. Your human feelings for her put us at risk," she continued, ignoring his dirty look.

"I have no feelings for—"

"The Vanguard need to die. All of them!"

War's eyes sized up the gothic beauty. He had seen Death play many roles over the millennia: liar, deceiver, manipulator. But warmonger was not among them. "What do you want, Kishar?" he asked, sucking the rolled tobacco like a straw and blowing out a white plume.

"We must act while the power still resides in us." Her face transformed from flawless complexion to decomposed flesh and then to exposed bone. "Before one artifact can be found," chattered the teeth within the Horseman's white skull. Death pointed a bony finger at War. "With the Vanguard eliminated, no one would stand in our way. Imagine the delicious fear and desperation we…you could feed upon."

"But for how long?" War asked, staring into the black, empty eye sockets. "We are nothing of our past selves; our power is that of a single drop of rain in the Sahara. With Famine's spirit banished once more, the power of 'The Four' no longer sustains us, and without power, we have no control...We have nothing."

War watched as muscles, veins and arteries, skin and hair covered Death's bony skull. Her eyes reappeared with a blink.

"What then?" the Warrior Horseman asked, puffing on the cigar and placing the smoldering log in an ashtray.

"You are a coward!" she declared. "Does the memory of your recent reunion with Famine still haunt you?"

War's memories flashed to eight months earlier, to Faye Monroe, the host of the spirit of Atra...the host to their lost Horseman, Famine. He remembered how her human soul had fought to control the supernatural power, whipping him with her stygian tendrils, the smoky aura draining the last bit of strength from his limbs. He, the supreme warrior, had been bested in battle by a mere human.

War's eyes narrowed, full of rage.

His hand crackled. A bright flame erupted around his fist. Then the fire dwindled as if choked of air.

Death fixed her gaze on the pathetic flame. "So weak..."

War slammed both hands on the desk, and his hands and arms burst into a bright orange flame.

Death's appearance shifted from skin to bone. With a wave of her hand, the office shook and the chandeliers clinked and swayed from side to side as her power over the elements sent an earthquake underneath the foundation of the dilapidated building.

The Warrior Horseman stared at Death, his lips curled into a sneer. "I see through your taunts, Kishar," he said, extinguishing his flame. "Your efforts to redirect my anger toward the Vanguard shall not succeed." He leaned back in the leather chair. "I do not know how deep your deception goes, but you will regret any betrayal."

You have nothing to fear from me, brother," she said, her beauty returning.

"We shall see."

"And what of the artifacts?" Death asked.

"You need not to worry about the artifacts. They are of no consequence, and neither are you. Leave me," he commanded, pushing an intercom button and waving her away as he would shoo a fly.

"I will not be dismissed like one of your lackeys," she replied, her skin peeling away from her face. Another trembler rattled the desk.

"Don't test me, Kishar!" War threatened and he directed his eyes down to the map on the desk.

The office door swung opened and two of War's henchmen entered the room.

"My guest is leaving," War declared.

The ground quieted. Death's guise fell away, replaced with a copy of the seated Horseman. The doppelganger plucked the smoldering cigar from the ashtray and turned to exit, stepping to the door, glancing at one gunman guarding the doorway.

With a wicked grin, the Horseman twin stepped up to the tall man, grabbed the bodyguard's chin with one hand, and spun his head around, breaking his neck. Death gestured over the fresh corpse, and the newly created black-eyed death walker stood at attention.

"Take him," the Warrior Horseman declared.

The mock warrior shrugged his shoulders and exited the room, zombie in tow.

«« —»»

Death walked out into the abandoned warehouse. Six Los Pagarones gunmen lay dead on the cement floor.

"Do not test me, he said," Death whispered mockingly, gothic beauty replacing stony features. "Brother, you shall be tested soon enough."

She spied the white limousine, driver-side door wide open, and strolled up to the stretched car, her meat puppet staggering behind. Death caressed the smooth metal and spied the keys hanging in the ignition. She faced her dead companion. "Hold this," she said, sticking the chewed cigar into the walking corpse's hand. "I'll drive."

«« —»»

War stood alone in his dark wooden office staring at his painting. He remembered his bliss on that bloody day as the fear, pain, and hate of thousands of French and Prussian soldiers, gripped in his warring enthrall, fed his Horsemen spirit to its overflowing.

He stepped up to his portrait, gripped the frame, and pulled. The painting swung from its hinges off the wall, exposing a large safe and white keypad. War's index finger jabbed in a six-digit code, the clasp sprung, and the metal door opened. The Horseman reached into the black void and pulled out a treasure covered with a silk cloth. He carried the hidden cache back to his desk and sat down.

A fierce anticipation washed over War's face as he pulled the silk swathe away. The golden Ād tribal axe sat on a small pedestal and glowed with a subtle radiance in the dark room.

The Horseman looked at his hands as mystical flames licked across his fingers and across his palms. His tired eyes looked at the meager flames, questioning his Horsemen reserves and the exertion that was to follow. War reached out and encircled the golden blade with blazing hands. Gripping the metal, he infused his power into the axe, the warring essence flowing like a blood transfusion from him into the yellow metal. As the golden hue glowed more brilliantly with every passing second, the Horseman's flame dimmed, and he cringed with pain. The process, as it had over the past weeks, bled the Warrior Spirit nearly dry.

War gritted his teeth and closed his eyes as he forced more of himself into the axe. His hands shook as the blade shimmered until, finally, the Horseman succumbed to the pain and let go of the scalding blade.

The Horseman slumped in his chair and looked at his hands.

"What have I done?" he asked the empty room, staring at the glistening axe as it returned to its normal golden luster.

A bodyguard entered the office and stared at the Horseman. "Sir?"

The man at the desk looked at the gunman, his blue eyes wide, softer, the cruel intensity abating. He blinked hard and shook his head from side to side as if trying to wake from a bad dream. His gaze fixed on the man. "Who are you? Where am—where's Faye?"

"Sir?" the gunman asked again, unaware of the internal struggle raging inside the man at the desk: human soul and Horseman Spirit in a winner-take-all tug-of-war to determine the fate of the man once known as Ben Sasson.

"I," the man began, drooping his head. "I will not be denied," he yelled, slamming his balled hands on the desk.

War had almost taken it too far, expended too much supernatural energy and allowed the human soul to retake control, pushing the Horseman Spirit aside.

"Send it," War ordered, pushing the golden axe forward on the polished wood. He plucked a Montblanc pen and a pad from the desk and scratched out a note: *Steve P. Schimmel, Curator, New York Metropolitan Museum of Art.*

CHAPTER 5

"These tank O-rings are pretty worn out," Carl said, sitting on the deck of the *Excalibur*, an empty scuba tank in his lap, five other drained cylinders lined up like soldiers waiting for inspection.

"Add it to the top of the list," Michael responded, his legs crossed, inspecting a regulator.

"I'll go into town today and get some replacement rings after I fix those leaky BCs," the deckhand said, pointing to the black vests in the corner.

"I'm surprised that I haven't drowned," Michael joked.

"Why do you think I send you down with a pony bottle?" Carl replied.

"Yeah…about that—"

"You left it at the bottom again?"

Michael shrugged and tilted his head, a guilty smile staining his face.

The rising high-pitched whine of an engine curtailed the morning banter. Michael and Carl looked up from their dive preparation to see the two pontoons of a white single-engine Maule M-6 Float Plane as it cleared the ship's bridge.

"Who the hell is that?" Carl yelled, ducking his head reflexively as the plane skimmed overhead. "Are they insane?"

Both men stood at the railing and watched the seaplane skid along the calm turquoise surface and coast to a stop in between the *Excalibur* and the oil rig. The plane's pilot door swung open, and a woman, wearing sunglasses, shorts, and a bikini top, stepped out onto the float. A flash of sunlight reflected off the pendant dangling from her neck as she set the floatplane's anchor.

Michael immediately recognized the pilot. With his hands clasped on the railing, Michael straightened his arms and leaned down, his face staring at the white planks. "Why her?" he whispered, his eyes darting from side to side, searching for an answer that just wasn't there.

Michael straightened up, turning his back to the new arrival. "She's not insane, just a little crazy," he responded.

"Who is it?" Carl asked.

"Faye Monroe."

Carl glared at Michael. "THE Faye Monroe? The one you always talk about?"

"Always?" Michael said with a shy grin. "Go get her."

The deckhand hopped down onto the ship's landing and stepped aboard an inflatable dinghy. A smaller sibling waited in an adjacent slew.

"Oh, this should be fun," Carl said, starting the outboard motor, his lip curled up.

Michael turned around and watched Carl steer the skiff out to the seaplane, leaving a small V-shaped wake behind.

Fun was the furthest thing from Michael's mind. It had been more five months since he'd seen Faye, and their parting had been, well, less than cordial. He remembered how he'd warned her to stay away from the man once known as Ben Sasson, who was now a Horseman of the Apocalypse.

Michael's memories flashed to his last meeting with Faye. "The Horseman inside him is unpredictable. He is not the same man you knew...we knew!" Michael proclaimed in the Vanguard library, Faye seated in a leather-backed chair pouring over ancient writings.

"I'm not going to give up on him! He never gave up on me. He never gave up on you," she responded fiercely.

Michael was a man divided, torn between his kinship with the man who had once been Ben Sasson, his friend, and Ben Sasson, the man possessed: the Horseman, the enemy.

It was the hardest thing he'd ever done. He'd never wanted to turn his back on his friend. But his friend was gone.

Michael remembered looking up into the stone-cold stare and wicked grin of Ben as he stood over him, the Horseman's wicked threat pouring over him like icy water. His team of four Vanguards was dead, and he lay flat on his back. The attack had been so sudden, so ferocious, that Michael could only watch in horror as his friend killed each of his fellow Vanguard as easily as swatting a fly. Michael recalled fighting for breath: "Ben, Let me hel—" And then blackness.

Michael's next memory was of him waking in a Vanguard infirmary, with four black body bags lying on cold steel examination tables under the dull white lights. Every fiber in his aching body was telling him that the Ben he knew was lost. His being left alive was a message: the vessel had changed, but the Horseman had not. He had never said a word about the covert operation to Faye.

Michael watched as Carl pulled alongside the floatplane. Faye tossed her backpack into the center of the skiff. Carl reached out his hand and helped Faye into the dinghy.

Old memories flooded back into Michael's mind like tumbling surf. He remembered how Ben, the old Ben, had reached out to Faye, holding her, comforting her.

Michael rubbed his thumb anxiously along the waxed railing surface. Another wave crashed over him: the image of Faye, burned into his memory, as she accepted Ben's tender embrace and returned his affections.

Michael's stomach was fluttering. Why did he feel like such a schoolboy around this woman? He clenched his teeth and squeezed the railing, forcing away the butterflies in his stomach.

Michael was attracted to her, of course. Faye was beautiful, she was strong, but it was her passion, her zest for life, which was what attracted him most, like a moth to a flame. And Ben, his friend, was also Ben, his rival.

Michael hit the wooden rail with his hand. He shook his head, ashamed of the jealousy that still brewed inside him, even now. Whether it was Ben Sasson, friend, Ben Sasson, Horseman or Ben Sasson, suitor, he couldn't help the way he felt. The memories flooded through his mind like a rising tide.

"Stay away from him! He's not Ben! He will kill you and kill those around you," he'd insisted, hoping his plea would dissuade her stubbornness.

"I don't care. I have to try save him."

"I don't want you getting hurt...or worse."

Michael tried to hide his true feelings for Faye, but Zachariah Prond, his mentor, knew, saw through him like a window. Hell, the old man knew Michael better than he knew himself sometimes. Zachariah was like a father to him, had rescued him from Camp Gabriel, a correctional facility for wayward boys, brought him on as his apprentice, and taught him everything of the Vanguard and of the Horsemen. The old man had spotted Michael's impending train wreck.

"Lessons learned are lessons felt," Zachariah said. "And lessons of the heart are the hardest learned of all."

Michael remembered how desperate he was to protect Faye. "Stay away from War."

"Are you ordering me?"

"If that's what it takes."

"Not a single Vanguard will lift a finger to help me...and now you?"

Michael was silent. His heart ached to help Faye, but the image of the four body bags haunted his memory.

"You're a coward! If you were half the man Ben is, you'd—"

"He is not a man, Faye. Not anymore."

"You're the only one I have left."

Michael turned and walked away.

"Go, walk away. You bastard," he remembered her saying, her voice softening, wavering, but cutting him just the same.

The *put...put...put* of the approaching outboard motor stemmed the tide of Michael's memories.

As the skiff drew closer, Michael raised his hand, his lips pressed together in a half-hearted smile.

"But why is SHE here?" he thought, and then he remembered his call to Zachariah.

"Well, I'll have to send some luck your way," Michael remembered the old man saying on the phone.

The wily bastard had planned to send along another set of hands to help with the artifact search, only Zachariah wanted a set that he could trust, regardless of the awkward and painful moments soon to be inflicted on his apprentice.

Michael stood on the landing. His butterflies were back, but now transformed into pterodactyls, and from the scowl transforming her face, Faye was just as surprised and as uncomfortable as he was. "Thanks, Zachariah."

As the dinghy slid next to the *Excalibur*, Faye's backpack smashed into Michael's chest, the bag falling to the deck.

"Is this some sort of sick joke you're playing, Michael?" Faye spat, stepping on board the research vessel.

"I had nothing to do with this," Michael pleaded. "This was all Zachariah's doing."

"That son of a bitch," she said.

The small engine revved, and the skiff bounced against the ship.

"I hate to interrupt this touching homecoming, but we need to get new O-rings, so…hell, while I'm floating here, I might as well shoot into Paphos and get them."

"Mind if I tag along?" Faye asked, jumping back into the skiff, wanting to avoid any further awkwardness.

"Good idea," Michael added.

"Hold on a second," Carl began. "If I don't get to the BCs, no one is diving today. Hmm," he said, touching his chin. "I'd better stay on board and get to work." The deckhand leapt out of the dinghy and onto the *Excalibur*, snatching up the leaky black vests from the planks. The deckhand turned around and stared at Faye bobbing alone in the skiff. "But wait, Faye doesn't know Paphos," he announced. "It could take her hours to—"

"Okay, okay, enough already," Michael said, stepping into the dinghy, surrendering to the deckhand's obvious ploy.

Faye looked at Michael with an icy stare.

Michael cast a dirty look at Carl. "Just have those BCs ready to go by the time we get back."

"Hey," Carl began, ignoring Michael's dirty look and grabbing two empty scuba tanks. "You might as well get Stelios to replace the valves on these two and fill 'em while you're there," he said, passing the two cylinders over to Michael.

"Anything else?" Michael said sarcastically, grabbing the empty tanks.

"A gyro would be fantastic."

"Dream on," Michael said, twisting the throttle and steering the dinghy away.

For six agonizing minutes Faye and Michael motored in silence toward the line of fishing boats docked in the small marina. Michael's conscience was the only one speaking to him, and it was making him feel like shit.

The Vanguard twisted the throttle handle to its limit, but the little skiff struggled against the outgoing tide and the strengthening breeze. Ten minutes was an eternity, twelve was Michael's breaking point.

"I'm sorry for what Carl said back on the *Excalibur*," he said, staring out across the barren blue desert.

Faye sat silent at the front of the skiff, motionless, her eyes fixed on the destination ahead.

"I'm sorry for a lot of things," Michael said, releasing the throttle.

Faye turned around.

"Five of us went to Argeles-Gazost." The engine sputtered and cut out, and the dinghy rocked back and forth through the swell outside the harbor. "Sunada, Sechler, Hecht and Stone," Michael noted each name solemnly.

"The plan was simple: infiltrate the compound, snatch the sword, and use it to free Ben, but he was waiting for us."

"What are you doing?" she asked, her cold and bitter eyes fixed on Michael's sorrowful countenance.

"Their deaths are on me. All because I thought I could save him. I believed that there was still time, that Ben was inside somewhere, still fighting against the Horseman, that we had a chance." Michael looked across the rolling blue dunes. "I was wrong, and my overconfidence killed four Vanguard." Michael turned, his eyes fixed on Faye. "Ben is a captive, a prisoner in his own body. The man taking his place is a ruthless killer."

Faye was silent. Her thoughts leapt to Julian Adeyemi, her murdered partner.

"I don't want any more deaths on my hands. I don't want your death on my hands. I couldn't live with that. The Vanguard would not sanction any further actions to free Ben, because of me, my failure, so I left to find another way. I left to find an artifact."

Michael stared down at the water as it lapped along the edge of the skiff.

"Thank you," she said, the chill falling off her words.

Michael smiled, as both his conscience and stomach had quieted.

"Now get me off this rocking bathtub before I lose my breakfast."

After another ten minutes on the whitecaps, the inflatable dinghy bumped alongside the Paphos pier. Faye leapt out of and bounded onto the wooden dock. "I'm so happy to have my land legs under me again."

Michael passed up the two empty scuba tanks, tied off the skiff, and, carrying one cylinder over each of his shoulders, he walked with Faye into town.

Faint music floated on the warm afternoon breeze up Dionysou Boulevard just as Michael and Faye turned onto the abandoned narrow street. Tall buildings rose straight up from the sidewalk and loomed above shorter kin, dark, dead windows that stared out from yellow-green walls or else slumbered with closed shutters.

"Do you hear that?" Faye asked. "It sounds like a party."

"It is Kreatini," Michael answered.

"What is Kreatini?"

Michael smiled at the confused look on her face. "You'll see."

With each passing step through the shadowed avenue, the music grew louder and more vibrant.

As Faye and Michael stepped into the sunny square, the sights, sounds, and smells of the festival overwhelmed their senses. Costumed minstrels wandered the streets with guitars and mandolins playing Greek serenades. In the center of the square, masquerading revelers, wearing dazzling home-made costumes, danced in an open grassy courtyard. Bordering the square, vendors sold an assortment of meats, bread, fruit, and wine.

Michael passed cart after cart. The sizzle of sausages, steaks, and pork ribs captured his attention. White smoke wafted up from the grills. His senses delighted in the peppery aroma.

Michael's stomach gurgled. "Oh, that smells good."

One shopkeeper on the sidewalk, a thick and bull-like man in a white tank top, was pulling down a corrugated steel gate over his door as Michael hurried up to him. "Stelios!"

The merchant turned. "Michael," he bellowed, a big grin on his face, a black gap where three top front teeth should have been. "Have you come to celebrate Kreatini? Ah, the festival is so wonderful."

"Kreatini?" Faye asked.

"Michael, who is your very beautiful friend?" the shopkeeper asked, turning to Faye.

"This is Faye Monroe."

"It's a pleasure," the shopkeeper said, taking her hand and shaking it. "I am Stelios Paparizos."

"I was hoping you could—" Michael began, lowering the tanks to the ground.

"Please, Michael," Stelios interrupted. "I would be happy to explain to Faye," he said, touching her elbow and shoulder and guiding

59

her onto the street and into the mass of revelers. "Kreatini is the most spectacular festival in all of Cyprus. Everyone is here for the celebration," he said proudly, his big arms wide open. "The festival lasts two weeks. The first week is Kreatini or Days of Meat," he said as he inhaled deeply, relishing the savory scents in the air, "Ahh...and the second is Tyrini, Days of Cheese—"

"Stelios—" Michael interjected from the sidewalk.

"Which is also so delicious," Stelios continued. "I hope you can stay for the entire celebration."

"Stelios!" Michael shouted, cutting off the shopkeeper's flirtatious advances.

"Yes, my friend?" the shopkeeper answered, ignorant of the Vanguard's frustration.

"We need you to replace the O-rings in the tanks and fill them. Please."

"It's no problem," he said, a lopsided smile on his wide face. Stelios walked to the sidewalk, picked up both cylinders, and tucked them both under one arm. "Come back in one hour." The big man lifted the steel corrugated door and entered his dive shop.

With time to kill, Faye and Michael strolled through the crowded courtyard.

"You haven't changed a bit," he said.

"I don't know if I should take that as a compliment or an insult," she answered.

"No, no," he responded, raising his hands in defense. "Any other person would have chartered a boat, but you, a floatplane?"

"Yeah, well, it's not often I get any time behind the stick."

Michael furrowed his brows.

"My flight instructor had the same look," she said smiling. "Ah... right, I never told you. A souvenir from Famine: a photographic memory," she said, tapping her temple. "And an understanding of ancient Sumerian."

"Good to know."

The two Vanguards left the festivities behind and walked along the beach. In front of them rose two massive rock formations. The first cliff, jutting out of the foamy surf, was bordered with hair of grass and wild flowers. In the center of the stone face was a gaping mouth lined with stalactites and stalagmites. A dozen spelunkers fitted with hard hats stood at its mouth like offerings to the rocky deity. The second formation, rising thirty meters away in the blue sea, was a massive stone worn down to the center of its right side by the ceaseless battering of waves.

Faye's eyes soaked up the craggy view. "It's beautiful."

"The Maiden's Cry," Michael said. "Legend has it that a princess, in love with a fisherman, called out across the sea to her beloved each night. A rough sea stole away the fisherman, but the princess still beckoned every night. The sea, taken aback by the lost love, created this."

"It's amazing."

"Every evening when the tide comes in, waves crash into the underground cave, forcing seawater up through the rocky recesses, producing an eerie wail you can hear for miles."

"So those people up on the ridge...cavers?"

Michael nodded. "That whole place is a huge catacomb, but only when the tide is out. At night, the Maiden is deadly."

Faye looked across the turquoise horizon dotted with cotton and the ship rocking against the light blue backdrop. "We should head back. It's getting late."

"Good idea, before Carl thinks you tossed me overboard," he said with a grin.

"Don't think it didn't cross my mind earlier," she cracked.

After retrieving the scuba tanks from the square, Michael motored the skiff back to the *Excalibur*. Fifteen minutes later, Faye and Michael stepped aboard the Vanguard research vessel, staring at the white caps slapping against the hull.

"Visibility is going to be less than three feet with this churn," Michael said. "No dive today."

"Figured that much," Carl chimed in.

"So much for fieldwork," Michael said, walking toward the deck table and chairs. "Faye, let me show you what we've discovered in the Chronicles."

Michael sat at the table in front of his laptop and with the press of a button brought the computer to life. A few keystrokes later, he turned back to Faye and motioned to her to join him. She stepped across the deck and, leaning over the table, read the ancient text on the screen. "The Medusa and Bedouin guardian bar the paths." She stood up and looked down at Michael. "Two entrances?"

Michael nodded, his lips pressed together.

The two Vanguards were consumed, ignoring the third wheel

standing on the deck and clasping his hands in front of him like a girl at the prom waiting to be asked to dance.

"I guess I'll get dinner started then," Carl said. Failing to elicit even the slightest response from the duo in front of him, he walked off the deck.

Michael's fingers tapped the keyboard. "I can understand how the Medusa would be a powerful deterrent. This region was full of Greek influence and mythology. But the Bedouin guardian," he said. "I can't figure how warriors from Arabia played a role."

Faye looked away. Her mind's eye scanned the volumes of Vanguard writings in her head. And after a moment, there it was.

"Bedouins were fierce hunters." Faye leaned over and maneuvered her hands in front of Michael's, taking control of the keyboard. "Around the eighth century BC."

Michael turned his head and stared at Faye. The puzzlement plastered on his face was the same as his earlier tweaked expression.

"There was a notation in an old text of War using Bedouin hounds in battle, salukis," Faye said. Feeling Michael's piercing gaze on her face, she turned and looked at him with a half smile. "Sorry, photographic memory."

The computer screen was full of illustrations of a bloody battle scene: soldiers stabbing enemies with pointed spears as tall, long-haired dogs tore foes apart.

Faye straightened up. "Bedouin warriors were the first to use saluki hounds in battle."

The ghostly wail of the Maiden's Cry enveloped the Mediterranean twilight.

Faye stepped to the rail and stared out over the waves at the rocky cliffs.

"Do you ever get used to it?" Faye asked.

"I never have," Carl answered, returning with an assortment of smoked and marinated meats, light garnishes, and exotic dips on a platter. "Faye, I pulled together some Cyprus delicacies. I think you'll love them."

"I'm sure I will, thank you."

Michael stood up from the table and plucked his dive bag from the nearby deck chair. Reaching inside, he moved his scuba mask and weight belt to one side and pulled out a handful of fluorescent glow sticks.

"A little dinner ambience," he said as he cracked and shook each rod. The sticks came alive like fireflies and lit the deck.

*Boom...boom...boom...*echoed across the sea, announcing the beginning of the Limassol night festivities.

Faye, Michael, and Carl looked up and were greeted with floating red, white, and green chrysanthemums that disappeared with the gray sky.

"Dinner and a show. I'm impressed," Faye said with a wink to the deckhand.

Carl returned a welcoming grin and placed the tray on the table.

Boom...boom...boom.

As the blue and red cascade faded, the breeze died away. Suffocated by the hanging darkness, the waves dwindled and brushed the hull of the ship.

Michael snatched up a pair of binoculars and watched as the next round of fireworks streaked into the sky.

All the while, the wail from the Maiden's Cry accompanied the pyrotechnic spectacle.

Boom...boom...boom.

The surface of the ocean reflected the orange and red hues from the sky.

Boom...boom...boom.

The abandoned oil rig cast a shadow across the floatplane and *Excalibur*. His attention drawn to the silhouette, Michael swung his field of view onto the steel girders of the oil derrick.

Boom...boom...boom.

With the platform lit from above, Michael spotted a purple and silver costume on the rig. He lowered his glasses. "Why would a reveler be on the rig during the festival?" he thought.

Boom...boom...boom.

Faye watched the explosive artistry on the gray canvas, unaware of the white bell bobbing below her on the surface of the water like a discarded milk carton.

"That oil reserve had dried up more than two months ago," Michael thought.

A series of small fireworks erupted in the sky. Michael turned to Faye to see her face illuminated with a soft green glow.

Another milk carton broke the surface and bumped the ship's hull.

"It's Sunday, and nobody in Cyprus works weekends," Michael thought, struggling with the new puzzle in his head.

Boom! Boom! Boom!

Taking advantage of the bright starburst, Michael refocused on the girder where he'd first seen the reveler in purple. His jaw dropped and his heart raced as he focused on the two dozen square gray blocks and red blinking lights.

Michael rushed at Faye, snatching up his dive pack as he passed.

"What are you—" she started.

Michael slammed into Faye, his momentum carrying them both over the side of the *Excalibur* and into the blackening water, his scream, "Bomb—" drowned out by *boom...boom...KABOOM!*

CHAPTER 6

"This is the last one. Get it loaded!" ordered the foreman standing in the shadow of the warehouse at the edge of the Milan Malpensa tarmac. He inspected the paperwork on his clipboard and then looked up at his overweight freight handler in a lime green vest sitting at the helm of the idle cargo tractor. "Now, Angelo!" he shouted over the whine of a jet engine.

"On it," Angelo answered. With a shrug of his slouched shoulders and twist of a fat wrist, the tug's diesel engine rumbled to life. Spewing black plumes out its tailpipe, the tractor towed the train of plastic-wrapped cargo trailers toward the waiting Boeing 727 bound for LaGuardia.

With his flabby knees at five and seven o'clock, Angelo lifted his headphones from around his thick neck and positioned them over his ears. Grooving to the latest pop music sensation and dancing in his meager seat, his knees bobbing up and down, the freight handler captained the cargo caravan over the black tarmac.

In the warehouse, the foreman stood in front of the automatic stretch wrapper. A partially wrapped palette of cardboard boxes, stacked eight feet high, sat unattended on the circular turntable.

"What the hell? Why isn't this shit bundled?" he shouted, looking around the empty warehouse. "Lazy assholes! I should fire all of you!"

*Click…click…click…*Steps echoed in the freight depot.

The irate supervisor turned around, prepared to unload his full repertoire of verbal pejoratives. "You fu—"

The stranger, his hair pulled back in a ponytail, stopped at the warehouse entrance.

"Hey, asshole, you can't be in here! This is a restricted area!"

The goateed stranger smoothed the creases from the sleeves of his black Armani jacket. Shifting his weight in his borrowed Brutini loafers, he fixed his eyes on the foreman.

"What are you...a fucking idiot? Get the hell out of here before I call security to haul your ass away!" the foreman spat, releasing his pent-up venom on the unsuspecting visitor.

One side of the stranger's mouth curved up, and he walked toward the foreman.

Click...click...click...

"Asshole, you've made the biggest mistake of your life," the supervisor began, rolling up his shirt sleeves over his hairy, clublike forearms.

Click...click...click...

"I'm going to wipe that fucking smirk off your face," the supervisor bellowed.

Click...click...click... The tapping of the dress shoes on cement, like a dawdling drum roll, further heightened the foreman's angst and anticipation.

"And shove it up your ass!" he added, balling his fists.

As the stranger stepped up, the foreman launched a right cross, landing the powerful punch squarely on the man's cheek.

The foreman's jaw dropped, his eyes as big as saucers, as he witnessed the stranger accept the blow as if were a kiss. The foreman unleashed an otherwise nose-breaking left and right combination and might as well have hit the warehouse wall, as the stranger stood unmoving, the same mischievous grin plastered on his goateed face.

"Who the fuck are you?" the supervisor questioned, fear crawling up the back of his spine as the stranger stepped toward him.

Click...click...

"Get away from me," he said, backing up but finding his path blocked by the wall of boxes on the automatic stretch wrapper.

Click...click...

"What do you want?" he pleaded.

The stranger raised his eyebrows, his smirk deepening to an evil sneer.

The stretch wrapper sprang to life with a whirr. The palette of boxes spun on the turntable, as did the foreman leaning against it, the stretch wrapper firmly applying plastic wrap with each revolution.

Whirr...whirr...

"Stop!" the foreman cried as plastic sheets wrapped tightly around his torso. "I can't brea—" he gasped and then mumbled, his eyes bulging as the transparent gag covered his nose and mouth.

Whirr...whirr...

With each revolution, the stretch wrapper covered the warehouse foreman from head to toe with a layer of plastic, like a spider cocooning a fly, until the man and cargo were one.

In the next instant, the stranger spun on his Brutini heals and clicked his way out of the warehouse and onto the tarmac toward the Boeing 727.

At the rear of the three-engine jetliner, Angelo finished loading the last of the LaGuardia cargo and had pushed the red "Close" button on the large aft cargo door. The fat freight handler was back on his tug and listening to DJ Antoine even before the hinged access hatch had moved.

With his mind on a rendezvous with his friends and an aperitivo at the local club, Angelo steered the tow tractor away from the transport plane, passing a well-dressed stranger. "The guy with the ponytail and goatee could have been ENAC, EASA, or customs. Hell, he could have been INTERPOL," the freight handler thought. "I'm not stopping, none of my business. Why pass up good Campari?"

As the tow tractor headed into the warehouse, the stranger stepped through the narrowing black gap in the aft cargo door as the jet engines rumbled to life.

〈〈〈—〉〉〉

The massive yellow-orange plume overshadowed the Limassol fireworks finale and like a fist reached up and punched the Mediterranean night sky. The explosive cloud, traveling eight thousand meters per second, enveloped the floatplane instantly and, adding its forty-gallon gas tank to the blast, rolled over the *Excalibur* like a locomotive over a tricycle.

Burning pieces of plane and research ship fell from the sky and splashed on the water. The old abandoned oil rig belched black smoke into the sky and groaned like a mortally wounded giant. A few crippled steel girders gave way and splashed into the sea.

Faye broke the surface, followed by Michael.

"Oh my God!" she exclaimed, treading water, small waves spilling over her head. She grabbed a length of wreckage, part of the fiberglass float from the seaplane, and, bobbing on the surface like a cork, eyes wide, she soaked up the chaos from the wreckage. "Michael?"

Before the Vanguard could respond, Carl erupted twenty feet away. "What the fuck happened?" he screamed, spitting out sea water and gulping air.

"Is everyone alright?" Michael asked, holding on to a charred piece of *Excalibur* decking. He pulled the heavy pack from around his shoulders and laid it on top of the wide makeshift raft, thankful that the fifteen-pound weight belt inside hadn't carried him to the bottom. He reached into his bag and pulled out his dive mask and two fluorescent glow sticks.

"All right?" the deckhand questioned. "All right?" he screamed, clutching a floating plank. "What the hell happened?"

"Someone was on the rig…it was C4," Michael said, pulling the dive mask to the top of his head. He turned and stared at the moaning steel behemoth. Wreckage from the floatplane and *Excalibur* covered the rolling waves like an undulating hardwood floor.

"Why the fuck would someone want to blow up that old rig?" Carl exclaimed, fear raising his voice an octave higher.

Michael turned and looked at Faye, intensity burning in his eyes.

"They didn't," she answered.

Carl's eyes grew wide, his brows raised. "Oh, you're shitting me!" he screamed. "Who'd want to kill us?"

Michael cracked both fluorescent glow sticks, lighting his concern. "He and the Vanguard Order were the only ones who knew," he thought, his mind recalling the telephone call with his mentor: "We're getting close, Zachariah. With a little luck, we may have an artifact soon."

"Now what?" Carl's panicked voice cracked.

"Looks like we're in for a moonlight swim," Faye announced, staring up at the glowing white orb in the darkening sky.

Michael looked toward the Cyprus coastline. "The tide is strong now, pushing inland. It shouldn't take us more than fifteen minutes," he agreed as he pushed away wood, stacking broken planks on top of one another. The more timber Michael piled, the more it amassed around him. He looked to the shore again, this time taking a bearing using the massive rock formations, the Maiden on shore, her lover at sea. "If we keep the first cliff face at our ten o'clock and the second at our one o'clock, I—"

Stacks of debris rolled in front of Michael's view, and for a brief moment the two cliffs formed a single effigy: something familiar, but the memory was just out of reach.

The ghostly wail filled the still air.

"I'd just wish that fucking howling would stop," Carl spat.

Michael turned to Carl. "What did you say?"

"I wish it would stop."

"No, before that," Michael said.

"I wish that fucking howling wou—"

"Howling," Michael repeated, the word electric. Michael's mind reeled, the puzzle pieces falling into place. "It was right in front of me all the time," he said, slapping the water.

"What was?" Carl asked.

Michael stacked the floating wood in front of him, wreckage filling the gap between the two rock formations. As the waves gently rolled across his view, the image took shape and the head of the guardian emerged.

"There!" Michael announced.

"What?" Faye asked.

"The Bedouin guardian," Michael exclaimed.

The wail from the shore carried across the sea.

"That!" he said, raising his finger into the air. "That sound. It's not a maiden's cry, but the howl of a Bedouin guardian. It's a watchdog!"

Faye and Carl looked at Michael, their eyebrows raised.

"I'm betting that the two cliffs were once a massive bluff in the shape of a saluki hound. The howl was enough to scare off trespassers, and over the centuries, the waves eroded away the guardian."

Faye and Carl looked toward the rocky monoliths.

"There's the entrance," Michael shouted, pointing to the cliff face. "That's where we'll find the artifact."

"Then let's get a move on and find it," Carl said, abandoning his float and taking two strokes toward the shore. "I'm getting water-logged."

On the third stroke through the calm Mediterranean, Carl's face twisted in pain. "Aaah!"

"What's wrong?" Michael asked.

"My arm! Oh my God! My arm feels like it's on fire! Aaah!" The deckhand's face turned white, and his eyes bulged.

Carl lifted his arm from out of the water; slime draped on it like strands of cooked spaghetti. The deckhand screamed again and sank beneath the waves.

"I'm coming," Faye shouted and started toward the struggling deckhand.

"Don't move!" Michael yelled, throwing one of the fluorescent glow rods. The yellow stick turned end over end and splashed where Carl's head had been.

"Carl?" Faye shouted.

Michael slipped the dive mask over his eyes and dropped under the water. His heart skipped a beat as he watched as the mass of glowing jellyfish engulfed the deckhand and the glow rod, their shimmering bioluminescence lighting the dark sea.

Michael kicked his feet furiously, his head crashed through to the surface. "Jellyfish!"

"What?"

"Box jellyfish! Hundreds of them!" he said, clutching the piece of singed wreckage.

"Where's Carl?" she asked, her head pivoting, her eyes searching for any sign of the deckhand.

"He's gone."

The howl of the defaced Bedouin guardian accented Michael's somber tone.

"No," she said in disbelief.

Michael buried his face in the water and spun three hundred-sixty degrees, his eyes frantically searching the blackness of open water. But the sea was an ocean of glowing cube-shaped blooms.

Faye looked down at the water as if she were trying to peer through a dirty window. "Where are they?" she asked.

A glowing square bell bobbed to the surface four meters from her raft.

"Everywhere," Michael answered.

Faye splashed at it. Another bell breached the surface…and then another. Faye's eyes darted along the surface of the water. Circles of fluorescent yellow light radiated all around.

"Shit!" she yelled and paddled over to Michael.

The glow from the swarm lit the water like an underwater sun. With each passing moment, the marine invertebrates drew closer. Michael sank below the surface, desperate to find a way out, a gap through the glowing wall. He watched as Carl, the deckhand's mouth twisted in a silent scream, was dragged deeper within the prison of tentacles. And then, Michael looked down: darkness.

"One way," he said, splashing to the surface. "We go down to the bottom." He pulled his dive bag around his shoulders.

The box jellyfish pulsed closer. On every side, three meters separated Faye and Michael from the stinging arms.

"What?"

"Take a deep breath, hold onto my bag, close your eyes, and kick like hell!"

"We'll never make it!"

"Now!" Michael ordered and sucked in a deep breath.

Faye clutched the bag around Michael's shoulders and inhaled. In the next instant, she was under the surface, salt water stinging her closed eyes.

Glow stick in hand and Faye in tow, Michael kicked hard, his hands sweeping the water out of his way. He was thankful for the weight belt in his pack as he sped downward toward darkness. As he stared down into the darkness below, the walls of tentacles closing in, his mind was focused on two thoughts: "The Medusa and Bedouin guardian bar the paths." There was an entrance down here somewhere. He was close. And: "You left it at the bottom again?" The pony bottle was there, below in the darkness. He just had to find it.

Four meters from the bottom, Michael cleared the tube of tentacles. With the dull radiance of the glow stick lighting the sloping bottom, Michael scoured the sand like a prospector searching for nuggets in a pan. Michael's lungs burned, and he realized that Faye must be completely out of breath.

From the corner of his eye, the fluorescent yellow bottle stood out like a firefly on a moonless night.

Michael raced to grab the small reserve tank and pushed the pony bottle's regulator into Faye's mouth. She pulled in three deep breaths. As he watched, Faye's image began to blur, and he knew he was on the edge of losing consciousness.

With one hand Michael tapped Faye's shoulder and with the other pulled the regulator from her mouth. He sucked in two large breaths, stemming the shadows creeping in from the sides of his mask, and wedged the regulator back into Faye's mouth, tapping her arm twice. The pair buddy-breathed for the next minute, Michael tapping Faye's arm with each two-breath exchange.

As Faye inhaled, Michael glanced at the small tank's pressure gauge: the indicator needle had passed from yellow to red. He then tipped his head up and watched as the box jellyfish closed the circular gap from which Michael and Faye had swam. Tentacles blanketed the water above their heads in every direction.

Out of air, Michael put the regulator in his mouth and pulled in two breaths. He gulped at the air, and his heart slammed in his chest as he watched the tentacles begin to descend, floating down like paratroopers. He turned to Faye and watched as she drew in her breaths. He pulled one deep breath from the pony bottle, knowing there was only a few hundred pounds of air left in the small canister. His eyes darted up and down the sloping bottom. His mind raced, considering every escape route: down the slope, run out of air and drown; up the slope and into venomous barbed tentacles, painful paralysis and drown. Neither option was much of an option.

Spinning to his rear, Michael fixed his sights on a huge coral shelf. The fan and brain corals grew along a curved stone shaped like an upturned letter *C* or a tail, Michael thought. His eyes followed the contour of the shelf as it headed inland and toward the surface. He imagined the Bedouin guardian's tail, its haunches and back. It was a long shot, he thought, looking at the glowing jellies above, but it was the only option.

He sucked hard for another breath as the regulator began to resist the pull of his lungs. Michael wedged the mouthpiece between Faye's lips and swam for the shelf, pulling Faye behind.

Reaching the coral lip, Michael reached his arm under the overhang. A speckled green parrotfish, hiding under the shelf, darted out and up the coral bank, only to be speared by the stinging barbs of a box jellyfish. The fish quivered and rolled, its body shaking like it was being electrocuted.

Michael swept mounds of sand out from beneath the overhang, glancing over his shoulder at the tentacles drifting down, now two meters above their heads. His hands shook as cool water sucked precious heat from his body, but he knew he'd either be out of air or jellyfish food long before hypothermia killed him.

After sweeping another armful of sand aside, the space under the shelf wide enough to slip under. Michael shot a quick look at Faye, who sat unaware of the tentacles that dangled within one meter of her.

Michael removed the dive bag from around his shoulders and removed another glow stick. Pulling the pack back over his shoulders again and cracking the fluorescent rod, he pulled one last breath from the pony, placed the regulator into Faye's hand, and dragged her by her shirt under the stone lip.

Pulled forward by Michael, her hands wrapped around the pony bottle, Faye kicked hard against the cold water. The more force she exerted, the more her lungs craved a fresh breath. She sucked hard on the regulator.

The chill raked across Faye's body, and she felt goose bumps rise on her skin. Thoughts were her only companion in her blindness, thoughts of Ben, and of an artifact to free him from the Horseman. It was those thoughts that stoked the engine pumping her legs.

She inhaled hard: half a breath. It wasn't long before her lungs burned and her hands and legs were numb. "Michael hasn't' taken a breath in over a minute," she thought. But she needed one breath. Faye bit down hard on the mouthpiece and sucked. But the pony bottle resisted her embrace. She sucked again...nothing, and again. Then even Ben slipped away.

The dull light from the glow stick reflected off the red and green algae on the underground cavern walls, casting an eerie incandescence on Michael's bare skin. With one hand clutching the glow stick, feeling above, along the top of the rocky ceiling, and the other clamped on Faye, Michael swam hard though the narrow underwater passage. Faye's body felt like dead weight in his hand, and the cold had made him sluggish. He kicked until his legs cramped. His heart raced, adrenaline pumping through his veins, and he felt like his head was going to explode. Michael's air was gone. The path ahead: a blur.

Then the hand above his head broke the surface of the water.

Michael exploded out of the water, screaming and inhaling at the same time, the underwater cave echoing his dire cry for life. He slapped the surface of the pool with both hands, trying to force air into his deprived lungs.

Floating on his back and gasping aloud, Michael's head was spinning, all thoughts, beyond the next breath, clouded. With each cool breath, the smell of seashells and salty water filling his lungs, his mind cleared. He lifted his light stick up into the giant air pocket; the dim glow reached up but was unable to pierce the shadows of the subterranean refuge.

Michael's eyes shot open wide as his thoughts of self-preservation were replaced with…"Faye!" he screamed. Shock rocketed through his body, his precious air stolen from him like a punch in the gut. Faye was lying facedown in the dim pool. Michael hurriedly turned her over and felt for a pulse and a breath. But there was nothing.

"Faye, stay with me," he shouted, dragging her limp body to the ledge and up onto the rocky bank.

His lips sealed on hers, his thumb and forefinger squeezing her nose, Michael blew in two rescue breaths. Faye's cheeks expanded like a balloon. Her chest rose. He then positioned himself over her chest, interlocking his fingers, and pressed into her, the compressions deep and rhythmic. He stopped and gave her two more breaths.

"Come on, Faye! Wake up!" he shouted, the dim light from the glow stick fading.

He straddled her waist and performed thirty more compressions, his arms tiring. Michael moved back to her lips and cupped the back of her neck with his palm and gave her another deep breath.

Faye coughed out salt water and gasped.

"Ben?" she weakly urged.

Faye inhaled and coughed again.

The panicked expression on Michael's face was replaced with cold dejection. He winced hard, stood and pulled off his dive bag. He retrieved two more glow sticks from the bottom of the bag and cracked them to life.

The underground grotto was a massive limestone dome spanning fifteen meters across. At the center, a stalagmite chandelier hung above the dark pool, the stony fixture casting shadows instead of light.

"There's fresh air," Michael announced, inhaling deeply. "We rest, wait out our gelatinous friends, and then I'll try for the surface."

"We'll try for the surface," she amended, standing, her eyes fixed firmly on his.

Michael nodded with a smile.

"The Medusa and Bedouin guardian bar the paths," Michael quoted, his eyes darting across the rocky room.

"The artifact?" she asked.

"It has to be close," he said, handing Faye one glow stick.

Michael raised the light bar. He scanned the grotto and then tilted up his head and focused his eyes on the center of the cathedral ceiling, captivated by the stone candelabra.

74

Faye stepped to one side of the grotto dome. Within the dull radiance of the fluorescent light, she ran her fingers along the gray limestone and brushed across moist blue-green algae that coated the flat stone. She passed her hand across a small fissure, and a slight breeze stroked over her skin.

"You're right, there's a breeze," she said.

"This chamber is likely one within a labyrinth that runs all the way to the shore," he surmised.

As Faye stepped along the craggy wall, the surface darkened with black soot.

"This wall was torched," she announced, fingering the blackened area.

Michael turned to Faye, unaware of the glowing transparent bell that had breached the surface of the dark pool at his feet, and walked over to her.

"That's not all," she continued. "The ceiling collapsed," she said, staring at the massive boulders frozen like a stone waterfall.

"Or was made to collapse," Michael added, stepping next to Faye and inspecting the cave-in.

Michael spun around. "There is nothing here," he declared, scanning the barren grotto.

Boom!

The sound echoed through the chamber, and the ground quaked.

"What the hell was that?" Faye asked.

Fifteen meters above their heads, another two-ton metal beam groaned and broke loose from the abandoned derrick and plunged into the Mediterranean. The steel dart shot through the water like a torpedo, plunging through the sandy bottom and stabbing the limestone.

"I don't kn—" Michael began.

BOOM...

Water sprayed in through the crack at the top of the grotto like a fire sprinkler, dousing Faye. Liquid cascaded down the charred wall like a fountain.

"We've got to get out of here," Michael shouted as he raced to the pool's edge, pulling the dive bag over his shoulders.

Outside, the crippled oil rig fired another torpedo. The I-beam slammed into the coral shelf.

BOOM...

At the top of the domed grotto, the limestone chandelier broke free and plummeted down, water pouring in from the wound like water from a hose.

Michael dove and rolled to the grotto wall as the stone fixture crashed into the pool. A wave of water splashed over the bank.

Along the far wall, Faye looked down at her shoes, already buried in salt water. "This bowl is filling up!"

Michael's heart raced as he watched the water lap over the edge of the grotto bank. Getting to his knees, Michael's stomach sank as bell after bell oozed out of the expanding pool, the spineless hunters oozing on the floor.

"It's worse than that," he answered.

Faye stared at the wormlike appendage spreading toward her shoe. "Shit!" she exclaimed, stepping back to the blackened wet wall, her hand pressed up against the sooty limestone water fountain for support.

"Michael, come here!"

He turned and sloshed his way across the jellyfish minefield and approached Faye from behind. She was engrossed on the wet grotto wall, rubbing it with her hand.

"What are you doing?" he asked and then watched as each stroke of her wet hand exposed more of the ancient inscription.

"It's Sumerian," Faye began. "Wary the Lost One," she recited, the fluorescent glow stick illuminating the etching.

Working from left to right, she wiped the soot. "Brave the path…" Faye scrubbed the grimy wall. ". . . of burning ice…" She rubbed clean the last section. ". . . in the moving mountain."

Michael turned and peered at the translucent grotto floor, now covered with deadly invertebrates. "Anything about how to get out of here?" he asked.

"That's everything."

"Not helpful," Michael said, jumping up onto the first of the scattered boulders at the base of the cave-in, pulling Faye along with him to higher ground.

The two Vanguards extended their light bars and watched the domed room fill. Faye and Michael climbed upon each row of stacked boulders as the jellyfish-laden water rose.

"We're running out of rocks," Faye said, stepping atop the last tier.

At the top of the heap, the pair pushed against a massive boulder, their arms straining, but the stone blockade would not yield.

Water and stinging tentacles surged up over the lip of Faye's ledge.

She turned to Michael and sat down on her stone seat in silent acquiescence.

"No!" he screamed, his brows furrowed. Michael jammed his back against the top of the limestone wall, braced his feet against one boulder, and pushed. He clenched his teeth. The veins in his neck, in his forehead, even in his hands pulsed as he shoved against the massive stone.

BOOM...Another man-made metal intrusion slammed against the ocean bottom and rocked the grotto.

The wall supporting Michael, weakened from the girder assault, cracked, and, with the upper section giving way around his back, Michael, eyes wide, fell backward through the limestone wall.

"Michael?" Faye called out, climbing down into the new chamber.

"I'm okay," he answered breathlessly, lying flat on his back.

Faye raised her glow stick; even in the dim light, she could see the curve on his lips.

With water spilling into the new chamber, Faye and Michael trudged up a narrow, sloping passageway. Along the craggy corridor, the Vanguards passed coils of old climbing rope.

Before long, the howl of the Bedouin guardian resonated through the rocky corridor, and within moments the two Vanguards stepped into a moonlit stone vault that opened, through jagged stalactite and stalagmite teeth, to the night sky above and the pounding white surf below.

Faye stared up at the starlit blackness through the serrated orifice, her eyes focused on the single white orb. "Swallowed by the Maiden," she said.

Michael turned to her, his eyebrows raised.

"We're inside the Maiden cliff. We've made it to shore," Faye said, her face flushed with relief.

In that moment, a huge wave crashed through the rocky gap, filling up the basin and spilling over onto the ledge where Faye and Michael stood.

In the churning foam, Faye spied part of the *Excalibur*'s skeleton rolling back and forth with the tide. A six-foot breaker stormed in at twenty miles per hour and tossed the wooden debris high up on the rocky backstop, splintering it to pieces.

Faye's jaw dropped. "How do we cross that?"

Michael ran his hand down the algae-covered walls and realized that the crushing waves were not their only concern. "Whatever we do, we need to do it fast. This entire chamber will soon be underwater."

Another rogue wave, larger than the previous one, crashed into the cavern. The white wave crested over the ledge and swept Michael's feet out from under him. Lying prone on his stomach, Michael spun like a human propeller as the force of the wave pushed him toward the edge.

"Michael!" Faye screamed. She leapt forward, grabbing his arm, stopping him from splashing into the churning basin.

The howl of the Bedouin guardian grew louder, the sound deafening in the rocky cathedral.

"The surge is treacherous," Michael said as he and Faye backed away from the ledge. "Cavers don't dare come near the Maiden cliff after dark."

"Cavers!" she repeated, jostling the dive bag from around Michael's shoulders and retrieving the last light stick. Cracking the rod, Faye disappeared into the corridor.

Another wave barreled into the cavern. Standing alone on the ledge, Michael stared at the dark shape flopping in the churn, bouncing across the jagged rocks.

"Carl," he said solemnly, watching the deckhand perform a gruesome ballet with each swell.

As Carl's body washed close to the ledge, Michael reached into the white foam, grabbed the deckhand's wet shirt, and pulled the corpse out of the surf and into the passageway.

Meanwhile, within the dim glow of the narrow corridor, Faye soon came upon the piles of frayed nylon rope abandoned by cavers. She grabbed as much of the least-worn coils of rope that she could find and hurried back to Michael, only to see Carl's tentacle-scarred face and unrelenting stare greeting her return.

"He escaped the jellyfish prison and washed in with the tide," Michael said, kneeling next to the deckhand.

"I'm sorry."

Michael nodded and wiped his hand over Carl's face, shutting the dead man's eyes.

Waves thrummed. The ghostly shriek echoed louder as the pounding surf blew through the cavern mouth like a cacophonous saxophone. The tide surged higher, and waves crested up over the ledge, spilling into the corridor.

Faye dropped the braided sections to the wet ground. "Let's get the hell out of here," she said and began tying pieces of rope together.

Michael weaved one end into a loop and stared at the chasm and the huge stalagmite pointing up like a post in the ground two feet below the cavern entrance. "I guess thirty feet across." He coiled up the knotted lasso and, with the waves receding off of the ledge, stepped to the ridge and threw the lariat, only to have the loop fall short of the stalagmite and splash into the churning basin.

"Shit!" he exclaimed.

Again and again he tossed the knotted lasso. Each time, he caught only water.

"I can't get it there," he said, his shoulder aching.

Another wave crashed into the cavern and poured into the corridor.

"If we can't get this to the other side, we're dead!" Michael said.

"Dead," Faye repeated, looking at Carl's corpse. Her eyes grew wide as the idea sprouted and took root. Faye snatched the lariat out of Michael's hand and tied it around the waist of the dead deckhand, handing the other end to Michael. She grabbed Carl under his arms and hauled him out of the corridor.

"What are you doing?" Michael questioned.

Faye looked up. "Helping Carl save our asses," she declared, straining against the dead weight as she dragged the corpse to the ledge and pushed Carl over into the water. "Have you ever gone fishing?"

The deckhand's body bobbed on top of the surging surf. As the next breaker streamed in, Carl was tossed up against the rocks. Each time his body rolled down into the retreating surf, like a child tumbling down a grassy knoll.

Michael held the knotted rope as Carl's corpse was cast upwards onto the rocks, the Vanguard letting out or pulling in slack like a fisherman casting a line.

The next whitecapped wave smashed into the cavern. Michael and Faye struggled to keep upright in the gushing torrent as the water cast the deckhand's body up and onto the stalagmite, the corpse wedging between the stone spikes.

"He did it," Michael said, pulling the rope taut.

"Thanks Carl," Faye uttered.

"Now the easy part," he said, looking at Faye. "You're first."

"Easy?" she asked.

Michael wrapped his end of the rope around a boulder and held it fast. Faye grabbed the nylon with both hands, kicked her feet up, and wrapped them around the horizontal line. With her face staring up at the craggy cathedral ceiling, she pulled with her hands and pushed with her feet and worked her way over the crashing torrent. In less than a minute, Faye had crossed over the chasm and stood on the upper ledge of the cliff opening.

"Hurry," she cried. "Watch ou—" The deafening howl of the Bedouin guardian drowned out Faye's warning, and her heart skipped a beat as she watched the swell rise up and wash Michael over the ledge.

Hanging down above the foamy churn, his hands burning against the course nylon fibers, Michael struggled to find stable footing on the slime-covered stones. The next wave crashed over him, pummeling his body: he felt like a prizefighter's heavy bag.

Michael had never enjoyed climbing ropes in gym class as a child, and this was worse than any gym class he had ever endured.

"Hurry!" echoed the voice in his ears.

Hand over hand, he pulled himself up.

One foot from the stalagmite anchor, the rope broke. The knotted length of frayed rope fell into the churning waves. Michael dangled over the tidal cauldron, holding on to Carl's cold arm, saved from a watery death by death itself.

Faye's high-pitch scream, "Michael!" cut through the wail of the churning waves.

He stared up into the deckhand's vacant eyes. With adrenaline pumping in his veins, Michael reached up, grabbed Carl's wet shirt, and pulled himself up to the stalagmite. Moments later he hauled himself onto the upper ledge of the cliff.

Outside, the cool Mediterranean breeze blew across Michael's wet face as he stared out over the black sea.

"What now?" Faye asked.

"Now we find out just how deep the Vanguard treachery goes."

CHAPTER 7

A single streetlamp governed over twilight and the empty lot. In the corner of the Minnesota business park, stainless-steel lettering reflected the dim authority and shimmered its appellation for the parking-lot specters: Chimeracon.

Inside the private biotechnology company, the sterile laboratory was a buzz of activity. On one wall, round petri dishes, lined end-to-end like cars stuck in a traffic jam, rode a conveyor belt within a large biocabinet. With each intermittent whirr, a new car paraded forward and stopped in front of two mechanical arms that swung back and forth like a cop directing stop-and-go traffic. The first robotic arm lifted the lid from the dish; the second limb dispensed a stream of purple nourishment. With its lid replaced, the plate moved forward on the assembly line, and another took its place.

In another corner of the lab, a human skeleton, mounted on a rolling stand, looked on with hollow eyes and a toothy, ironic grin at the automated culture-dish highway.

Taking center stage, two glass tanks bubbled with glaucous ooze that almost concealed the strange embryonic forms suspended within. Each humanlike organism, curled in a fetal position, had a bulbous head dominated by large, lidless black eyes. In the middle of the head, a long canine snout stretched forward, the sleepy snarl on its muzzle incapable of restraining long canine teeth. Two hands floated in the goo, both with five fingers, all ending in well-developed claws. A long tail wrapped around each developing fetus like a blanket.

In front of the artificial wombs, a set of robotic arms raised levers and twisted dials, adjusting temperature and monitoring fluid and nutrient levels of the DNA soup. A steel finger of the mechanical midwife rapped one transparent cauldron, like a child might tap the glass of a fish tank: the mutated embryo twitched.

On the far side, a door labeled Exam Room 1 slid open with a whoosh, and a thin, brown-haired man in his late twenties wearing a white lab coat entered the mechanized laboratory. The door slid closed, and the HEPA-filtered space within was sealed once more.

The scientist plucked a cell-culture dish from the conveyor belt and, walking up to the lab bench, slid the dish onto the stage of a low-powered microscope. He peered through the eyepieces, focusing on the globular patterns.

A rattling from the far side of the lab pulled his attention to the bony figure standing along the side wall. His eyes rolled over the skeleton and then across the lab. Finding nothing out of the ordinary, he resumed his inspection of the microbial designs.

The scientist was unaware of the movement behind him; he didn't lift his gaze from the microscope lenses as the bony digit brushed his ear.

With little more emotion than the robots tending to the mutated embryos, the scientist turned around and stared into the white sockets of the skull.

"Your experiment preoccupies you, brother," the toothy jaw chattered.

The young man's expression was a blank canvas. No shock, no terror, not a single crease appeared on his face, only an icy stoicness that could have been painted on.

"Are you not surprised to see me?" the skull mouthed as muscle and tendons and then skin covered the bony scaffolding until the Horseman, Death, stood naked in the lab.

"Why don't you answer me?" the bare gothic beauty asked.

A forked tongue flicked in and out from between the scientist's lips, and then it was Death whose hard expression cracked. "What madness is this?"

«««—»»»

Inside Exam Room 1, a twenty-six-year-old woman awoke on a long table to find her arms strapped down and her legs spread apart, up in stirrups. An IV tube, needled into an arm vein, was attached to a small drip bag filled with a clear fluid. She had no covering, nothing soft between her pale skin and the cold metal of the sterile table.

As she rolled her head from side to side, she blinked her eyes hard, and the gray blur sharpened into the back of a white lab coat.

"Where am I?" she murmured, her voice trembling.

The faux doctor turned around with a smile, injecting sedative into the IV port.

"Where am I!" she screamed, thrashing her arms, straining against the restraints around her wrists.

"In the lab," Pestilence casually answered.

"What happened?" she asked, slurring her words as the sedative took effect. "I remember interviewing for a job and—"

"Oh, you got the job, Kim," the Spirit of Disease interrupted. "No one was more qualified."

"I can't feel my legs."

He pulled a long aspiration needle and syringe from its package, attached an ultrasound probe, and sat down on a wheeled stool, rolling between the woman's legs. "That's because you're paralyzed," he said, poking the needle and probe into her vagina.

"What's wrong with me?"

"Wrong?" he echoed. "Nothing's wrong, but I can't have you jostling around during the procedure, now, can I?" He focused on the needle's image in the ultrasound display as it pierced the woman's ovary.

"Procedure? What happened?"

"I severed your spinal cord," the Horseman answered matter-of-factly. "You don't feel a thing from the waist down." Pestilence straightened up, "You certainly have lots of questions today."

"Oh God," Kim said, sobbing. "Why?"

"Eggs," he answered, drawing up clear fluid into the syringe.

The woman's eyes grew wide. "Wha...what?"

"I'm harvesting your eggs," he said, pulling the needle and probe from between her legs. "I've found that the most viable clones"—he tapped the syringe—"are made with fresh specimen."

"No...please," she sobbed.

"Come now, Kim, you are healthy and well fed," he said, adjusting the drip bag. "You can live this way for years."

"No," she pleaded.

His eyes turned cold, and a sneer washed away the pleasant bedside manner as easily as a wave washes away footprints in the sand. "You will live this way for years."

The Horseman turned to the sliding door, raising his eyebrows, the sides of his mouth curving up into a smirk. "It appears that an old friend has come to pay me a visit."

He tucked the sample into his side coat pocket. "I'll see to my guest and let you rest so you can provide more of your lovely eggs for me."

The naked and unwilling patient opened her mouth to scream, but the sound froze in her throat as Pestilence jabbed a syringe full of sedative into her leg and pushed the plunger.

She glared at the needle sticking out of her leg.

"See, you don't feel a thing," the Horseman declared.

The sedative took effect in seconds. Kim struggled to keep her heavy eyelids open as the white lab coat blurred gray once more.

«««—»»»

Amidst the confusion burgeoning in the main laboratory, the exam-room door slid open with a whoosh, and Pestilence stood framed in the doorway. "Not madness, Kishar, science," Pestilence declared, watching his doppelganger's forked tongue flick in an out in of its mouth.

The Horseman stepped into the lab, walking up to his duplicate. "What do you think of my clone? Good enough to fool even you, I think."

"I am not amused, Reesef," Death answered, folding her arms.

"Still upset because your own ruse failed?" he commented, glaring at her nakedness. "Sulking doesn't become you, Kishar."

Death rolled her eyes and dismissed the remark with a haughty lift of her chin.

"A simple experiment really," Pestilence continued. "DNA from this vessel," he said, patting his chest. "And add in the genetic material from a king cobra." The horseman grabbed his double's lower jaw, pulling the expandable mandible down and exposing two long hypodermic needle–like fangs that curled back inside the copy's mouth. "A nice combination, don't you think?"

Death walked around the huge glass cylinders bubbling with ooze.

"Include a touch of my essence," Pestilence said, releasing his clone. He extended his arm, and beetles and scorpions engulfed his limb, some dropping to the floor and disappearing in a black mist. "And my double is perfect...bait."

"Treachery becomes you, my brother."

"And what of your treachery, Kishar?" Pestilence asked,

Death produced a clear baggy, the chewed stogie resting inside, and tossed it to the Horseman.

The scientist's face was flushed with excitement, and his hands trembled as he snatched the prize from the air, tucking it away inside his lab coat.

Death peered through the bluish-gray ooze. "Another science project?" the Horseman asked, tapping the vat. The embryo, its face a mutated facsimile of its Horseman creator, squirmed inside the simulated womb like a shark in its egg sack. "I can see the family resemblance."

"My Blood Beasts, grown for one week. When fully developed, they'll track prey from ten kilometers away, and the sabers will be eight inches long. In three days, my pets will be born."

"I prefer my pets dead," Kishar interjected, stepping out from behind the incubation chambers.

"Your mindless death walkers are nothing compared to my chimeras. These aren't mere puppets; they will be smart, autonomous, and lethal."

Pestilence stared at Death's naked body. Kishar's form was beautiful, for a human: taut breasts and tight ass. But it was far from perfect. "Maybe a hyena or a vulture hybrid: eaters of the dead. How appropriate for Death," he thought. He'd need only a small sample. A cruel smile washed across his face.

"Would you like a clone of your own? All I need is a flake of skin," he said, stepping toward Death, his eyes rolling over her exposed flesh.

The lab began to quake. The glass petri dishes rattled off the conveyor belt, smashing into shards on the ground, as Kishar delivered her answer. "I think not, brother."

Feeling his intrusive gaze on her bare skin, Kishar furrowed her brows. Skin and muscle dissolved away, while at the same time her black hair grew to the floor and transformed into a long dark cloak which covered her bony form.

"Why have you come, Kishar?" Reesef asked. "You've never cared about my work before."

"The Vanguard is a threat, a threat that should be eliminated while the mystic power still resides within our mortal shells."

"It has always been a threat, but no more so than a flea on the hide of a hound." He looked at Death quizzically. "Four millennia, and you're concerned with the Vanguard now? Why?"

"Farrow is gone. The Order has control of the Chronicles and hunts for artifacts which can be used against us. They must be destroyed."

"You approach the wrong Horseman, Kishar. I'm not interested in fighting the Vanguard. It is Seth you seek, if warring is your design."

"Seth reeks of that putrid mortal soul. He is not fit to be a Horseman of the Apocalypse," Kishar spat.

"Be careful where your loyalties lie," Pestilence warned. "War is many things: deceitful, cunning, manipulative, but most of all vengeful."

"And where does your allegiance lie, Reesef?"

"Only to that which makes immortality most entertaining."

"The winds of change are blowing, brother. Are you too arrogant a fool to hear them?" Death asked, stepping toward the laboratory exit, bony heels clicking on the tile floor.

"Even a fool knows that the wind can be both a gentle breeze and a deadly hurricane," Pestilence announced as Death left the room.

The scientist stared at his copy, whose forked tongue flicked in assenting response, and then looked down at the small beetle crawling across the floor, up his leg, over his arm, and into his hand.

"Kishar never felt a thing, did she my pet?" Pestilence said, plucking the black wisp from between the beetle's mandibles. "Winds of change indeed," he said, blowing against the thin strand of hair.

«««—»»»

"There is a mole in the Vanguard!" Michael announced, standing in front of the huge semicircular table. His gaze, full of marked accusation, fell across the faces of the twelve people in the boardroom: Zachariah Prond, Diana Waterford, the four heads of the Vanguard houses: War, Death, Pestilence, and Famine, and their respective bodyguards.

Whispers filled the room until the quiet murmurs grew into a swell of angry roars.

"He can't be serious!"

"Impossible!"

"Liar!"

Michael shrugged, shifting his weight from one foot to the other. Why the hell did he feel like he was on trial?

"My report," Michael began.

"We've read your report, Mr. Cantal," Diana Waterford interrupted. "And I will advise you not to make rash allegations without proof."

"Proof!" Michael shouted. "Is a dead Vanguard and the wreckage of the *Excalibur* scattered across the bottom of the Mediterranean proof enough for you?"

"It is one thing to acknowledge an unfortunate accident involving an oil rig," the Dragon Lady stated. "It is another to allege that someone in the Order is a traitor."

"Accident? Is that what you think happened?" Michael retorted, his temper rising. "Explain that to Carl's family."

"Let's not forget Milan," Faye chimed, stepping forward into the semicircle.

Michael turned to her, his brows furrowed. "Milan?" he asked.

Faye stood next to Michael. "Milan is down, all agents retired." Faye stared at Diana Waterford. "Wasn't that the report?"

"Let us not forget that the explosion occurred hours after your arrival, Ms. Monroe," Diana Waterford countered.

"Are you accusing me of being the mole?"

"People have a tendency to die around you, Ms. Monroe."

"It would not have taken much for someone to have followed Ms. Monroe to Cyprus," Zachariah announced, ending his silent observance. "And she could not have been in Madrid," he added.

"More attacks?" Faye asked.

"Or Berlin, today," the head of the Vanguard Order announced gravely, his gaze shifting to Diana Waterford as he watched the blood drain from her face.

"Berlin?" the blond Vanguard questioned in shock. "All agents?"

"I'm sorry, Diana," he said, his tone consoling. "Your son—"

"My son was a Vanguard," she interrupted proudly.

Zachariah nodded. "We have a traitor in our midst."

Michael's mind raced with thoughts both coherent and fantastical. "The danger is not merely a mole within the Order," he thought, his eyes washing over the faces in the room. "No, the real danger is what it has been for millennia: the Horsemen of the Apocalypse."

"A Horseman spy," Diana Waterford said, voicing Michael's thoughts. The leaders of the four Vanguard Houses nodded in agreement.

Diana Waterford pushed out her chair and stood. "For so long, we have protected humanity," she said, "given our lives for the sake of people we will never know, and taken the secret to our graves with no memorial, no tribute. My son is dead," she said with outstretched arms to the Vanguard assemblage. "Your friend is dead," she declared, turning and pointing at Michael, the timbre of her voice dark and wavering with each passing second.

More head nodding from the council members. Diana Waterford walked around to the center of the room, pausing for a moment, regaining her composure.

"But this is not about individuals, or self-sacrifice," the Dragon Lady continued, her eyes addressing each seated Vanguard elder.

"We should continue the search for Horsemen artifacts," Michael interjected.

Murmurs of discontent echoed from around the semicircle. Michael glared at Zachariah, his eyes pleading for the Vanguard leader to be the voice of reason, but the voice was mute.

"Or personal crusades," Diana Waterford continued, glaring at Michael.

"We must," Michael began.

"We must act!" the Dragon Lady asserted.

Faye watched as the number two Vanguard steamrolled Michael's plea. Her temples ached as the words "The Dragon Lady always gets what she wants" panged in her head.

"We cannot tolerate this murderous betrayal," Waterford declared, pacing in front of the panel. "It is an affront to the honor of all Vanguards, now and those who have come before."

The seated Vanguard nodded, turning to one another in a simple and singular affirmation.

"I beseech all of you. We must lock down all Vanguard facilities until the Horseman traitor can be flushed out and found!"

Michael lowered his eyes in frustration as heard the Vanguards' whispered agreement.

"Return to your houses and institute the lockdown," Waterford ordered. "As of midnight tonight, no one enters or leaves this or any Vanguard facility."

«««—»»»

The eighty-seven-year-old apartment building creaked and groaned as evening and drizzle descended on Sutton Place. The prestigious New

York City oasis, with its river views, parks and playgrounds, fantastic restaurants, and plentiful shopping, had seen the likes of Marilyn Monroe and Michael Jackson. Newly renovated apartment 1A was nearly everything the Meyers wanted; everything except the uninvited ponytailed visitor who now reclined in the lounge chair watching TV, his Brutini loafers propped up on an ottoman.

Mr. and Mrs. Meyer, clothes soaked from standing in the downpour struggling with their front door lock, now sat propped up on the loveseat, staring blankly at their host.

The intruder shifted his gaze away from the news broadcast and onto his hosts. Mr. Meyer, his face gray-blue, had flicked on the light switch, unaware of the frayed wires and failed ground. The arc had reached out and licked the wetness on his finger, electricity coursing through his body. The once-prominent attorney and New York state assemblyman had fallen to the floor, fingertip burning, his heart still. Mrs. Meyer, her complexion white, had rushed to her husband's aid, but wet hardwood is slick, so dangerous, and her temple had met the square corner of the granite coffee table. Her skull had fractured, and the fluid in her brain had leaked out like an egg cracked into a pan.

Joyous screams erupted from the television screen and interrupted the intruder's droll reminiscing. His eyes moved from his decaying decor and focused on the digital images.

He watched as the throng of people cheered in the streets, but it was the picture of the glistening gold object that shocked his body upright, his eyes wide and unblinking. He glared at the golden axe head, recognition in his eyes, his lips pressed tight.

The reporter's words echoed in his ears. "Omanis rejoiced today in the capital city of Muscat as a golden axe head dating back to the sixth century BCE was returned by an unknown benefactor to the ruling family of Oman by the New York Metropolitan Museum of Art."

The house guest clenched his fists hard, the veins in his arms throbbing. He slammed one fist down on the arm of the chair. He squeezed his eyes shut and twisted his mouth as vivid memories as thick as clouds of wasps stung his mind. Their stares poured disdain down upon him like water, and the words "You are lost" stabbed at him as the sun was blotted out. The house guest cast his gaze on the television but looked through the spectacle. Arching his brow, he whispered, "Lost no more," as his fingers tore through the leather of Mr. Meyer's Barcalounger.

CHAPTER 8

Sentries, each with a MAC-10 submachine gun slung around broad shoulders, stood like twin Christmas nutcrackers at every entrance. It had taken less than an hour for the Vanguard headquarters to be placed on lockdown. The air was thick with the taste of distrust.

Two-man patrols prowled the Vanguard corridors like hungry lions. The rhythmic stomp of their boots on the floor echoed like a bass drum through the hallway.

A new female recruit, freshly persuaded off the grounds of Cambridge University, hurried down an empty hallway, papers and a tablet clutched to her chest.

Tromp...tromp...tromp. The bass drum of the hunters beat louder, drowning out the *click...click...click* of her heels. Her face flushed red as she glanced behind at the empty hallway; she quickened her pace.

Tromp...tromp...tromp.

Her heart pounded in her chest, and she exhaled deeply, trying to stem the shaking in her hands.

Nearly sprinting around the corner, her body came to an abrupt stop as she stood face-to-chest with the Vanguard patrol.

"Humph," one big man growled.

"Excuse me," she stammered, squeezing her petite frame between the wall and one of the predators, her doe-eyed gaze firmly directed on the grout lines at her feet.

"Just keep walking," she recited in her head, the hairs standing on the back of her neck as the patrol's suspicious stares crept over her.

She glanced back and saw the gunmen turn around and start to follow behind.

Tromp...tromp...tromp.

Passing the large oak double doors of a private Vanguard library, she again quickened her pace, suppressing the mounting urge to bolt down the corridor.

Tromp...tromp...tromp. The tempo increased.

She held her breath, thinking that the stern command "Stop!" was a moment away.

Tromp...tromp...tromp.

"He's a fucking coward!" The loud declaration permeated through the double doors and into the hallway.

The bass drum stopped.

As the female Vanguard recruit turned another corner, she spied the armed patrol lean into the double doors, eavesdropping on the heated exchange within.

On the other side of the oak double doors, Michael Cantal and Faye Monroe stood opposite one another inside the private library. Floor-to-ceiling shelves, stuffed with books and newspapers, lined the walls and looked like an unfinished crossword puzzle. Three flat-screen monitors hanging from the ceiling glowed brightly, windows to global news broadcasts.

"A mole hunt? She wants to waste our time with a goddamn mole hunt!" Michael roared, slamming his fist on a nearby oak table and sweeping books and papers to the floor. "Are they blind? Can't they see what's going on?" he added, pacing across the hardwood.

"But why now?" Faye asked.

Michael furrowed his brows. "Now?" he asked.

"Why infiltrate and attack the Vanguard now and not centuries ago?" Faye asked. "The Horsemen surely had opportunities. Why now?"

"My guess is that they've always had eyes in the Order," Michael responded.

Faye raised her eyebrows, crinkling her nose.

"You never knew about Farrow?" Michael asked.

Faye shook her head.

"How could you?" he answered. "You were out cold."

Faye tilted her head, her gaze penetrating into Michael.

"Famine had succumbed to the power of the artifact in the Tower of Babel, and by the time you joined the Order, the Vanguard had buried all knowledge of Farrow's betrayal."

"There was a traitor within the Vanguard?" Faye exclaimed.

"As high as it goes," Michael replied. "Jonathon Farrow was the leader of the Vanguard and in league with the Horsemen for his own selfish ambitions, as was his father and his father's father. Farrow and his family were no better than dirty cops that looked the other way or misplaced evidence for ill-gotten gains. Farrow used the Horsemen as assassins, shaped global governments, and influenced world policy. And in return—"

"Looked the other way," Faye added. "Why bite the hand that feeds you?"

Michael nodded. "Well, the son of a bitch got bit, and his body now lies buried under thousands of tons of rubble."

"And without Farrow, the Horsemen would need a new spy to gather intelligence on Vanguard activities," Faye concluded.

"We watch them, they watch us."

"Horsemen détente," Faye expressed.

Michael continued to pace the library. "The question is, who and at what level? A low-level mole would have access to a limited amount of classified material in his or her section. The real threat would be a traitor high enough up in the Order to have access to a wide array of operations and plans."

"Worse," Faye replied. "A mole that could influence other Vanguards, breed distrust and suspicion, turn Vanguard against Vanguard, and undermine the very foundation of the Order. That would be a real threat."

"Milan, Madrid," Michael noted.

"And Berlin," Faye added. "But doesn't the Vanguard screen all of its agents?"

"Of course. The Order has an elaborate system, including psych evaluations, background checks, and…the Game."

"The Game?"

"A test of skill, character, loyalty, and obedience," he replied. "Pass and you become a Vanguard. Fail and you die. The Game was originally a holy ritual conducted by and for monks, a trial of faith. Remember, the Vanguard started as a religious order. Over the millennia, it has evolved into what it is today, a—"

"A sadistic fraternity hazing?" Faye interrupted.

"A means to protect the Order and to protect humanity," he answered.

"I never played any Game."

"For you, there was no need. Your possession and the Horsemen: yours was never a game. It was real life," Michael stated.

"Of course," she interjected sarcastically, her lips pursed. Faye's mind flashed back to Zachariah's words, "There is no going back"—his invitation to join the Order—and only now did she realize the seriousness of membership to this exclusive guild.

"Did you play this game?" she asked.

Michael nodded, his brows furrowed, his mind delving back to the night Zachariah had revealed the Vanguard. The old man had explained the "reality of things" and the monsters and the guardians shrouded from the public. Michael first thought the old man was joking, but the creases on the man's stone countenance told otherwise. The joke was less funny when Zachariah asked him to become a Vanguard. Michael remembered asking, "What if I don't?" The bald man's cold dark eyes shot the answer through his body like a bullet: "Once revealed, there is only one choice."

Michael remembered how Zachariah's car skidded to a stop, and he stepped out onto the wet New York sidewalk at 2:00 am. The bald Vanguard wanted to give Michael some "time to think." It was drizzling, and he crossed the street, two blocks away from his rented shithole in East Brooklyn: a bathroom down the hall and moans from the whores and their johns echoing through the paper-thin walls, but at least it had a bed, a dirty one at that. At ten bucks a night, he couldn't complain.

As Zachariah's car turned out of sight, Michael saw patrons leave Lefty's Bar. He watched three of them, two men and a woman, cross the street and turn down the alley in front of him. Then he heard it: "You fucking tease!" And then the scream. As he stepped in the alleyway, he turned and saw the woman on her back, the two men standing over her. One man was unfastening his belt, and the other was ripping off the woman's panties.

Michael's mind flashed to his own childhood: his abusive dad who raped his alcoholic mom and who beat him nightly. His body was running down the alley before his mind knew what it was doing.

Adrenaline pumping through his veins, his mind a blur, Michael buried his fist into the cheek of the first man, breaking his jaw. He kicked the second attacker in the gut, following up with an upper cut to the man's nose. Michael's legs buckled when the glass bottle met the back of his skull. He never imagined the woman would attack him. He was naïve. It wasn't long before the fists and kicks of the three Vanguard operatives rained down on him. Before blackness consumed him, he heard sirens in the back of his mind. He woke up, beaten and bruised, two days later in a Vanguard infirmary with Zachariah's smiling face and bald melon staring down at him.

"Yeah," he said now. "Different for each recruit, it's personal. Only one in three survives the game."

Faye clenched her teeth. "It's unimaginable the number of Vanguard recruits killed over the centuries, those failing the final exam."

"Without an artifact, we're going to lose even more to the Vanguard traitor, and that's why we're going to find it, for the Order, and for—"

"Ben," Faye added.

Michael nodded.

Faye twisted the gold band on her finger.

Michael's memories flashed to months prior in this very library, when he had walked away from her, ignoring her plea to help the man, save the monster.

"You heard what the Dragon Lady said, this place is locked down," she said.

"Yeah, I heard her. I heard a lot of things, but I'm not listening to any of it."

Muffled screams resonated from one of the digital screens. Michael shifted his gaze to the television and then touched a control console. A reporter's voice echoed through the library: "Shocking developments today. A golden axe blade, centuries old, was returned to the Sultanate of Oman by the New York Metropolitan Museum. This gesture is sure to strengthen US and Arabic relations. The artifact is on display at Oman's National Museum."

"Well, at least something good is going on in the world," Faye acknowledged.

"Great goodness often conceals wicked intent." A deep voice resonated in the room.

Michael and Faye wheeled around to see Zachariah Prond standing in the doorway.

Michael silenced the broadcast with a tap of his finger. "Oh, now you have an opinion?" he spat. "Where was your wisdom an hour ago?"

The Vanguard leader stepped into the library.

"I understand that you're not happy with my disinclination, but my actions were what they were, for reasons of my own."

"You hung me out to dry!" the former apprentice cried.

"There is more at stake than you know, Michael."

"I know that the Horsemen are the greatest threat, not some fucking mole," Michael countered.

"And what I know is that the Vanguard is at a crossroad, fragile like a crystal vase in a hurricane. Ambitions run strong, and the council is divided."

"Divided in what?" Faye asked.

"Some on the council wish to remain vigilant in our responsibility," Zachariah said. "Maintain our anonymity, continue as watchers of the Horsemen, acting only when needed. Others, however, others strive for change, a more active role."

"Fight the Horsemen?" Faye asked.

Zachariah shifted his gaze to Faye's upturned face. The stoic intensity in his eyes conveyed the unspoken answer.

"A war with the Horsemen of the Apocalypse is incomprehensible," Michael added. "It's been tried. The Horsemen are immortal. Modern weapons are useless against them."

"Agreed, but some within the Vanguard wish to try to contain the menace," Zachariah countered.

"Contain?" Faye asked. "You mean imprison them."

Zachariah nodded at the two Vanguards.

"An open confrontation with the Horsemen would expose the Vanguard to public scrutiny," Michael said.

"And you better believe that the authorities around the world would get involved. Just wait until the media gets wind of the story," Faye added.

"Worse," Zachariah responded, "the global widespread fear and panic would only feed the Horsemen, strengthening their supernatural powers. Even without the Awakening and the return of Famine, the Horsemen at less than full strength, they would be uncontrollable, unstoppable."

"Seven billion people—it's the perfect Horseman feast," Faye quipped, trying to lighten the gloomy mood.

Michael turned to Faye, his jaw clenched. "A lot of innocent people are going to die."

The Vanguard leader walked to the double doors and turned around. His penetrating stare made Faye's skin crawl. "I will do everything in my power to prevent it, but if I should fail, God help us all. The Vanguard will need all the help it can get," he proclaimed, opening the doors and exiting the library.

Faye turned to Michael to find him scooping up books and papers from the floor and stacking them on the table. He cracked open one volume and started to pour through the text.

"What are you doing?" Faye asked.

"You heard Zachariah. Let's find the artifact."

«««—»»»

Seth stepped onto the balcony of his Georgian Colonial and looked out over the Connecticut countryside. His saluki trotted out, its nails clicking on the wooden deck. The one-hundred-pound hound reared on its hind legs and rested its forelegs on the balcony railing as if to have a casual conversation with its master. He smiled and reflected back to 10th century BC and his first saluki hound. At that time, the Horseman was Ad ibn Kin'ad, and he was ruler of the Kingdom of Ād.

The dog's whine stirred memories long forgotten. As War reached over and patted his furry companion, his thoughts turned to hunting during the cool summer mornings in what was now the Omani peninsula and how his Persian greyhounds had been closer to him than anything or anyone: obedient and loyal, affectionate but deadly.

Seth glanced at his watch. It was seven o'clock in the morning in the Greenwich suburb, and while the heat of the day was still hours away, the Horseman knew that the inferno that was the Omani afternoon was burning down upon Muscat, the capital of the sultanate.

More ancient memories seeped into his mind, and he remembered how, after a century of rule in Ād, he'd tired of kingship and diplomacy and craved the intimacy of combat, the vivacity of slaughter. War's lips curled as he remembered how he'd faked his own death, his body lost to the sea. He reappeared in Oman a century later, a stranger in the kingdom, but stepped into a new role, that of Headsman of Ād.

The Horseman's smile broadened as he recalled the way the King of Ād would applaud, one finger stroking another, each gruesome spectacle. Seth relished his role and perfected his craft, honing it over centuries of brutality: he was a master executioner.

Death by fire, hanging, and drowning, all methods the Horseman had perfected but found too impersonal. Death by sword and axe he did with grace and bravado. Yet death by sawing was his personal favorite: he hung the criminal upside down and, using a large saw, cut their body in half, starting with the groin, all the way to the head. Because the person was hanging upside down, the brain received sufficient blood to keep them alive until the saw reached the main blood vessels in the abdomen. With every cut of each saw tooth, the victim's screams filled the Horseman with energy.

So proficient was his skill, and the king so delighted, that War was presented a royal gift: a golden axe. War laughed out loud, for it had been the same golden blade that ended that king's reign.

With the death of another king, and weary of defenseless butchery, War returned to the battlefield. Undefeated in personal combat, he rose to the rank of general. With his golden consort, sword nestled in a bejeweled scabbard, and his beloved salukis, he and his army of Ād warriors laid waste to all neighboring kingdoms.

War watched as wind blew leaves across the manicured lawn, each yellow and red wave disrupting the beauty, and with it new memories pained the Horseman's mind.

"Kishar," he whispered through a tight jaw. As if on command, his saluki snarled, its jowls pulled back, long canines exposed.

It was after one yearlong campaign that the Warrior Horseman was reunited with the Horsemen of Death. It was also a time of the Awakening, a time when the Horsemen's lost supernatural power surged anew, albeit ephemerally. He watched through his mind's eye as Kishar walked into the Kingdom of Ād and used her wiles on the gullible king. So smitten was the royal fool that he made Death his new queen.

War balled his hand, his fist engulfed by orange flame. He fixed his gaze on the dancing flame, remembering how the beguiled king, fearing that his army's loyalty was not to him, had sentenced his general to death. The Warrior Horseman knew it was the trickster, Death, who had planted the seed of dissention in the King of Ād.

War's memories stoked his rage, and his hand burned brighter. He remembered how the king and a dozen royal guards, led by Kishar, had come to seize him in the middle of the night. The master warrior and strategist, expecting such a visit, had turned one man on another, and soon the royal guard and the king were dead.

War then sought to unleash his fury on Death, but the trickster had set loose a new ploy and a new weapon: all of the inhabitants of Ād. Men, women, and children, slain by the Mistress of Death, mobbed him. Wave after wave of mindless servants piled upon the Horseman. Buried under tons of death walkers, War's rage burned hot, as did his mystical fire, and within seconds, the corpse blanket was reduced to ash.

He remembered the smile in Kishar's eyes as she stood petting his beloved salukis, now dead shells of fur; and how, in an uncontrollable frenzy, he unleashed a fire storm that engulfed the entire city.

Death answered War's ferocity with a final insult, wiping away the existence of Ād with a yellow tsunami of sand that swallowed the entire kingdom. Days later, War emerged from the sand, sword in one hand and golden axe in the other. Kishar was gone, as was his renewed mystical power.

War's fire dimmed. His eyes narrowed, jaw clenched as he strained to stoke the sputtering flame that died, starved of its mystical fuel. Seth gripped the balcony banister and looked out past the pristine gardens, beyond the rock wall bordering his land. His fingers crushed deep into the railing, splintering the wood. His saluki growled. "Yes, Quwwa, I see them," he said. "The Vanguard are quite diligent, but even they can't foresee what is soon to befall them."

«««—»»»

Obaid Barwani was happy to be inside the air-conditioned room. He knew that one hundred and sixteen degrees Fahrenheit was conducive to drinking and not a Masters in Antiquities. While he had to finish his dissertation, there was always time for beer. He had become a regular patron at Oman's National Museum, but never had he seen the exhibit rooms filled to capacity. Nor had he seen such heightened security: armed security guards, closed-circuit cameras, and motion detectors. He, like everyone else in the museum, had come to see the same exhibit: the ceremonial axe blade of the lost Kingdom of Ād.

Obaid had arrived early to see the blade. It was to be the highlight of his dissertation. But the sheer number of people ahead of him in line to see the axe had put him at odds to even make it to the exhibit door before closing. The guard counted off twenty patrons for the last showing, and, as luck would have it, Obaid was number nineteen. With a smile on his face, Obaid, along with the rest of the group, led by the guard and a docent, entered the tiled room. In the center, a lighted glass case was roped off in velvet. At the center of the display case rested a golden axe blade on a white satin pillow.

Unseen to the mortal eye, a thin strand, no thicker than fishing line, slowly played out from its golden spool, writhing like a snake, growing longer each passing second, passing in and out of the glass enclosure as if it were air.

Over the next twenty minutes, Obaid sketched the axe, capturing the detailed etchings, noting historical facts from the docent's lecture. He'd have to forego his beer a little while longer as he'd need to further research the Kingdom of Ād if his dissertation was to be supportable.

All the while, the invisible strand overflowed its confinement, stretching its radiance past the velvet ropes and across the exhibit room floor.

"The exhibits are now closed. Please proceed to the exit," sounded the announcement over the loudspeaker. Grumbling echoed in the tiled room as the docent led the group out through the exhibit door, save one.

"Sir, it is time to leave," ordered the guard.

Obaid ignored the request and continued to shade his sketch, unaware that the mystical line had wound around his leg.

"Sir, this exhibit is closed!" the guard said, grabbing the student's shoulder. "Please take your belongings and leave the mus—"

Before the guard could finish, Obaid spun around and plunged his sharpened pencil deep into the museum guard's heart.

CHAPTER 9

"Wary the lost one," Faye recited from between the bookshelves. "I remember a reference," she said, calling out to Michael. "It was"—she hesitated, her eyes bouncing from one weathered leather spine to the next—"from one of the earliest references on War. Here it is!" she exclaimed, snatching the dusty reference from the shelf.

Faye emerged from the bookstacks, a triumphant smirk on her face.

She sat down at the table across from Michael, whose wide eyes popped up over the paperback buildings like Gulliver in Lilliput.

She opened the book, visualizing the page in her mind's eye, leafing through the sheets until stopping at the correct page.

She read through the page, finding the reference she sought. "The Lost One is abandoned, never to be free from War's prison," she quoted. "It's the only reference." She read more of the ancient text. "There's nothing in here about who the 'Lost One' is or why the Horseman War imprisoned him."

"Or who carved the warning into the undersea cave wall," Michael added. "From the warning, it's not someone who was popular with the Horsemen."

"The enemy of my enemy," Faye affirmed.

Michael nodded.

"Did you find anything on the 'moving mountain'?" Faye asked.

"Brave the path of burning ice in the moving mountain," Michael recounted. "Not much."

"Burning ice could hint at severe cold. Maybe Russia, Antarctica, Canada, or Scandinavia," Faye surmised.

"That narrows it down to millions of square kilometers," Michael responded. "Moving mountain could be a reference to earthquakes or shifting tectonic plates."

"Or a glacier," Faye added.

"A glacier, hmm," Michael contemplated, his mind sorting clues like a recycling plant sifts through glass, aluminum, and cardboard.

"Burning ice! That's it!" Michael shouted. He shot out of his chair and charged over to a map rail.

Michael thumbed through the atlases, and, finding his objective, he pulled the colored chart free from the rack. "The Vatnajokull Glacier," he exclaimed, walking back to the table and laying the map of Iceland flat on its surface. "The Vatnajokull covers about 8 percent of the country," he began, pointing to the white area at the southern tip of Iceland. "The ice flow sits over a deep subterranean magma chamber and several large active volcanoes. One of them, Grimsvotn, erupted recently."

"Burning ice," she acknowledged.

"Exactly."

"But how do we find an artifact in a burning glacier?" Faye asked.

"We start here," he said, uncapping a red pen, writing the word *artifact* in the center of the white splotch, and circling it. "At the Grimsvotn crater."

Michael's stomach growled, reminding him he hadn't eaten all day. "Interested in dinner?"

"I'll pass. The Vanguard cafeteria makes a PB&J look like fine dining."

"I'm thinking more of spicy lamb madras at a little place in Knightsbridge."

"We're locked down," Faye countered. "Waterford would lose her mind."

"Just knowing that it'd get under the Dragon Lady's skin is reason enough," Michael replied and headed to the door. "I know a couple of sentries who owe me a favor." He stopped and turned to Faye. "Are you coming?"

Faye cracked a mischievous smile and followed Michael out.

One floor below the library, a person knelt in a shadowed corner, hands molding gray clay onto a wall like a baker shaping dough. The baker halted his preparation, distracted by the vibration in his pocket. The man tapped his earpiece and, continuing his nefarious recipe, slid a detonator into the explosive loaf.

"Kill everyone and bring me the Chronicles," ordered the voice in the baker's ear. "Do not leave a single Vanguard alive."

Above the baker's head, Faye and Michael walked down the empty Vanguard corridor, the sound of their footsteps drifting out of sync. Turning the corner, the duo approached a lone sentry standing in the hall. As they approached, the guard's brown eyes layered disdain over Faye. Graeme LaSalle gripped the MAC-10 tightly, his right index finger moving toward the trigger.

Faye stopped and stood in front of the big black guard and stared up into his eyes. Graeme's jaw tightened as hard as metal bands.

"Save your ire for the Vanguard traitor, Graeme," Faye declared. "I'm not your enemy."

The big Vanguard snorted his discontent.

"Just watch your back," Faye warned. "And don't trust anyone."

Graeme grunted and trudged down the hallway.

«««—»»»

The waiter slid the plate of garlic naan and hummus dip down the center of the white linen table.

Michael tore off a piece of the flatbread and dipped it into his lamb madras. His mouth watered as he anticipated the taste of the savory meat and spicy curry.

Faye scooped up a mouthful of chicken vindaloo with her own flatbread spoon. "Ah, this is so much better than cafeteria food."

"Better than a PB&J?" he quipped.

Faye held up her hand with a small amount of space between her thumb and index finger. "This much," she answered, smiling, a bit of orange-colored sauce on the side of her mouth.

Michael took a long draw from his glass of lager, looking at Faye from over the rim. His stomach growled like a grizzly bear.

Faye looked up from her curry dish, raising her eyebrows.

Michael could feel the heat from his face and rubbed his stomach. He took a deep breath and stared at Faye for a few moments, enjoying how her face brightened the dim room. Michael's gaze was transfixed while his mind was screaming "Look away, look away," but his body was frozen. He was captivated by her light blue eyes, the way her colossal eyelashes danced on her cheeks when she blinked, and the way her nose crinkled when she smiled. "She's like that one perfect present," he thought, his mind wandering into the hallway of his past and into the family room of a seven-year-old boy's birthday party. The gift, big as a person and wrapped with colorful paper and bow, but inside was the real treasure and the very best part: the anticipation, the sheer unbridled excitement felt before opening that gift. There was no better sensation in the world. And this was how Faye made him feel.

Michael took another sip from his beer and sat up straight. "To think that the Order would even try to imprison the Horsemen," he began, trying to draw attention away from his rumbling stomach. "It's insane."

"I've got to believe that capture has been tried before," Faye replied.

"And failed," he interjected. "But as technology improves, so do the means and desire. The Vanguard will do as the council commands."

"Even in their weakened state, their supernatural powers can't be underestimated," Faye noted. "The Vanguard must know that."

"What do they expect Kishar will do when a hundred Vanguard pull up? Greet them will milk and cookies?" he said with biting sarcasm.

"No, the Horseman will slaughter them, and those that are killed will rise up to become her death walkers. The killing will only escalate," she responded.

"Can you imagine what War would—" Michael started, lost in the moment, forgetting his company, but the statement was delivered like a punch in Faye's face. "I'm sorry, Faye. I—"

The waiter brought over another lager and asked the bothersome question, "Will there be anything else?" He was plainly trying to entice the words "Just the check" and clear out the last dinner patrons, but instead Michael dismissed his invitation: "Nothing for now."

Michael watched the waiter sulk away, and turned to Faye. "We're going to find that artifact, Faye, stop this war, and free Ben."

"It's a burning volcano?"

"We will find a way."

"What if we can't?"

Michael was silent, his thoughts lost in the bubbles rising from the base of his beer.

"What if we can't?" Faye repeated. "What if Ben is lost to that monster inside him?"

"I don't know," Michael answered.

"What if the Vanguard captures him? The thought of Ben in prison for an eternity…I can't imagine a more cruel existence. Life in a hole, the isolation, the loneliness, it would drive anyone mad. I can't allow that. I won't."

The glow on Faye's face faded, and the edges of her lips curled down as she pondered the possibility.

Michael reached out and covered her hand with his. "If we can't, I…I want you to know that I—"

Faye pulled her hand away. She stared at him with deep sadness; her light blue eyes now darker. "Michael, stop," she said in an empty tone. "It's—"

"Ben. Always Ben," he thought, struggling to keep his inner voice quiet. "Yeah, I know," he answered aloud, trying to bury the feelings tearing at his heart. He stared at his lager and watched the bubbles float up from the bottom to the top of his glass again. It was then that he realized that saving the man from the monster was everything. Nothing else mattered.

There was no room inside her for anything or anyone else.

《《《—》》》

The red hair was a stark contrast to the Spartan white walls of the Vanguard corridor. Eric Stoneridge slowed his gait so as not to spill the two cups of coffee resting atop the cafeteria tray. The strong aroma of freshly brewed coffee wafted up his nose, and he looked down, the worst thing he could have done, and black waves crested over the Styrofoam edges and onto the long pastry box.

"Shit," he exclaimed. He shifted his right palm underneath the tray; his left fingers grasped the plastic lip, and soon his precious cargo was balanced again.

Eric cast a bright gaze forward. "You guys in need of some fresh coffee and day-old doughnuts?" he asked, his momentary lack of concentration spilling more coffee. "Oh crap."

The guards grinned, amused at the antics of the clown shuffling down the hall toward them. "All he's missing is a red nose and big floppy shoes," one sentry thought.

"Sorry, it's a little soggy," Eric said, stepping up to the guards.

Each guard grabbed a white cup from the tray and sipped at the steaming brew.

"Wasn't expecting a coffee break, but this is a nice surprise," one sentry remarked.

"The surprise is still to come," Eric noted, grinning. "Open the box."

As the invitation left his lips, the redhead clutched the side of the tray with his left hand just as his right palm fell away. Dropping with it, concealed between his hand and the cafeteria tray, an M&P .45 caliber handgun.

With the straight face of a poker player and the dexterity of a magician, Eric caught and manipulated the falling weapon into firing position, pointing the gun at the groin of one guard as the other sentry lifted the lid to the pastry box. The guard's eyes were as large as saucers, expecting to see the shine of glazed sweets but instead looked upon the cold black metal of a Steyr 9mm machine pistol.

"Is this some kind of joke?" demanded the sentry.

"No joke," Eric said, smiling cruelly as he squeezed the trigger.

Bang!

The bullet blew away the guard's cock and testicles, castrating the man and dropping him to the floor.

In the next instant, and with a raucous moan echoing in the hallway, Eric raised the M&P to the other sentry's forehead, his crimson eyebrows lifting. "You're dead."

Bang!

The back of the second guard's head exploded, his brain splattering on the immaculate white wall.

Eric, cafeteria tray in hand, stared at the downed guard lying on his side and holding his empty crotch.

"You bastard!" the eunuch cried, blood pouring out from between his legs.

"Let me reunite you with your manhood," Eric said, grinning wickedly and pointing the barrel at the sentry's head.

Bang!

The shot cleaved the man's skull, silencing his howls.

Eric closed his eyes. His ears were filled with the sound of shouts and hasty footsteps, but all the redheaded assassin noticed was the calm beating of his heart. He placed the pistol up on the tray, reached into his pocket, and removed a wireless remote detonator. His nimble thumb manipulated the keypad, and, with the press of a red button, a thunderous explosion erupted from the rooms at the far end of the corridor, blowing doors from hinges, rocketing bodies through the air, and tossing body parts into the tiled passageway.

Eric's lips parted into a toothy grin as detonations advanced sequentially down the corridor, wiping out rooms in order, like the bass drum from a Souza march.

With another feat of prestidigitation, Eric dropped the detonator and cafeteria tray and, in the same motion, snatched the M&P handgun from atop the tray and the Steyr 9mm machine pistol from within its cardboard confinement.

With arms extended out to his side, a weapon in each hand, the redheaded assassin stepped past each smoldering room, firing a volley of bullets and silencing the groans and pleas of Vanguard survivors.

Having purged the first floor of life, Eric holstered his handgun behind his back. He reached into his pocket, pulled out a 9mm clip, and snapped the magazine into the empty machine pistol. He exited onto the staircase and climbed the stairs up to the second floor.

Eric flung open the second-story door and stepped into a smoke-filled passageway. There hadn't been enough time to rig each room as he had done below in the Vanguard living quarters, but he had planted explosives in two of the most populated rooms on the floor: the cafeteria and the gymnasium.

Eric rounded a corner and moved down the hallway, shooting Vanguard agents as they stepped into view.

Graeme LaSalle pushed through the smoke, sucking in shallow breaths. He turned into the hallway from the far side and, seeing the redheaded gunman through the haze, ducked back around the corner just as Eric fired, the metal spray tearing apart the wall in front of Graeme's face.

Graeme stuck the barrel of his MAC-10 around the bend and fired back blindly, unleashing thirty hollow-tip rounds. Eric scrambled back around a protective bend.

"You fucking traitor!" Graeme shouted from around the corner. He pulled out the empty clip and snapped in a fresh magazine.

At the same moment, Eric inspected his weapon: empty. He tossed away the machine pistol and drew his handgun from the small of his back.

"You can't stop me, Graeme. I'm smarter than you, smarter than all the Vanguard."

"Just watch me!"

"Are you going to shoot me?"

"Just stick out your head, asshole!" Graeme responded.

"You get your nuts cracked by some bitches, and now you don't want to get your hands dirty. Who's the pussy now?" Eric baited.

"We'll see," Graeme answered.

"That cunt Monroe sure did a number on you," the assassin taunted. "Everyone is talking about how you got beat down by a woman."

"Shut up!" the big Vanguard cried out, squeezing the barrel of his weapon, envisioning the scrawny neck of his redheaded adversary.

"You're the laughingstock of the Order," Eric said, grinning. "But don't worry, the Vanguard always needs help in data entry."

"Shut up! Damn you!"

"Come on," he said, stepping out from around the protective corner. "Wouldn't you like someone to help you work off that frustration?" Eric asked, tucking the M&P behind his back. "I'm right here, unarmed."

Graeme peeked around the corner to see the wiry redhead standing in the center of the corridor, arms extended out, walking forward.

The big Vanguard stepped into view and walked toward the traitor. "Or I could just shoot you where you stand."

"How satisfying would that be?"

"It has its advantages."

"Yeah, well, a woman could do th—" Eric's words were cut off as Graeme jabbed the butt of his MAC-10 into the redhead's gut. "Now we're getting somewhere," Eric groaned, doubled over, smiling, knowing the fool had taken his bait.

Graeme laid his MAC-10 on the floor and, rotating quickly, followed up with a right cross to Eric's face.

The redhead spat blood onto the floor.

"You're right. That is satisfying," Graeme said, pumping his arms in the air.

"Too easy," Eric uttered.

"What did you—" the big man started.

Before Graeme could finish his query, the wiry redhead's fist shot out toward the black man's throat, but before the killing blow could crush the Vanguard's windpipe, Graeme dropped his chin to his chest. Eric's four knuckles smashed into the big man's jaw.

"So, you did learn something, you stupid lout?" Eric declared.

"Learned how to protect my air," Graeme replied, rubbing his chin.

"Well then, I'm going to kill you slowly."

"Kiss my—" Graeme's head snapped back. He was shocked at the speed of the redhead's fists. "The guy has had training, boxing," he thought as another fist crashed into his temple.

The assassin's hands were too quick, landing four punches to Graeme face before the Vanguard could launch a single strike. Graeme lifted his hands to protect his head. "He's toying with me," the big man thought and winced as the pain now radiated from his abdomen.

"How does it feel?" Eric exclaimed, slamming his fist into the big man's stomach.

The big man gasped.

"To know that all your strength means nothing?" Eric's punches peppered the Vanguard's backside.

Eric relished every groan he inflicted.

Graeme rushed forward and threw a quick jab. Eric threw a right cross over Graeme's lowered left hand. The punch hit the big black man in the face, causing him to stagger backward.

"Why won't you go down!" the assassin cried.

"Just stupid, I guess." Graeme said, staggering on his feet, "But not as stupid as you," he slurred.

Eric furrowed his brow.

"While you're wasting time with me, your advantage has disappeared as quickly as your smoke."

The horrible realization struck Eric like a punch to his stomach; he knew he'd made a mistake. He'd become so consumed in his personal sadistic drama that the hallway had cleared. He could now hear the heavy stomp of boots down the hallway.

Graeme's lips curled up in a spiteful grin. "Asshole."

Eric pulled the 9mm M&P from behind his back and shot Graeme twice in the chest. The big man crumpled to the ground. The redheaded assassin picked up the MAC-10 machine gun and continued his killing spree down the hallway.

From the far side of the corridor, two Vanguard sentries rushed forward. Eric cut them down with one pull of his index finger.

Around another bend, Eric spied Zachariah in the passageway and sprayed a lethal greeting to the Vanguard leader. However, Kenji, Zachariah's tattooed bodyguard, spotted the redheaded gunman and pushed the bald man into the library as gunfire peppered the door.

Inside the private library, Kenji threw a table on its side, spilling text, maps, and books. He and Zachariah knelt behind the makeshift barrier, guns drawn, barrels pointed at the depository entrance. Zachariah reached into his coat pocket and pulled out the worn leather book. He brushed the Chronicles with his free hand like a protective father patting his son. This was the prize the traitor sought, a treasure worth dying for.

A faint scratching noise sounded outside the room.

"What the hell is that?" Zachariah began, but the sight of the flash-bang grenade shaped like hockey puck sliding into the room silenced the Vanguard leader.

"Down!" Kenji commanded, pushing Zachariah toward the book-stacks just as the concussion grenade rocked the room.

Zachariah's body was numb. The old man knew the effects of a stun grenade weren't lethal, but they hurt like hell. Even with the ringing in his ears, he heard the gunshot echo through the library. "Kenji," Zachariah murmured.

Mustering all of his strength, his face glued to the ground, Zachariah crawled, arm over arm, through the bookstack, trying to put as much distance as he could between himself and the gunman. Zachariah was unaware that the size ten boots stood just in front of his shiny bald head.

Eric reached down and pulled Zachariah by his shirt, sitting him upright.

"Give me the Chronicles," Eric demanded, kneeling and patting down the Vanguard leader, finding nothing.

"Stoneridge?"

"The book, where is it?" the redhead asked, staring into the Vanguard leader's eyes.

"You're the mole?" Zachariah asked, his head clearing, the effects of the stun grenade fading. The old man took a deep breath. "The book? Safe from the likes of you," he answered, his gaze falling onto thousands of volumes on the shelves.

"Tell me where you hid the book," Eric threatened, cocking his M&P and driving the barrel into the bald man's sternum.

"Better I die a Vanguard than live as a Horseman's pet."

"You fool."

Bang!

Zachariah's eyes opened wide, his mouth agape. The pain radiated from his chest throughout his body like electricity. With a groan, he slumped over to one side.

Eric looked about the book stacks, sweat beading on his forehead. "Where is it?" he asked, frantically searching for a clue. "Where'd you hide it, old man?" His gaze jumped from binding to binding, his breath coming in quick gasps.

No answer was forthcoming. Zachariah, blood pooling around him, was silent.

"Fuck!" the assassin roared, tearing down a bookshelf and then another and another.

Turning, Eric stormed out of the bookstacks, but stopped midstride, a colored atlas at his feet capturing his attention. The assassin peered down at the floor, staring at the red ring and the word *artifact* within.

CHAPTER 10

The acrid smoke stung Faye's eyes and nostrils as she crossed the threshold of the first-floor entrance.

"What the hell happened?" she exclaimed, putting her hand over her nose and mouth.

She watched as Vanguards, donned in fire-proximity suits, lined black body bags in the smoky corridor like Hell's Unclaimed Baggage Center.

"Our mole wasted little time making his presence known," Michael responded.

"With the lockdown and the tightened security, I can't fathom it," she replied. "The traitor knew when, where, and how to hit us."

"And who!" he shouted, his voice filling with anxiety.

"Zacha—"

Before the last syllable left Faye's mouth, Michael had raced through the door and bounded up the flight of stairs. He pushed into the second floor to see Zachariah lying prone on a stretcher surrounded by medics. The Japanese bodyguard stood silent and solemn over his fallen master, his shame and dishonor more painful than the bullet hole in his side.

"Zachariah!" Michael yelled, rushing up to the gurney.

"Zachariah," Michael repeated, grasping his mentor's still hand.

"He's been shot, lost a lot of blood," spouted the medic, and wheeled the stretcher away.

Michael stood watching. He winced in pain as the knot tightened in the pit his stomach.

He could barely hear the muffled sound of Faye's voice calling to him, anguish rolling around him, surrounding him like a fog, stifling his breath.

"Michael?"

As he turned and faced her, she could see the tight lines of concern etched on his face.

"Is he...?"

"He's alive." Michael walked along the corridor, the sound of his footsteps and Faye's consoling words drowned out by the screaming inside his head. "I should have been there! Damn it! I could have stopped it, could have saved him!" With each guilt-ridden thought, Michael clenched his teeth harder, until his jaw ached.

"He'll make it," Faye said, placing her hand on his shoulder, her words and touch cutting through his anguish.

"Did I tell you the time Zachariah and I were on assignment in Berlin?" he began, his eyes focused on the tile ahead of him, his mind stepping back to the past. "We walked into this dive to meet an informant, but it was a setup. Five lowlifes were waiting for us." Michael looked up and turned to Faye. "Do you know what Zachariah said to me?"

Faye raised her brows.

"He just smiled and said, *Warten in der kabine,*" that was it. "Wait in the cab," like he was just going to have a nice little chat with them. Three minutes later, the bastard waltzes out of the bar without a scratch."

"He's strong, Michael," Faye responded.

"He taught me so much, and I never told him I—"

"He knows," she declared. "And he'd want us to do our jobs."

Michael managed a smirk and a nod.

He and Faye stepped into the private library.

"Shit," Faye exclaimed, her eyes soaking in the room's devastation.

Michael righted the overturned table and chairs and sat down. He rested his elbows on the table and lowered his head, running his hands through his hair, dragging his fingers through it as if he were in pain.

Faye reached down and picked up the map. She saw the crimson stream trickling out between the book stack, like a creek, the sight of which spurred her next question. "Michael, the Chronicles...Where—"

"The Chronicles!" boomed Diana Waterford's voice. "Where is it?" she demanded, stepping into the ransacked depository with two muscular guards.

Michael shook his head.

"Where is it?" she repeated.

"How the fuck should I know," he spat. "Go ask Zachariah."

"Zachariah is unconscious in route to London Bridge Hospital," the Dragon Lady replied.

"No," Michael uttered.

"Arrest her!" Diana Waterford ordered.

Faye's heart skipped a beat. "What for?" she exclaimed.

"Treason."

"You're out of your mind. You think I did this?" Faye answered.

"People have a way of dying around you, Ms. Monroe."

"We weren't even here," Michael answered. "Faye was with me."

"Arrest them both."

"The hell you will!" Michael declared, shooting out of his chair, his despair turning to rage in an instant. He never saw the huge fist shoot out from the bodyguard, but he heard the knuckles crash into his chin, the same sound when a bat meets a ball, and his head was a fastball in the center of the strike zone. Michael's knees buckled, but not before the other bookend grabbed Michael's hair and smashed his face down onto the table.

Blackness consumed Michael, drowning out Waterford's final command: "Take them away!"

«««—»»»

Three floors down, in the Vanguard basement, Michael woke up on the cold cement to see Faye's face above him.

"Are you okay?" she asked as he stared blankly up from her lap.

"Yeah," he said, forcing a smile. Groaning, he rubbed his head with one hand, pushing himself up with the other.

"Where are we?" he asked, his eyes adjusting to the low light and focusing on the vertical stripes surrounding them. "Oh, right."

"Welcome back to the nightmare."

"What'd I miss?" Michael asked.

"We are to stand trial for treason and murder."

"Oh, and I thought it was going to be bad," he quipped, getting to his feet.

Michael looked out through the bars. The room was mostly shadow, lit by two weak fluorescent bulbs.

Faye stood up. "Michael, this is serious. Waterford's got her moles, and now she going to get her war."

"All because we went out for Indian food?" he said, smiling at her and then grasping the metal bars. Michael focused on the cold steel in his grip. He envisioned his fingers around the traitor's neck, and he squeezed. "It's someone with access to all parts of the facility."

"During lockdown? A sentry, maybe?"

"No, someone with a working knowledge of Vanguard operations."

"Michael, do you know what you're saying?"

He nodded, his eyes fixed on the veins pulsing in his hands. "Where was Waterford during the attack?"

"I was holding the cold, lifeless hand of my son." The voice cascaded through the cellblock. Diana Waterford stepped from the shadows. "His body arrived at Heathrow this evening."

"You have no right to hold us!" Michael shouted, pulling on the bars. "Check the surveillance video."

"The video that you disabled?" she asked.

"No one is going to believe that this is anything more than a witch hunt," Michael added.

"No, Mr. Cantal, the Vanguard will believe exactly what I tell them. You and your accomplice sabotaged this facility, killed dozens of Vanguard, and critically wounded the head of the Order."

"Liar!" Michael cried.

"And escaped, only to return later to dispel suspicion," the blonde said. "You are the Horsemen traitors, the threat that Zachariah was too blind to see. The threat that I had warned him about. Now the Vanguard are going to put an end to the threat, once and for all."

"You're insane," Faye uttered.

"We go to war with the Horsemen of the Apocalypse," Diana Waterford declared, walking into the shadows, the blackness devouring her.

《《—》》

Sidab Sumahram was a kind man, a happy man, a fisherman. It was a life he'd known for forty-nine years, a life of long hours and bad weather in the Gulf of Oman, a dangerous life, a meager life, but a life that supported him and his younger brother, Malik, and their families.

His life this morning started early: three o'clock. He had nets to repair and hooks to tie: hundreds of them, and as captain of the *Nomad*, his mortgaged thirty-foot trawler, it fell on him to see that the work got done.

He sipped kahwa, Omani coffee mixed with cardamom powder, looked at his hands, oil permanently outlining fingerprints and callus-blanketed palms, and reflected on the day ahead. The big-bearded fisherman smiled, knowing his brother would be at the docks to help him, and they'd be on the water well before sunrise. He and his brother had fished together all of their lives, and Malik was more than a sibling: he was a trusted deckhand and his best friend.

Sidab swallowed the last mouthful of the bitter brew, gathered his nets, loaded his truck, and set off for the harbor. He whistled as he made good time rolling through the deserted Muscat roads and within minutes had turned down Main Street, passing the National Museum. "It's going to be a good day," the big fisherman thought.

Unknown to Sidab, another angler had cast a mystical line into the dry sea that was Muscat. The invisible thread, a warring essence from its Horseman master, extended out from the antiquity depository and bounced through the air, moving down the center of Main Street, passing seamlessly through parked cars, lampposts, and trees: the invisible scalpel cut through all inanimate objects in its path, leaving each unscarred. It slithered like a serpent, searching, swaying, and growing longer with each passing second...waiting.

Sidab was the first fish to touch the line as he unwittingly drove his Toyota through the bouncing thread. The loose cord jerked taut as it passed into and through the fisherman, only to slacken again and bounce free once the car and its passenger had passed by.

Minutes later, Sidab's truck rolled into the marina. The fisherman navigated to a stop next to Malik's parked El Camino. "Aye!" the big man shouted, smacking his open hands on top of the steering wheel. "How did Malik beat me to the docks?" he thought, his smile gone, his mood soured.

Malik, a thinner version of his brother, was on board the *Nomad*, mending the gill nets and singing an old Omani fishing ditty.

"How dare he be on my boat without my permission," Sidab muttered, uncharacteristically, the tone of his brother's melody increasingly grating on his newly frayed nerves.

"*Sabah el khair,*" Malik called out, waving from the deck, a grin plastered on his face.

"There is nothing good about this morning," Sidab thought, ignoring the gesture and stepping aboard his ship.

"How is Daarina?" Malik asked.

Sidab ignored his brother, tossing the torn nets on the deck.

"She is well, I hope."

The big fisherman didn't answer, only asked, "Are you saying that I cannot provide for my family?" He rushed up to his brother and stabbed a thick finger into Malik's bony chest.

"What?" Malik replied, pushing his brother's finger aside. "You're an asshole, Sidab."

The bigger brother turned away with a sneer. He stepped to the dash panel and started the trawler's two hundred horsepower outboard motor.

"When did you become so serious?" Malik asked, weaving new nylon line into the net, like a spider mending its web.

The younger brother stared at his older sibling, who stood motionless at the trawler's controls. Malik shrugged and returned to his work. Before long, Malik's voice reached up into the morning again, breaking the awkward silence.

As his brother's melody speared the air, Sidab's big hand squeezed the black ball that was the boat's throttle control.

'Sidab, you need to be more like your brother," he said, interrupting his ballad and pulling on the fishing line, testing the strength of the knot. "And don't let every little thing bother you." Malik glanced at the statue standing at the trawler's controls and resumed his tune. Sidab revved the engine once, the motor's voice screaming "Shut up!" The tune was not deterred. Sidab revved the engine again, his hatred a building torrent. Malik continued to sing, louder, intent not to be bullied by his older brother.

Overcome with rage, the big fisherman pushed the throttle control down, and the *Nomad* lurched forward, its progress halted by the strained mooring lines wrapped around dock cleats.

Malik was tossed backwards onto the deck. "What are you doing, Sidab?"

The big fisherman pushed the throttle to its hilt. The prop spun wildly, the engine whining.

"Wait!" Malik cried, racing to the stern, struggling to free the braided lines. "I need to untie us!"

Sidab pushed away from the dash, grabbed a hand gaff from the rail, and started walking aft to where his brother toiled with the ropes.

"Throttle down!" Malik pleaded.

"Let me help you!" Sidab replied, looming up from behind his brother.

The fisherman raised the gaff above his head and slammed the sharp, pointed hook into the middle of his brother's back.

Malik screamed, his body frozen with pain.

"A much better tune," the big Omani said, venom in his voice, numb to his brother's cries.

"Sidab, help me," Malik begged. "Please! Stop!"

"Sing, brother! Sing!" Sidab answered, hoisting his screaming brother up and over the stern and lowering him into the spinning prop until Malik sang no more.

«««—»»»

Two hours slipped away, and Michael still paced back and forth in the cell like a caged animal. With each pass, he stopped and pulled on the cell door with the same result as the last ten times. "We need to get to the Vatnajokull Glacier and find the artifact."

He wrapped his fingers around the metal bars and buried his head in his hands.

"Reykjavik is three hours away," Michael said under his breath. "We'll need a guide once we get there."

"Might as well be three days away," Faye muttered.

Michael spun around. "Have you logged any time in a Gulfstream?" he asked.

"What? Sure, but—"

"London Biggin Hill," Michael said, hatching his plan. "It's a private airport to the southeast of London."

"Michael," Faye interjected, unable to stall his exuberance.

"Zachariah has a Gulfstream G150. We can use his authority clearance to get into Reykjavík Airport," he added.

"Michael!" Faye interrupted. "We're not going anywhere unless you know a way to open this cell. She pulled on the steel bars for emphasis.

"I can do that," answered a deep voice as Graeme LaSalle limped out from the shadows.

"It was Eric Stoneridge," the big Vanguard declared, stabbing the key into the lock.

"The little redhead recruit?" Faye asked.

The bruised Vanguard nodded, unlocking the cell and pulling the swinging door open.

"He did that to you?" she asked, staring at the dark welts decorating his face.

"Not the pussy I took him for. The bastard killed a lot of Vanguard, a lot of my friends."

"Why are you helping us?"

"Returning the favor," the big man replied, pulling open his shirt, exposing the Kevlar vest and the slug embedded into the armor. "Call us even."

«« — »»

"The Horsemen have never been so vulnerable. We attack in two days," Diana Waterford declared in the boardroom. The eyes of the Vanguard council members were glued to the digital atlas on the screen. "Strike team one will be on the Eastern Seaboard, here," she said, pointing to a small region in Connecticut. "Team two in the Midwest, here," the blonde added, pointing to an area outside of Minneapolis. The Dragon Lady pressed a button on a console, and the atlas was replaced by the wavy contour lines of a three-dimensional holographic topographic map. "Team one, I want a one-mile buffer between us and the warrior Horseman. I don't want a single Vanguard coming under his murderous influence. Even weakened, War will kill us all if given the chance." Waterford pressed another button, and the curved lines disappeared, replaced with a floating image of a building and its floor plan. "Team two, Pestilence is cunning, so expect the unexpected. Stealth and speed are our greatest weapons."

"Capture is futile! It's been met with failure every time," stated one silver-haired council member. "What makes you think this attempt will be different?"

Diana Waterford nodded, her gesture answered with the clatter of metal fastenings on the table. "Electromagnetic force," declared a younger council member, streaks of gray at his temples. "Weaponized."

"Thank you, Dr. Barrett," Waterford answered.

"Futile!" the elder member repeated.

"Maybe a demonstration is in order," prompted Waterford.

"Certainly," Dr. Barrett began, snatching up the shackles from the table. "Perhaps our naysayer will volunteer."

The Dragon Lady nodded, smiling as the silver-haired council member's eyes grew large, his jaw dropping. Dr. Barrett snapped the bracelets onto the man's thin wrists and, pulling a black box from his pocket, activated the remote control.

"Electromagnetism is the second strongest force in our universe," the doctor stated. "It has both attractive and repulsive properties," he said, twisting the control knob. As the dial rotated, the metal shackles sprang to life and leapt away from each other.

"Ahh!" cried the elder council member, his arms extended outward in a sick parody of crucifixion.

Dr. Barrett glanced at Diana Waterford, who answered with a smile and a nod.

"Strong repulsive properties," the doctor said, turning the knob again. The silver-haired man's screams muffled the sound of his shoulders popping out of their sockets.

"That will be enough, Dr. Barrett," Waterford chimed.

The doctor nodded and deactivated the electromagnets. The silver-haired volunteer collapsed to the ground unconscious.

"And when we've captured the Horsemen?" asked another council member.

"We cage them, like the animals that they are," Waterford exclaimed.

"The polymer is revolutionary, the cell unbreakable," bragged Dr. Barrett.

"I want it tested," Waterford ordered, the flash in her eyes punctuating the severity of her tone. "Do you understand me?"

The group nodded in unison.

"Testing has been ongoing for months," the doctor added. "The enclosure is fireproof to four thousand degrees Celsius, and strong enough to withstand ten thousand pounds per square inch of pressure. It will not fail."

Nervous smiles sped across the room.

"And best of all, there is no door," Dr. Barrett continued. "The entire enclosure is molded around the monster. There is no way out, no escape."

Excited murmurs filled the room like a breath filling a balloon, only to deflate when a young Vanguard entered the private room.

"Madam Waterford," the young man began.

"Yes, what is it?" she asked.

The young Vanguard, feeling the eyes of the senior members crawling over him, was unable to utter the words.

"Out with it!" Waterford commanded.

"The prisoners have escaped," he bleated.

"What!" she exclaimed.

The room filled again, but with worried murmurs.

"Mobilize our patrols, sweep the building," Waterford ordered.

"Sentries have searched the entire facility. The prisoners are nowhere to be found."

"Check the surveillance vid—" she began, but killed her words, remembering that the security system was useless.

The young man shifted his weight, waiting for orders, the awkward silence in the room unbearable. Diana Waterford looked into the face of each council member. "There is only one course of action," she announced to the senior members, turning to the young Vanguard. "Launch retrieval teams, contact our informants, find the traitors and—"

The young Vanguard waited for the final order he knew was forthcoming.

"Use all measures necessary to terminate the threat," Waterford ordered.

With a nod, the young man turned and exited the private chamber.

Less than an hour later, the meeting adjourned, and the Vanguard council members flowed out of the room.

Diana Waterford stepped down the tiled hallway, her bodyguards in tow. At the end of the corridor, she dismissed her escorts and exited the facility. Moments later, she was behind the wheel of her Bentley, driving through the streets of London, deep lines creasing her alabaster face.

After thirty minutes on the M25, Diana Waterford guided her car off the motorway and onto a narrow street. Two kilometers and five tight turns later, she steered onto the empty parking lot of the meat-packing plant, abandoned and left to fall into ruin.

The Dragon Lady stepped through the opened steel door and entered the slaughterhouse. The smell of decay and chlorine assaulted her senses. Her eyes scanned the area and fell upon a dilapidated bone saw, its blade rusted, covered with dust. The Vanguard leader imagined the ghostly echo of the whirring saw filling the empty warehouse.

A faint humming interrupted her thoughts. She followed the soft noise to the far side of the slaughterhouse and stood in front of a large walk-in freezer.

"It's about fucking time," Eric Stoneridge announced, leaning against the warehouse wall.

"Where are the Chronicles?" Diana Waterford asked, stepping toward the redhead. "Give it to me, traitor."

"I...I don't have it."

"How disappointing."

"The old man, he—"

The Vanguard leader raised her hand, stopping the redhead's words cold.

"I said to kill everyone and bring me the Chronicles. Was I not clear?"

The Dragon Lady turned away from the redhead and opened the freezer door. Inside the ice box, men and women, clad in black uniforms and frozen stiff, hung from meat hooks. One man, his arm broken, the bone protruding out, hung frozen in his underwear.

"Then why aren't that bastard Prond and the whore, Monroe, hanging from hooks!" she screamed, spinning around, facing the traitor.

"I don't—" Before Eric could utter another word, Diana Waterford's hand shot out and grabbed the redhead by the throat.

Gasping, Eric felt his feet leave the ground. He watched as the Vanguard visage of Diana Waterford melted away, replaced by a white skull.

Mistress," he murmured, the bony digits of Death's hand tightening around his neck.

"You've failed me," Death chattered.

Blackness rushed in from all sides, and with his last breath, Eric whispered, "Ar...ti...fact."

The bony noose loosened, and Eric collapsed to the ground, clutching his throat.

"They seek an artifact," he coughed.

"Find them and kill them," the Horseman ordered.

The redhead nodded.

"And Eric," Death added, her face now covered with the mask of Diana Waterford, "you know what awaits you if you should fail me again."

Eric stared wide-eyed at the bodies hanging like slabs of meat in the freezer.

CHAPTER 11

Even in the dim light, swathed with a heavy fog of cigarette smoke, Gunnar Gudmunsson could see the bills on the counter. He had no reason to be in the bar, short of begging for more time to pay off his unsettled debt, but the promise of an easy score was too much to resist.

At six foot, he was a pine bordered by withering weeds. His blond hair and Viking-like features stood out from the gray, wrinkled patrons surrounding him. Gudmunsson was likeable, an adrenaline junkie with a lackadaisical attitude toward work. If he didn't get a rush, then why bother, he just wasn't interested: not in school, having dropped out of Reykjavík University six years ago, not in driving forklifts, a job his father landed for him, and not in women. Sure, women were good for a night's romp in the sack, but relationships were boring.

What Gunnar Gudmunsson was, was a conman. His were penny-ante schemes, taking advantage of the tourists coming in droves to Iceland, and best of all, it was the one thing that gave him his adrenaline fix.

His favorite hustle, the thing that gave him the purest rush, was to dress up like a cop, approach a tourist, and inform them of counterfeit bills circulating in the area. Having the unsuspecting mark open their purse or wallet, he would then spot some bills and take the paper into custody. On a good day, he could have enough false arrests to bag him a hotel for a week, three square meals a day, and enough beer to wash it all down.

As good as that con was, Gudmunsson was not going to pass up lonely kronor sitting on a bar.

The conman's eyes shifted to the bartender, a big man with a crooked nose, pouring drinks at the far end of the scratched wooden counter. Gudmunsson hunched down, blending in with the other tired, wilted drinkers. He slid off the black vinyl stool and hopped up onto the next, one seat closer to his prize.

He was always a "grass is greener" type of guy, always in search of the next rush, thinking of the next con, but his grass was more weeds these days, tourists more suspicious. He hadn't eaten a decent meal in three days, and this was the first time he'd been back to the bar since his release. "Where's the trust?" he mused, thinking of the ninety-day jail time he'd just finished. He could still hear his mother bitch at him, having bailed him out. "Gunny, you need help." Instead, he'd helped himself to the cash in her purse and headed to the watering hole.

With his head frozen, the hustler's eyes shot up and scanned the room. In the next instant, he slid from his perch and parked his ass onto the next stool. Nobody cared. The drinkers stared into their tinted windows of beer or bourbon or sat mesmerized by the wall full of ribbons and pictures paying homage to one man's accomplishment in Iceland's National Sport: glima.

Gudmunsson lifted his head; the black-and-white brutality, framed above the shelved spirits, reached out like a headlock and trapped his gaze.

The matted wrestler was built more like a machine, with hard plates of muscle running up and down every appendage. Veins bulged from the massive mitt wrapped around his opponent's neck; the other clasped onto the unfortunate man's leg. The victor's face was a glaring image of rage and exhilaration as he held his adversary above his head.

The photo was that of a perfect warrior specimen. Perfect, except for one flaw: the man's crooked nose.

Gudmunsson's eyes ran down the far side of the bar, and to the man wiping off spilt booze, his gaze creeping up the bartender's barrel chest and onto his broken beak.

"Shit!" he said under his breath.

He knew the risk, but loved the rush. He couldn't help himself, and he scooted onto the next stool, his eyes locked onto the notes.

With his head buried into an empty shot glass, his hand crept along the wood like a spider. His eyes shifted back and forth between the glass and the bills. His mind was focused on the prize. . . glass...bills... easy money would solve a lot of problems...glass...bills. His heart pounded in his chest, his palm rested on the pile...glass...SLAM!

The wrestler turned bartender's massive hand smashed down, crushing the spider. The cushion of money didn't ease the pain radiating through Gudmunsson's fingers. The big man's claw squeezed Gudmunsson's hand, lifting it from the pile of bills. His other hand meanwhile swept the kronor away. The caught con looked up into the face glaring down at him, an image of rage sans exhilaration.

"Where's my money!" the bartender said, squeezing the hustler's hand,

"Ow...ow...Otto, how have you been?"

The bartender's gaze burned into Gudmunsson.

"I just got out of—"

"Don't care," Otto uttered through clenched teeth.

"Right," the captive declared. "I have a deal. I will get your money."

The bartender spun his grappling hook, sending needles of pain rocketing up from Gudmunsson's hand into his arm. The former wrestler leaned in on the hustler. "Don't con me."

"I'm not. You'll have your money, this week, I promise," the hustler pleaded.

"Double it or I'm going to twist this off," Otto added, applying more pressure to the conman's appendage, the pain shooting up Gudmunsson's shoulder and into his neck.

"Okay...okay...don't worry, you'll have it."

The big man released his hold, stemming the stinging current flowing through Gudmunsson's arm.

The conman rubbed his shoulder while his mind frantically searched for a con that could save his ass, his arm, and the rest of him.

Outside, a black Range Rover rolled up to the wrestling shrine.

"Twenty-seven Hverfisgata," Michael announced, pulling the rented SUV to the wet curb.

Faye looked at the dripping sign hanging above cracked and peeling walls, the wooden plaque adorned with the voluptuous and scantily clad namesake astride a winged horse. She cast a skeptical glance at Michael and guessed that this was the traditional workingman's bar, not frequented by the Fairer Sex, complete with a motto: "Good Beer, Lots of Bullshit, and No Women."

"What?" he asked.

She shook her head, opened the car door, and stepped out onto the rain-soaked sidewalk of downtown Reykjavik.

"It's an old haunt. We're likely to find someone to take us to the crater, discretely," he said, coming around the front of the car, his eyes transfixed on the endowed billboard.

"Right," Faye answered and walked inside the Valkyrie. Michael trailed behind with a grin splitting his face from ear to ear.

As Faye and Michael pushed into the wall of smoke, it was as she imagined: a grungy little hole-in-the-wall, hard-liquor bar crammed with a lot of trinkets and whatnots from someone's glory days. The watering hole was at death's door, with an old jukebox playing songs long forgotten.

Gunnar Gudmunsson spied the pair. They didn't look like lost tourists, but, his mind was already on the con.

Faye and Michael walked past an old patron reading a newspaper. The headline occupying the entire front page read: *"Kreppan í Mið-Austurlöndum"—Crisis in the Middle East*. It was as clear as day, written in black and white…and Icelandic, and both Faye and Michael passed by; to them, it may as well have been scrawled in hieroglyphics. The old man looked at the picture of a town in chaos and squinted and read the fine print: *Riots engulf Muscat, the capital of the Sultanate of Oman. The Arab state on the southeast coast of the Arabian Peninsula threatens to close off the Strait of Hormuz. Iran has threatened war. The US Secretary of State is traveling to Oman to defuse the situation.*

Faye and Michael bellied up to the bar.

"*Hvað viltu drekka?*" asked the bartender.

"English?" Michael asked.

"What will you have?" he repeated.

"Two dopplebocks," Michael said.

The bartender turned away and grabbed two pint glasses from the shelf, filling each under the beer tap.

"And a guide to the Grimsvotn crater," Michael said, putting a stack of kronor on the bar.

From three stools down, Gunnar Gudmunsson's eyes were two beacons in the smoke-filled cave.

The bartender swung two glasses of beer with healthy heads in front of Faye and Michael. "No guide here," he said, wiping down the bar and stepping away.

Michael turned to Faye. "That didn't go as I had hoped."

Gunnar Gudmunsson slipped off his seat and bounded over three vinyl cushions. "Excuse me, I didn't mean to eavesdrop," he said, inserting himself between Faye and Michael. "But did I hear you're looking for a guide to the crater?"

"That's right," Michael responded

"You know that it's active—off-limits and very dangerous."

The Vanguard nodded.

"Someone could get into a lot of trouble."

"Do you know that someone or not?" Michael questioned.

"Why do you want to go up?"

"Our second honeymoon," Faye said, intervening.

Gudmunsson eyed the pair. "It will be expensive, and it's a four-hour drive, in the dark."

"Do you know of someone?" Michael asked again.

"Yep, I've skied all over Grimsvotn. Call me Gunny," he said, extending his hand to Michael. "Meet me out front, one am."

«‹‹—›››

Not one of the three white coats in the Chimeracon laboratory noticed the wasp crawl through the ventilation screen and launch into the sterile cloning environment. The whir of the petri-dish conveyor belt drowned out its motorized buzzing. The micromechanical insect, guided by an unseen hand, landed on the coat, crawled up to the collar, and plunged its venomous stinger into the neck of the unsuspecting scientist. Having delivered a painless neurotoxin payload, the robotic drone set off toward the second lab coat.

Outside the lab, standing in the adjacent hallway, a Vanguard agent's agile wrist edged the remote-control joystick forward, his eyes glued to the small digital screen like a video-game addict. The checkerboard tile floor filled the display as the drone dove to knee height then leveled its trajectory, passing lab workstations and custom glass cabinets until the second white lab coat filled the screen. In the lab, the scientist, concentrating on the pipette in his hand, was oblivious to the mechanized intruder that landed on his rubber-soled shoe and crawled up his pant leg, and to the hair-thin needle that pricked his skin.

A hand rested on the shoulder of the video gamesman, who looked up into the smirk of the Diana Waterford disguise. The drone operator and seven-person Vanguard assault team had no idea that a Horseman was the chessmaster, and they unlikely pawns.

"Target three in motion," the gamesman whispered. "Standby," he uttered as he guided the robotic wasp through the laboratory maze. As the drone zeroed in on the last scientist, a flash of white filled the display, and with a blink the video screen went black.

"Negative on target three," the drone operator said.

Death, under a Diana Waterford guise, held up a fist followed by two fingers. Two Vanguard agents pulled the pins from their flash-bang grenades, while a third agent cracked the door leading into the laboratory. The two bowlers rolled their metal spheres down the checkerboard alley.

Bang! Bang!

The explosions rocked the room, and smoke filled the sterile space as the Vanguard assault team swarmed into the laboratory. The faux Diana Waterford stood in the hallway, dark eyes stabbing into the ensuing chaos, searching for the quarry.

"The winds of change blow against your door, brother," the blond Horseman said.

Two Vanguard agents tackled a white lab coat, dragging it to the ground. "Horseman down!" the lead agent called, forcing his weight onto the back of the scientist.

"Shackles! Now!" Waterford cried, stepping into the lab.

Before the lead agent could extract the metal bracelets from his pack, the scientist, belly on the floor, spun his head around one hundred eighty degrees.

"What the hell?" the agent muttered.

In the next instant, the scientist elongated his neck two feet, like a child stretching playdough. The agent watched wide-eyed as the man in the lab coat unhinged his jaw, exposing two long fangs, and bit down into the Vanguard's shoulder. The lead agent fell to the ground screaming in spasms as the concentrated venom flowed to his racing heart. The man-serpent then turned his attention to his second handler, spitting a bolus of venom into the Vanguard's eyes, blinding him.

Across the lab, two Vanguard grabbed the arms of another lab coat, forcing the scientist to his knees. "Horseman down!" a third agent cried, manacles in hand, stepping up to the captive. But before the approaching agent could apply the cuffs, two new limbs on the left and right sides emerged from the scientist's body; hands laden with suckers lined with teeth grabbed the restraining agents' faces and tore the men's flesh from their skulls. The third Vanguard was motionless as first fear penetrated his body, followed by the chimera's squidlike beak that shot out of the scientist's mouth like a piston crashing into the Vanguard's brain.

The blind Vanguard's screams added to the mayhem as he stumbled into laboratory workstations, his flailing hands pulling free the smoke grenade pin dangling from his vest and dragging a trail of fluffy plume behind him like an airplane contrail.

"They're clones!" Waterford cried.

"Clones immune to your tricks, Kishar," whispered a voice through the smoke.

Waterford spun around, eyes scanning the white veil. "Reesef!" the Horseman fumed.

"My chimeras are immune to all known venom. I cloned them that way," added the voice through the mist. At the same moment, the squid chimera cleaved the white blanket of smoke in front of Diana Waterford and grabbed the Horseman with its six lethal appendages. As the doppelganger opened its jaws, Death's bony hand speared the scientist in the mouth, pulling out the lethal beak.

"But not immune to my power, brother," Kishar declared, discarding the cephalopodic prize.

"You play a dangerous game," whispered Pestilence.

"Reesef!" the blonde Horseman cried into the white cloud.

"I like to play games, too," Reesef said.

Under the cover of the fading smoke, the door labeled Exam Room 1 slid open and two new scientific atrocities crept into the main laboratory.

A staccatic burst of machine-gun fire rang out in concert with the disharmonious cry from a panicked Vanguard as the agent fired her MAC-10 into the cobra chimera. The agent stood glaring at the fallen atrocity. She blew out a full breath, her cheeks puffed out like a trumpet player's. She blew out again, exhaling the remains of her fear and panic. It was her last breath before two eight-inch canines tore into her stomach, disemboweling her.

Inside the adjacent examination room, Pestilence packed a small medical satchel. "Come here, my darlings, we'll find a new nursery for you," he said sweetly, plucking two particular test tubes from the rack and securing them into the bag. The Horseman turned and stared at the woman sedated on the exam table, her legs spread in stirrups.

"What a waste," Pestilence said, shaking his head.

The Horseman of Disease pulled another glass vial from a shelf and threw it at the concrete wall; the stone and steel fell apart like it was papier-mâché. Pestilence stepped to the makeshift exit and leapt out of the hole, landing on the parking-lot asphalt as easily as a gymnast off a trampoline.

Inside the hazy laboratory, a second sabertooth watchdog tore into the blind Vanguard, ending his disability.

"Capture the beasts!" Waterford exclaimed.

Two Vanguard agents launched electrified nets from handheld catapults, wrapping the Blood Beasts like spiders cocooning flies. High voltage sparked across the mutated hounds, forcing the abominations into unconscious submission.

«««—»»»

It was one o'clock in the morning. As the headlights scared back the shadows on 27 Hverfisgata, Michael pulled the Range Rover to the curb. Gunny Gudmunsson, dressed in a down parka and wearing a black knit hat, stepped out from the fleeting darkness and into the headlights, a backpack over his shoulder.

Gudmunsson opened the passenger-side rear door and slid inside the SUV.

With the fluorescent lights of Reykjavik a distant memory, the Range Rover's headlights stabbed at the early morning gloom. Within moments, the road transformed from concrete to ash-ridden trail as the SUV ascended into the highlands.

Faye stared out the window. The fading night burned pink along the jagged horizon. "Looks like a different planet," she said. "We could be on the moon and wouldn't be the wiser."

For two hours, the trio crossed the alien landscape in silence. Then the car bounced, bucking like a bronco.

"We're on the ice fields," Gunny said. "Follow this trail for an hour."

"This is a trail?" Michael asked, gripping the wheel, trying to control the mechanized bull.

"One away from prying eyes."

Faye looked out her side window to see a red stream winding through the earth.

"You got to be kidding me. That's lava!" she said pointing at the window.

"It's a volcano," the guide answered.

The car bounced hard on the makeshift road for forty minutes. Ahead, the sky brightened with the sunrise.

"Stop here!" Gunny shouted.

Michael slowed the Range Rover, and the black SUV came to a stop.

"We're here. One-hundred meters right up there," he said, pointing to the mountainside. "Now, where's my money?"

"Half now," Michael answered, passing back two thick stacks of bills. "And the rest when we're safely back in Reykjavik."

Gunny flicked through the stacks of bills, eyes widening with each bill he touched.

Michael looked at Faye, who answered his questioning glance with a nod. Both Vanguards exited the SUV and, with their conman turned guide in tow, walked toward the back of the car.

Michael opened the trunk. Inside, lit by the SUV's interior light, were silver suits, metal air tanks, and a wooden crate.

"Honeymoon?" Gunny questioned, skepticism dripping from the word.

"Yep," Faye answered, pulling out one silver jumpsuit.

Gunnar Gudmunsson pressed the paper bricks into his chest, knowing that his "tourists" weren't what they appeared to be. But the hard cash in his hands was all too real.

Moments later, donned in silver fire-protective suits, their helmets and air tanks resting aside the wooden crate, Michael and Faye looked down into the glowing cauldron that was Grimsvotn crater.

"Hide an artifact inside an active volcano," Faye said, raising binoculars to her eyes. "Very clever."

"But where?" Michael asked, focusing his glasses on the red witch's brew of bubbling and sputtering earth. "What we need is," he began, panning his field of view across the cauldron, "an entrance."

Faye inspected the pot's brim, watching red-yellow lava splash high onto the black caldera walls only to ooze down like blood from an open wound. One glowing splatter that disappeared into the shadows caught her eye.

"An opening," she exclaimed. "Three o'clock."

"I see it," Michael responded, refocusing his attention on the coordinates. "It looks man-made."

"Or Horseman-made," she added.

"They never guessed that the entrance would be pushed up to the surface."

"Problem is that there is no way to get to it. Even with the silvers, we'd burn up like two French fries. If we could put a lid on the pot, maybe we could get to the entrance."

Faye continued to scan the cauldron, and then directed her view far above, to the massive glacier cliff resting above.

"I see our lid," Faye said.

Michael focused his binoculars onto the ice shelf.

"Then let's cap it," he said, smiling. Michael lowered his glasses and opened the wooden crate. Gray bricks were nestled next to flashlights, ropes, pick axes, and other mountaineering gear. "And get our artifact," he announced, lifting up a brick labeled C4.

«««—»»»

Below the caldron, Gunny Gudmunsson leaned on the black Range Rover and pulled his black knit hat down over his ears.

"Should've taken all of their money," he muttered, pulling an automatic pistol from his backpack and brandishing the gun. "Left them up here on their honeymoon," he said, kicking the ash-laden dirt.

He peeked inside the pack. "At least this will get Otto off my ass."

"Can you help me?" sounded a voice from the other side of the SUV.

"Who the hell?" Gunny exclaimed, turning around and peeking over the hood of the Range Rover.

"I need help," a stranger exclaimed, trudging up the makeshift trail twenty meters away.

Gunny raised his pistol, leaning against the side window. "No help here. Take your ass down the mountain."

"I can't do that," the stranger answered, continuing to press upward.

Gunny Gudmunsson never heard the muffled shot. What he did hear was the soft "plink" as a bullet passed through the SUV's side windows. What he saw was a fluffy plume of feathers exploding from his down jacket. What he felt was the sting of a bullet piercing his chest.

The con man reached to the pain throbbing in his torso and felt the blood flow warm across his hand. His legs buckled and he slid down to the ground against the side of the SUV.

Tap...tap...tap...

Gunny sluggishly looked up to see a redhead tapping a handgun against the car, a smirk on his face.

"Hurt, don't it?" Eric Stoneridge asked.

The con man's lips curled up at the wiry assassin as realization flooded in. No, not pain but numb exhilaration. Gunny blinked hard trying to force back the growing darkness. All of his cons were nothing compared to this ultimate adrenaline rush blanketing his body.

Gunny clutched the backpack full of money to his chest. He needn't worry about Otto or his next hustle; he didn't have to worry about anything again, ever.

«‹—›»

High on the glacier above the boiling pot, Michael finished carving out a hole in the ice and arming the clay brick with the detonator. He then deposited the explosive varmint inside its burrow. Faye did the same, ten meters farther along the ridge.

"That's the last one," she shouted.

"Okay," he answered. "Let's get off this ice shelf."

Faye and Michael trudged off the white overhang and converged around the wooden crate.

"We have one shot at this, and we need our lid intact," Michael announced extracting a remote detonator from the box. "Blow the charges at the exact same time and—"

"And then repel down into an active volcano," she added, turning the screws into the solid ice. "Find an artifact we've never seen before, to use to stop a secret Vanguard-Horsemen war." Faye snapped a carabiner onto each metal screw and clipped a nylon rope into each carabiner. "Save the man I love who wants to murder the world, and all without burning to a crisp. Yeah, no problem."

Michael smiled. "Simple."

Faye and Michael pulled on their air tanks. "We have one hour of air," Michael announced.

Faye reached into the crate and extracted two flashlights. "Then let's get it done in half that time," she said, handing a torch to Michael.

"Ready?" he asked.

Faye nodded, and Michael's thumb stabbed the red button on the remote detonator. The C4 charges detonated in unison, and a mass of snow and ice leapt into the air like a fountain at a posh Las Vegas hotel.

Faye could feel the vibration travel up her legs, and her body shook like she was gripped in an epileptic seizure. Then an eerie silence followed the deafening roar.

The Vanguards stared at the unflinching ice shelf; its silent resilience seemed to mock them.

"Nothing," Michael declared.

Faye turned to Michael. "Can we set—"

"There are no more charges," he muttered.

"No!" she cried, her plea echoing off the ice sheets. "There has to be a way. There has to!"

The ice shelf answered with a soft moan and a pop, the cracking sound building like an ice cube fracturing when put in a glass of water. Then came a sharp shot. Faye's legs shook again. The ice split, and the cloudless sky was full of loud thundering as the two Vanguards watched the ice shelf fall down into the caldron.

Faye slipped on her suit's helmet, tugged on her rope, and stepped off glacier. In less than fifteen seconds she had repelled down and stood on the fallen ice shelf.

Michael followed suit and stood next to Faye like an alien groom on a white wedding cake.

"Let's find it," she said hollowly through her mask, unclipping her harness from the line.

Suddenly, the rope danced in Faye's hand like a slithering snake. She looked up to see another body, clad in a down jacket and black knit hat, repelling down into the caldera.

"What's that fool guide doing?" she asked.

"You're going to get yourself killed," Michael yelled up at the descending figure.

"Me? No," said the man, landing on the ice a moment later and spinning around, pointing a pistol at the two Vanguards. "You, on the other hand, will most certainly die."

CHAPTER 12

Michael stepped toward the man in the down jacket. A boom echoed off the cauldron walls, and a bullet ricocheted next to Michael's boot, throwing ice shards into the air.

"That's far enough," the gunman ordered.

"You're not Gunny," Faye said, her voice muffled under her helmet.

"No," the gunman answered, pulling the black beanie from his red head.

"You!" Faye cried. The memory of her last meeting with the recruit in the Vanguard library flashed through her mind. "How did it feel… to be one with a Horseman?" the redhead had asked between the book-stacks, and she remembered how his covetous gaze had made her skin crawl.

"Off with the lids," the gunman commanded.

The Vanguards removed their protective helmets. "Eric, what the hell are you doing?" Faye asked.

"Isn't it obvious?" the redhead said, brandishing the pistol. "I'm tying up two loose ends."

"You're the mole!" she declared.

"It was a miracle that you both survived the oil-rig explosion in the Mediterranean and my little surprise in London," he said with a sneer. "But your charmed lives end today."

"Murderer," Michael snarled.

134

"You're the murderer!" Eric shouted, directing his fury at Michael with a pointed finger. "You!"

Michael's questioning glance stabbed at the gunman.

"Charles Stone?"

Michael furrowed his brow, searched his thoughts, but the name, while familiar, was just out of reach.

"Just like the Vanguard to piss away good men on a fool's errand and then forget about them like yesterday's garbage."

Without warning, an assaulting memory hit Michael like a gut punch: Sunada, Sechler, Hecht, and Stone. They were all dead. Michael sucked in air, blinked hard. But he couldn't force out the old memories bombarding his mind.

"Chuck," Michael said, remorseful recognition washing over his face.

"Now you remember," Eric said.

"Michael?" Faye asked.

"Tell her," Eric demanded. "Tell her how you murdered my brother."

"Your brother?"

"Tell her," the redhead ordered, sighting his pistol on the Vanguard's head.

Michael looked at Faye.

"Argeles-Gazost. Five of us were part of a covert Ops team dropped into Argeles-Gazost. Our mission was to obtain the Horseman's artifact.

"Steal it, you mean," Eric countered. "The Vanguard are murderers and thieves." The redhead's eyes covered Michael with a blanket of contempt. "Did you think he'd let you take his sword from him again? Do you think the Horseman a fool?"

Michael was silent.

"You're the fool!" Eric declared. "Because of you, War slaughtered my brother like a pig."

Faye shot Michael an unknowing glance.

Eric noted Faye's response. "He didn't tell you how he let the Horseman gut my brother?"

"Chuck died," Michael uttered, the memory slamming into his mind like a car crash. War, fiery blade in hand, looked over the dead Vanguard like a crazed lumberjack surveying severed tree trunks. He had come up behind Chuck Stone like a ghost and, with one arm holding the

Vanguard captive around his neck, cut open Chuck's stomach like a butcher. War had thrown the corpse to the ground and in a callous exclamation stomped down on the side of the Vanguard's gray face, crushing his skull like an egg. Michael blinked hard, trying to cast out the image of gray matter spilling out from its fragile shell. "He died bravely," Michael said.

"Fuck you! You, the only pig not slaughtered," Eric spat, lowering his weapon. "Do you think you're better than my brother?"

Michael stared at the crazed gunman.

"Do you!" the redhead exclaimed.

At the same time, and unnoticed by the embattled men, the ice cracked between Faye's feet. A small wisp of steam escaped from the tear. Faye's heart pounded in her chest as she realized that their makeshift lid wouldn't last much longer over the boiling cauldron.

"Well, I'm here to correct that," Eric continued, redirecting the muzzle at Michael's head.

"Can't you see we are trying to stop a war?" Faye asked, directing the gunman's attention away from Michael. "The Vanguard and Horsemen will kill millions of innocent people."

"Let them die...let them all die."

"Die like lobsters in a pot of *boiling* water?" she said, emphasizing the one word, starting her code, sliding her foot backwards toward the shadowed wall opening.

"What?" Eric asked, raising his eyebrows. "Lobsters? Yeah, I love it when they scream."

Michael's eyes shifted to Faye's, whose gaze flashed to the ice.

"And how their shells *crack*," she continued as she slid back her other foot toward the hidden vent.

Michael glimpsed the wisp of steam and understood immediately. He slid one foot backwards. "You know you have to put a lid on the pot or the lobsters will try to crawl out to *save* themselves," Michael added, his other foot retreating.

"All this talk about lobsters is making me hun—"

The gunman's retort was interrupted by a rumbling that echoed around them like thunder.

Eric looked up to the sky, unaware that the danger lay beneath his feet.

Faye's mouth drew into a fierce line, her face wrinkling up like the ends of a drawstring purse.

Michael and Faye inched toward the vent, its dark entrance smoking like a mouth exhaling cigarette smoke.

The thunderstorm returned in earnest, accompanied by the sound of breaking glass. The redhead glanced down to see a fissure growing between his feet, unaware that his two captives were sprinting for the wall. Eric spied his fleeing quarry and raised his gun, sighting it on Michael's back just as the cauldron lid broke with a loud pop, kicking up thirty degrees and toppling the gunman off his feet. Steam erupted out of the icy kettle. Eric slid screaming down into the crevice.

At the far side of the caldera, Michael and Faye dove through the shadowed vent as molten magma gushed up through the icy lid, reclaiming the Grimsvotn crater. They tumbled down into the dark abyss.

In the darkness, a wave of heat slapped Faye across the face. She could smell her hair burning, could feel the heat consume her. Her cheeks burned as if demons were clawing at her skin, dragging her soul down into the pit.

«««—»»»

Michael toppled out alone, eyes shut, rolling on the ground, swatting at his hair and clothes. He sucked in one cool breath and stopped his seizure. "You're hil...larious," a voice called out to him, and Michael popped open his eyes.

"Light?" Michael thought. He turned his head and stared at a young boy sitting on a log next to a campfire.

"You're a riot, Mickey," the boy called out.

Michael stood up, his eyes wide, soaking in the spectacle before him: a campfire, woods in the background and...

"You okay, Mickey?" the boy asked.

...a camper, with roasting stick, a white marshmallow adorning its tip.

"Where am I?" Michael asked.

"Duh," was the camper's retort.

A cool breeze whistled through the trees, the scent of pine pervasive. The chill felt good, and Michael reached up to rub his singed cheeks. He stopped short and stared at the small hand he had raised, removed of creases, calluses, and scars.

"How can this be?" Michael murmured, stroking his cheeks and chin, expecting to find his five o'clock shadow but finding a smooth face.

The Vanguard shifted his eyes down and looked at his clothes. His silvers had been replaced with shorts and a short-sleeve shirt: a summer camp uniform with an embroidered moose on the chest.

He turned around and stared up at the totem pole.

"Camp Waksolatchi?" Michael uttered.

"Mickey, smore?" he heard the boy say.

"Billy?" Michael asked, staring at the boy in front of him. "Billy Sulleman?"

"Double duh," the boy wisecracked.

Euphoria swept over him, and he smiled. He was ten, it was summer, and Camp Waksolatchi was one of the best times of his life: a simpler time, a time when his mom wasn't drinking, a time when his dad was still his dad and not the deadbeat father who used him and his mother as his punching bags.

"Am I dead?" Michael asked.

"Come on, Mickey, quit fooling, roast one," Billy Sulleman said, throwing a marshmallow to the ten-year-old Vanguard.

Michael caught the confection with one hand and picked up a long stick. "Yeah, okay," he said, impaling the Magic Puff with one smooth stroke.

«« — »»

Seconds after Michael skidded into Camp Waksolatchi, Faye rolled out of the tunnel onto her back. Coolness. The joy of not hurting was so intense it was nearly its own kind of pain. Faye focused her eyes; a dim light greeted her. Surprised at her unusually soft landing, Faye swept her hand across the plush ground. "Carpeting?" she thought.

"Where am I?" she asked, sitting up and scanning the room until her eyes fell upon a familiar silver framed photo of her father and herself.

The sight of her father's den rocketed Faye to her feet. Her head swung back and forth as she soaked in the image that was burned into her memory: the bookcase, her father's desk and leather chair, even the old coat rack where he hung his button-up cardigan.

Faye walked across the carpet, leaving footprints on the flooring like it was sand, and touched the wool sweater. She was seven the last time she had seen her father wear it.

Faye lifted the fabric to her face, rubbed it on her cheek, and inhaled. "Old Spice," she thought. "Dad's favorite." Faye's lips curled at the memory.

From behind Faye, one yellow and one red eye watched her every move.

"Faye?" echoed a deep voice from outside the room.

"Dad?" she muttered.

Faye's mind flashed back to her childhood. She was a young girl of seven, wakened in the night by loud voices. A booming sinister voice muffled her father's words. Terrified, Faye crept to the hallway, hiding behind a door and peeking through the crack. A big man clamped his gloved hand around her father's throat, and, with a quick twist of his wrist, the stranger snapped her father's neck.

"Faye, can you come into the kitchen, dear?"

The voice shattered the horrific memory.

"It can't be," she declared.

She'd always felt comfortable in her dad's study but something felt wrong, "off" in the room like a shirt tag scratching the back of her neck.

《《—》》

In his own illusion, Michael stepped to the campfire with his sugar-tipped spear, like a knight prepared to battle a dragon, and pushed the marshmallow close to the glowing embers. But the white treat did not brown. Michael plunged the treat deeper into the fire, but its sugary coat still did not yield. His hand was hot, his fingers stinging.

"What is wrong with this thing?" he questioned.

Billy sat unmoving, smiling in exuberant anticipation.

With a shrug of his shoulders, the summer-camp knight pushed the marshmallow until the flame licked the confectionary.

《《—》》

Back in her father's study, Faye stepped passed the big desk and a standing Tiffany-style floor lamp, its shade cast of red, green, and yellow tiles. Faye stopped, her eyes searching for something just out of sight. The hair on the back of her neck stood on end.

"This looks like my dad's study," she said aloud. "But my father never had the same crappy lamp I had in college." She spun around, her roundhouse slamming into the Tiffany-style lamp.

As the lamp crashed to the ground, the illusion of her father's study dissolved away like a chalk drawing in the rain.

Sprawled unconscious on the dim, lava-lit ground was a naked man. He was old, weathered by time. Folds of skin hung loosely about his frame like wet clothes on a line. His face was a roadmap bunched in deep wrinkles. Dark brown spots, like stars, lined along his thin forehead and down his cheeks.

Faye turned to see Michael's silver gloved fingers, held close to a pool of lava, on fire. "Michael, stop!" Faye charged the Vanguard, slamming him to the ground.

Camp Waksolatchi dissolved before Michael's eyes.

"Michael, wake up!" Faye cried, smothering his burning glove with her own.

"Faye?" Michael asked, looking up at her. "I was at summer camp."

"I know," she said and looked over at their naked host prone on the ground. Faye stood up and helped Michael to his feet.

"Where are we? What happened?" Michael asked.

"Not what, but who?" she answered, directing Michael's attention to the old man with a nod.

"Illusions?" he asked.

Faye nodded.

"It was so real, I couldn't stop."

"I know," Faye answered, remembering her father's voice calling out to her.

"How did you break free?"

"*Redum lu genii,*" the old man said, lifting his head up, pointing a shaky finger.

Faye stared at the hermit.

Michael reached out. "Faye?"

"I was touched?" she said, returning Michael's gaze. She turned back to the old man. "It's Sumerian or some close dialect."

"*Redum lu genii,*" the old man repeated, and added, "*Bit sisu.*"

"I was touched by the Riders," Faye translated, stepping toward the man.

The hermit's eyes grew large, his wrinkled brow creased, and he scrambled backwards like a cornered crab.

"*Ti salamu,*" she said in Sumerian, "You are safe. *Ti mannu?* Who are you?"

"*Ta Egisnugal,*" the old man spouted, looking left and right, his eyes wide, searching for an escape.

"I don't understand," Faye responded. She turned to Michael. "He said something about a House of Light."

"*Emu adaru damqis. Ulta ulla tanaddasi. Ro'esnugal,*" the old man said, his words running together as one.

Faye kneeled in front of the naked form. "Slow down," Faye said in English. "*Balu awatum.*"

"*Adi tanaddassi basu bubutu bit sisu isatum hursag.*"

"You're speaking too fast. I can't keep up."

"I am the Reliquary," the naked man said in perfect English.

Michael's eyes grew to the size of dinner plates, and his jaw dropped.

"You can speak English?" Faye asked.

"No one, save the Riders or those touched by their darkness, can escape Zilittu, the Walk of Oblivion," the hermit said, ignoring her query. "Are you in league with the Riders?"

"It is true that I was touched by Atra," Faye said.

With a panicked look, the hermit bolted away behind a large rock.

"But Famine does not control me now," she shouted. "I am free from the Horseman."

"Leave me!" the hermit cried out over his keep. Faye's words provided no reassurance to the old man.

"We just wish to speak with you," she called out over the stone. Silence answered back.

"Now what?" Michael asked.

Faye furrowed her brows.

"He's terrified of you. We're the first people he's seen, ever, and probably the strangest looking."

Faye's face lit up like a lightbulb as the words slipped out of his mouth. "Yes!" she said, unzipping her silver jumpsuit and shedding it like a butterfly cocoon.

"What are you doing?" Michael asked.

"A peace offering," she answered.

Faye stepped toward the hermit's hiding place. "Reliquary, I present you a gift: a special fabric that protects from fire and the burning power of War."

Faye tossed the silvers, gloves, and boots onto the rock. The ensemble slid away behind the stone. After a moment, the silver-clad hermit stepped into view and paraded the shiny offering like a proud peacock.

Faye smiled warmly.

The Reliquary approached his two guests and sat down. Michael and Faye followed suit.

"You have questions," the Reliquary began.

"I am Faye," she said, patting her chest. "This is Michael. Do you have a name?"

"I am Ro'esnugal. I am the Reliquary."

"Yes, but what do your friends call you?"

"Friends?" he responded quizzically.

"Oh, boy," Faye muttered.

"I've never been called anything than but what I am."

Faye leaned in. "It's customary to have a name with people close to you, friends, and we'd like to be your friends. How does the name Roy, sound?"

"Roy?" the old man repeated. "Yes," he said, smiling, "I like that very much."

"Okay, Roy. How did you come to be in this place?" Faye asked, her eyes roaming the rocky cavern.

"I have been here for what seems like a lifetime. Cast aside by the Riders, imprisoned by my brethren."

"You're a Horseman?" Michael asked.

"No." The old man shook his head. "I walk a path of light and not in darkness, like the ones you call the Horsemen."

"Why did they imprison you?" Faye asked.

"I am the maker of gifts. Those of light: humanity's goodness; and of darkness: evil, man's hatred contained. I am balance to an imperfect world. Where there is war, I am peace. Death...life."

"You controlled the Horsemen," Faye concluded.

Roy nodded. "My gifts can diminish the power of the Riders or strengthen it, and it was for my refusal of the latter that I was exiled to this forgotten place."

Michael scanned the empty chamber. "Where are the gifts?"

"My power infuses light or darkness only into objects touched by the hand of man, and as you can see, there is nothing here but frozen or boiling earth." The old man reached down, running his hand along the cold ground. "I am the only relic in this prison."

"Can you still make your gifts?" Michael asked.

The hermit tilted his head, listening.

"Roy, Michael and I are part of a group that for millennia has sought to protect humanity from the Riders. We are here now in search of your gifts to stop a war," Faye said, turning a somber face to Michael. "And to save a man," she added.

"I have not wielded the light for such a long time, and never more than one, or—" Roy pressed his hands together in a ball and then gestured them up and out.

"An explosion?" Michael asked.

The Reliquary nodded.

Michael turned to Faye, the two Vanguards striking upon the same idea.

"Roy, we need you to make two artifacts now," Faye asked.

Michael pulled two flashlights from his suit and extended them to Roy.

The Reliquary stared at the metal torches. "They will destroy us."

"Your gifts are our way out of here," she said with a reassuring smile.

"I will try," the Reliquary said.

Surrounded by the glow of lava, the old man grabbed the flashlights and closed his eyes in fierce concentration. Soon a subtle radiance pulsated from his withered hands, growing brighter with each passing second. The Reliquary winced, his wrinkled face creasing deeper. His hands shook until the brilliance flowed from him into the flashlights like water.

Roy dropped to his knees. The pulsating gifts rolled out from his open palms.

Michael scooped up the glowing torches, his eyes fixated on the flashing rhythm. Moving the flashlights away from one another, each torch radiated a slow dull white light, but as he brought them together, the wands pulsed brilliant red like warning beacons.

Michael scanned the rocky chamber, taking his bearings and choosing one vent from the dozens scattered throughout the chamber like the honeycomb of a beehive. "We need to tie these together," he said.

Faye ripped a strip of cloth from her shirt and tied the shimmering torches together.

"It's time to go," Michael declared and, cocking his arm, threw the glowing gifts to the far wall and into a small hole.

Michael and Faye lifted the Reliquary up to his feet, and the three raced behind a rocky outcropping. In the next instant, an explosion roared through the chamber; the cavern transformed into a cloud of ice and steam. Faye was thrown to her back, and her ears were filled with high-pitched ringing that her own voice could not penetrate. "Michael!" she coughed.

"Here," came the reply. "I have Roy."

Faye stood up and watched as a beam of light pierced the dirty veil and a cool breeze filled the icy prison. Michael cleared debris from the newly made exit and stepped out into the Icelandic afternoon.

Faye helped Roy out of the tomb. The old man cringed at the new surroundings and fell to the ground. "I'm sorry my friends, but I have not the strength to move these feeble legs."

"I have strength for both of us," Michael said. Scooping the Reliquary into his arms, he trudged down the glacier.

After a few steps, Michael looked down at the old hermit. "How is it that you can speak English?"

"When you walk the Walk of Oblivion, I travel the path with you. I learn what you know, but while the words are familiar, their meaning is often lost to me," he said with a grin.

Michael stared at the old man's face, feeling a tinge of familiarity. "Billy Sulleman?"

The Reliquary's grin broadened. "What is a smore?"

Michael smiled. "It's one of life's little pleasures."

"I look forward to having one."

Faye sighed as the black Range Rover came into view. When she stepped around to the driver's side, their guide, Gunny Gudmunsson, greeted them from the ground with a blank, wide-eyed stare.

"I see the ways of man have not changed over the ages," Roy said.

Faye looked at the corpse slumped to the side of the car. "No, they haven't."

CHAPTER 13

The delivery truck, looking like a brown box on wheels, crested the hill, gathered speed on Round Ridge Road, and entered the exclusive Greenwich neighborhood. Residents were familiar with the clatter of the diesel engine in the late afternoon, ears perking at the telltale sound of an impending delivery. The UPS freight truck slowed around a curve and passed a parked Chevy Volt. The driver snickered at the New York vanity plate that read *GR8MYERS* and thought, "Leave it to the uber-wealthy to piss pompousness on everything, even a thirty-thousand-dollar hybrid."

Continuing on its route, the brown box soon stopped in front of large iron gates. The delivery man pressed the intercom, and, with the power of a muted Ali Baba, the metal doors swung open.

As the truck cruised up the long paved driveway toward the French-style brick chateau, the driver glanced through his open cab at the sprawling estates to each side. To his left: rolling hills of wild flowers parading up to an English country house. To his right: a large manicured lawn, framed by a Civil War rock wall, basking in front of a regal Georgian Colonial.

The rolling brown box squealed to a halt in front of the French mansion. The delivery man, sporting a matching brown uniform, jumped out and lifted the roll-up back door of the truck. He plucked six shoebox-sized brown squares from the cargo hold, stacking one atop another, and deposited the packages on the grand doorstep. In less than a minute the truck roared back to life, rolled down the drive, and exited the estate. The UPS driver watched as the iron gates closed, musing that there'd be no more deliveries today.

"Packages delivered. You are clear to deploy," he announced into his shoulder microphone.

On the grand doorstep, the six brown packages started to move, rocking back and forth like mini-Houdinis in handcuffs trying to break out during a performance. The sides of the shoeboxes bulged until silver appendages stabbed through the wrapping. One by one, metal hatchlings tore through their paper containers like steel chicks hatching from square eggs.

The mechanized newborns looked like miniaturized train cars: shiny bricks with two silver all-terrain wheels positioned underneath. The body of each brick was not a single stationary piece but was comprised of hundreds of smaller components that moved, each individual piece shifting position and orientation, like live fish scales, and then were glued into place by an invisible force. On each brick, one scale held a small lens.

On the doorstep of the French estate, the first brick morphed into a globe, and, as if leading a game of Simon Says, the others mimicked the transformation. In subsequent moments, Simon and its five siblings transformed into a tall letter *T,* a letter *H,* and then returned to their original four-sided forms.

One mile away in a remote command center, six Vanguard agents sat in front of flickering control consoles. One Vanguard swung his chair and turned his attention to the blonde standing at the center. "Electromagnets functioning at one-hundred percent," he reported. "Video surveillance and cloaking generators operational and drone diagnostic complete."

Diana Waterford nodded. "Initiate Operation Tartarus."

Moments later, the wheels of each brick spun and the mechanized drones rolled off the doorstep and onto the adjacent garden path. The six train cars crunched on gravel and then grew muted as hard pebbles gave way to the thick sod of the decorative backyard landscape. The French garden was more than plants and flowers; it was outdoor architecture, extending the rooms of the chateau to the space outside its grand walls. The garden was designed like buildings, with a succession of rooms which guests could pass through like hallways, and vestibules with adjoining chambers. The walls were composed of low-clipped hedges laid out in geometric patterns. On the ground were carpets of grass, embroidered with blooms, and the fruit and nut trees were swaying curtains. Pools of water replaced mirrors, and fountains sparkled like chandeliers.

Statuary of Greek themes dotted the garden. One figure standing amidst the cherry blossoms was neither stone nor mythology. The goateed stranger in Brutini loafers stood like a perennial and watched the old Georgian Colonial house with wanting eyes.

The stranger's nails raked against the tree bark as his thoughts retreated to the past. Memories resurfaced, crashed around him, images of the earth rising up, engulfing his being as easily as a fish swallowing a fly. He remembered looking up at his four betrayers. "Why, my brothers?" he had pleaded. The bitterness in his heart soured in his mouth. He could still feel how their stares stabbed at him, how they looked down upon him with disdain. He was cast from the same dark mold as them, but the four never embraced him as one of their own. "You are reckless," a voice had answered.

Surrounded by the floral beauty of the French garden, the stranger shut his eyes, his mind at peace in the darkness. "Yes, I was reckless," he reflected, but that was his essence, his being. He was the embodied Spirit of Disorder. His name was Lateris. His name was Chaos. His power had always tipped the scales of order in favor of bedlam and mayhem. In his presence, the impossible was probable, the predictable...unknown, the definite...random.

His mind's eye blinked, and he saw the yellow seas of Mesopotamia dotted with dark armor. He remembered how he had poured out reverence to the Riders, only to drown in their scorn; and in that swell of contempt, a tsunami of death had risen up from his feet and swept the legion of warriors away like a broom. One by one, the Riders had acted against the sandstorm only to find the power of Chaos acting against them: barriers of earth and pest fell to pieces in the shifting sand. Famine's ghostly vapors dispersed in the cutting wind. War's commands were drowned out by the howling gale.

The stranger remembered the words that had panged his ears and stung his soul. "You are blight upon the land, an affront to the Riders, an accursed abomination to be shunned for eternity," the Warrior Horseman had cried. "You are reckless, and now you are lost." And the earth had consumed him.

Chaos opened his eyes, his gaze falling back on the opulence at the top of the sprawling lawn. He reflected back to the more modest Italian villa he had looked upon a week prior and how within that confine the Vanguard knowledge had flowed into him. While his mind swam with understanding, centuries of wonders once lost to him, now regained, his heart was full of rancor and vengeance.

The sight of the metal caravan rolling past the diamond-shaped hedge derailed his train of spite. As the column proceeded past, Chaos stepped into the floral hallway and touched the last car.

The mechanized steel box stopped in its tracks.

In the mobile command center one mile away, a Vanguard agent stared at a blank screen. "Number six is off-line," he stated.

"Run the diagnostic," was the reply.

"I did," the agent began. "It's completely de—"

Before the last syllable left the Vanguard's mouth, Chaos touched the metal brick again, reactivating the drone.

"Never mind," stated the Vanguard in the dim operation center. "Number six is back on line."

"Proceed to target," echoed the order through the command center.

Among the backdrop of green, yellow, and orange hues, the stranger's lips formed a twisted smile as he looked at his hand. "I'll show them reckless," he thought. He'd breed bedlam and anarchy in this world, and he'd have his revenge on them. The Four Horsemen of the Apocalypse would pay for their treachery.

«««—»»»

Inside the Georgian Colonial, War sat alone in his study. His business suit was immaculate, his black hair neatly combed in place, but the tall Horseman wasn't busy with battle strategies or tactical maneuvers. He sat slouched, his back to the curtained glass door, in his high-backed swivel chair, his eyes closed, the rich harmonies of Richard Rodger's *Victory at Sea* filling the room.

The tonetic poem inspired memories of the Pacific theatre. It was a hot June, 1942. The Warrior Horseman was masquerading as a pilot aboard the American aircraft carrier USS *Yorktown*, steaming two hundred miles northeast of Midway Island. He remembered his fervor at the blaring siren as General Quarters sounded while the roar and smoke of aircraft engines filled the flight deck.

The melodic mix of high and low notes resonating through the dark wooded room spurred images of him, his hand caressing the flight stick of his SBD Dauntless dive bomber. Two miles above the Pacific Ocean, he pushed the stick forward, and his plane dove at three hundred knots through ferocious flak, the image of the Japanese aircraft carrier *Akagi* growing ever larger in his windscreen. As the music reached its crescendo, bullets from a Japanese A6M2 Zero fighter speared the cockpit and his rear gunner. Blood and wind whipped his face, but still he dove, his hand steady on the stick, until at 1,000 feet, two seconds before running out of sky, he dropped his payload and pulled out of the dive. The one-thousand-pound bomb pierced the flight deck; the massive explosion broke the back of the Japanese flagship.

A disquieting familiarity crept over the Horseman like icy fingers, interrupting his harmonious reflection. War popped open his eyes and shifted his gaze around the room, his eyes fixed on the open doorway leading to the hall.

With a flick of his thumb on a remote, War muted the military ballad. A wisp of ancient kinship stirred in the room.

War balled a fist, sparking to life a supernatural flame. He sat up and leaned forward in his chair, prepared to launch his fury, as a long-haired Persian greyhound trotted into the study, its nails clicking on the hardwood floor.

"Quwwa," the Horseman declared, extinguishing the flame.

The golden hound trotted to the chair and rested its muzzle on its master's knee, its dark eyes saying "Pet me."

War stroked the soft yellow fur, yet the Horseman's eyes were uneasy.

"Kishar," he surmised, clenching a fist; but the Horseman dismissed the thought and unfurled his rage. The essence he felt was ancient, but it was not Death; the difference was subtle but distinct, like the taste of scotch and bourbon.

His eyes scanned the cracks of the mahogany bookshelves and the crevices of the stone fireplace, searching for a memory buried over the ages, but he was unable to exhume it.

"Weakling!" he shouted, slamming his fist down on the armrest. The saluki yelped and cowered at its master's feet.

The Horseman's gaze crept to the center of the sanctuary, to the lighted glass case and the barren space that was both reminder and warning: a lost kingdom soon regained. The warring seduction of his golden Ād axe was at work, yet his grip on the human host was faltering. He had transferred all but a sliver of his supernatural essence to the blade, leaving little power to hold possession of his host, and the battle with the human spirit inside the mortal shell was constant.

The Persian greyhound lifted its snout and pointed its ears. The dog turned its muzzle to the shrouded balcony window and growled.

"I sense it too, Quwwa."

The saluki stood, its alarm vibrating through the study, and padded across the Persian knotted pile to the glass. It pushed its keen nose through the curtains, steaming up the pane with its hot breath.

Outside, the drones rolled across the manicured expanse leading up to the Georgian Colonial. With the touch of a button in the distant Vanguard command center, the silver scales on each drone rolled over like a wave of dominoes, its lustrous skin replaced with a light and dark array of emerald hues that matched its grassy surroundings. With its camouflage active, each mechanical chameleon disappeared into the ocean of green.

Quwwa's bark echoed through the study.

War stepped to the glass, pulled back the thick curtain, and cracked the balcony door. The anxious hound nosed the door open, forcing its bulk through the widening gap, and shot out onto the wooden balcony.

The golden saluki reared on its hind legs and placed its forelegs on the balcony. It perked its ears, its sharp canine sight surveying the dusky scenery like a castaway scanning the horizon.

The Persian greyhound sounded its alarm again, accenting its bark with a worrisome howl.

The Horseman stepped out onto the balcony. "What do those keen eyes show you?" he said, patting his companion's blond head, his own penetrating gaze scanning the landscape.

The saluki growled.

As the Horseman's image appeared on the six video screens, "All units stop" rang out in the Vanguard command center.

The train of chameleons rolled to a stop.

The Horseman closed his eyes, concentrating, and cast his warring essence out across the field of green. He sensed no anger, no fear. There was not a single spark of human fire that he could hook and reel in. But still the chilling sense of familiarity continued to claw at his mind.

Quwwa fired off another threatening growl.

"I know," War said with a final pat, and returned to his study.

"All units proceed to target," echoed the order in the dark Vanguard command center. The drones continued their forward progress.

Quwwa pushed off the railing onto four legs, eyes locked on the moving grass.

In the curtained study, War sat back into his chair, pressed the remote control, and roused the *Song of the High Seas*. He closed his eyes. His thoughts returned to the dead stick in the cockpit of his Dauntless dive bomber. Quwwa's warning stanza filled the dim room. War turned the volume higher; the orchestral shells riddling his mental canopy.

On the balcony, the Persian greyhound crouched down, its body quivering. With a bark that could have been saluki for "Geronimo!" Quwwa leaped over the balcony, landed on the green cushion, and darted forward.

The hound honed in on the drones within seconds: ears tracking the soft hum, nose hunting the faint ungrasslike odor.

Within the confines of the remote command center, the Vanguard operator watched as the four-legged smart bomb bore down on the drone. "Complication on three," he announced.

"Kill the mutt," ordered Waterford. The Horseman behind the Vanguard mask smiled, reflecting upon an ancient memory, an ancient time when another saluki died at her hands.

On the emerald expanse, Quwwa bit down on the camouflaged brick.

Before the row of white daggers could penetrate the metal exterior, the drone's scales shifted. Dozens of pieces slid out of the saluki's mouth, countless more extending over the hound's nose and jaw. Quwwa squirmed, using its forepaws to try to pull free of the expanding muzzle, but within seconds the drone had enveloped the greyhound's entire head, like an old-fashioned diver's helmet, muffling its wails and yelps.

Inside the armored hood, two metal spikes extended forward like pistons, piercing the dog's eyes, stabbing its brain. With a final muffled yelp, Quwwa's golden body lay still on the green grass.

Above, symphonic serenade filled the study and the Horseman's mind. With his eyes closed, War was immersed in battles: Coral Sea, Guadalcanal, and Eastern Solomons.

Lost in thought, he wasn't aware of the bracelet closing around his wrist until he heard a sharp click.

War's eyes popped open. In the next instant, he was on his feet.

The Horseman stared down at the small metal brick.

"Vanguard?" he questioned, stamping his foot down on the brick, but before leather met metal, the drone had morphed into a circular ring and avoided the crushing blow. As War's boot crashed onto the floor, splintering the hardwood, the robot encircled the Horseman's foot with another shackle.

Click!

War's cry overwhelmed the soft melody coursing through the study. "Do you think your shackles can hold me?" he boasted.

With fierce concentration, he clenched his captured fist, igniting his mystical Horseman flame. The fire engulfed his balled hand and metal band, but the shackle resisted the heat.

"What magic is this?" War questioned, his eyes widening with not a single rational or coherent thought able to pierce through his haze of surprise. It was then that the Vanguard attack pressed on.

Click!

War stared at the new jewelry adorning his other wrist. His face reddened, and his jugular veins swelled.

"This ends now!" the Horseman declared, stepping to the lighted display case at the center of the room, his cuffed hand reaching inside for the spiked mace. But before War could wrest the morning star from its cradle, his hand was driven down toward his foot, the shackles' attractive nature manipulating his movement.

"No!" he screamed, pulling against the electromagnetic force, standing upright. The Horseman's hand shot through the glass case, and his fingers wrapped around the handle of the mace.

As another drone reached out toward his unencumbered ankle, War brought the spiked club down onto the metal brick, smashing the robot.

Gloating in his victory, the music crescendoing in the study, the Horseman failed to see through the wooded camouflage rolling between his legs.

Click!

Enraged, War raised the Morning Star, unaware of the Vanguard order resonating in the mobile command center one mile away. "Reverse polarity."

As the Horseman brought the mace down on the drone, the electromagnet stopped the club's crushing momentum, and the weapon leapt from his hand. The Morning Star crashed into the audio theater, silencing the wartime symphony.

"This is not poss—" But before War could complete his rejection, the invisible force grabbed his wrists, compelling his hands together.

"No," he said, pulling his hands apart, resisting the force. "No more!" the Horseman cried, stepping to the two cross-mounted blunderbusses.

Away from the battle, in the mobile Vanguard command unit, the blond Horseman stared at the drone video monitor. "New tactic," ordered Waterford.

War peeled one muzzleloader from the wall, but before he could cock the hammer, the morning star slammed into the side of his head. Rocked by the mace, the blunderbuss slid through his hand onto the floor. War reached for the second mounted shotgun as the medieval suit of armor, standing empty in the corner of the study for centuries, crashed into him.

Again the morning star attacked with invisible force, slamming its forged spikes onto the back of the Horseman's head. War's study became an arsenal against him, his body bashed by the armaments he cherished, until he fell prone to the hardwood.

As the bombardment fell silent, the shackles around his wrists and ankles sprang to life, splaying the Horseman's hands and legs on the floor. His reserves had run dry, and he knew that to continue the battle would have meant losing his host. War clenched his teeth and submitted to the forces pulling at him.

The Horseman watched with a scowl as one drone merged with another, the two morphing into a gurney. War felt himself being lifted up by his hands and feet and then transported out of his study.

The mechanized cart rolled the captured Horseman out the grand door.

War watched as a black truck pulled up.

"You are fools!" he shouted, casting out his warring essence. "You can't hold me! I will fill your hearts with rage until you rip out the throats of your—"

War's line fell slack as he looked into the driver side, to see it empty. The rear door rose, the ramp extended, and the mechanized dolly rolled its payload into the empty cabin.

"No!" he cried, his frustration and rage igniting a small mystical flame that soon dwindled and died.

The supernatural perennial stood amongst the cherry blossoms watching, gloating like the moon at sunset.

CHAPTER 14

"What about the Vanguard? Won't they have eyes on this place?" Faye asked as Michael inserted the key into the lock.

"This place is off the grid," Michael answered, turning the doorknob. "Something Zachariah liked to call our safe-safe house."

"And if ten armed agents are in there waiting for us?"

"I'd be shocked if they could fit five," Michael replied, stepping across the threshold. Faye and Roy followed him inside.

Faye's eyes took in the room. The four-story walk-up was a coffin, typical for flats in the artsy and somewhat less tourist-trodden Central London neighborhood. It had only the basic necessities: couch, table and chair, small refrigerator, television, two single beds in an adjacent shoebox bedroom, and a water closet.

"Homey," Faye mused.

Michael disappeared into the one bedroom and returned with a bundle of clothes topped by a pair of shoes nestled like a child in his arms.

"These were Zachariah's," he said, handing the garments to the old man. Michael's narrowed eyes and pressed lips reflected the concern he felt for his friend and mentor. "They might fit and will attract fewer glares than your silver space suit."

Roy stood. "Thank you."

"You can change in there," Michael said, motioning to the water closet.

The Reliquary disappeared behind the wooden door.

"Let's see if the Vanguard have popped up on any US newswires," Michael said, stepping to the satellite television and pressing the remote.

Faye sat on the couch and listened to the broadcast.

"The US Secretary of State met with the Omani Deputy Prime Minister today to discuss US relations with the Arabian Sultanate…"

Michael paced across the room, walked to the window, and, pulling the shade back, peeked through the decorative iron bars and out into the London night.

The water closet door opened and Roy stepped into the room. His shirt was buttoned to the top, his slacks wrinkled, and the old man nervously smoothed the bottom of his tweed jacket.

Faye looked at Roy, the edges of her lips forming a smile. "Very nice."

The broadcast continued to reverberate through the matchbook-sized residence.

"In US news today, PETA activists attacked Chimeracon, a Minnesota-based biotechnology company, yesterday afternoon. No arrests were made…"

Faye's thoughts turned to Ben, and her mood saddened. He was an unwilling passenger in his own body, human and Horseman souls fighting for control of one heart.

Her mind flashed to her own past nightmare as host to Famine. "Get out of my head, God damn it!" her thoughts screamed.

"This mortal shell is the host of Atra, Spirit of Famine and Suffering," the voice in her head answered. "I will do with it as I please."

Faye remembered how all she had wanted was to close her eyes and push the voice out, but all her efforts were in vain. Like a spectator in her body, she felt how her will weakened, her mind retreated. The possessive Horseman soul was smothering, a wet blanket on her glowing life ember, but still she fought for control until…

"In other news, New York state assemblyman Jon Meyer and his wife were found murdered in their apartment late today. The assemblyman's car was found in Connecticut on Round Ridge Road."

Faye's head shot up at the sound of the words, her eyes sparkling with recognition.

"Round Ridge Road?" Faye mumbled.

"Faye, what is it?" Michael asked.

"Ben," she added.

"Then the war with the Horsemen may have already begun."

⟨⟨⟨—⟩⟩⟩

The steel door slid away, and a spear of light stabbed into the darkness of the abandoned warehouse. The blond woman entered, heels clicking, a little bounce in her step, her gait a stark contrast to her gray-faced escort shuffling behind.

Waterford stepped beside a large steel crate.

"Hello, my little darlings," she said, knocking on the metal box.

The box jumped and shifted to the left, the occupants answering the greeting with ferocious roars and snarls.

"All you hoped they'd be, brother," she said, reflecting upon Pestilence's handiwork and patting the steel cage.

Waterford glanced back at her companion. "Come," she commanded and set off deeper into the darkness. The escort staggered behind, dragging one foot after the other.

From the shadows, a circle of light shone down from the ceiling like a theater spotlight. At center stage, the Warrior Horseman stood, arms and legs outstretched like a Broadway singer gripped in a musical finale, surrounded by a robotic entourage.

The blonde stepped alone from the blackness and took the stage next to the captured artist.

"Kishar," War whispered, his head hanging low.

Black streams ran through the flowing blond strands. Waterford's face dissolved away, the visage of the gothic Horseman taking its place. Death stared at War. "Do my tricks amuse you now, brother?"

War looked up, his sneer palpable.

Death extended a bony finger and stroked the captured cheek. "There is nothing worse than a warrior defeated, is there, brother?"

War clenched his teeth and strained against his bonds, his weakened supernatural state no match for the power of the electromagnetic shackles that imprisoned him.

"You are quite the spectacle," Death taunted.

War lowered his head.

A shuffling noise from the darkness snatched the captured Horseman's attention. War's eyes peered into the darkness.

The visitor skulked into view.

The Horseman cast his murderous essence onto the new arrival.

"Don't bother," Death said smugly. "He's not even alive."

"Stinking death walker," the chained warrior spat.

"No...stinking Vanguard death walker," Death corrected, stepping to the ashen-faced visitor. "I have to give you credit, you know," she said, sauntering around the death walker. "Slaughtering the Vanguard was passé, and although I still enjoy the old ways, I've found controlling the Vanguard meat and their technology a far more enjoyable endeavor." Walking up to one attack drone, Death patted the robot like it was a golden retriever. "You see, brother, I have my new Horsemen: thousands of Vanguard to do my bidding, enough to breed fear in this world to feed my hunger for centuries."

"Then what do you want of me?" the shackled warrior asked.

"You? You're obsolete," Death charged. "An antique, a prize to be locked away, flaunted on special occasions," she sneered. "I've got a very extraordinary trophy case in mind for you."

"What of Reesef? What plans do you have for Pestilence?"

"That fool is more resourceful than I gave him credit for," she spouted, grinding five bony fingers together in a fist. "No matter, Pestilence will soon join you on display."

War's face turned crimson as his rage boiled over. He pulled against the invisible force, his foot sliding toward his captor, his arm pulling across his chest.

The mechanized handlers hummed loudly as more power was directed to the electromagnetic shackles, positive and negative forces pulling and pushing against Horseman's power.

War balled his hand, his fist engulfed in supernatural flame. "I will not be caged like some beast." But soon his flame sputtered and died, starved of Horseman essence.

"The power of the Four abandons you already. How pathetic you've become," Death taunted.

In the next moment, the Vanguard death walker fell to the ground.

"Eventually, the power abandons us all," War declared, his laughter filling the dank warehouse.

With a defiant grimace, Death assumed the Diana Waterford façade, spun on a heel, and stormed away into the shadows.

«««—»»»

The morning sunlight cast a haze through the safe house. The sound of muffled gunshots rang out in the small apartment. Michael, prone on the couch, popped his eyes open and stared at the white ceiling. He turned his head, focusing on the chair and the old man sitting in front of the television. The Reliquary's eyes were glued to the set like those of a child watching Saturday morning cartoons.

The news broadcast filled the small living room, the volume too low for Michael to hear clearly, let alone comprehend, the sound more similar to white noise than clear commentary.

Michael closed his eyes, concentrated on the floating words, but was able to discern fragments of information: "Oman...stability... exported oil...The Sultanate...critical sea-lane...US Secretary of State requested...President...Strait of Hormuz..."

Michael dismissed the gibberish, sat up and rubbed his eyes. He looked around before resting his gaze on the old man. "Did you watch TV all night?" he asked.

Roy pressed the remote, silenced the box, and turned around. The Reliquary beamed, a childish smile crossing his face. "This television is remarkable," he began. "Did you know that the Towel-o-Wow can soak up ten times its own weight—wine, coffee, and soda are no match for the power of Towel-o-Wow. But wait, there's more! Call right now and we'll double your order!"

"Infomercials?" Michael said with a grin.

"What is soda, anyway?" the Reliquary asked.

The door to the bedroom creaked opened.

Michael turned to see Faye, a determined look on her face.

"Let's go," she announced and headed for the door.

Within an hour, the two wanted Vanguard and discarded Reliquary stood at the entrance of a side alley in the misty London morning. Faye and Michael watched the motionless revolving door within the brick veneer.

"Tell me again why we are staring at the building full of people who want to shoot us?" Michael asked.

"Information," Faye said, her gaze frozen on the reddish stone edifice.

"And how do you suppose we get that? Walk in and ask them for it?"

"Something like that," she answered with a grin.

Peering out into the main street, the Reliquary's gray head bobbed and weaved as his virgin gaze roamed the city block, eyes wide in wonder like a kid in a toy store.

"Humanity has done so much, it is wondrous," the old man said.

"Just progress…and technology," Michael answered.

"Your technology is astounding, but…"

"But what?" Faye asked.

"All this," the Reliquary said, his arms sweeping around the alley. "This is but an extension of man himself. Peel away the progress, strip clean the technology, and man stands as he always has, alone, flesh and blood, at the mercy of the dark and light within himself, at the mercy of—"

"The Horsemen," Faye added.

The Reliquary nodded. "The Riders are but an extension of man's dark side: the murderous, filthy, and deadly intent, all of which makes man…man. This war you speak of, it is in your nature."

"But you, your gifts, they can help us stop it. If darkness is in our nature, then certainly there is also light, mankind's kindness, and goodness," Faye countered.

"My gifts can weaken or strengthen the Riders but temporarily. It is humanity's fear and wretchedness that feeds them, that gives them true lasting power."

"Can you kill them?" Michael asked.

"Destroy the Riders? No," the old man answered. "There was a time when the first gifts could destroy—"

"The sword," Michael inserted.

"Yes!" Roy exclaimed excitedly, bounding from one foot to another. "The Warrior's sword is the gifted light to his darkened soul."

Faye's mind pushed out the London morning, welcoming the memory of a dank cave. She felt again the hilt of the sword in her hand as she'd plunged the blade into the Horseman's back; saw again the blinding light, after which the Warrior Horseman had been gone. Or so she'd thought. Her thoughts flashed to Ben: a memory of the two of them holding hands in the rocky den.

"Ben?" she'd asked, pulling against his iron grip. "Ben, you're hurting me!"

Ben released her and retrieved the sword. She remembered his tone, dark and foreboding. "Tens of thousands have greeted death from this sword. Boudica and her Inceni Celts, the Germanic tribes at Aquae Sextiae and Raudine Plain."

"What are you talking about?"

"Faye, get away from him!" Michael had commanded. "He's not Ben anymore!"

The sound of Roy's voice escorted her thoughts back to the here and now. "But the spirit of the Rider remains, the dark essence seeking out another vessel, a host," the Reliquary concluded.

"Can your gifts free a host possessed by a Horseman?" Faye asked.

"Two souls, one vessel?" he asked. "Free the human from the Rider?" Faye's expectant gaze focused on the old man in anticipation.

"I don't know," Roy answered. "I suppose it is possible."

Faye and Michael returned to their vigil on the brick building.

Roy's eyes, however, fixed on the gold band encircling Faye's finger.

"What is this?" Roy asked, reaching out a crooked finger and brushing the polished gold.

"A reminder," she said. "It is a ring from someone close to me. He's—" Faye spotted the big black man exit Vanguard headquarters in a gray tracksuit.

"The Loop, so predictable," Faye muttered, watching Graeme LaSalle start a slow run.

The Park Loop was a thirteen kilometer run that Faye, like all Vanguard runners, was all too familiar with: down Grosvenor Street to Park Lane and into Hyde Park, through Green Park with its view of Buckingham Palace, into Saint James Park, and then back again. She could do the Park Loop in forty-five minutes. Faye guessed that it would take the big Vanguard close to an hour to complete the loop. She would catch up to Graeme at The Diana, Princess of Wales Memorial Fountain at the southwest corner of Hyde Park: it was open and populated, easy for her, Michael, and Roy to disappear into the crowd if necessary.

Faye hailed a black cab, and the trio piled into the backseat.

Congested street traffic and the Reliquary's wobbly legs cost more time than Faye anticipated, and she was lucky to spot the black mountain moving like a glacier alongside the fountain's flowing water.

Faye stepped across the Cornish granite in front of the sweating black Vanguard.

"You're out of shape, LaSalle," she sniped.

Graeme LaSalle broke from his gate and stopped. "Oh fuck," he started, gulping in breaths. "You've got to be the dumbest bitch on the planet. You know they want you dead."

Faye answered the Vanguard's "duh moment" with a piercing gaze. "What do you want?" Graeme spat.

"We just stopped by to tell you that your redheaded friend is resting at the bottom of the Grimsvotn Crater."

"I hope the bastard screamed all the way down."

"He did. Tell Waterford that—"

"Can't," the big man interrupted.

"Why not?" Faye asked.

"Operation Tartarus."

Faye cocked her head to the side.

The big man's eyes widened. "Waterford is in the US. They already got your boyfriend," he said with a smirk.

Faye's body froze, jaw slack, her breaths coming in short harsh gasps.

"Yeah, they got him, and he's coming in tomorrow, midnight, London Biggin Hill Airport. From what I heard, the Vanguard got some robots and unmanned transports. That Horseman can't do shit against anything that ain't breathing."

"It's not possible," Faye dissented.

"Believe it," he answered. "And get this, once the Vanguard put him in his cell, there's no escape."

Faye's head was spinning. She swept a hand across her head, hoping to brush away the words.

Graeme pushed forward, resuming a slow trot. The big man turned around, jogging backwards. "Once he's in that box, he's never getting out," he yelled, a smile lighting his face. Satisfied with the impact of his verbal assault, the Vanguard spun forward and picked up his pace.

Faye's mind thawed, and she turned wide-eyed to Michael. "We have to stop them. If they put him away, he'll—"

"Then we get to him before they do," Michael declared. "But we're going to need some help."

Two sets of Vanguard eyes swept to the side of the park and stared at the old man playing in the fountain with the other children.

CHAPTER 15

Faye stood on the park grass. Her knees were weak, and she winced as her stomach did another back flip. "Robots and unmanned vehicles…it's too hard to believe. Is that technology even available?"

"It is," Michael answered. "Radio-controlled cars and planes, just on a massive scale. The US military has had automated transport technology for years, and the Vanguard, decades before that. Vanguard scientists must have perfected attack and capture drones, and developed a technology to neutralize the Horseman's powers."

"What the hell can we do against attack drones?" she exclaimed. "There's no chance to beat robots that defeated one of the Four Horsemen of the Apocalypse!"

Michael pondered Faye's question, but an immediate epiphany eluded him. "I just don't—" he began, but stopped as children's laughter snagged his attention; he turned and watched the mob play hide and seek. "Eighteen…nineteen…twenty…ready or not, here I come," piped a little blonde, a girl of six or seven. As the little seeker skipped to one obvious hiding spot after another, her call "Got you!" rang out. Michael's interest focused on a dark-haired boy sneaking from hiding spot to hiding spot. He watched as the little ruffian lay down on his back like a corpse behind a row of strollers, the baby carriages lined up like parked cars.

"Why you little ch—" Michael uttered, just as inspiration slapped him in the face. "We cheat," he said, turning to Faye.

"What?"

"We have an edge and don't even know it," he declared.

"Edge?"

"We go to the man who spearheaded the Vanguard research and development for the last thirty years, and that man isn't in any guarded Vanguard lab. He's in a hospital."

"Zachariah Prond?"

Michael nodded.

"But Zachariah is in no shape to—"

"We have to try. It's a chance, a slim one at that, but it's our only chance."

Michael cast his gaze to Roy, splashing in the fountain. "We're also going to need one of the Reliquary's gifts."

"But Ben is—" she countered, raising her arms, her body tense.

"No!" Michael stated, serious intent shifting into his eyes and burning into Faye. "I'm not going to set free the greatest mass murderer in human history without a little insurance. One or both of us could fall under his murderous influence, and I'm not taking that chance."

Michael glanced again at the old man. Both of Roy's pant legs were now soaking wet. "And we don't know how the Horseman is going to react to seeing the Reliquary above ground."

Faye glared at Michael, considering her options, and then, with a small jerky nod, acquiesced.

Moments later after coercing the four-thousand-year-old child out of the fountain with the promise of pizza, Faye, Michael, and Roy exited Hyde Park and headed toward the nearest London Underground station.

"What's pizza?" Roy asked.

"You'll see," Michael replied.

"Is it like a smore?" Roy added.

"Almost as good," Faye answered.

"What's a hospital?" The old man continued.

"It's a place where sick people go to get better," Faye said. "We're going to take the Tube to visit a sick friend."

"What's a Tube?" the Reliquary inquired.

"It's an underground train," Faye replied as the trio stepped down the stairs into the Tube station.

"What's a train?" Roy asked.

Michael lips curled, and he stifled a laugh. "Our little Reliquary is growing up so fast," he mused. Roy's barrage of questions was a looking glass into what parents endure day in and day out, but it also offered a rare glimpse of Faye's character, a part of her that he and likely no other soul had ever seen. Beneath her iron "get the hell away from me" exterior, she was maternal, nurturing.

"That's a train," she said, pointing at the line of metal cars pulling in front of the platform, a high-pitched whistle cutting through the station clatter. "A train transports people and things from one place to another," she said, feeding coins into the ticket kiosk and plucking off the travel passes.

"Let's go for a ride," she said and handed Roy and Michael their tickets.

On board, Roy peered outside from his cushioned seat as the train pulled away from the lighted station, its horn blaring. His eyes darted from one immense walled advertisement to the next until the car plunged into the tunnel's waiting darkness. Quickly losing interest in the outer blackness and flashing rail lights, the Reliquary turned his attention to the passengers, some of who were reading, others chatting or snacking. Across from him was an old woman who had nodded off, her mouth half open. From the gap protruded a displaced set of dentures. Roy tapped his own teeth, unable to shift even one ivory.

Soon the train was born into light as the other side of the tunnel gave birth, heralded by a monotone "The next station is Westminster Station." The Reliquary gawked at every subway spectacle as the metal car pulled into each platform: jugglers and white-faced muted clowns at Waterloo, dancers and musicians at Southwark. "Remarkable," he uttered, his nose plastered to the glass.

Before the train doors closed, a tattooed hooligan, his head shaved, slid into the carriage and plopped down on the bench across from the old man. Roy watched as inked hands pulled white lines from each leather jacket pocket and stuck them into pierced ears. The hooligan sneered at the inquisitive onlooker and then closed his eyes, his head filled with pounding hardcore punk beats, thrashing tempos, and abrasive lyrics.

The muffled tune drew Roy forward like a moth to a flame. The Reliquary leaned forward, grabbed one white thread and pulled. The white bud popped out of the pierced ear.

The hooligan's eyes popped open.

"Is it hurting you?" Roy asked.

"What's your deal, you fucking git?" the hooligan cursed, pushing the old man backwards into his seat.

"Sorry, our friend is—" Michael started.

"Bugger off," the hooligan spouted, grabbing Roy's tweed lapels.

"You mess with my stuff, I mess with yours," the lout spat, raising his arm.

Faye launched her foot in between the hooligan's legs, catching the man square in the balls.

"Arrggh!" the man cried, doubling over, the gut-wrenching pain tipping him over like a chair.

Michael stood, pulled the hooligan up by his leather collar and hauled him into the next subway car.

Roy turned to Faye. "Was what I did wrong?"

Faye grinned. "Well, people like their personal space."

"And what you did to him?"

"It's what you do to assholes who grab you."

The old man cocked his head. "Hmm."

With the drama concluded, Faye spun in her seat and faced the old man. "Roy, do you remember when I asked you if your gifts could free a host possessed by a Horseman?"

Roy gave a quick nod.

"Someone…a friend, we need to try to free him from the Horseman soul. We need a gift," she pleaded, eyes wide, a glimmer of hopefulness on her face.

"I will try. Do you have something of his, something familiar to him?"

Faye pulled the ring from her finger. "This was Ben's," she said, placing the gold band in the center of Roy's withered palm.

The Reliquary's hand closed around the ornament. The old man narrowed his eyes in fierce concentration, and a soft radiance began to pulse from his fist.

"The next station is London Bridge," boomed from the carriage speakers.

The glow from the Reliquary's balled hand faded with the last word.

"I'm sorry," the old man said. "My power has dulled, weakened over the millennia. I am not as strong as the Riders or the Other. May I keep this and try again?"

Faye nodded, and Roy slid the gold circle onto his own finger.

"London Bridge Station, that's our hospital stop," Michael announced, returning to his seat.

The train soon stopped at the platform, the carriage doors opened, and Faye, Roy, and Michael exited the car. After a short flight of stairs, the three left the Tube station and started down Duke Street Hill.

Faye was happy to be in the fresh air and took in a deep London breath, hoping to clear her head. But the nagging question remained, pinging at her mind.

"Roy, who's the Other?" she asked.

Roy was silent, fear and concern covering his face like a mask.

"Roy?" she repeated.

"He is the Lost One," the Reliquary answered, shuffling his feet.

The words resonated like notes of a familiar song. "The Lost One," Michael repeated.

"The Lost One is abandoned, never to be free from War's prison." Faye quoted the ancient passage from memory. "Is he like you?"

The Reliquary shook his head. "No."

"Another Horseman?" Michael asked.

"He is and he is not," Roy answered. "He is crushing ice and burning vapor to the drowning fury that is the Riders."

"Wary the Lost One," Faye recited, the image of the words carved into stone clear in her mind.

Roy nodded, his face ashen. The Reliquary's eyes darted from side to side, searching for an escape from the questioning.

"Why, was he—" Michael started another line of questioning, his excitement blinding him to the old man's anxiety.

"How about that pizza?" Faye interrupted, grabbing Roy by the arm, escorting him forward, and shooting Michael a disapproving look.

Roy's face flushed, and the hard worried mask softened.

Faye spotted the street vendor a block down, and within moments she and Roy stepped up to the counter.

"Two slices of Neapolitan," she ordered, casting a questioning glance to Michael, who declined the gastronomic invitation.

Faye slid a purple note on the counter.

Roy stared at the colorful bill. "What is this?" the old man asked, brushing the twenty pound banknote.

"We use currency to buy things, like pizza."

The Reliquary's eyes fixed on the image of the British monarch. "Who is this woman?"

Michael stood behind and snickered.

"She is...," Faye began, but recanted, hoping to avoid an endless line of questioning on a topic she knew nothing about.

Faye was relieved to see the banknote disappear under a big palm and the steaming gooey triangles slide out onto the silver counter.

"Try it," Faye said, handing one plate to Roy.

The old man raised his brows as he looked at the gooey yellow and white islands floating in a sea of red.

"Like this," she said, biting into the slice, pulling away a long stretchy string of cheese.

The Reliquary stared in awe as Faye slurped up the gooey line. Her jaw jogged back and forth as she chewed the morsel.

"Now you," she said.

Roy bit down warily, lips drawn back like a rabid dog. The old man pulled away a thin thread of cheese, which hung down from his jaw like a fishing line. His jaw gyrated slowly and gathered speed like a steam piston.

"How do you like your pizza?" she asked.

"Mmm," he murmured, his eyes bright. With his next bite, Roy engulfed half the slice.

"And that's just cheese. Imagine the party in your mouth when you add toppings," Michael quipped.

"Toppings?" the old man asked.

"Pepperoni, ham and pineapple, mushrooms, olives, sausage, almost anything," Michael answered.

"I'd like to try them all," the old man replied. "And smores, yes, I want to try smores."

"Next time," Faye said. "We need to go."

Having finished the cheesy endeavor, the trio turned the corner onto Tooley Street and were bombarded with the rich, vibrating tones of pipe organ music.

"What is that?" Roy asked. "It makes my skin tingle."

"It's choral music," Faye answered.

"Southwark Cathedral is just around that corner, close to the hospital," Michael added as the deep baritone tune was peppered with high melodic voices.

"Never have I heard anything so marvelous," the old man declared.

"Dinner and a show...Roy, I think you've just had your first date," Michael cracked, throwing a smile at Faye to lighten the mood.

"I think I like dates very much," the old man answered.

"One of mankind's greatest accomplishments," Michael replied, and within moments the three arrived in front of London Bridge Hospital.

Michael led the way through the glass doors, followed by Faye and Roy. Surrounded on all sides by the white, sterile walls, Michael's body tensed. The look, the smell, the feel, the patients: there was just something about hospitals that made the skin on the back of his neck crawl. "God, I hate hospitals," he thought.

Having taken the lift to the third floor, Michael and Faye, with Roy in tow, stepped past the oncology ward and arrived at the intensive care unit nursing station.

"We're here to see Zachariah Prond," Michael told a heavyset nurse dressed in dark blue scrubs.

The ICU nurse glanced at her computer screen. "Mr. Prond is in room seven," she answered. "Only two visitors at a time," she announced and then buried her face in another patient chart.

Faye turned to the Reliquary. "Roy, please wait here for us."

The old man nodded, and Faye and Michael walked away.

The two Vanguard counted the numbered doors along the tiled hallway. Coming to number seven, they opened the door and entered the large private room.

Zachariah lay unconscious in the bed, a mechanical ventilator filling his lungs. A jangle of tubes hung from his frail body like clear garland around a wilted Christmas tree.

Michael stepped to the near side of his mentor; Faye, the far side.

Faye's gaze trickled over Zachariah's comatose form like water, from his bald head, over the light-blue hospital gown opened on the side, exposing his pale skin, along his arm and down to the IV stuck in the top of his hand. Faye reached over and pulled a polished ivory Buddha from the Vanguard leader's senseless grasp. Faye stared at the little smiling deity, amazed at the craftsmanship, her thumb rolling over the smooth belly.

Faye remembered Zachariah's account of his Japanese bodyguard in the Vanguard library. "He is more than what he appears...a master of netsuke."

Michael stared at his former mentor. Sorrow graced the sides of his lips, draining his face of color. "I was wrong," he proclaimed. "He can't hel—" Michael's words were chopped off, his brain short-circuited, as a fist plowed into the side of his head.

«‹«—»»›

Outside, in the sterile hallway, Roy slid his feet along the smooth hospital tiles, skating out of the ICU and into the oncology ward.

"Do you want to play?" a skinny ten-year-old boy asked from inside one room, staring at the old man.

The Reliquary stopped and peered at the bald-headed boy playing with blocks.

"I'm not contagious," the boy added.

"Okay," Roy answered, stepping into the room and sitting down next to the jumble of plastic bricks. "My name is Roy."

"My name is Paul McNamara. I have cancer."

"Cancer?" Roy asked, picking up a block.

"Leukemia, actually," Paul corrected, snapping a green brick into a red one.

The old man stared at the little boy. "The wickedness of the Plague Rider knows no bounds."

"You talk funny," Paul teased.

«‹«—»»›

In ICU room seven, Faye turned to see Kenji Watanabe standing over Michael, a protective rage in his eyes.

"Kenji, stop!" Faye cried.

With his head spinning, Michael kicked and swept the bodyguard's legs out from under him. Kenji toppled over but landed on his hands and then brought an axe kick down onto the Vanguard's unprotected solar plexus. Michael deflated like a balloon.

Kenji kipped-up, flipping from the ground to a standing position, and threw a jab across the bed to Faye's face.

Faye anticipated the punch and brushed aside the blow.

"We're not your enemy," she proclaimed.

Kenji spun around with a reverse roundhouse, the kick passing over Faye's ducked head.

"We need help," Michael wheezed.

Kenji's eyes shifted for a second, but it was enough of a distraction for Faye's roundhouse to collide into the bodyguard's cheek, sending Zachariah's guardian to the floor.

"We need his help," Faye declared, gesturing to Zachariah's prone form.

"He can't help himself, let alone you traitors," Kenji said, standing up and rubbing his face.

"We're no traitors. The Vanguard mole is dead. We saw to that," she said, sitting down in the wooden chair. "Here I am," she declared, arms extended. "Just do it. I won't stop you."

"No, Faye! There's got to be another way to stop the Vanguard drones," Michael uttered from the floor, holding his gut.

Faye stared at Kenji. His stance was relaxed, and it was at that moment that the bodyguard's stone countenance cracked.

"You know, don't you?" she asked, standing up from the chair.

"I am only a shadow," Kenji responded.

"But you know how to stop them," she concluded. "Of course, where Zachariah goes, you go."

Zachariah's guardian stared down at Michael, searching for the truth in the Vanguard's pained face.

"Kenji, we can stop the Horsemen, stop all the fighting, please," Faye pleaded.

The bodyguard cast a longing gaze to his master.

"Go to the pet store on Charlotte Street and ask for the rarest breed in the store," the bodyguard responded.

"Thank you," Michael grunted, getting to his feet.

Faye stooped over and picked up the ivory Buddha from the floor and handed it to the master of netsuke. "It's beautiful," she said.

Kenji Watanabe watched as Faye and Michael exited ICU room seven, unaware of the fleeting finger twitch on the hospital bed.

«« — »»

Down the hall, in a room in the cancer ward, Paul stood up and inspected the Lego castle with a satisfied smile on his face.

"I think our knights are safe, Roy," the bald boy said.

Roy nodded and smiled.

"Thanks for your help," Paul said. "I'm feeling a little tired," he added and crawled into his hospital bed and under the covers.

The Reliquary's eyes soaked up the boy's room. Cards, overflowing with banknotes, and flowers decorating every available countertop, balloons tied to bedposts, and presents, wrapped and unwrapped, dotted the floor. "Surely this can't be a place of death," the old man thought.

"It was my birthday two weeks ago, and I still haven't opened all of my gifts," Paul proclaimed. "Guess how old I am,"

"I—"

"Ten," Paul chimed. "How old are you?"

The old man paused. "Well, let's see, about four thousand."

"You're funny."

Roy picked up a wooden picture frame: Paul was smiling, wrapped in the arms of a man and woman.

"Mom and dad," the boy said. "They're dead. I lived with my grandma before she got sick."

The old man laid the frame down.

"Can I tell you a secret?" Paul asked.

Roy nodded.

"Sometimes I wish God would come and take me away so my grandma could get better. It makes me sad."

"Don't be sad," Roy answered, resting his hand on the bald-headed boy. "Your soul is so full of light. It gives this old body of mine new strength. You should be happy."

Paul smiled, a rosy hue coloring his cheeks.

"Do you like pizza?" Roy asked.

"Who doesn't?" responded Paul.

"I want to try pep…per…oni on my pizza."

"I like sausage best."

"Have you tried smores?" the Reliquary asked.

"Sure," Paul said, his face lighting up. "The best part is catching the marshmallow on fire. I used to tell my dad it was an accident, but I think he knew."

"I'd like to try a smore," Roy said.

"Me, too, but they won't let me have 'em here."

"What if I bring you some?"

"When?" Paul asked, grinning from ear to ear.

"How about tomorrow?" Roy replied.

"Okay, but don't let the nurses catch you. They'll take the goodies for themselves. Probably eat it all, the big cows."

"I will see you tomorrow," Roy announced and walked out of the room.

The old man shuffled on the tile and passed in front of the nurses' station.

"Sir?" one nurse called out to the old man.

The Reliquary stopped and turned toward the woman.

"It is nice for Paul to spend his last days with family. After his grandmother passed away, we thought him orphaned."

Roy smiled and nodded.

"He's a strong little boy. I wish I were that strong," the RN added.

"Me, too," the Reliquary whispered, turning away.

The old man stared at the gold ring on his finger, and his eyes narrowed. "Me, too," he declared, covering the balled ring hand with his palm. Roy drove his knuckles deep into his open hand, focusing his essence down his arm and into the gold ring. His clasped hands shook, and a dull radiance resonated from his skin until both hands glimmered. The image of the bald little boy with leukemia drove him on until at last, it was done.

The old man lowered his hands. He breathed hard past pursed lips. His shoulders slumped.

"Roy, are you okay?" Faye asked as she and Michael approached from the opposite direction.

"A gift," he said, pulling off the ring and handing it to Faye.

The Reliquary turned around. "He's a strong little boy," the old man said and shuffled away down the hall.

CHAPTER 16

The swaying carry box, covered in a blue and white checkered tablecloth, looked out of place among the boring black briefcases and trendy neon backpacks on the streets of Istanbul, but it was the spectacle above the large picnic basket that attracted the most attention. Wide-eyed stares peppered the young man as he strolled on the sidewalk, a black rat perched on the shoulder of his white lab coat. The scientist didn't mind the gawkers; he'd outlived them all four hundred times over.

Pestilence lifted the cage, pulled aside the patterned flap, puckered his lips, and smooched at the shaded occupants. The rat on his shoulder squeaked disapprovingly.

"Hush, don't be jealous," he said, turning his attention to his furry companion.

After a few steps, the Horseman stopped and set the cage down on the curbside, atop a sewer drain, and swung open the hinged door.

"Children…," Pestilence called.

Wiry whiskers rose out of the iron grate like antennae, heralding a pink nose, long yellow buck teeth, pink eyes, and black matted fur. The first sewer rat, the size of a dachshund, scampered out of its dank hovel, wiggled its nose, and crept into the cage.

"That's a good boy," the Horseman declared. "Where there is one…" he began, then watched silently as a stream of rodents crested the drain, pouring into the wire enclosure.

A woman pedestrian screamed at the sight of the pestilent swarm, spun around on her heels and dashed away.

Once the furry deluge ceased, Pestilence swung the door closed and hefted the weight.

"Are you all hungry?" he asked, speaking to the covered cage.

A chorus of squeaks answered back.

The Horseman lowered the basket of goodies to his side and stepped down the street. Dozens of thick scaly tails hung down through the wire cage and swung to the motion of the Horseman's gait.

Pestilence turned off the thoroughfare and walked down a shadowed alley. He stepped into a doorway, turned a rusted knob, and stepped into the front entrance with his rat-laden parcel.

Dim lights cast a yellow hue across the old laboratory. The air was thick with dust; cobwebbed instruments stood motionless, unused for months. The floor was covered with a knee-high fog.

White light flickered and died beneath the swaying smoke.

Crack! Pop!

Pestilence knelt down, setting the cage aside, and blew on the mist. The white blanket rolled away, exposing a web of red light beams. A white flash careened down one red line like a car speeding down a highway.

"Did you see that?" the Horseman said to the vermin scampering from one shoulder to the other.

Crack! Pop!

"Homemade lightning," Pestilence declared.

The Horseman plucked the rat from his shoulder and stroked its head. "Humans may never grasp the complexity of life's simplicity," he proclaimed. "Hell, lightning happens in nature all the time." He patted the black rat on its head. "I bet even you could understand it. Look here"—he pointed—"these lasers form a plasma pathway that steers lightning bolts to targets that conduct electricity better than that of the air or the ground. It's so simple."

Crack! Pop!

Pestilence set the rat on his shoulder and picked up the goody basket. He brushed the smoke back and carefully stepped between the crisscrossing beams. The Horseman stopped midstride, not stepping inside one crimson quadrangle. "Oops, I don't want to step there, do I?" he said grinning, placing his foot in alternative square. "Or there…or there," he declared, pointing to other spots on the smoky floor. "Empty, right?" he said to his shoulder companion. "Wrong, there are UV lasers."

After several more cautiously placed footsteps, the Horseman stepped free of the laser web. "Let's power down, shall we?" Pestilence said, reaching into a shadowed alcove and tripping a switch.

Clonk!

Setting down his parcel, Pestilence pulled the blue and white checkered cover from the cage. The wire enclosure was packed from top to bottom with an amalgamation of writhing hair, tails, and dark beady eyes.

The Horseman opened the cage and extracted one small thin rat. The little rodent squeaked in his hand.

"You must be starving."

He kissed the rat on the nose and put it down on the floor.

Pestilence's shoulder companion squeaked jealously, followed by raucous squeals from the sardine can on the floor.

"Just a little head start for the runt, okay?"

More discord sounded in his ear.

He pulled the rat off his shoulder, "Okay, you, too. Go ahead."

He watched both rats disappear into the mist.

"Let's get rid of the fog so you can see what you're having for lunch."

Pestilence reached into the alcove again and flipped another switch. Vacuum lines hummed, and the white gas disappeared. "That's better."

The Horseman's cheeks raised as his eyes fell on Vanguard corpses and dead attack drones littering the floor.

The two black rats scurried to the nearest corpse, one nibbling at a finger tip, the other feasting on an earlobe.

Pestilence took a deep breath and exhaled. "Dinner is served," he announced, opening the cage door and freeing the mass of rats to swarm over the dead bodies.

The two early diners, bellies extended with human debris, scurried up to the Horseman.

"Are you full already?" Pestilence said, picking up both rats and speaking to them like children. "Let Kishar try to attack us again and send us more fresh meat. She doesn't think us clever, but we are far cleverer than she will ever know."

Resting one rat on each shoulder, the Horseman stepped to the far wall, opened a door, and entered a back room. The whoosh of the air jets and vacuum inside the decontamination room was deafening. Each rat dug its claws into the fabric of the lab coat, struggling against the tempest, until…silence.

"Contaminants remain," sounded the hollow female voice from overhead.

"Don't you listen to her, boys," he quipped, and the Horseman opened a second door and entered a second laboratory, a massive tiled room. On one side, a pristine white wall provided a blank canvas to a multitude of objects: microscopes, DNA-sequencing and flow-cytometry units, culture hood, and a refrigerator-freezer. On the other side, a menagerie: a half-dozen iron cages consumed half of the wall, and a large salt-water fish tank devoured the rest.

The Horseman approached a large metal cage that contained a wooden box.

"Crocuta?" he asked, liking to refer to his non-human subjects by a more formal scientific designation.

The spotted hyena cackled and bounded out of its makeshift den, a human skull between its jaws.

"You haven't finished your dinner," he said, "and here I am with your desert." He pulled one squeaking rat from his shoulder by the tail.

Behind the bars, the hyena paced in anxious anticipation.

Pestilence tossed the rodent end over end between the bars. The rat's body was reduced to bloody pulp between the powerful bone-crushing jaws.

"Good boy."

The Horseman turned to the five-hundred-gallon salt-water tank and stepped up to the glass enclosure. The watery pen glistened with blue, red, green, and yellow coral hues but looked to be utterly devoid of life.

Pestilence glanced down at the bottom of the tank and then shifted his gaze to his lone hairy companion. The rat squeaked and twitched its nose, its beady eyes pleading for a stay of execution. The Horseman shrugged and tossed the rat into the aquarium. The rodent paddled along the surface, its movements attracting attention from below. Within a coral crevice, a giant moray eel inched forward, its mouth agape, as if waiting for the punch line to a joke. Large white eyes stared up at the small feet pawing the water.

"Come on, Javinicus."

In the time it took for the Horseman to utter his last word, the three-meter eel shot upward. Its two sets of jaws grabbed the hairy morsel by its stomach, and the eel dragged the flailing rat down into its rocky lair.

With feeding time over, Pestilence focused his attention on the two transparent tanks at the center of the room. The Horseman stepped to the incubators and cast a critical gaze at the sleeping children, each suspended in its own bubbling blue ooze.

"So like your mother," Pestilence said, tapping the first tank. The infant squirmed and yawned, extending two sets of jaws from its small mouth.

The child opened one eye. Pestilence raised his brows, smiling. "Hello, my gothic beauty," he said, grinning.

The scientist turned to the other tank and the sleeping boy. "And you, young man," he said. "How is my little warrior doing?"

The Horseman stared at the far laboratory door and contemplated the human and technological carnage strewn on the other side. "Far cleverer than she will ever know."

《《——》》

Evening burned along the London horizon.

"It's time to go," Michael announced, stepping into the safe-safe house, clad in dirt-stained orange pants and a green fluorescent coat, a brown bag in his hand.

"What's with the getup?" Faye asked.

"It's nice of you to notice. Here's your costume," Michael added, tossing the brown bag at her.

"What? Why?"

"A gas main mysteriously broke near London Biggin Hill Airport."

"Mysteriously," she repeated.

"Yep, and road crews have been dispatched to fix it. I figured we could give them a hand."

"Okay, let's go and get our hands dirty," she said. "But we'll need to stop by and pick up our new pet on the way."

Faye looked over at the Reliquary, engrossed in the television. "Roy, come on! You're going to love your first pet store."

"What's a pet?" the old man asked, standing and walking to the door.

Michael looked at Faye, and they both smiled at Roy.

《《——》》

177

Forty minutes later, a white highway service van pulled to the side of Charlotte Street and stopped in front of Pet Palace.

Faye looked up at the lighted sign from the van's passenger side. "Well, it's the only pet shop on Charlotte Street. This has got to be the place."

The trio exited the van, and Faye, followed by Roy and Michael, entered the pet store. Pushing through the doorway, the Reliquary's senses were bombarded by the sight of wire cages, stacked to the ceiling, full of furry animals pawing their enclosures, the ear-piercing sound of screeches and barks that echoed throughout the store, and the fresh smell of cedar shavings covering the scent of stale urine. Roy gestured to the caged puppies clamoring for attention. "Is this all food?" he asked.

"God, no," Michael replied. "Pets are for companionship, not for eating."

"Can I help you?" interrupted a thick Japanese accent.

Faye and Michael turned to the shop owner. Their eyes were wide with surprise upon seeing a wrinkled and balding version of Kenji Watanabe. Faye's thoughts raced back to ICU Room seven.

"Can I help you?" the pet shop owner asked again, from behind the counter.

"Sorry," Faye said. "We're interested in your rarest breed."

The shop owner raised his brows, Faye's request striking a chord. He paused a moment and then spun around, disappearing into a back room, returning moments later with a shoebox.

"This breed doesn't live long," the shop owner said, handing the box to Faye.

"Does it have a name?" Faye quipped with a smile.

"Emp," the owner replied stone-faced.

"Imp, that's a cute name," she said, patting the cardboard container. "But how will it stop—"

The shop owner turned away as Faye realized the phonetic mistake. "E…M…P," she uttered, and watched the store owner return back behind the counter. She lifted the shoebox lid and stared at the TV remote–sized electromagnetic pulse generator. "It's time to go."

Back inside the van, Michael spread a local city map across the dashboard. The overhead lights shed barely enough light to see the squiggly lines.

"There's only one direct route from London Biggin Hill Airport to Vanguard headquarters," Michael said, his fingers snaking across the paper. "The unmanned transport will be on this road." His finger jumped to a smaller curving line. "And it just so happens, this is the same road that has the broken gas main."

"Interesting coincidence," Faye noted.

Michael shot her a wily grin. "So, there is likely going to be a detour, here," he said, pointing to the map.

"Waterford is not going to follow any last-minute detour," Faye replied. "She'll suspect something."

"Exactly," Michael remarked. "You ready to go to work?"

«««—»»»

Twenty-five kilometers away, the whine of jet engines echoed off the tarmac of London Biggin Hill Airport. Landing-strip lights cast a dim haze on the parked Vanguard mobile command center and SUV escort.

Diana Waterford looked up into the night sky and watched the blinking navigation lights of the unmanned transport plane as it banked left on its final approach.

"Let's go," she commanded, stepping inside the converted lorry. Within moments, the long black semi-trailer truck and SUV escort exited the airport.

From inside the command center, Waterford stared at the image of the shackled Horseman, his body slack, standing like a puppet on a string. A spotlight shone down on him like he was the star of the show.

"The poor fool," the Dragon Lady whispered.

"We're in position, Madam Waterford," a Vanguard lackey reported.

"Bring it down," she ordered.

A Vanguard agent, eyes glued to his monitor, flicked a switch on a control panel. "Automatic landing protocol initiated."

The unmanned plane lowered its landing gear. Within seconds, the aircraft touched down on the private airstrip and taxied on the runway.

"Unload the cargo," she ordered.

The plane stopped, and the rear ramp swung down. An unmanned transport truck rolled down the decline, headlights on. It sped out onto the tarmac and exited the airport onto the service road.

"Front mounted cameras operational," sounded one Vanguard agent from within the dim confines, his screen filled with passing roadway.

"Capture drones at one hundred percent efficiency," noted another.

After one kilometer, the truck's headlamps fell upon a triangular yellow sign, illuminating the reflective warning: Road Work Ahead.

Moments later, the image of a road worker clad in orange pants and green reflective coat and waving an octagonal STOP sign, filled the Vanguard monitor.

"Madam Waterford, we have a problem," the agent announced.

"What is it?" she spat, the Vanguard distracting her from the entertainment on her screen.

"Looks to be a detour," the agent reported.

"Was there any highway work scheduled?" she asked, standing up, glaring at the screen.

"No, nothing scheduled."

"It's a trick," she said. "Disregard it."

"A trick?" the agent asked.

"Go through it!" Waterford bellowed.

The Vanguard agent jammed the joystick forward, and the unmanned transport accelerated through the detour, the road worker diving out of the way of the oncoming truck.

Waterford sat down, the Horseman mind under the Vanguard mask at work. "What are you doing, Seth?" she mused, looking at the defeated brethren on her monitor. "Impossible," she concluded.

Words from a smoky lab resonated in her head. "You play a dangerous game, Kishar," whispered Pestilence. "I like to play games, too." Waterford cocked her head. "The fool is probably in chains by now."

"Get me status on assault team Gamma," Waterford ordered.

"Gamma missed its 2130 SATCOM," was the reply.

"Find them!" the blond Vanguard ordered.

Moments later, the Vanguard monitors were lit up with halogen work lights. A road crew, clad in orange and green, muscled jackhammers and crowbars through a broken street and toted away concrete chunks.

"The detour seems to be authentic," one Vanguard replied.

The Dragon Lady stood and spied the spectacle on the video screen: one worker, seeing the approaching truck, stepped forward and raised his hand, twirling it in the air.

"Turn around!" Waterford ordered.

Within the mobile command unit, an agent pulled back and twisted the joystick. The unmanned truck slowed and completed its U-turn.

The blonde watched the Vanguard complete his task. "Head back to the detour. I want this Horseman caged in an hour."

The agent nodded, pushing the controller forward. He watched the road flash by on his screen as the truck rolled down the road, unaware of his newly acquired passengers: Michael, crowbar in hand, on the driver's-side running board; Faye and Roy sitting on the truck's rear step bumper.

«««—»»»

Michael swung the curved end of the crowbar and shattered the window. He reached in through the shards, unlocked the door, and jumped into the driver's seat.

He gripped the wheel, but the column resisted his right and left advances. Stomping down on the square pedal was also an exercise in frustration. "Damn it," he shouted. Michael's eyes jumped across the truck dashboard, his mind unable to determine rhyme or reason to the multitude of flashing lights, illuminated displays, and buttons and switches.

Michael floated his right hand back and forth over the console, hoping for a wisp of inspiration to guide him to the right button or lever.

"The hell with it!" He picked up the crowbar from the passenger seat and bashed the console. The display went black. The engine choked and coughed like a forty-year smoker, and then conked out.

«««—»»»

Inside the mobile command center, one Vanguard agent shot to his feet. "The transport video is dead."

Wide-eyed stares blanketed the agent.

"Diagnostics check out. The problem is in the truck."

Another Vanguard stood, stepped to the rear of the vehicle, and approached the blonde.

"Madam Waterford," the messenger said, his face pale. "We've lost control of the transport."

"What have you fools done?"

"Diagnostics confirm that there's a problem with the vehicle."

"It *was* a trick!" Waterford screamed.

"Use the drone lights and cameras!" Waterford ordered. "I want to see what's happening inside that truck!"

《《—》》

Inside the cab, Michael steered the truck to the side of the road until it came to a stop. He opened the door, jumped out of the driver's side, crowbar in hand, and made his way to the back, where Faye and Roy sat on the rear tailgate.

"You both okay?" Michael asked.

"Fine," Faye answered, and she and Roy hopped down to the road.

"Ready?" Michael asked, raising the crowbar.

With Faye's nod, Michael stabbed the metal pry bar into the rear door lock, breaking it. He grabbed the handle and opened up one door of the rear compartment.

《《—》》

"You!" Waterford's cry filled the Vanguard command center as Faye's image filled the video screen. The blonde's heavy pants fanned the fury burning within the Horseman. Waterford watched as Michael Cantal stepped into view. "I should have suspected Prond's meddling apprentice would be in tow with that bitch."

The fleeting image of the old man stopped the veiled Horseman on the spot. The blonde rushed to the monitor, her face inches away from the Reliquary's face. "Ro'esnugal," she whispered. "It cannot be. After all this time, how did you escape?"

"Madam Waterford?"

The blonde cranked her face up to the agent.

"Kill the Vanguard traitors and bring me the old man. Alive!" she commanded.

"What of the Horseman?" asked the Vanguard lackey.

"Are the drones still operational?" she asked.

"All electromagnets and counter-measures are at full power."

"Good, now go."

The Vanguard agent and three cohorts snatched up MAC-10 submachine guns from the weapons rack.

"Leave them," the Dragon Lady commanded.

The agents looked at each other.

"Do you want War to put a bullet in your tiny brains?" she asked.

The agents dropped their automatic pistols to the counter.

"All of them," Waterford added.

Each man pulled his sidearm from its holster, laid the Glock 9mm on the counter, and exited the command center into the night.

«« — »»

At the back of the now-manned transport truck, Michael opened the second cargo door, guiding the old man to the side of the transport in the process. Faye stared at the spotlighted Horseman surrounded by his four robotic consorts.

War lifted his head and watched Faye climb into the cargo hold. The Horseman smiled, shaking his head. "Woman, how many times must I tell you that this host is mine? He'll never be free of me."

"Well, if we don't get you out of here, you're going to spend an eternity in a hole in the ground getting to know your host," Faye replied.

She turned back to Michael, who had followed her into the makeshift cell. "Imagine a world without war or murder," she said.

"Imagine the greatest warrior of all time, caged like an animal in a zoo," Michael answered. "I'd pay to see that."

War narrowed his brow. His eyes focused rage onto Michael like a child's magnifying glass focuses burning sunlight onto a pill bug. "I told you what I would do to you if I saw you again."

"Looks like you're not in a position to do much of anything," Michael replied.

The Horseman strained against the unmovable force, the veins in his arms bulging like spaghetti.

"We're here to free you," Faye said.

Faye's words were muted like battle commands over artillery. The ancient presence crashed into the Horseman, snatching his breath, rocking his mind. He shook his head from side to side, refusing to let the memories in.

War looked up, sensing a presence and seeing the old man peer in from around the corner of the truck. "Ro'esnugal!" he cried. "How?"

The Reliquary climbed up into the lighted truck and shuffled up to the Horseman. The two stared at each other in consternation.

"You are old," War declared.

"And you are chained," Roy replied, the edge of his lips curving in defiance.

"I'll toss your worthless shell down a deeper hole next time," the

Warrior growled, gritting his teeth, straining against the electromagnetic bonds, and moving his manacled hands toward the Reliquary.

The old man stood unmoving, like the shadow of a stone, his eyes peering into the Warrior.

«« —»»

"Implement countermeasures," sounded Waterford's order in the mobile command center. The Horseman's wrist and ankle bracelets lit up as electromagnetic energy coursed across War's body.

"Batteries are at sixty percent," announced one agent.

"What's the ETA on the pursuit vehicle?" asked the blonde.

"Three minutes," the Vanguard answered.

«« —»»

In the back of the transport truck, Faye stepped between the ancients. "We can help you, if you let us," pleaded Faye, her eyes embracing the Horseman's.

"Ha!" War laughed, staring past Faye. "The Reliquary can help me by making the gift I asked for four millennia ago."

"I will not," the Reliquary replied.

"We have a gift, but not the one you seek," Faye interjected, pulling the ring from her pocket.

War stared at the glistening metal. The Horseman sneered at Faye's offer. "I prefer another way," he declared, casting out his warring essence.

Michael's screams filled the metal box as the Horseman ensnared the Vanguard's mind. "Stop it!" Michael begged, dropping to his knees and lowing his head. "I won't," he cried, his eyes slamming shut, his jaw clenching.

"Release him!" Faye pleaded.

The Horseman answered with haughty laughter.

Michael's pleas fell silent.

Enthralled by the Horseman, Michael raised his head and then stood. He snatched up the crowbar, eyes ablaze.

"Michael, no!" Faye cried.

«« —»»

All eyes in the Vanguard mobile command center watched as an enraged Michael Cantal lumbered toward the first drone.

"Countermeasures," bellowed the command, and, with the press of a button, sparks lit up the Horseman. But War's puppet continued forward.

"Redirect static discharge onto Cantal. Shock the son of a bitch!" A bolt of electricity jumped out, knobby and branched, and sparked across Michael's body.

"Batteries are at forty percent," reported an agent.

"He's still coming," announced another Vanguard. The image of Michael lifting the wrecking bar over his head filled the command center video screens.

"Reverse polarity of drone one," Waterford ordered.

«««—»»»

In the transport truck, Faye's mind was numb, her body frozen as she watched the choreographed melee. The Horseman's shackled limb swung across his body like he was directing traffic. Michael's arm, crowbar in hand, swung wide. The electromagnetic pulse shot the steel tool away, along with the Vanguard holding it, slamming both against the truck's metal side wall.

Michael crumpled to the floor. The crowbar skidded out of the truck, pushed by the repulsive force.

Faye rushed to Michael and helped him to his feet. "You okay?"

"Head hurts," he mumbled, standing tall. "But I'm fine," he added, his grin masking the pain coursing through his body.

Faye could hardly catch the husky whisper over the raucous roar of the engine outside.

Michael staggered to the open rear door to see approaching headlights. "We've got company!" he said, pointing to the oncoming SUV.

Faye spun around to the Horseman.

It's either this," she said, holding up the yellow band, "or a Vanguard hole. Your choice."

War's dead eyes stared at Faye, full of hate, lacking any hint of warmth or familiarity. His piercing look was like an icy breeze that made the hair on her arms stand on end. And then the Warrior stuck out his ring finger.

Faye stepped up the Horseman. "Let him go," she declared,

keeping her eyes locked on to his as she spun the ring down his finger. But there was no thaw in his icy stare; only hatred flourished.

"Now free me!' War commanded.

Faye turned to the Reliquary. "Roy, it's not working," Faye exclaimed.

The old man stood silent, staring at the Horseman.

The screech of rubber on gravel signaled the Vanguard arrival.

"They're coming!" Michael declared, watching four Vanguard exit the pursuit vehicle.

Faye pulled the EMP unit from her pocket, pointing the remote at one robotic keeper. She pushed the Charge button and watched as the green indicator bulb blinked green.

"Faye don't," Michael cried. "We don't know if Ben is—"

Faye pressed the button, triggering a directional EMP burst at the robot. The metal sentry flickered and died. The metal cuff opened and dropped off War's ankle.

"Again!" War commanded.

Faye charged the handheld EMP and fired at another drone. The robot shuddered and froze, the Horseman's wrist manacle dropping to the floor.

«««—»»»

The sound of frenzied orders and raucous activity filled the inside of the mobile command center. "Drones two and three are down. Horseman containment has been compromised."

"Full countermeasures," Waterford barked. "Fry the Horseman."

Electrostatic shock lit up the inside of the truck, electricity covering the ancient warrior like a coat. As the last bit of static charge dissipated, one agent turned to Waterford, his face pale. "Batteries are dead."

«««—»»»

"Free me!" the Horseman cried, the sound of his words bordering on pain.

"Ben?" Faye asked, her tone soft, hopeful.

"Free me," he repeated weakly.

Faye pointed the EMP at another drone and pushed the Charge button.

"Shit!" she cried.

She repeatedly tapped the button, but the indicator bulb remained dark.

"The EMP is dead," Faye shouted.

Michael leaped out of the back of the truck.

"Where are you going?" Faye asked.

"Buying you some more time," he answered, snatching the crowbar from off the ground.

"Drag them out," War shouted.

Faye stuffed the EMP unit into her pocket, grabbed onto a drone, pulling against the metal sentry with her weight, but the robot was frozen in place.

She looked over at the Reliquary. "Roy, help me, please," she exclaimed.

«‹‹—»»

On the side of the road lit by the SUV headlamps, Michael launched himself sideways onto two Vanguard agents, knocking them to the ground. He scrambled to his feet and raised the crowbar. "Who's next?" he snapped, squaring off against the two standing attackers. Michael charged forward, swinging the steel bar, and caught one Vanguard, thick copper mustache and a ragged scar running down the side of his face, square in the gut. The mustached man bent over and crumbled to the ground.

Off balance, Michael couldn't turn to block the punch careening toward his face, and the Vanguard fist caught him square in the jaw. Michael's head snapped backward, and he staggered against the force of the blow. The punch stung his mind, all thought beyond his next breath, gone. Shaking the haze from his vision, Michael glanced left and watched two assailants stand. A quick look to his right revealed another contender pulling back his arm, launching a fist. With one quick breath, Michael raised the crowbar in time for Vanguard knuckles to slam into the solid steel rod. The surprised agent howled, pulling back his stinging hand, giving Michael the opportunity to counter with a kick to the man's gut.

Michael allowed himself a triumphant grin. "Four on one, not too bad," he thought. He lifted the wrecking bar for another swinging barrage as two assailants tackled him to the ground.

«‹‹—›»

"Roy, help me save him," Faye called.

Roy stepped up to the drones and placed his hands on the metal.

"Pull!" she said, struggling against the unmoving resolve. "Move, damn it!" Her mind filled with desperation that quickly changed to frustration as she realized that she was the only one exerting any force on the robots. "Roy, hel—" Her words were clipped at the sight of the glowing metal under her hands.

"What have you done?" she asked, watching the old man exit the rear door and hop down onto the dark road.

"You fool," War roared. "Free me!"

I can't," she said, backing away from the flashing lights.

"I'll kill you," the Horseman declared.

Faye made no noise, but her cheeks were awash with sorrow. She turned and ran, jumping out the back of the truck, War's threat echoing behind.

Outside, Michael lay in a bruised and bloody heap. "Go! I'll finish this puke," said the mustached agent, plowing his boot into Michael's stomach.

The other three Vanguard assailants hurried to the truck and peered inside, their gaze falling onto an irate Horseman. "I'll kill you all," War bellowed.

"Forget him, find the old man and—"

Boom!

The unmanned transport was engulfed in a massive fire ball that lit the night and dismantled the truck and the three Vanguards into jagged pieces.

Faye raced to the smoky heap with Roy trailing behind. "Ben!" she screamed.

At the sight of the explosion, the remaining Vanguard crashed his fist into Michael's cheek, and started toward the truck. The old man pounced on the mustached Vanguard like a mouse on a tiger's back. The agent spun and threw the Reliquary to the ground, tearing the tweed jacket from the old man's frame.

"You!" the Vanguard declared. "Waterford wants you."

With his last vestige of strength, Michael staggered to his feet and threw himself forward, tangling up the Vanguard. Both men toppled to the road. Michael strained against the oncoming blackness.

The Vanguard straddled Michael's neck, pulling a butterfly blade from his pocket. "I'm going to cut out your eyes and bring them back to—" The mustached assailant's words were cut off as he slumped to the side. Roy stood over the unconscious man, crowbar in hand.

"Thanks," Michael murmured.

Along the fringe of the wreckage were pieces of bloodied, dismembered bodies.

"Oh, Ben, I'm sorry," Faye said, tears welling up in her eyes. "I couldn't save y—" Her atonement was interrupted as shards of smoking metal slid away, and a ringed hand, reflected in the remaining light, pushed through the debris.

Faye raced up to the heap as a man emerged like a phoenix.

"Ben?" she asked, her voice breaking. She stared into his blue eyes, searching, hoping for a clue to whether he was man or monster, but it was his cough and wince, the human frailties, that finally defined him. "Ben!" she cried, her mouth stretched open into a wide smile.

Faye rushed up to Ben and helped him to his feet. "I can't believe it. The ring, it must have saved you!"

"Faye? What are you doing here?" Ben asked.

"Do you remember anything?"

"Not much," he said shaking his head. "A cave, an office…some weird dreams, fire. Everything is kind of fuzzy."

Faye clenched her jaw and tilted her chin up. "You were host to one of the Four Horsemen of the Apocalypse, but now you're free."

"What?" he asked, the timbre of his voice shaking.

Faye nodded.

"War?" he muttered. "I thought them terrible dreams, but they were…real. How long?" he shouted, his blue eyes growing colder.

"Seven months."

"Oh God, no," he pleaded lowering his head.

"You're Ben Sasson," Faye said, cupping his face in her hands. "You're Ben Sasson," she repeated and kissed him hard.

Michael and Roy watched as Faye and Ben approached.

Ben stepped toward Michael. "I remember you with a lot less blood and bruises," he said.

Michael smiled, rubbing his cheeks. "Comes with the territory," he replied. "Welcome back."

Ben nodded. His grin spoke volumes of gratitude.

"Ben, this is Roy," Faye said, stepping to the old man. "We'd never have freed you without his help."

The Reliquary's eyes stared at the man, holding fast to Ben's face, but the old man saw past the weary countenance.

"I'm in your debt," Ben said, extending his hand.

With eyes wide and eyebrows raised, Faye watched the Reliquary step backwards from the gesture. Fear and distrust molded his face like clay.

"Roy, Ben's free of the Horseman," she said, looking flabbergasted.

No," the Reliquary said, shaking his head. "The Rider is not gone, only buried. You survived that tempest," he said nodding at the smoking debris, "but only because of the Rider within you."

The old man's words rocked Ben. "What?"

"Remove the ring"—his shaking hand pointed at the yellow band—"and the Rider would rule anew."

《《《—》》》

A deafening silence filled the Vanguard command unit. All eyes looked up to the blonde standing in the middle of the room, lost in thought, almost in a daze, staring into a dark video monitor.

CHAPTER 17

"We bring you breaking news from the Sultanate of Oman, where the US Secretary of State, in a dramatic turn of events, is calling for US military strikes against surrounding Arabic nations…" The commentator's words and slanting sunbeams of late afternoon crept through the London safe house like thieves, passing over the TV and the old man sitting in front of it like an obsolete and valueless fixture.

". . . Terrance Sitkoff is in the capital city of Muscat with this live report…"

Static filled the television screen like snow. Roy raised his brows, more from annoyance than curiosity. His eyes shot open in surprise as gunshots rang out like a bell, and screams pierced the air like a siren, all of the sounds: the paint, the white flurry on the screen: the canvas, where imaginations ran wild.

"Terrance? Are you there?" the anchor asked.

Static…"He's coming!" Static… "All of you bastards…" Static… "…will all die under the…" Static… ". . . heel of the master!"

The Reliquary leaned forward, flipped the channel, and stared at the culinary prowess on the screen. He pressed the remote again and again until a pitchman's plug for anti-aging cream trapped his attention.

Michael lay motionless on the couch. The disturbing news, cookery, or infomercial didn't make a dent in his mind-numbing sleep.

After another hour, Michael opened his eyes, and pain rolled upon him like a tide, starting from his feet and moving over his body, crashing finally into his head. "Shit," he moaned. The beaten and bruised Vanguard took five minutes to sit up, another two to rise off the couch, staggering to the bathroom. He moaned and groaned with every step, and with every breath. Leaning over the basin, the cold washcloth on his head, was little relief.

Michael exited the tiny water closet, and his stomach roared for attention. He glanced at his watch: four o'clock. Stepping to and opening the refrigerator, he grabbed the day-old Indian takeout. Michael scooped up a mouthful and worked the bite, grunting around his swollen cheek, loose tooth, and split lip.

Between agonizing bites, Michael stared at the closed bedroom door like a dog staring devotedly, waiting for his master's imminent return, imagining what *he* was doing to Faye. "It should be me," he thought.

In the dark corner of his heart, Michael's green-eyed monster reared its ugly head and kicked him in the nuts. He froze in place, slamming the brakes on his thoughts and bringing everything to a complete stop until he was still, hardly breathing. "He's not good enough for her," he spouted. Michael shook his head and blinked hard.

"Where the hell did that come from?" he said, shaken by the words that had passed his lips. But the mere thought of Faye with anyone, even Ben, turned his stomach, and he struggled to keep his Indian food down. How could it not? Faye was more than his friend. She was the Lois Lane to his Clark Kent, the one person he could always rely on, and he didn't want anyone getting near her, let alone someone who was half man, half monster, someone who could wake up one day and stick a knife in her throat on a whim and then set off a nuke for kicks. No, she deserved better than that, deserved someone who could always be there, someone who knew what she liked and what she didn't, someone who could surprise those intoxicating little grins out of her. "Someone like me," he whispered.

The door swung open.

Michael tried to ignore her disheveled hair, the pillow creases on her face, and the ear-to-ear, "I had sex" grin smattered across her post-coital glowing face. He dove into his carton of chicken tikka marsala, but his peripheral green-eyed monster captured the way she reached out her finger to connect with Ben. Ben extended his hand, and their palms touched, fingers interlaced. Ben lifted their hands and gazed at the gold band around his captured finger. "If last night wasn't obvious, I accept your proposal," he said, his blue eyes peering into hers.

"My prop—"

Ben drew Faye close and kissed her.

"Looks like you're stuck with me," he said, his lips brushing hers.

Michael's eyes narrowed, and his chest tightened. "You're fucking kidding me." The whispered words were harsh on his tongue, but he couldn't help it. The image was pure pain, an inner agony overshadowing his already throbbing body. He sighed and tried to look away from them, but he couldn't help but stare.

"Maybe we should find you a matching band and make it official," Ben announced.

Faye stepped back, her cheeks flushed, eyes wide, and then she threw her arms around Ben's neck, her lips finding his.

Michael's throat burned as he gulped down his vomit.

«« — »»

Chains rattled in the darkness of the dank meatpacking plant.

The blonde sat on a wooden stool beside an examination table and peered into the darkness. Waterford grabbed the shaft of the gooseneck desk lamp, directing its glow toward the shadows, pulling back the blackness and exposing pale skin. The naked man knelt in front of the woman as if in prayer.

"You failed me," the disguised Horseman declared.

"No, I did what you asked," the man pleaded. "Oh, God, it hurts, it—"

"Where is Ro'esnugal?"

"Who?"

"Where is the Reliquary?"

"Please make it stop. I—" The bare soul whimpered.

Clink! Clink! Clink! The sound of clattering metal chains was unmistakable.

The naked man twisted his neck. "What…what's that?" he asked, trembling.

"I told you to bring me the old man," the Horseman said, lifting up the tattered material from the table. "And all you brought me was this!" Death shook the ripped tweed jacket in front of the kneeling disciple.

"I can't see anything. What did you do to me?"

"You don't know what an old man looks like, so your Vanguard eyes are of no use to you. I took them out."

"Aargh!" the naked man screamed.

"And you weren't listening when I asked you to bring him to me, so your Vanguard ears aren't working. I fixed those."

"Oh God!" the bare man cried, hunching over.

"I don't know how much more I can help you with," Death declared, the wicked grin broadening on her face.

"I...I...can't move my legs, my hands."

"Oh, right, you were beaten by a man four thousand years your senior. So what use are your Vanguard hands and legs?"

"Please...make it stop...please," he pleaded.

Death bent the gooseneck, pulling the shadows from the naked man's face. "Stop? But there is still so much we can do," the Horseman declared, staring at her handiwork.

The man with the copper mustache and scar running down the side of his face was unrecognizable. His ears were cut from the side of his head and the lobes stitched to the spot his eyes once occupied. His arms and hands and legs and feet were stitched together, as if the Horseman had surgically repaired the evolutionary breach.

"Please...please make it stop. Please," he cried.

"Clearly your Vanguard mouth is of no use to you either," Death declared. Plucking a surgical needle and thread off the examination table and grabbing the man by the jaw, the Horseman started sewing the Vanguard's lips shut.

The mustached agent's cries were distorted and muffled by the needlework.

Clink! Clink! Clink!

"I see that the employee benefits haven't improved in this dump," sounded a voice from deep within the darkness.

"You should be dead," the Horseman responded, pushing the needle through the Vanguard's top lip and delicately finishing up the final stitch like some prized embroidery.

"Thought I was," Eric said, stepping into the light. Half of his red mane was burned off. White blisters dotted his bloodied and blackened face.

"I like the new look," the Horseman said flirtatiously. "It's becoming."

"Who's the soon-to-be stiff?" Eric asked.

Death's blond façade dissolved, replaced with gothic beauty. "Let me show you what happens to those who fail me," Death answered, grabbing the altered Vanguard by his hair and lifting the mustached man to his feet. "My masterpiece."

"So he's art?"

"Well, not a Picasso, but it has a certain *je ne sais quoi*, don't you think?"

Clink! Clink! Clink!

Eric shrugged, peering past the Horseman, searching the shadows for the source of the jangling chains.

Death stared at the disfigured body. "You're right," she declared pushing the naked Vanguard down to the cement. "I can probably do better with the proper subject." Death cast a wicked and wanting gaze toward the redhead.

The Horseman's whistle pierced the air like an arrow. The sound of clanking metal grew louder until two fanged monstrosities emerged from the shadows. They sank eight-inch canines into the tortured Vanguard, tearing the naked man apart.

"What the hell are those?" Eric yelled, stepping back from the feeding frenzy. Each mutated hound had its heavy jowls pulled back, exposing long canines and teeth glistening with pink foam. The shaggy bodies, the size of a lion, were accented with a pair of large taloned hands, clawed feet, and a long bushy-tipped tail.

"I call that one War, and that one is Pestilence," the Horseman announced. "I keep them on a strict Vanguard diet."

"I see that."

"Why have you come back?" the Horseman asked, watching her pets lap the last of the blood off the floor. "Are you staying for lunch?"

"I'm back, isn't that enough?" Eric responded, taking another cautious step back.

"It might be," Death replied, stepping toward the charred man. "You look different, Eric, better," the Horseman said sensually, rubbing bony fingers over his blackened skin. "Mmm," Death moaned. "I like scars on my men, lots of scars."

Eric winced as his skin peeled away with every carnal stroke.

"I need you to do something for me," Death said.

She grasped his head with both hands and licked his face

Her fingers prowled the charred man's body, wandering between his legs and lingering over his groin.

She stepped to the table and picked up the ripped fabric. "Do you know what this is?" she said, holding up the torn tweed jacket and stepping up to the burned redhead.

"A bad fashion choice," he said with a grin, enjoying his smartass remark.

The Horseman slapped him hard across his blistered face.

"This reeks of the Reliquary, an old man. Find him!" Death commanded, tossing the tweed jacket in front of the Blood Beasts. The creatures tore the garment to shreds.

"My pets will track down the Reliquary," Death proclaimed, placing the beasts' chains into the burned man's hands. "I want the bitch Monroe and her sidekick, Cantal, dead. Do what you want with what's left of the Warrior's host, but I want Ro'esnugal. The power of the Reliquary must be mine. The old man comes back alive," she said, digging her fingers into Eric's bloody mask. "Do you understand me?"

Eric nodded, blistered lips pursed, his eyes shifting back and forth between the two sabered killers.

"You need not fear them. They smell me all over you," she said, her lips curling with sensual wickedness. "But I'd recommend you not change your clothes or take a shower."

The scarred redhead tugged on the chains. The Blood Beasts answered the leash command with baleful growls.

"Don't disappoint me," the Horseman said, her tone biting. "Otherwise, you will become my greatest work of art."

«««——»»»

"Is this the happy ending?" Michael asked Faye bitterly, his green-eyed monster stepping into the center of the safe house, the small room dimming with the fading sun.

"Michael?"

"I want to know, Faye. Is this the fairy-tale ending you hoped for?"

"Michael, what are you doing?" she asked.

"Me?" he blurted, his voice rising. "What the hell are you doing?" Michael added, his pitch caustic, body tense, pain and anxiety fueling his growing anger.

"Michael, I don't under—" Ben began.

"Shut up!" the Vanguard spat.

Michael directed his narrowed brow to Faye. "He's still one of the

Four Horsemen of the Apocalypse," he said, pointing at Ben. "Do you think that by fucking him, all of the world's ills will just go away? Wake up, Faye!"

"That's enough, Michael," Ben said, stepping forward.

Michael launched a right cross, his knuckles connecting with Ben's face, knocking the Mossad agent to the floor.

Faye raced over and knelt next to Ben. She looked up at Michael. "Stop it!"

Michael stepped backwards. "I...I'm sorry," he exclaimed, looking at his balled hand like it didn't belong at the end of his arm. "I don't know what came over me."

The Reliquary sat in silence, watching the human display. Roy sighed, turned off the television, and walked toward the door.

"Roy?" Faye asked, watching the old man step to the safe house entrance.

The Reliquary turned the doorknob and cast a sorrowed look back. "Even when the Horseman slumbers, his power corrupts."

Faye turned and looked into Ben's unknowing stare.

"Wait," Michael said, rushing up to the old man. "Where are you going?"

"I promised that I would visit a friend and bring him some pizza," Roy answered.

"A friend?" Michael asked, taking Roy by the arm and guiding him to the other side of the room.

"Yes, at the hospital, s dying boy. His name is Paul McNamara and—"

Roy's words were cut off as the window shattered and a taloned hand swiped across the open space like a kitten batting a ball of twine, the hooked claws tearing cloth.

"Aargh!" Roy cried, falling to the ground, blood seeping through his torn shirt.

"What the hell is that?" Michael exclaimed, watching the long saber-toothed snout push through the window, pushing aside the metal bars.

The Blood Beast's howl shook the small room.

Another fanged snout crashed through the window, breaking apart the window frame.

"Run!" Michael shouted. "I've got Roy!"

Faye and Ben dashed to the door and swung it open. Faye shot a quick glance back in the room.

"We're right behind you!" Michael cried.

Faye pushed through the threshold and rounded the banister, her foot stepping off the landing.

"Not down, they'll be waiting for us. Go up to the roof," Ben said, and he and Faye charged up the stairs.

Inside the apartment, Michael lifted Roy to his feet and sprinted for the door, dragging the hobbling Reliquary along, just as the first mutated hound crashed through the wall.

Michael maneuvered the old man out of the room and down the stairs. "Come on, Roy, you've got to help me," Michael said, making it down the first flight and onto the third-floor landing.

One flight above the shattered safe house, Ben and Faye clambered up the stairs and pushed open the metal door leading to the roof, slamming it behind them, then scanned the flat, barren concrete.

"We've got to get off!" Faye cried.

Ben ran to the roof edge and looked down five stories. "No fire escape!"

"What about another building? Over to another roof."

Ben's head panned to the adjacent structures. "Too far, and even if we could, that thing would follow us."

"Then we have to stop it!"

Slam!

The metal door bulged. The brick frame shook.

"Stop it how?" Ben exclaimed, glancing around, his eyes falling onto the empty roof. "There's nothing up here!"

On the fourth floor, the second Blood Beast careened through the open apartment door, tearing out the wall. The hound howled in the hallway, its roar echoing through the hollow stairwell like a bull horn. It sniffed the air, catching the scent of its prey, licked its slobbering jowls, and lumbered down the stairs.

Michael stared up through the stairwell, hearing the crash and roar of the beast on the landing above. The old man teetered on the banister, dragging himself along the wooden railing.

"We have to keep going," Michael said. He looked over the slatted barrier and down at the remaining three flights, knowing that he'd never make it down with the wounded old man.

Michael's mind was buzzing. Hide and the hound would sniff them out, he thought. Run and it would pounce, killing them as easily as a lion kills a gazelle. His eyes scanned the hallway. Three apartment doors, a fire hose, and a window adorned the third-floor corridor. An oak banister separated the wooded walkway from the gaping staircase chasm. "How, Michael?" he silently demanded of himself. "Think!"

Two stories above Michael's impasse, Ben's eyes rolled over the flat rooftop. He spied the thin metal satellite antenna, but nothing else. He walked to the edge of the building again, peering over the side, and then cast a quizzical glance above Faye's head.

"Maybe," he said. "It just might work."

Ben rushed to the satellite antenna and tore it from its base, thrusting the narrow metal tube like a spear.

Faye arched her brow. "That isn't going to do much good against—" The door banged, and the brick doorway rattled. "Against whatever that is," she said, backing away from the roof entrance.

Ben dropped the makeshift spear and stepped to the brick doorway. He kicked the corner, loosening a brick, and pulled the block from the cracked mortar.

"What are you doing?" she asked, watching the Mossad agent battle the brick stoop.

Slam!

Faye spun around to see another crack appear in the door frame.

Ben, brick in hand, stepped to the edge of the building and lay on his stomach. "Hold my legs," he said. With Faye acting as a counter-weight, Ben shimmied over the edge of the building.

Slam! A fissure weaved its way through the red blocks.

As Ben's upper body dangled five stories above the ground, he pounded the brick into the hinges of a narrow skylight, tearing the little window free. He handed the glass pane up to Faye.

Then, back on the flat surface of the roof, Ben broke one side of the frame and shattered the edge of the glass.

Slam! Broken bricks popped out of formation and crumbled to the rooftop.

"That thing is coming through," Faye announced, grabbing the antenna and pointing it at the door.

Ben climbed on top of the brick entryway. He could feel the vibration of the animal inside. The red blocks clinked together as the mortar was pounded to dust. The fissure slithered past Ben's feet.

Slam!

The door tore open, and the Blood Beast's snapping jaws and sharp sabers tore through the center of the door like a can opener. The mutated hound pushed its head through the breech, thrashing its head from side to side, clearing room for its massive bulk.

Faye jabbed the monster's face with the antenna.

The Blood Beast pushed forward, its foreclaws carving deep grooves into the rooftop.

Ben jumped down, legs straddling the hound's massive shoulders. He drove the jagged glass down on the beast's thick neck like a guillotine, severing the black eyes and snapping jaws from the thrashing shaggy body. Ben rolled away from the spewing blood and looked up to see the brick stoop collapse, burying the headless carcass.

Two floors beneath the pooling blood, the second Blood Beast stalked down the stairs, pouncing onto the third-floor landing. The monster's black eyes fixed onto the old man trembling in front of the hallway window.

The hound padded along the wooden corridor, ears flat, jowls tight and fangs exposed, ignoring the opened fire-hose cover and the one door, ajar. The scent of its prey in front of its powerful nose drove its massive body forward.

Roy stared at the abomination bearing down on him. He took a deep breath, gulped down his fear, and did as Michael had instructed. "Did you know that the Towel-o-Wow can soak up ten times its own weight?" the Reliquary asked, clenching his fists to steady his nerves. "That's right…wine, coffee, and soda are no match for the power of Towel-o-Wow."

Michael watched through the slit, his heart pounding in his chest, as the hairy beast passed his door.

"But wait! There's more!" Roy called out. "Call right now and we'll double your order!"

In one fluid movement, Michael swung open the door, jumped over the Blood Beast, lassoing its neck with the makeshift fire- hose lariat, and, holding onto the other end of the hose, vaulted over the side of the railing

"Please hold!" he shouted, falling into the stairwell.

As the slack tightened, the Blood Beast was swept off its feet and slammed against the banister. Michael's body dangled at the end of the hose like a fish on a line. The hound gasped, the thick collar squeezing off its air, its long sabers useless against the garrote around its neck.

Michael pulled down on the hose, tightening the noose. "Die, you son of a bitch," he cried, gritting his teeth.

The monster pulled against Michael's weight, and then the railing broke.

The banister toppled onto its side, extending over the three-story gap. Michael bounced at the end of the hose, almost losing his grip on the woven linen. The Blood Beast thrashed against the thick leash. Four bent nails held the slatted wood from collapsing into the chasm.

Michael looked down two stories to the concrete below. "Bad idea," he said, his heart slamming, sweat beading on his brow. He begun to swing like a pendulum, then dove over the second-floor railing just as the slatted plank above his head collapsed.

Michael wrapped the hose around the second-floor banister and pulled, watching the Blood Beast fall past, twisting and turning like a trapeze artist.

"Be short...be short, be—"

The hose jerked in Michael's hand, and he heard the muffled sound of bone snapping over the creak of the strained wood. Michael looked down into stairwell chasm and saw the Blood Beast hanging by its neck, its black tongue sticking out of its sabered mouth.

Michael released the Blood Beast from its fire-hose gallows and charged back up the stairs to Roy.

"Are you okay?" the Reliquary asked, his voice wavering.

"Fine," Michael answered, stepping up to Roy. "How is your—" the Vanguard's words were lost as he stared at the Reliquary's blood-soaked shirt.

"You need help," Michael said, eyes wide, brows arched. "We have to get you to a hospital."

"There is nothing that can be done, my friend," Roy said.

"There's another one of those things around here, and I'm not waiting around for it to find us," he said, moving into the open second-floor apartment door and disappearing into a back room. Moments later, Michael emerged, a black hooded sweatshirt and a blue baseball cap in his hands. "Put these on."

After a quick inspection of the rear entrance, Michael wasn't surprised to find it sealed tight. Pheasant hunting, he thought. And they were the pheasants. The hounds were here to flush the game, driving it from its hiding place for the hunters to shoot or capture. Michael knew that the killers were in the front of the building, waiting. They had disabled the fire alarm and had likely led local law enforcement on a wild-goose chase miles away. No, he was alone.

"All hell is going to break loose, and I want you to go out the front door, turn, and run," Michael said, dragging the dead Blood Beast across the foyer of the apartment building.

"You're coming with me?" the Reliquary asked.

"No." Michael hefted the hound's carcass into his arms and, holding the beast like a dance partner, ran screaming to the window and dove, Blood Beast first, through the glass pane.

Rolling on the sidewalk, Michael cried out in pain, hoping the mock battle would provide enough distraction for Roy to slip away.

Eric watched the drama, starring Michael Cantal, from behind a taxi, his mouth wide, a smile speeding across his face.

Michael pushed the hound's muzzle up and brought it down on his chest. Michael screamed in agony. His performance may have not been Oscar-worthy, but Michael smiled as he watched the black sweatshirt and blue baseball cap turn the corner.

Eric's grin morphed into a scowl as he stood up from behind the taxi. The redhead had seen the Blood Beasts tear into a body in seconds. This mutilation was taking too long. He stepped into the street and walked toward Michael's routine, chambering a round in the automatic pistol.

Slam!

The Blood Beast's head crashed into the top of the cab, its black eyes staring blankly at the redhead. Eric spun and stared at the decapitated head and then looked up to see Faye's scowl bearing down on him in the dim light. The redhead unleashed a burst from his automatic pistol, the spray of bullets peppering the side of the building.

Five stories up, Faye raced to the collapsed rooftop stoop. "We've got to get down there and help Michael and Roy," she cried, pulling bricks from the pile.

Down on the street, Michael's strength was all but gone, and he collapsed under the dead animal's weight.

"Quite the performance," Eric spat, standing over the fallen Vanguard.

"What…what the hell happened to you?" Michael asked, his tired eyes opening wide, the combination of fear and surprise almost choking his words.

"Where's the old man?" the redhead demanded.

Michael looked up at the charred face and then stared down the snout of his dead dance partner. "This fucking thing is a beauty queen compared to you," Michael cracked.

Eric slammed the barrel of his pistol down onto Michael's forehead; the Vanguard went limp. The redheaded stuffed Michael's unconscious body into the back of a stolen taxi and drove off.

«««—»»»

After twenty minutes of clearing the stairway of bricks, Faye and Ben raced down the steps and exited the building onto the empty, darkening street. "Roy?" Faye called. "Michael?" The Reliquary, Michael, and the redheaded assassin were gone.

"Could they have gone after the asshole with the sunburn?" Ben asked.

"Eric," Faye muttered, the image of the charred face fresh in her mind.

At least we know this fucking thing didn't get them," Ben said, kicking the dead Blood Beast.

Faye scanned the sidewalk and spotted the red trail leading around the corner of the building. "No, but I'm afraid something far worse did."

CHAPTER 18

R oy didn't know how long he'd been sitting on the curb, and he didn't know how long he would stay, but he wasn't ready to leave just yet. The new sensation running down his back was as if a part of him were tearing itself free from his body. With each breath, his strength dripped away. He could barely keep his eyes open, but he didn't dare to close them. His time was short.

Through pain and fatigue, the old man reflected on his recent journey and those who walked the path of the Reliquary: memories of Faye and Michael seeped into his mind, as did thoughts of water fountains, trains, pizza, and infomercials. Still, it was one bright path that was to end soon that captured his thoughts.

"Paul," Roy whispered, his smile melting away. The nurse's words— "He's a strong little boy. I wish I were that strong."—ran through his mind.

The old man looked up and down the dark street. "I will be strong now," he thought. Pushing his weariness into the bloodied gutter at his feet, Roy mustered his strength and stood. He limped forward, beads of sweat rolling down his withered face, his body's tears defying the cool breeze blowing against his flushed cheeks.

He struggled to put one foot in front of the other. His mind that so urgently cried to be strong and keep going, now urged him to stop. To lie down.

"No more time," the old man whispered and collapsed to the cold sidewalk. The old frame trembled, struggling against pain both new and from millennia past. Roy rolled over onto his back, his face twisted, jaw clenched, as the phantom talons tore into his back again and again.

From the quiet of the back street, Mozart's Requiem in D minor floated into his ears. Michael's words joined as colloquial accompaniment: "Southwark Cathedral is just around that corner, close to the hospital." The music infused him with renewed energy. Roy opened his eyes, rolled to his knees, and climbed to his feet. The old man shuffled forward, turning his cheeks from side to side, letting the soothing harmony guide his every hobbled step.

The old man followed Mozart's melody and then cast the choral tune aside for the glass hospital doors up ahead.

Roy staggered into the hospital foyer and onto the elevator.

Bing!

«««—»»»

Michael winced at the sharp, piercing light that lanced deep into his head from beyond the thin veil of his eyelids. It was as if someone had hammered a nail into his skull, and it had lodged there, raw and painful, making his temples pound and his head spin. He screwed his eyes shut, but the world exploded into pain and then forgiving blackness. His consciousness gradually extended out into the world again as lights, sounds, and smells crept into the room. His head drooped as the scent of his mom's burning meatloaf surrounded him. It took Michael another moment to remember that it was his skin burning. The pain was lancing and deep on his face, and he could hear his heart pounding in his ears.

"Aargh!" Michael cried, the pain sparking his consciousness.

"Wakey, wakey," Eric chimed. "I can't have you passing out at the good parts."

Michael pushed and pulled against the restraints that held him to the chair. His face was black and blue, and a white blister had grown out of the charred patch that was his cheek.

"Release me, you asshole!" Michael roared at the redhead. "Where's the old man?"

"My old man? Jersey and jail, most likely," the captive Vanguard cracked.

Eric turned and picked up a stainless-steel scalpel. "Let me ask you the question again," he said, holding Michael's head still and reaping the blade across the blistered skin.

"Aargh!"

"The Reliquary—where is he?"

"Go fuck yourself!"

Eric threw the scalpel to the ground and grabbed the acetylene torch, sparking a blue flame to life. "Let me show you what it's like to kiss a volcano," he said, stepping forward.

Michael's heart thumped so hard it felt like a sledge hammer smashing through his chest cavity. He couldn't breathe, and his eyes widened in horror. It took every bit of courage to stifle the scream clawing its way out.

Just before blue flame reached pale skin, the torch sputtered and died.

"Shit! Shit! Shit!" Eric clamored.

Michael's eye darted to the blade on the ground. His mind worked the puzzle pieces into place: "Get the blade, free yourself, kill the asshole," he thought.

After trying futilely to reignite the flame, the charred redhead dropped the torch to the ground. "The fun's just starting," Eric said, trudging away.

Michael stared at the scalpel. His body tense, his mind working through the steps playing in his head: "Topple the chair, grab the blade, cut the—"

"A penny wise and a pound foolish." The assassin's voice cut through Michael's thoughts. Eric snatched blade off the floor. "I'll be back," he said with a wicked grin and left the room.

"I'll be right here waiting for you, asshole," Michael answered, dropping his head, thankful for the reprieve. Minutes passed. The Vanguard focused on contingencies, but each new possibility was no better than the previous one.

"Michael?" sounded a voice from the doorway.

The bounded Vanguard's head snapped up. He blinked hard and shook his head, trying to throw the image of Faye from his sight.

"Michael?" the vision called out again, creeping forward. "Thank God I found you."

"Faye?"

Faye dropped to one knee in front of Michael. "Are you alright?"

"Faye, I'm sorry. I didn't mean what I said."

"I know," Faye replied, staring up into his battered face. "Let's get you and Roy the hell out of here. Ben's waiting outside." She loosened one leg bond.

"Roy's not here."

"Where is he?" she asked, freeing his other leg.

"He wanted to go back to the hospital, visit that cancer kid," Michael replied. "Faye, Roy's hurt."

"Which hospital?" Faye asked, continuing to work on the wrist restraints.

"London Bridge," Michael answered, staring up into Faye's dispassionate face, and then realized his mistake. "But you'd have known that if you were Faye."

Faye's face morphed into the countenance of Zachariah Prond. "I thought I taught you better, Michael, to see through the Horsemen's ruses. You're thinking with your wrong head, boy," the mock Zachariah said, grabbing Michael's groin and squeezing.

"Aargh!" Michael screamed.

The bald imitation pressed into Michael's face, the old man's visage melting away until only bone remained. "The Reliquary's gift will be mine, and when I have it, all of humanity will be nothing more than my banquet, the Vanguard, my toys, all because you're chasing some bitch you'll never have," Death declared, her gothic beauty restored.

Eric sauntered back into the room, acetylene torch in hand. The redhead stepped up to the chair and lit the torch, adjusting the flame from orange to blue. "I told you that the fun was just starting," he said.

"I will let you boys get reacquainted," the Horseman said. "I need to visit an old friend in the hospital. I might as well kill that bastard Zachariah Prond while I'm there."

«««—»»»

The old man hobbled clear of the hospital lift doors and onto the oncology wing. Roy straightened up and smiled down the hall at the pretty blond attendant tucked behind the ICU nurses' station, her blue scrubs unable to contain her ample bosom.

"Paul McNamara," the old man said.

The blond RN nodded and returned her gaze to her patient charts.

The Reliquary staggered to the boy's room and cringed in the doorway at the sight of the bald-headed boy: thinner, haggard, his face a pallid mask. Paul had a breathing tube now. The tape holding it in place was contorting his normally smiling face. Tears were pooling in the corners of his eyes as he coughed against the tube.

"No," Roy uttered, staring wide-eyed at the numerous bags and dripping tubes of medication holding the boy together.

The old man stepped to Paul's bedside. "I have no pizza," he said.

The boy reached out and squeezed Roy's hand tightly and nodded and mouthed words around the tube. "O—kay."

Beep...beep...beep. The electrocardiogram machine was like a bird that sang its melancholy song in the room.

"We've done little in this world," Roy began. "Lights once so bright, now grow dim."

The hospital bird's chirp slowed.

"We've only now begun to experience life's pleasures. It is not right that our being be squelched like water on a flame."

Beep...beep...beep.

Paul's eyelids fluttered as the cancer and chemotherapy stole more of his life away.

"Alone, we face our shadows. The darkness overcomes us both, but together." Roy dropped to his hands and knees, his strength gone.

Beep...beep...beep.

The Reliquary pulled himself up to Paul's bedside. "But together, we can bring back the light," the old man proclaimed. "I ask this of you, to accept my final gift."

Paul raised his head, using every last bit of strength in his ten-year-old, cancer-stricken body to nod his head.

Roy reached up and placed a glowing hand on top of Paul's smooth head, just as the little bird in the hospital sang its final note.

Beeeeeeeeeeeeeeeeeeeeeee...

The radiance enveloped the little boy's body like a blanket.

Beep...beep...beep.

Paul's eyes snapped open. His cheeks rosy, the dark rings that once held his eyes captive gone. The little boy pulled the tube from his throat and disconnected himself from the bags dripping relief into his body.

Beep...beep...beep.

He threw the covers off and swung his legs over the side of the bed. Paul inched down to the cold tile. Next to his foot, a heap of ash as still as the miniature mountain it resembled.

The bald boy stepped toward the hospital songbird and silenced it. His eyes swept over the room: the picture frame, the procession of gifts and toys, and the block citadel. Memories, old and new, blew over him like a strong wind. He remembered his mom and dad, and how they need not worry about him any longer; he remembered his tenth birthday, but understood that he was far older than that; he knew of Faye and Michael, his new friends, and the Riders: a cold chill held him in an icy hug at the thought of them. He remembered his gifts. Paul extended his hands, turning them palm up and staring at the narrow roadways. The ten-year-old knelt down next to the block castle and, extending two index fingers, touched two neighboring blocks. The plastic bricks started to glow, the brilliance growing more brilliant with each passing second.

Paul stood up, grabbed a card full of birthday money and an opened box of clothes, and peered out of his room to the nurses' station. The nurse, back turned and face buried in her routine, didn't notice a very healthy Paul McNamara dart out of his room, creep down the hall and push into the stairwell.

Boom!

‹‹‹——›››

Faye and Ben turned the corner and followed the trail of crimson bread crumbs leading around the building.

"The old guy will be okay. Michael's with him," Ben announced.

Faye remained silent, ignoring the declaration. She focused all of her attention on the painted spots in the dim light.

"You know he loves you," Ben added.

Faye pulled up and turned toward the Mossad agent. "Roy?"

"Michael."

"It's not important," she replied flatly and continued along the trail.

From down the street, a procession of cars raced past, engines roaring like a herd of charging elephants.

"A little late for a funeral," Ben thought.

After another block, Faye stopped, her gaze pooling into the gutter running along the sidewalk.

Ben watched another herd race past, whipping loose papers across the street in its wake.

"I was serious this morning," Ben said, standing beside Faye, spinning the yellow band on his finger. "I want us to be together. I want—"

Ben stopped, his feet frozen on the cold concrete.

"You want?" Faye asked.

Ben's eyes were locked upon a tall edifice across the street.

"What is it?"

"That building. It's so familiar."

The revolving door spun, and the hotel doorman, dressed in a bowler and long coat dotted with a white carnation, stepped out from the portico. "Mr. Smythe, it is good to see you again, sir," the man said with a broad grin.

"I—" Ben muttered.

"No car? Don't blame you much, with the mess that's going on," the doorman added.

Squealing tires and an engine roar echoed blocks away and punctuated the man's comment. "See, it's been like that all day. Damn hoarders."

Ben narrowed his brows. "Okay," he answered. He didn't have a clue what the man was talking about.

"Please excuse my informality," the doorman said, and he straightened his hat and smoothed his coat. "Will you be staying with us tonight?"

"What?" Ben answered, unprepared for the assuming yet courteous greeting.

"What I mean to stay is, shall I prepare the penthouse for your arrival?"

"Penthouse?" Ben asked, his mind spinning, unable to string a sentence together.

"I will see that the fifteenth floor is ready," the doorman announced. "Plus one?" he added, glancing at Faye.

"Yes, myself and three more," Mr. Smythe responded, Ben now assuming the role.

"I will see to the accommodations," the doorman said, tipping his bowler and returning inside the hotel.

Ben faced Faye's arched brow.

"What was that all about?" Faye asked.

"Damned if I know, but thanks to Mr. Smythe, we all have a place to stay tonight," Ben replied.

"We have to find them first," Faye countered, her gaze redirected down to the stained sidewalk.

"Where could they have gone?" Ben asked.

"He—" Faye sounded. "This is one man. It's Roy," she declared.

She thumbed through her memories, all of the places where Roy would have gone: park, train station...

Choral music echoed high above the street, the deep base notes clouding Faye's concentration. But then, clarity.

"This trail leads to London Bridge Hospital."

«««—»»»

Bing!

All gazes flew to the swaying white lab coat like moths to a flame as the gothic beauty exited the lift and strolled down the smoke-filled hallway. The Horseman's chilling apathetic stare crushed the spirit of the hopeful police, firefighter, or paramedic admirers endeavoring to bolster courage enough to approach the attractive hospital resident.

Death strolled up to the ICU nurses' station, interrupting a policeman's flirtatious advances to the buxom blond RN with a disapproving look. The discouraged uniformed admirer walked away, joining the other badges inside the charred hospital room.

"Can I have the chart for ICU room seven," Death asked the nurse, whose blue scrubs were barely able to contain her generous bosom.

"I'm sorry, Doctor, but all ICU patients were cleared to St. Matthew's after the explosion."

The disguised Horseman looked down the hallway and watched as authorities marched in and out of the burned room like ants.

"What happened to that patient?"

"Like I told the police, the old man walked into the room and then—"

"An old man?" the Horseman interrupted.

"I guess it was the boy's grandfather. He looked nice enough but—"

"Who was the patient?" Death asked, cutting off the blonde.

"Paul McNamara," the ICU nurse answered, pulling the chart from the rack. "Poor boy."

The Horseman looked at the picture of the boy and then snatched the photo from the clipboard.

"The whole thing is pretty strange," the buxom RN added.

"How so?"

"No bodies. The inspectors have checked the room and outside on the street, but we can't find the little boy's or the old man's remains anywhere."

"Could the old man have moved…," the faux doctor asked, casting a wide-eyed questioning glance to the RN and stepping into the nurses' station.

"Paul," the blonde answered.

The Horseman grinned. "Could the old man have moved…Paul to another room? Another floor, perhaps?"

"I don't see how. The boy was on a ventilator. My alarms would have sounded, so he couldn't have." The nurse sobbed. "I left my station only once to check another patient," she said frantically.

"Thank you," the mock physician said, reaching out and hugging the blonde.

"I'm sorry, Doctor," the ICU nurse whimpered against the white coat.

"I know. Me, too," Death remarked, lifting the nurse from her feet and constricting the blonde between two powerful arms.

As onlookers disregarded the doctor-nurse consolation, the blonde's breast implants popped like two water balloons, her lungs collapsed, and the RN lay limp within the Horseman's deadly embrace.

Death glanced about, picked a moment devoid of prying eyes, and dropped the dead weight to the floor behind the counter. The doctor's guise transformed within seconds: blond hair, blue scrubs, ample bosom.

《《——》》》

Faye and Ben raced off the dark street and into the hospital foyer, passing a bald-headed boy clad in crisp clothes and eating a slice of pizza. So focused on finding their wounded friend, they both missed the fact that the ten-year-old was barefoot.

Bing!

The Horseman smiled behind the ICU nurse's station as the bitch and warrior husk stepped onto the hospital wing. She thought better than to kill the two, which would have been easy, and resigned herself to playing dress-up a little bit longer. "The humans may prove useful," she mused. She would kill them later.

Faye stepped into the threshold of the blown-out room. The outside wall was gone, and a breeze was blowing in. "OSHA investigation. What happened here?" she asked a fireman kneeling down and inspecting debris.

"Some type of explosion. It wasn't electrical, not chemical. We just don't know yet," the fireman answered.

Faye pulled back into the hall and faced Ben. "It was Roy," she whispered.

"How do you know?" he asked.

"I've seen his gifts in action, and these were his little presents," she said, remembering the concussion under the Grimsvotn crater and the explosion inside the unmanned transport.

The fireman collected his samples and soon left the scene. Faye stepped into the hodge-podge. She picked up a burned picture: a boy, smiling, wrapped liked a blanket in the arms of a man and woman.

"What?" she exclaimed, the photo chipping free a recent memory. The image of a boy filled Faye's mind eye: his toothy grin and round cheeks. It was the same face, but with the hair. "Shit!" she exclaimed and shot out of the room and hurried down the hall.

"Faye?" Ben called out, following behind.

Faye pressed up against the nurses' station. "Excuse me," she said.

The Horseman masquerading as the buxom blond nurse turned. "Yes?"

Faye showed the picture to the buxom blond nurse, who stared at the picture

"Who was the boy in that room?" she asked, handing the charred picture to the blonde.

"That's Paul. Paul McNamara, poor boy."

Ben stepped forward and smiled at the nurse. He struggled to keep his eyes north of her endowments, like driving past a twelve-car pile-up, and instead of fighting his DNA turned in the opposite direction.

"Did you see a man…eighties, this evening?" Faye asked.

"You know, there was an old guy here, before the explosion," the faux nurse answered.

"Thanks," Faye replied.

"Excuse me," the blonde called out to Ben.

The Mossad agent turned around.

"Have we met?" the mock nurse asked.

"I don't think so," Ben answered.

"I'm sure of it. I never forget a face," the blond Horseman said, a seductive grin creased on her face. Death was enjoying the game. "Was it at Houlihan's, the little bar on King Street?"

"No, I'm sorry. I've only recently returned to England."

"Oh, okay."

"Thanks again," Faye said. She pushed off and headed toward the elevator, Ben in tow.

Faye narrowed her brows and looked back at the buxom blonde and then cast a set of questioning eyes at Ben.

"What? Please tell me you're not jealous?"

Faye rolled her eyes and shook her head, pushing the down arrow. Within a moment, they both stepped into the elevator. As the lift doors closed, the faintest of words, so familiar, drifted past Ben. "So weak..."

Bing!

CHAPTER 19

The ten-year-old chewed his last mouthful of cheesy goodness, savoring the morsel like a cow chews its cud. He stood motionless on the Tooley Street sidewalk, a splatter of tomato sauce on his chin, his eyes fixed into the darkness. Inside the smooth skull, thoughts from an ancient soul mingled with that of the child, and two voices, Paul and the Reliquary, conversed inside one mind like children playing in an afterschool playdate.

"The pizza was good," thought Paul.

"The sickness is gone, but this body is still so weak," the Reliquary responded.

"More pizza?" the child asked.

"No, something better," the old soul answered.

"Smores!" piped Paul's voice.

"Yes, but where?"

The boy planted one bare foot after another and began to walk up the street.

"We ask someone," Paul thought. "They'll know," and he approached an elderly man and woman strolling side by side.

"Hello, can you—" the boy began, trying to attract the attention of the older couple, but the man and woman hustled past the street urchin, noses in the air.

Paul watched the gray hair turn the corner. He dropped his chin to his chest, staring at the dirty feet below, and shuffled down the pavement.

"Well, that didn't work," the old soul thought. "Let's try again."

The boy scanned the darkened street and spied a woman wearing a short skirt hiked up to her ass, a low-cut top, her white face adorned with shades of blue, purple, and pink. Her spiked neon red heels clicked as she walked back and forth on the sidewalk.

"This woman will help," thought the younger soul.

"Excuse me, do you know where they make smores?" the boy asked.

"Beat it, kid," the whore responded. "See me in six years, maybe five, if you're really horny."

"But—"

"Butt, pussy, tits, everything from the neck down, the whole playground is open, as long as you can pay for it," the streetwalker said, scanning the inside of passing cars for prospective johns.

The boy twisted his head, watching the woman cross the street to begin hooking again.

"Hey, kid?" The voice leapt out from the alley.

Paul turned and stared into the narrow sidestreet, his eyes bouncing from one shadowed object to the next in search of the sound's origin.

"I know where you can find smores," the voice said, dragging a short, fat frame into the dim light. "Oh, the gooey marshmallows—"

"Where?" Paul asked, turning, stepping across the darkened threshold and into the narrow passageway.

"—and the milk chocolate," the fat stranger added, stepping back into the shadows.

"I've never tasted chocolate. I've had pizza, but not chocolate," the old soul thought as the boy followed the stranger deeper into the alley.

"Don't forget the crunchy graham crackers," the tempter added.

"Where can I get some?" the boy asked, stepping farther into the passage, closing on the stout shadow.

"I was just at the sweet shop near Piccadilly Circus. I have a smore right here." The voice oozed persuasive pretense, topped with a maniacal snicker.

"A circus?" the old soul thought. "What's a circus?"

"It's not a real circus, with clowns and elephants and stuff," Paul answered with a thought. "It's a place. I've been there. I can take us."

"Here," the voice urged, but the boy stood frozen in the alleyway, his eyes glazed, his mind immersed in the mental banter. "Come get it," the voice ordered with high-pitched sadistic desperation.

Paul stepped forward, and the fat mugger emerged from the

shadows like a shark from the depths and grabbed the child by his crisp new birthday shirt.

"Got ya!" the mugger barked, his breath stinking of cheap whiskey, stale cigars, and gingivitis. Sweat dripped from the fat man's acne-riddled face, and his lips parted, showing yellow teeth. Loops of gold hung from the man's thick neck rolls.

"Hey, you're in my personal space!" the boy shouted.

"We're about to get a lot more personal, you and I," the mugger answered, his tongue wagging across his chops.

Paul pulled his arms and shook his shoulders, but he could not break free of the fat man's grip.

"You're a feisty one. I like feisty!" the fat lout proclaimed, his cheeks red with excitement.

"Bugger off," Paul shouted, the older soul remembering the hooligan from the train.

The bald boy reached up with both hands and grabbed a gold chain in each hand. Within seconds, the yellow metal loops began to shimmer.

"I'll show you how I bugger off," the fat man proclaimed, unfastening his belt.

Paul shifted his leg and drove his right foot into the mugger's balls. "That's what you do to assholes who grab you!" the boy cried.

The man crumbled down to the alleyway, his hands around his crushed jewels, the chains around his neck sparkling like starlight.

Paul dashed out of the alley.

"I'm going to kill you! You little bastard!" the mugger groaned, his muffled threat echoing through the narrow street.

"Piccadilly Circus is this way," Paul declared, pointing down the sidewalk.

Moments later, a roar boomed through the street, and a wave of crimson splashed out from the darkened alleyway.

«« —»»

"He was right here," Faye said, her reflection in the glass hospital doors panning right and left. "He was standing right here no more than ten minutes ago."

"Are you sure it was the same boy?" Ben asked.

"Bald with a slice of cheese crammed in his face, yeah, it was the same boy. It was Paul...I mean Roy," she replied, her eyes closing, nose crinkling. "The kid is Roy!" she exclaimed. The supernatural implication made her head hurt. "We need to find him and fast. Those monsters at the safe house were there for Roy."

"The Horsemen," Ben uttered.

Faye nodded. "Roy said his gifts could diminish the power of the Riders or strengthen it. Imagine the devastation and widespread panic if the Horsemen were returned to full strength. The Vanguard couldn't stop that type of threat."

"The kid couldn't have gone far," Ben stated.

As Faye followed behind, stepping out of the fluorescent glare, the buxom blond ICU nurse exited the hospital, gaze locked on the departing Vanguard. A policeman, his nose too big for his face, walked past the nurse, a grin on his face, his eyes admiring the passing cleavage. The endowed nurse snubbed the appreciation and hurried into the yellowish hue of the London streetlights, her visage melting away to be replaced by a copy of the big-nosed bobby. The duplicate policeman stepped lively down the street and within moments was within earshot of Faye and Ben.

"What would a ten-year-old Reliquary want?" Ben asked.

"I don't know. Anything…everything."

"Where would he go?" the Mossad agent pushed.

"I don't—" Faye's words fell flat as the memories swept into her mind like leaves on a breeze.

"What is a smore?" she remembered the old man asking Michael on the slope of the Grimsvotn crater.

"It's one of life's little pleasures," Michael had replied.

"I look forward to having one," the Reliquary had answered.

Faye stopped mid-stride, standing expressionless, her mouth agape.

"Faye?" Ben asked, noticing that she had dropped behind.

Another memory floated past, an image of cheese and tomato sauce, and a moment on the sidewalk blocks away.

"Toppings?" the old man had questioned.

"Pepperoni, ham and pineapple, mushrooms, olives, sausage, almost anything," Michael had answered.

"I'd like to try them all," the old man had replied. "And smores. Yes, I want smores."

Faye's frozen form thawed, and she raced forward. "I know what a ten-year-old Reliquary wants," she stated.

"What?" Ben asked, trotting to catching up.

"What every kid wants...treats."

Faye looked up the boulevard. "Wait here," she said and jogged across the street, disappearing into a local grocer. A moment later, Faye returned "The nearest sweetshop is in Piccadilly Circus. My guess is that's where we'll find him. It can't be more than a couple of blocks away at best."

The big-nose cop, standing in the background, smiled wickedly.

The clang from the thirteen-ton Big Ben bell seemed to shake the light fog that settled over London's West End.

《《———》》

An old-fashioned bell jingled as the sweetshop door opened into a bright interior filled from floor to ceiling with every kind of cake, cookie, soda, bubble gum, and candy imaginable. The fragrance of strawberry, the rich smell of vanilla, the comforting scent of chocolate, and the smell of dairy fresh butter reached out like warm hands and grabbed hold of Michael. He turned a bruised cheek. To the right was the cake and cookie counter, dead center housed the soda-fountain bar, and to the left were shelves of candy that stood out like a cavity among the three walls of teeth. Rows of Jolly Ranchers, whoppers, Pixy Stix, Pop Rocks, peppermint sticks, butterscotches, and a multitude of taffies and lollipops were good and plentiful.

"There," he muttered, his eyes falling on the shiny white head and the boy sitting at the soda bar. One marshmallow, chocolate, and graham-cracker sandwich sat on his plate. Another was in his hand, on the way to his mouth.

"Paul?" Michael asked.

The little boy turned around, raising his eyebrows in mild surprise, his mouth overflowing with the campfire treat.

"Are you are okay? I was worried," Michael said.

"It's Michael," the old soul thought. "But...but something is wrong."

"Michael?" the boy replied, fastening his eyes on the man's face.

"That's right, it's me, Michael. We have to go."

"I can't. I just ordered another plate of smores, and, you know, they're going to make me one special."

"We're leaving now," he said angrily, grabbing Paul's arm and wresting him from his seat like a doll. Michael's shifty eyes darted to the large store window; he released his grip on the tiny arm as he spied the two passersby heading to the sweetshop entrance, and hurried into the nearby restroom.

Jingle! Jangle!

Faye scanned the sweetshop counters and spotted the bald boy from the coiffured patrons enjoying their sugary snacks. Faye's lips curled, watching the boy's face light up as the waitress slid the plate of smores in front him. A small laugh escaped her mouth as the boy buried his face into the treat and devoured the gooey goodness.

"Roy?" she asked, stepping up to the seated boy, failing to notice the policeman exit the bathroom and sit on the stool one seat over, his long nose pointed down to the counter.

"That's Faye, the other is Ben," noted the old soul. "They are our friends."

The boy turned to Faye, bits of graham cracker dotting his lips. "My name is Paul."

"Sorry...Paul."

"I like your necklace," the boy said, pointing to the turquoise floating in a gold teardrop.

"Thank you," Faye replied, stroking the pendant.

"Did you know that they make wonderful smores here?" the boy asked.

"I can imagine," she said with a grin.

"Did you see Michael?" Paul added. "He was just here."

"Michael?" Faye asked. She spun her head, and her gaze slid across the sweetshop.

"What?" Ben muttered, his eyes flashing to the exits.

"Yeah, but he was mad—wanted to leave—even pulled me right off my chair. I didn't like that one bit."

A wave of realization crashed over Faye. "It wasn't Michael," she thought, fear pounding in her chest like a drum. The hairs on her arm stood on end like a chill that reached inside and touched her very soul.

"It's okay. We'll find Michael later," she said, patting Paul's back comfortingly. "Finish your treat," Faye added, her eyes darting from the boy and then across the room. "We have to go soon."

"Go where?" asked the boy.

"The Lanesborough Hotel," Ben answered.

"Is it nice?" Paul asked.

"Can't remember, but I think it's safe."

The policeman sitting one stool over stood and stepped away from the counter, passing in back of Faye. The bobby leaned his shoulder into Ben, bumping him.

"Excuse me," Ben chimed. Moments later, he heard the familiar whisper. "So weak..." The Mossad agent whipped his head around, only to see the sweetshop door jangle and close tight.

«<—>»»

Faye, Ben, and Paul each stepped out of the revolving door and into the hotel lobby. The doorman, immaculately dressed in a charcoal-gray suit, matching vest, and green tie, stepped to the trio.

"Good evening again, Mr. Smythe. Welcome back to the Lanesborough. Your rooms on the fifteenth floor are prepared as you requested. Your kitchen is fully stocked," the man said with an accommodating grin.

"Thank you," Ben stammered.

"It's Monte, sir."

"Thank you, Monte."

"It's my pleasure, sir."

The doorman looked down at the dirty bare feet scuffing his polished tiles.

"A crazy scavenger hunt," Faye explained. "The kid waded through the park fountain, and the next thing we knew, his socks and sneakers were gone. Can you believe it?"

"I can. I've seen everything at the Lanesborough and remember nothing," the doorman answered with a devilish grin. "I will see to it personally that a size"—the doorman glanced down at the boy's twitching toes—"a size four pair of sneakers are brought up to the fifteenth floor along with socks and a sweatshirt."

"Thanks, Monte," Ben replied.

"It's my pleasure, sir."

Faye herded Paul toward the elevator and pressed the up arrow with her index finger. As the doors parted, Ben smiled awkwardly and entered the small lift. The doorman stood smiling back, staring at Ben, who hoped the elevator doors would close and rescue him. One excruciating moment passed after the next until Ben glanced at the elevator panel and recognized that the penthouse floor was key access only.

Ben patted his pants. "Monte, I seem to have forgotten my key. Can you help me?"

"Of course, Mr. Smythe," the doorman responded, walking to the elevator and pulling a card key from his coat pocket. "If I may inquire, how is your brother?" Monte asked, stroking the rectangular access card with his thumb.

"My brother? Oh, he's still away on business."

"Well, give him my best," Monte said, reaching into the lift and inserting the access card into the key slot.

"I will." Ben nodded as the doors closed. The lift accelerated upward. Seven stomach-jarring seconds later...*ding!*

The lift doors opened, and the three passengers stared into a luxurious living space: marble tile entry, floor-to-ceiling glass walls, hand-crafted upholstery, antiques, and a wrap-around terrace with three hundred-and-sixty-degree views of the London skyline.

Faye stepped across the marble foyer and onto the hardwood floor, shuffling to a far wall and an oil-on-oak panel painting.

"*The Righteous Judges,*" she proclaimed, her brows raised, face bright with astonishment. "This painting was stolen in the thirties. It's priceless. There are a dozen more masterpieces hanging here."

Ben and Paul stepped into the lavish penthouse.

"Mr. Smythe has been a naughty little Horseman," Ben quipped. "I'm sure the Vanguard will be more than happy to take these off his hands and return them to their rightful owners."

The Mossad agent slid open a tall glass door and stepped out onto the terrace. "Whoa," Ben uttered. "He didn't steal this view from anyone. It's amazing."

Faye walked out onto the terrace. Placing both hands on the railing, she stared out into the twinkling city skyline.

Ben slid behind Faye and encircled her waist with one arm. "We're safe," he said.

"Not all of us," Faye countered.

"He'll be okay. Michael can take care of himself."

"I know," she murmured unconvincingly.

"We found Roy...or Paul," Ben said, glancing back into the penthouse and at the ten-year-old bouncing from one antique couch to another.

She turned and faced Ben with a half smile.

"How do you feel about a ready-made family?" he asked.

She looked in at the boy, realizing, as did Ben, that they were the only family the Reliquary would ever have.

Faye smiled and kissed Ben hard.

Inside the penthouse, Paul bounced off the couch, grabbed a remote and turned on the large flat-screen television. He sat down on the floor and began to surf the channels as Faye and Ben stepped in from the terrace.

"Hey," the boy called. "This thing has got the Internet. You want to try it?" The words "Breaking News" flashed across the screen.

"Wait, leave it here," Faye answered, freezing the boy's tapping thumb.

"Here in London, fuel shortages and long lines at the pump have led to brawls and riots across the city," piped the anchor. "In other local news, a devastating fire erupted in Brighton today when a charter jet from New York crashed. Witnesses report one survivor walked away from the scene. There is no further information at this time."

The screen filled with the image of warships cutting through a deep azure sea. "And finally, in international news, tension continues to escalate in Oman as the President of the United States agreed to use military force to close the Strait of Hormuz in defense of the small state on the southeast coast of the Arabian Peninsula. Two aircraft carriers, the USS *Wasp* and *Forrestal*, are patrolling the area, as is the ballistic submarine, the USS *George Washington*. Gas prices are rising all over the world. Here in Britain, prices could triple over the next week. The Sultanate of Oman first garnished public attention with the return of a priceless artifact, but now it seems that oil is more precious than gold."

Ben's eyes froze on the golden image on the TV screen.

"What good is that thing without the handle," Paul said, staring at the yellow blade. "My dad used an axe once, when we went camping, and it had a long handle."

"Ben?" Faye asked, seeing the pallid look wash across the Mossad agent's face.

"That axe needs a handle," the boy said.

"That blade," Ben exclaimed, rubbing his temples, trying to recall an old memory. "I've seen it."

"Well, it's been on the news. It—"

"No!" Ben interrupted, angrily. "In my hands, I've held it!"

"What?"

"Aargh!" Ben cried. "The more I think about it, the more it feels like my skull is ripping apart," he groaned, slamming his eyes shut.

"The Rider inside," thought the old soul inside the child. "He is trying to take back his host."

"The bad man inside of you, he wants to come back," Paul stated.

"The axe *is* War!" Ben exclaimed.

"Ben? You're not making sense," Faye declared. "Sit down," she said, taking his arm and directing him down on the couch.

Ben breathed hard, sweat beading his forehead. "The Horseman, he's put himself into the blade, his strength and warring essence." He winced, trying to push back the flood of pain. "Anyone close to it will fall under its murderous influence." Ben fixed his hard, concerned gaze on Faye. "Oman controls the flow of over sixty percent of the world's oil supply. It's going to cripple economies, push countries to the brink."

"The Horseman's own private apocalypse," Faye uttered.

"It'll start a global war," the Mossad agent affirmed.

"What can we do?" Faye asked, her eyes locked on the man who may have unknowingly orchestrated Armageddon.

"I don't know," Ben panted. "I just need to rest a bit." He lay back into the cushion, his face wet with perspiration.

Faye pressed the remote, and the television screen went black.

"Well, I still think that axe needs a handle," Paul repeated.

"Come on, Paul, let's take a walk and give Ben some time alone," Faye said, and she and the boy walked out of the room.

Moments later, Faye and Paul walked in silence along the hardwood floor.

"You okay?" the boy asked, noticing Faye's warm demeanor had chilled.

"Something is making people do bad things," she answered.

"Then take away the badness," Paul stated matter-of-factly.

"Wish it were that easy."

The duo turned a corner and the narrow hallway opened up to a large room filled with medieval weapons: battle-axes and polearms, armor and swords and shields in one corner, ancient hand cannons and early age flintlock rifles, breechloaders, and more modern automatic weapons in another.

"It's an armory," Faye noted.

"Cool," Paul answered.

"Yeah, cool," Faye replied sarcastically, smirking at the boy's response. "Don't touch anything."

Faye and the boy pressed into an adjoining room full of animal heads, horns, tusks, and skins mounted on dark walls. A black rhino stuffed and mounted posed menacingly in the center of the room.

"This room is super cool."

"Not cool," Faye answered, her gaze falling upon a massive bull elephant head with enormous tusks. She looked at Paul and then up at the pachyderm's ivory. "I have an idea. Hop up on my shoulders," she said, kneeling down.

"What for?"

"We're going to take away the badness."

«‹‹—››»

Fifteen stories below in the hotel lobby, Monte piled a new pair of sneakers, socks, and a thick sweatshirt into a neat bundle on his concierge counter. He glanced up from his parcel to see a policeman spin through the glass revolving doors and enter the hotel.

"Can I help you?" the doorman asked, struggling to keep from staring at the man's prominent proboscis.

"I'm looking for a man. He'd be accompanied by a woman and a small boy."

"I don't recall such a group, but if you'll excuse me, I was about to make a delivery to the penthouse," the doorman said, patting the pile and pulling the card key from his coat.

The bobby stared at the pile of clothes, spotting the sneakers. "I can bring that up for you," he said, and in the next instant, his nose retracted into his face, his appearance and clothing remolding like clay on a potter's wheel until the doorman's duplicate stood smiling back at the original. The copy raised his right hand. Skin and muscle melted away from his digits until only a bony hand remained.

"Oh my God," Monte exclaimed, shock and awe freezing his body solid.

"Not even close," the concierge copy said, stabbing the five-finger spear into the doorman. As Monte's body quivered on the lobby floor, his double snatched up the clothes and card key and entered the hotel lift.

Ding!

The mock Monte stepped onto the marble floor of the penthouse foyer. "Sir?"

"Leave everything on the couch, Monte," Ben shouted from the kitchen. "Can I get you something cold to drink?"

"That would be nice," the pretend doorman answered, his eyes surveying the vacant living room.

"Sorry, there's not much to offer you besides a glass of cold water," Ben said, entering the foyer, cup in hand, his expectant gaze landing on a much shorter form. "Where'd Monte go?" Ben asked, raising his eyebrows in mild surprise. "Did he leave those with you?" he asked the boy, gesturing to the pile topped with sneakers.

Paul stood silent, motionless, holding the parcel. His small eyes bored deep into the Mossad agent.

Ben knelt down in front of Paul. "Are you okay?" He then looked past the boy to the open elevator door, his mind screaming, "Trap!"

The response was sudden and violent. A small balled hand shot out, crashing into Ben's face, catapulting the Mossad agent across the room. The bald boy stepped up to Ben's unconscious form. In the next instant, a perfect copy of Ben stared down with disdain. "So weak..."

The Mossad mimic walked down a hallway and through the kitchen, passing Faye without the slightest acknowledgment, his face expressionless.

"Ben?" Faye asked.

The Horseman padded into the next room, his gaze fixed on the boy sitting on the floor in front of the chatting television screen.

Paul turned. His eyes lit up at the gift bearer. "Are those Nikes?" he asked, jumping to his feet and grabbing the socks and sneakers, then plopping down on the couch to put them on.

Ben's double stared down at the boy. "The power of Ro'esnugal is mine."

"What?" the little voice uttered.

"That's not Ben," the old soul answered. "Run!"

"Run?" Paul questioned as Ben's hands clamped down on his arms like a vise.

"Hey! You're not Ben!"

"No," the Horseman said wickedly.

Paul reached up with both hands and touched the Horseman's clothes.

"There is nothing manmade on me, child," the Horseman proclaimed.

"No, but this is!" Faye cried, smashing a cast-iron skillet into the side of the fake Ben's skull.

Faye's eyes widened with fear, like a cat staring down headlights in the night, as the Horseman turned and faced her, unaffected by the blow.

"Your fear is a delicious taste of the banquet that is yet to come. With the power of the Reliquary, I will breed dread, pain, and despair among you, enough to feed a hundred Horsemen a thousand times over."

"The Vanguard will stop you," Faye cried, raising the skillet.

"The Vanguard! Ha!" the Horseman bellowed. "They are unwitting puppets for me to control." The Mossad agent visage fell away, replaced with the face of Diana Waterford.

"No!" Faye shouted at the blonde.

"Yes. It was so easy to manipulate you, you and that pompous ass, Prond."

"It can't be," Faye uttered.

"Humans think themselves so superior, but in reality you are no more than emotional cattle to me." Death's eyes stabbed at Faye. "I am going to hang you on a hook next to your little friend, Michael, and all of the other Vanguard meat—"

The skillet dropped from Faye's hand and clattered on the ground.

"And pull you out to play with your body when I'm bored."

"Play with this, bitch," Ben cried, stepping into the room, M4 machine gun in hand.

"You!" Death declared.

Faye rushed forward and dove on Paul, breaking the distracted Horseman's grip as Ben opened fire, riddling the blonde's body full of holes.

"So weak...," the Horseman declared tauntingly, invulnerable to the cascade of bullets.

Faye picked up the ten-year-old and leapt behind a couch. Ben cocked the M203 grenade launcher, mounted below the machine gun, and fired.

Boom!

The force of the blast punched Waterford backward through the glass penthouse window and out into the London night.

"You saved me," Paul said, staring up at Faye.

Faye sat up and touched the small turquoise teardrop pendant hanging at her neck. "This was my mother's," she said, reaching behind her head and unfastening the chain. "She gave it to me, and now I'm giving it to you." Faye hooked it around the boy's neck.

"Why?" the boy asked, stroking the neck ornament like it was a new pet.

"It's what family does."

Outside on the terrace, Ben stepped to the railing, glass crinkling under his boots. Cool mist sizzled on the smoking hot barrel as he looked down fifteen stories to an empty street below.

"Will that monster be back?" Paul asked.

"No," Faye answered, her eyes welling with uncertainty.

"Death is a deceiver, not a warrior," thought the ancient soul.

"I'm shutting down power to the penthouse elevator, just in case," Ben announced, stepping back into the room and walking toward the marble foyer, unaware of the tagalong at his heels.

Ben spotted the elevator controls on the hallway wall, opened the panel and flipped the switch. "There."

"There," repeated Paul.

Ben turned to see the boy standing in front of the lift, his small palm on a glowing elevator door.

"Just in case," Paul said, with a grin.

CHAPTER 20

A s the morning sun burned away the fog that lingered along the Thames River, Faye sat in the kitchen staring into her coffee cup as if the answer to the burning question that had kept her up most of the night might be read there.

"Where are you, Michael?" she thought. The image of the Vanguard and his words—"Is this the fairy-tale ending you hoped for?"—ran through her head.

"Not even close," she whispered and then sipped the dark brew.

Ben walked into the kitchen and poured himself a cup. He looked out into the adjacent room at the tiny figure curled up on the couch.

"Looks like this Reliquary actually needs to sleep," he said.

"Not really," Paul piped, jumping into the kitchen.

Ben jumped back, spilling his coffee onto the floor.

"Take Night-ZZZZ and sleep a better eight hours—it's so Ea-ZZZZ," the boy said, nodding his head to the side and closing his eyes.

"Another infomercial?" Faye asked.

Paul's stomach grumbled.

Faye stared at the bald-headed boy. "Hungry?"

Paul nodded. "Do you have any smores?"

"No smores."

"Then how about pizza?" the boy asked.

"With pepperoni," thought the old soul inside the child.

"With pepperoni," Paul added.

"No pizza, but I've got scrambled eggs."

The boy's stomach growled like a beast, and the sides of his face flushed like two strawberries.

"Sit down," she said rifling through the refrigerator. Faye pulled out an egg carton, cracked six eggs over a hot pan, lifting out the occasional bit of shell, and beat the yellow globs with a wooden spoon until they were golden and fluffy. She piled up some eggs on a plate and slid it in front of the boy.

"I'm so hungry, I could eat a cow," Paul proclaimed.

The word shocked Faye's body like two triple espresso shots in an all-night study session.

"Emotional cattle," she uttered, her gaze transfixed.

"Faye?" Ben asked.

The Horseman's chilling threat—"I am going to hang you on a hook next to your little friend, Michael, and all of the other Vanguard meat."—parked on her mind like a bus of dread hiding the revelation beneath.

"Cattle!" she declared, pulling the epiphany free.

Ben looked wide-eyed at Faye, unable to decipher her cryptic code.

"No cattle, thanks, just the eggs. They're great," Paul announced with his mouth stuffed.

"No, I think I know where Michael is," Faye declared, and she hurried into the other room.

She snatched up the remote control and accessed the Internet. The browser flashed on the screen, and Faye began to type in her query: *slaughterhouse.*

"What are you looking for?" Ben asked, stepping into the room.

The TV screen popped full of images of a hip-hop group of rappers and concert dates.

"No...no...no," Faye mumbled.

She cleared the screen and started again, entering another query: *abandoned meatpacking London.*

"Here it is," she announced. "Repeated E. coli outbreaks shut down McGregor & Son Meat Packing." Faye clicked on the link, and the image of a man, his white smock and boots splattered red, hacking a hanging cow carcass into quarters, filled the screen.

"The slaughterhouse was closed two years ago," Faye said. "The plant is in Caterham. That's no more than a half hour away."

"That's gross," Paul announced, stepping into the room, his gaze fixed on the gory scene.

Faye pressed the red button on the remote, and the mutilated bovine disappeared.

"That's where we'll find Michael, I'm sure of it," Faye replied. "Michael and—"

"The Riders," the boy interjected.

Faye nodded, a hint of worry showing on her face.

"Then let's be ready for them," Ben declared.

Moments later in the armory, Faye and Ben stuffed automatic weapons, grenades, and ammo into duffel bags.

Ben grabbed a crossbow and a handful of arrows.

Faye looked at him and nodded.

"Silent and deadly," the Mossad agent said.

Paul watched from the doorway.

"Michael's our friend, too," thought the ancient soul.

"But what can I do? I'm just a kid."

"You have my power," answered the Reliquary.

"I just don't know," Paul thought.

"Do you not have a strong arm? Did you not knock out Richie Grignon's tooth?" the old soul questioned.

"We can help save Michael," he thought and stepped into the weapons store and picked up a sword.

"What do you think you're doing?" Faye asked, packing a pair of binoculars.

"Coming with you," he said, cutting the air with the sharpened steel.

"No, you're not," Faye said sternly.

"But I can help," he said, slashing the air again. "I have the power of the Reliquary."

"And it is because of that power that you aren't coming with us. You're the one the Horsemen are after. We just can't risk it. We have to keep you safe," Faye countered.

"I'm safe with you," the boy pleaded

"Not where we're going," Faye replied.

"I'm not afraid," said Paul.

"I know," Faye said, zipping up the duffel bag. "But I've got a more important job for you, to take away the badness. You're the only one who can do it."

"But—"

"Faye is right," thought the old soul.

"Do you have what we wrapped last night?" Faye asked.

"Yep, it's in the living room," Paul answered.

Ben glanced at Faye, a questioning look on his face.

"Good, because without it, millions are going to die," she added, casting a concerned glance at Ben.

"Okay," Paul said, smiling with pride.

"I'm going to save millions," the boy thought.

"I still worry for our friends," the old soul answered.

"Me, too," Paul thought.

«««—»»»

The scream, an unmistakable mix of a lion roar and a pig squeal, smashed the silence of the Vanguard office like a hammer breaking glass. The Horseman, Death, stood in her Diana Waterford guise, shaking the battered agent by the neck.

"I had him in my hands," the Horseman bellowed. "I had Ro'esnugal!" Death cried, throwing the limp body against the far wall like a kid playing with a ball.

Five Vanguard corpses lay piled in a corner.

Kishar nodded to the redhead watching from the doorway. Half of Eric's blistered face was now scabbed over.

Eric stepped to the stunned Vanguard agent and pulled her to her feet.

"No more," the agent uttered.

"Better you than me," the redhead replied, dragging the Vanguard to the blonde's feet.

"That bitch Monroe. I am going to kill her slowly," Waterford declared, bending over and clutching the dazed agent by the throat and lifting her off her feet. "What do you think it would take to crush her skull like a grape?" the Horseman asked the struggling woman.

The choking agent gasped, smacking her lips like a fish out of water.

"What?" Never mind," the blonde chided and catapulted the Vanguard toward the wall. The woman's head crashed against the hard surface and cracked open, staining the wall with abstract patterns of reds, yellows, and grays.

"I need another ball," the Horseman spat.

"There are no more," the redhead responded, stepping back and looking with mingled fear and delight into the eyes of the blonde.

"Escaped?" the Horseman questioned, menace taking root in her gaze and growing outward like a weed.

Eric nodded.

"How?" the blonde asked stepping toward the redhead.

"I don't know. All of the exits were sealed, but the locks failed."

"All of them? That's impossible," she remarked, stepping closer. "Did you check surveillance?" she asked, her nose inches away from the man's scabbed face.

"Video is still nonoperational since the fire."

"Aargh!" the Horseman cried. The blonde's face melted away, and Death's bony countenance stood in front of the charred redhead. Five bony digits shot out and slapped Eric across the face, hurling his body backwards against the wall.

"That's not all," Eric said, sitting up, rubbing his face.

The Horseman's gaze screamed "What?"

"The R&D lab," the redhead began, getting to his feet. "All the attack drones. They're missing."

The Horseman paused, its body beginning to clatter as it trembled, trying to contain the fury burning within. "I need another ball," the skull chattered as the Horseman reached down and clutched Eric by the throat.

«««—»»»

The blue sedan pulled up in front of St. Matthew's hospital. A small boy, his bald head now concealed under a baseball cap, hopped out of the passenger side carrying a long brown paper package and scurried into the white building.

"I don't like hospitals," Paul thought.

He remembered what it was like, his cancer, both the first day and the last, one hundred nine days later. He remembered he was just a regular ten-year-old in the fifth grade at Sandpiper Elementary. His days we're pretty routine: school, homework, baseball practice and reading before bedtime. He remembered how when he got sick, everything changed. He couldn't go to school anymore. He couldn't go to baseball practice; it hurt him too much to run to first base, or to swing a bat.

He remembered his grandma talking to the doctors and him watching her cry. She didn't smile anymore; she was too busy working or pretending not to be sick.

"Yeah, I don't like hospitals."

"We're here to stop the Riders," answered the old soul.

Paul walked up to the information kiosk; he smiled at a blue-haired old woman sitting behind the counter.

"I'm looking for the ICU," he said.

"Second floor," she answered. "Is that a gift?"

"It will be," Paul replied, repositioning the brown paper present in his arms.

He walked up to the door label Exit, opened it, and scaled the flight of stairs. He pushed open the door, his gaze falling on the nurses' station.

"I don't like nurses, either" the boy thought. "Every time a nurse came in to my room, it was to poke or prod me. I hated shots the worst."

"No shots for you, today, or any day," answered the Reliquary.

"Mr. Prond?" the boy asked, stepping up to the counter.

"Room three," answered the nurse, her face buried in patient charts.

The boy walked down the hall, counting the numbers down in his head.

"Room three," he said and then entered the room, the brown paper–wrapped present under one arm.

As the door closed behind him, Paul stared at the bald man in the bed.

"Cancer," he uttered, unconsciously touching his baseball hat.

'Not cancer," answered a voice to one side. The tattooed bodyguard stepped out from the shadows.

Paul stared at the pictures on the man's arms. "You're Kenji."

The bodyguard nodded, raising one eyebrow quizzically.

"Faye Monroe wanted me to give this to you," Paul said, handing the long present to the bodyguard. "Something about you being a really 'nutty' master."

"Netsuke," Kenji corrected.

"Yeah, that's it. Net…suky," the boy stammered.

Kenji tore off the brown wrapping and stared at the ivory tusk.

"The axe on TV, it needs a special handle," Paul said, placing a finger on the ivory. The tusk began to glow in the bodyguard's hands. "It will take away the badness."

Kenji watched as the radiance dissipated. He turned around and set the ivory tooth on the counter.

"Who are you?" the bodyguard asked, turning back around, only to find that the boy was gone.

«««—»»»

The drive took longer than Faye or Ben had anticipated after a search for gas ended up being a wild-goose chase. After an hour on the road, they were still two kilometers away from Caterham and McGregor & Son Meat Packing.

"Come on, baby, just a little bit farther!" Ben coaxed the car as he headed down an exit ramp off the highway. The sedan was running on fumes, and Ben knew that it wasn't a question of if he was going to run out of gas, but when. The line of cars off to the side of the road didn't calm the tension in his gut.

"We're close," Faye said, her voice urging the car forward.

The car slowed down.

"Damn!" Ben cursed under his breath as he steered the blue sedan off to the side of the road and sputtered to a stop. "Looks like we're walking," he said, stepping out of the car. "Grab a bag."

Ben and Faye covered the two kilometers and knelt on a rise above the dilapidated meat- packing plant. It had been built into the side of a hill and was now overgrown with brush. Faye panned the binoculars to the right. "One sentry," she reported, then panned to the left. "Wait, two," she added as a familiar face came into view. "They're Vanguard, but something doesn't feel right." Faye lowered the glasses and looked at Ben. "Why would Vanguard be standing guard at an abandoned meatpacking plant?"

Ben furrowed his brow. "Let's get down there and take a closer look."

Faye slung a MAC-10 around her shoulder, then tucked a 9mm handgun into her waistband and a couple of clips in her pocket for good measure. Ben followed suit and holstered the crossbow behind his back, adding a small quiver of arrows around his shoulder.

The two snuck down onto the meatpacking lot, weaving between processing and packaging buildings. Ben crept away, focused on the two sentries patrolling the farthest side of the compound. Faye stood staring at the familiar face to her left. "He is not going to be happy to see me," she thought.

As the big man walked past, Faye stepped out from between the buildings. "Hello, Graeme," she said.

Faye's former sparring partner turned around. Instantly, she realized what she'd missed: Graeme was unarmed. All of the sentries were.

"When did Vanguard stop carrying?" she asked.

The big Vanguard fixed his eyes on Faye and drew his serrated knife.

"Waterford isn't who she appears to be," Faye declared. "She's Death. The Horseman has been playing the Vanguard for fools!"

The big man trudged forward, his face a blank canvas.

"Graeme! Did you hear me?" Faye shouted. "It's not Waterford. It's Death."

Graeme continued to advance.

Faye placed her hand on the butt of the submachine gun, hoping her move would halt the creeping man mountain. "Don't be stupid."

The Vanguard sentry slashed the air with the blade.

Faye backed away, pulled the MAC-10 from around her neck, and cocked it, pointing the muzzle at the Vanguard. Her threat had little impact, as the man mountain turned for another thrust. Faye's mind raced a mile a minute. She didn't want to kill him. Something seemed off about him. His movements were slow, too slow. This man couldn't be the Vanguard she knew.

Graeme pushed the knife forward. Faye parried the thrust with the barrel of the MAC-10, and the big man passed by.

"One way to find out," she thought. "Just don't die."

The sentry turned around like a robot in need of oil.

"I bet your mamma could've dodged that," Faye piped.

Graeme stepped forward again.

"Cat got your tongue, today?" she asked. "I doubt your Neanderthal brain could string two words together."

Faye's words fell on deaf ears. It looked like Graeme, even smelled like Graeme, but this wasn't Graeme.

"I don't know who you are, asshole, but you're not Graeme," Faye declared, launching a roundhouse at the man's knife hand and kicking the blade away. "If you were Graeme, you'd know what comes next." Faye leapt forward and plowed her foot into the black man's groin.

The Vanguard stood unfazed, raised his hand, and smashed Faye in the face, knocking her down to the ground.

"Not possible," Faye uttered.

«« — »»

Three buildings away, Ben snapped his head around and watched as Faye was hammered by the big Vanguard. The Mossad agent took one step in Faye's direction but was grabbed from behind and flung down on his back by the other Vanguard sentry.

Ben kicked his legs around the Vanguard's ankle and twisted. The man came crashing to the ground. Ben drew out his pistol and whipped the sentry in the head.

"What?" Ben gasped, as the sentry's hands grabbed the Mossad agent by the throat.

Ben reached back, snatched an arrow from the shoulder quiver, and jammed the little spear deep into the man's eye.

«« — »»

At the other side of the lot, Faye spotted the serrated blade on the ground. "Too far," she thought as Graeme knelt above her.

Thunk...

A metal arrow tip stuck out of the man mountain's forehead. A line of crimson dribbled down his forehead. The Vanguard collapsed forward like an avalanche.

Ben raced to Faye's side.

"They're not alive," she said.

"I know. It's the Horseman. It has to be!"

"Then let's find Michael," she said. "And get the hell out of here."

Ben replied with a nod, and he and Faye raced to the meatpacking plant. Once inside, the duo surveyed the dank surroundings. The smell of blood and rotting flesh assaulted their senses. Before they could take one step, the earth shook and the ground cracked beneath their feet. The abandoned warehouse rattled and clattered, dust drifting down from the rafters like snow.

Six black-clad sentries appeared from around a rusted storage container.

"More of the Horseman's death walkers," Ben stated.

"Time for stealth is over," Faye announced, cocking her MAC-10 and firing. The wall of walking corpses trudged forward, riddled by the stream of bullets, as Ben and Faye ran out of ammo.

"Go!" Ben shouted, and they raced toward the far side of the slaughterhouse.

"Michael could be anywhere," Faye said mid-stride.

"We'll find him," Ben answered.

The earth shook again, and a wall of concrete rolled up like carpet from the ground blocking their path

Ben slammed his fist against the barricade. "What the hell?"

"It's Death," Faye said. She turned and saw the row of Vanguard sentries march forward. Behind them was the blond hair of Diana Waterford. "She's too powerful."

"Split u—" But before Ben could finish his command, the ground reached up like a claw and grabbed his feet. The earth oozed up and around Ben and Faye's legs like an amoeba, holding them fast.

Death's skin and flesh ebbed like water in the desert until only a skeleton remained. The bony figure cut through the line of tall Vanguards like a kid through a cornfield. The Horseman did not lose a word.

Ben reached over his shoulder, pulling the crossbow and an arrow from behind his back.

"Faye, try to free yourself! Get out of here!"

"I can't move my feet!"

Ben fired the arrow at the Horseman's head. Death stared down the oncoming projectile, then opened its chalky jaw and blew as if blowing out candles on a birthday cake. The arrow deflected harmlessly away.

"No," Ben cried, and he hammered the crossbow against his stone shackles.

"A futile effort. I should have expected no less," Death said as she gestured to the floor in front of her captives.

Chunks of concrete and stone merged together in the form of a giant hand. The crusty appendage shot up and snatched the crossbow out of Ben's hand, crushing it.

"What?" Ben uttered.

Faye spotted the circle of turquoise floating effortlessly in a gold teardrop hanging around the Horseman's neck.

"My pendant," Faye uttered.

"No, my pendant," Death countered, stroking the turquoise tenderly. "A gift from the Reliquary."

"It can't be," Faye uttered.

The redhead, one side of his face charred and scabbed, the other black and blue, hobbled into view. "Get out here, you little shit," Eric said, dragging the boy.

"Paul?" Faye gasped.

The boy looked at Faye, his eyes streaming. "I'm sorry, Faye," Paul cried. "I took the train. I wanted to help," he added, struggling against the bonds that tied his small hands together.

"We both were duped," the ancient soul thought.

"The elements are mine to command once more," chimed the Horseman, its jaw open wide. "As are the dead who now obey my every command."

"Paul, tell me you didn't," she declared.

"But you told me to," the boy stammered. "But it was really her!" he cried, pointing at the Horseman, his high-pitched voice full of sorrow. "She told me to make it! She said it was the only way to save Michael."

"There is no way to save your precious Michael," Death spat, extending a bony hand to one side.

Michael stepped out from the shadows, his body slouched. His arms hung loose, his eyes transfixed with a piercing gaze on something unseen.

Faye tensed her body, and her heart raced as she waited for Michael…to be Michael, but Michael never came. There was no wise-crack or smart-ass retort, no call to action. This man was oblivious to the drama unfolding in front of him. This man was a walking corpse.

"He belongs to me now," the Horseman proclaimed.

"Michael!" Faye gasped. Her head spun and her stomach heaved, the taste of bile stinging the back of her throat.

"Do not lament for your poor Michael," Death declared. "You shall join him shortly."

CHAPTER 21

"With the power of the Reliquary," Death announced as the ground rumbled like the mighty "amen" at a Baptist sermon, "and the Vanguard and their technology at my disposal, I will rule this world."

"The Vanguard will never follow you," Faye said, her words laced with venom.

"Me, no," chattered the Horseman, pink bundles of muscle covering bone, now hidden under alabaster skin and blond hair. "But they will follow me," Death declared, the Waterford transformation now complete.

The blood drained from Faye's face, and her heart sank into her stone-covered shoes.

Ben tugged on his thighs, trying to pull his legs free from the rocky bonds.

"And those that don't, well—" Waterford gestured and a dozen more walking Vanguard corpses stepped into view.

Faye stared at the pale and bloated countenance of the real Diana Waterford as the Dragon Lady's corpse, skin peeling and one eye bulging out of its socket, stepped forward in answer to its master's command. Faye gasped at the next victim: a dark-haired Marcello Rizzo stood in his underwear, a bullet hole in his head, a jagged bone protruding out of his mottled gray skin like an exposed root.

"I can always use more meat puppets," the blonde added.

Faye tried wiggling free of her shoes, but the stone was unforgiving.

"And when I've had my fill of fear and desperation, my hunger satiated, say in a hundred years, I will pull you, my brother," the Horseman said, directing the threat to Ben, "out of your dungeon, and we'll play, well, Dungeon and Dragons, acting out days like today."

The blonde gestured to the floor, and the cement jumped to command, slotting into space like a jigsaw puzzle until two replicas of Faye and Michael stood like a monuments to the tragedy about to befall humanity. With a wave of Death's hand, the stone effigies stepped forward.

Faye stared at her twin; her gaze met with a blank stare.

"And when I'm done"—Death's eyes bore into Ben—"I'll put you back into the ground for another hundred years, along with this child."

Death nodded to the redhead standing silent to one side, his hands squeezing down like a vise on the boy's shoulders. Eric shoved Paul, who tumbled onto the ground in front of Faye.

"I'm sorry, Faye," Paul sobbed.

"It's not your fault," Faye replied.

"You are a fool," Death spat. The Horseman fixed cruel eyes on the boy. "Ro'esnugal, you will watch for millennia and realize that it was you who doomed humanity."

Paul stood, staring back at the blonde.

Ben was the first to hear the popping and cracking sound and then saw the fissures snake up the stone casts, shards of stone peeling away from his legs. The Mossad agent lunged forward and pulled his legs free from the earthly manacles. Likewise, Faye twisted her legs as the hard casing flaked away.

In front of the mock Diana Waterford, the stone figures broke apart as amputated arms and legs crumbled to bits on the ground.

"How?" Death exclaimed.

"Looks like your power has failed you," Faye said.

"What have you done?" the blonde said, distracted with the fleeting sense of something familiar yet unrecognizable.

"Grab Paul! Run!" Ben ordered, and Faye darted away, dragging Paul by the arm.

The Horseman turned to the charred redhead and the dead Vanguard. "Kill the woman. Bring me the child," she commanded.

Eric limped after Faye and Paul, Michael's corpse trudging behind. The Horseman shifted her attention to Ben. "My death walkers will make you long for your dungeon, brother," said the blonde, her tone vile.

"I'm not your brother, bitch." Ben bucked as the wave of walking corpses moved toward him.

«««—»»»

At the far side of the slaughterhouse, Faye hurried through a narrow hallway, Paul in tow, her eyes darting back and forth, frantically searching for an exit.

"You're dead, Monroe," cried Eric. "There is no way out."

Faye could hear the approaching slap of boots on concrete.

"Shit!" Faye exclaimed, her hands trembling, her breaths so shallow that no air seemed to reach her lungs. She felt like an animal cornered with nowhere to run.

"How about in there?" Paul asked, pointing at the metal freezer door.

"That's a good hiding place," thought the ancient soul.

"Hurry, inside," Faye urged.

Faye grabbed Paul by the wrist, hitting the light switch on the wall, and opened the walk-in freezer door. Bile flooded her mouth, stinging her throat, as the smell of death and fresh meat permeated the entire room. A shiver swept down Faye's spine and her lungs burned as the cold tightened its icy embrace. Faye could see Paul's frosted breath rise like steam from a geyser.

A line of large meat hooks, glistening in the artificial light, hung from the low ceiling, some still and rusted, others with bodies hooked down to their spines.

"Vanguard," she uttered, staring at the corpses, her heart pounding, the image of a butcher with a cleaver in his mitts racing through her mind.

"Move back," Faye said, and she and Paul waded through the line of dangling cadavers.

The door clicked opened and the charred redhead staggered into the meat locker.

"You're going to die in here, Monroe. I'm going to hang you on a hook and carve you up."

242

Paul, panic pumping his feet, tripped and bumped into a hanging stiff.

"Gross," he said.

"Shh," Faye whispered, moving a finger to her lips.

The corpse's hand reached down and grabbed Paul by the shirt. He gasped, thrashing, as the corpse opened its eye.

"Faye!" Paul cried.

As Faye reached over to pull Paul away from the death walker, a solid body hit her and sent her sprawling to the floor, knocking the air from her frozen lungs. She rolled to one knee to see Eric sneering down at her.

"You're uglier than the last time I saw you," Faye chided, getting to her feet. "The Horseman has been using you as her piñata," she added, trying to goad him into losing his temper and attacking recklessly.

"So predictable," Eric said, circling. "Your pathetic banter and stale moves aren't going to save you now."

Faye mirrored the redhead's motion, measuring him, looking for an opening.

"Then how about some new moves," she said, feinting a jab at his face and landing a hard punch in his solar plexus.

"You'll have to better than that," he said, rubbing his chest. "This is going to be too easy."

Eric limped forward, his fist slamming into Faye's face.

"Jesus," Faye thought, and for two seconds she couldn't see anything, couldn't hear anything. Eric's knuckles plowed into her eye and jaw. Faye's face felt like it was going to break in half. "Have to get closer," she thought. "He's too fast."

"Leave her alone!" Paul cried, wriggling away from the dead grasp and pummeling the redhead with his small fists.

Eric slapped the boy to the ground. "Death will deal with you," he said. "As soon as I finish wi—"

Faye's heel crashed into the charred and scabbed jaw. She recovered and planted her foot, driving her other knee up into the redhead's groin.

Eric punched down with his hands, blocking Faye's blow and pushing her leg to the side. Off balance, Faye twisted her body. In a split second, the redhead spun behind her and wrapped his arm around Faye's neck.

"So predictable."

With her next breath, Fayed reached up and plunged her thumb into Eric's open eye. She dug it in, feeling the wet pop as his eye exploded.

"Predict that, asshole!" she shouted, tearing free from his grasp.

Eric shrieked, limping backwards, hand to his eye, blood and clear liquid trailing down his face. "I'll kill you!"

"Faye!" Paul cried.

Faye turned to see Michael clutching the struggling boy's arm.

Cold maternal strength pumped through Faye's arms. She took two hard steps forward, planted her feet, and swung from the left into Eric's blind side. The punch landed at the joint of the man's charred jaw, solid and with all her weight behind it. The shock rocketed up Faye's arm, and the redhead didn't stumble backward but sailed up, landing on the sharp end of a hook.

"Aargh!" the redhead screamed, his feet dangling a foot off the floor.

Faye charged, throwing her weight against Michael's cold body, knocking the walking corpse down and freeing Paul from its grasp.

"I'm sorry, Michael," she said, her eyes fixed on the pale familiar features.

Paul stood and looked at the redhead wiggling like a fish on a hook. "I'll kill you all!"

Paul reached out and touched both of the fish's boots.

Faye shot to her feet, grabbed Paul, and raced toward the freezer exit.

"You fucking bitch, I'll kill you!" Eric screamed, struggling to free his skin from the curved metal.

Michael looked blankly at the dangling redhead. His boots beamed brightly, like two suns.

"Get me down, you fucking meat bag!" Eric bellowed at the death walker.

Faye and Paul bolted out of the freezer, slamming the door and silencing the redhead's cries. As the woman and boy raced through the warehouse, Faye heard the muffled boom, like distant thunder, as the frozen meat in the locker was broiled and blackened.

《《《—》》》

In the center of the warehouse, Ben, battered and bruised, tossed another animated corpse over his hip, stomping his boot down on the cadaver's neck with a crack.

Dead fists slammed across his face, leveling the Mossad agent.

"They can't kill you, but you'll wish for death," the blonde said as more punches rained down on Ben.

From within the downpour of fists, Ben spotted a silver brick rolling silently across the floor, and then another and another.

The Horseman, immersed in the trouncing, failed to notice the little brick until she heard the click as the cuff was fastened to her ankle.

Waterford stared down at the metal drone. "No!" she screamed.

"Who dares?" she exclaimed as another wave of fleeting familiarity swept over her.

The blonde cast angry eyes to Ben. "You did this, warrior," she said, speaking past the host to the Horseman within.

Ben stared up at the Horseman through the onslaught of putrid arms and legs in utter disbelief.

Death gestured to the ground at her feet, and the small robot was devoured by the earth.

More drones rolled onto the floor like cars on an assembly line. Ben heard the familiar *click! click!* He saw flashes of silver to his left. *Click! Click! Click!* More glistening metal to his right, and then his four assailants were dragged away by an invisible force.

A row of drones bore down on the blonde. Death shed the flesh and blood of her Waterford disguise. Black hair grew to the floor and transformed into a long dark cloak which covered her bony form.

"Ben," Faye called, running into the main floor and helping Ben to his feet.

"You're wearing the same bracelet that she has," Paul said, looking down at Ben's foot and then out across the floor to the Horseman. "Why?"

Ben raised his brows in surprise and then realized that it was he and the other Horseman who were the intended targets.

Another wave of drones rolled toward Ben. The Mossad agent widened his stance, steadying himself against the tug on his foot.

"What is Death doing?" Faye asked.

"It's not the Horseman," the old soul countered.

"It's not her," answered Paul.

"Then who?"

"The lost one has returned," the Reliquary announced to the boy.

"We have to go," Faye said.

"I have to stop her. I'm the only one who can," Ben replied.

"What do you mean?" she asked

"Rider against Rider," the Reliquary told the boy.

"The bad man inside you, he is going to come back," Paul said, pointing to the ring.

Ben nodded.

"No, Ben! I can't lose you again, I can't," Faye pleaded.

"A part of me will always be there, hidden beneath the monster," he said, his gaze fixed on Faye. "Remember me for who I was and not for what I've become."

"I will find another way, another artifact," Faye declared, holding him in a tight embrace. "I promise."

"I love you," Ben said and kissed her lips hard.

"I know."

Ben pulled the ring off and slid it onto Faye's finger. "Now run!" he ordered. "Get out of here."

Faye grabbed Paul's hand and started toward the side of the slaughterhouse. Paul pulled up, coming back and kneeling down at Ben's feet. The boy looked up at the Mossad agent, his eyes asking, Can I?

Ben nodded his approval, thanking him with a smile.

Paul touched each side of the silver band. "The power of your Horsemen will protect you," he said and then darted off after Faye.

"Stop them," ordered Death, and a mass of death walkers trudged toward them.

Ben leapt into the wave of dead flesh, the band around his ankle glowing like the tail of a comet.

Close to the exit, Faye and Paul stopped, their path blocked by the walking dead.

"Damn!" Faye cried, guiding the boy to the left and racing behind rusted storage containers.

From their vantage point, Faye and Paul watched as death walkers swarmed on Ben like maggots.

In the next instant, a blast consumed the horde, throwing dismembered cadavers across the floor. Faye breathed a sigh of relief to see Ben in one piece.

Kneeling at the center of the slaughterhouse, Ben glanced at his ankle, free of the metal encumbrance and thankful to still have his foot.

"You still stink of human, brother," Death said.

I'm not your brother yet," Ben replied getting to his feet. "I control this power," he said, creating a fireball in his palm and throwing it like a fastball at the skeleton.

Death reached out her hand, gesturing at the floor. A slab of concrete leapt up, obeying its master's command, and deflected the fiery attack.

The skull's jaw parted in a malevolent grin.

Click!

Death stared at the silver bracelet that bound her bony wrist.

"No!" the Horseman shrieked, stomping on the drone.

"Your plan to use my Vanguard robots against me will fail, warrior," Death yelled.

"I don't need robots," Ben answered, an orange flame dancing in his hand. "Not when I have pow—" And the fire choked and died.

"So weak..." Death spat.

Ben stared at his smoking hand as a big Vanguard corpse crashed onto his back.

"Strong enough," Ben said, lifting the corpse from off him and throwing it at the skeleton.

Death's hand reached up, but the chalky limb was drawn down as the electromagnetic power of two drones pulled against the Horseman's will.

The catapulted death walker slammed into its mistress, the corpse's flailing limbs snagging the pendant, breaking it off Death's bony neck.

Peeking around the metal storage container, Paul spotted the stone on the cement.

Paul looked up at Faye and touched her hand. "I have a gift," the boy said, "for your gift."

"What do you mean?" she asked.

"She is worthy, full of light and hope," thought the ancient soul.

"For sure," thought the boy.

"You'll see," Paul replied with a smile. "Good-bye," he added and then darted out onto the meatpacking plant floor.

Ben watched as Paul scurried over and picked up the pendant like a squirrel gathering a nut.

As soon as the boy's fingers clutched the greenish-blue rock, all of the death walkers dropped as if someone had shut off a switch.

"Looks like you've lost your edge, Horseman," Ben quipped.

Death's white claw reached up to her neck, only to find it barren.

"Aargh!" The skull let loose a roar that crescendoed to a squeal.

As the high-pitched howl echoed through the slaughterhouse, Faye charged over to Paul. The metal roof clattered and the ground trembled, shaking loose her footing and tossing her to the ground. She crawled over to the boy. "This place is coming apart," she shouted over the racket. Her words heralded the next moment as part of the dilapidated roof broke apart, metal beams and ceiling falling in, burying Ben and the bony Horseman.

"Ben!" Faye screamed.

After the dust cleared, Faye and Paul fixed their gaze on the pile of debris.

"Ben?" Faye cried, tears welling in her eyes.

The metal on the floor shifted to one side. A white claw pushed away roof remains.

"We've got to go," Faye said, pulling at Paul's arm.

Paul looked into Faye's blue eyes. "Thank you for pizza and smores," he said, gripping the pendant. The turquoise rock in his balled hand began to glow.

"And infomercials," thought the old soul.

"TV, too," Paul said, placing his other hand over his heart, the skin under his clothes shimmering.

Faye watched as the brilliance expanded over his body.

"It's what friends…family does."

Faye smiled, a mother's smile, a smile of courage and pride.

The wreckage quaked and rubble fell away as Ben emerged from the pile of debris. "The power of the Reliquary." Ben's rough voice cut through the tender moment like a knife through warm butter. "Give it to me."

"The gift is mine," chattered the skull, pulling free of the collapsed roof.

"Give me the gift, boy," the warrior Horseman commanded.

"Ben?"

"The Rider's reclaimed his host," the ancient soul thought.

"Ben's gone. You need to leave now," Paul urged, shoving Faye with glowing hands, then turning to the two Horsemen.

"Roy?" Paul asked, turning his words inward.

"I stand with you, child," thought the ancient soul. "I will walk the path now and speak in your stead."

"The gift! Boy!" War bellowed.

"We're not a mere boy, Rider, but the light of the ages. We are the Reliquary, and our answer has not changed from long ago," Paul declared, his skin pulsing bright. "My gifts are those of light. You cannot have them."

Faye exited the slaughterhouse and sprinted through the brush.

War turned away from the brilliance, his eyes shifting to Death. "It is I, not you, who shall rule over humanity, even without the Reliquary's gift," he uttered and disappeared into the shadows.

Death urged her bony limb forward, but the silver bracelet around her ankle held her fast.

"Coward!" Death chattered, pulling against the invisible force.

Outside, Faye gasped, reaching the top of the rise overlooking the slaughterhouse.

Boom!

CHAPTER 22

The ashen skull stared out through black sockets. The silver room sparkled like a diamond as light pulsed and then dimmed, the radiance metering the pain coursing through the Horseman's body. Death screamed, her bony arms and legs straining against the immovable force.

"Imagine that pain, but in darkness over millennia," said the voice beyond the Horseman's view.

Death stared at the silver bracelets encircling her wrists and ankles. "I am going to kill you a thousand times ove—" The Horseman's threat dissolved into a squeal as the brilliance again filled the small room.

"Your torment is nothing compared to the pain of longing, the never-ending ache of denial and rejections," added the voice bitterly.

With the wave of pain subsiding, a sense of enduring malevolence and wicked kinship wafted through the space.

"The Riders sought to cast me aside like scythed grass lost to the wind," the voice declared.

"La…Lateris?" the Horseman stammered.

"But I am lost no more," Chaos said defiantly, facing his Horseman captive.

"No," Death said, fear dripping from her voice. "Lateris, your anger is misplaced, your—" The Horseman cried as white bolts sparked along her bony frame, invisible ties stretching her limbs on the electromagnetic rack.

"Don't speak my name like it belongs in your mouth," Chaos spat.

"Your vengeance is not with me," Death pleaded, her voice trembling, "but with the War Rider, the one who leads the Horsemen. It is Seth that you seek."

"He, like you, will beg for forgiveness at the betrayal," Chaos said, positioning a small cube the size of a die at the Horseman's feet.

"What are you doing?"

"I am surprised that you don't recognize the Vanguard technology," he said, tapping the cube.

Death watched as the cube softened into an amorphous blob, burying the Horseman in its gelatinous mass.

"You will feel what it is like to be lost," Lateris scoffed. "And Chaos will rule this world like the Riders could never do."

"No!" Death squealed as the polymer crept into her mouth and over her head, encasing her body in an opaque and impenetrable prison.

«««—»»»

"Four hours," Faye thought, pulling her rental car to the curb. She was lucky that the three-hundred kilometer drive from Kalba in the United Arab Emirates to the Omani capital hadn't taken longer, having snuck across the Omani border, skirted the military checkpoints, and rolled into Muscat at dusk. She was damn lucky. Luckier still that most of the city, now under martial law, was at the Sultan Qaboos Grand Mosque for nightly prayer and not the National Museum twenty kilometers away.

Faye grabbed her cloth-wrapped bundle, patted the lumps in her coat pockets, and stepped out of the car. She could hear screams and gunshots as chaos and rioting gripped parts of the city. "One hundred yards to save a world on the brink. Luck don't fail me now," she said.

Faye pulled an EMP unit from her pocket, pointing the remote at the stone and glass edifice. She pushed the familiar Charge button and watched as the green indicator bulb blinked green, then fired the directional EMP burst at the museum. The outdoor lights flickered and died, and the museum was bathed in darkness.

"That takes care of the museum lights, surveillance cameras, and alarms," she thought, stowing the EMP unit in her pocket. From an inner coat pocket, Faye retrieved Vanguard night-vision glasses that looked more like designer shades than high-tech optics. As she looked through the specialized spectacles, the darkness gave way to green daylight.

Faye walked up the museum steps. Her mind was not on the museum towering in front of her or the lone guard shifting uncomfortably by its door, but on three people who had touched her life. Faye thought of Michael. She remembered his bighearted nature and wise-cracking bravado. He'd been a Vanguard through and through. It saddened Faye that Michael had loved her, all the while knowing that her heart would never be his. Her sadness deepened as she thought of Ben. Her heart ached at the thought of a good man, the man she loved, trapped inside a monster. She would find a way to free him from the Horseman or die trying.

At the top of the museum steps, Faye put her hand into her other coat pocket.

"Who's there?" the sentry asked in the darkness. "The museum is closed."

"The lights will be out for a while," Faye said in her sweetest feminine tone, "and so will you." She pulled a Taser from her pocket and fired at the guard.

Faye tucked away the Taser and retrieved the master key from the unconscious sentry. She stepped up to the locked doors of the museum, looked at the bundle in her hand, and thought of the Reliquary. Images of Roy and Paul were framed in her mind like photographs. Their child-like innocence and selflessness had saved humanity, saved her.

She unlocked the museum door and entered the grand foyer. Through the green light, she spotted the long stretch of post and rope barriers devoid of its queue of patrons. Faye stepped to the exhibit door and walked into the tiled room. In the center, a glass case was roped off in velvet. At the center of the display case rested a golden axe blade on a white satin pillow.

"Now the motion and pressure sensors," Faye thought, pulling the EMP unit from her pocket. She charged the remote and fired the pulse at the display case.

Using the EMP remote as a hammer, Faye smashed the glass enclosure, stripped the cloth from her bundle, and affixed the prize to the golden blade. She was amazed at the beauty of the long polished ivory axe handle, intricately carved into the shape of the Sultan Qaboos Grand Mosque Minaret, and thankful that the Reliquary's gift was protecting her from the Horseman's warring madness.

Faye stepped out into the Omani night, golden axe with ivory handle in hand, a sea breeze blowing against her face. The city had quieted as Muscat awakened from its nightmare. She had stopped the global crisis, so why didn't she feel so lucky?

«««—»»»

The town car driver loaded the suitcases in the trunk, rushed to open the passenger-side door, and, with his client situated on the plush leather seat, closed the door promptly. The chauffeur opened his driver's side door and slid behind the wheel, adjusted his rearview mirror and glanced at his passenger. The cold sneer on that face made him think twice about idle chitchat.

"Heathrow, isn't that correct, sir?"

"Yes," the client answered curtly.

"Travel much?" the driver asked.

The passenger stared out the side window, ignoring the chatter.

"Last week," the driver continued obliviously, "it'd take an hour to go just two miles, for Christ's stake, but now, since that mess in the Middle East is all done, thirty minutes tops."

"Done?"

"Peace."

The driver glanced back at the cold steely eyes in his rearview mirror. The hair on the back of his neck stood on end.

"Yep…" The car slowed to a stop at an intersection. "All that's left is the clean u—" The driver's words froze in his throat as the warrior Horseman's fingers tore through the back of the driver's seat and into the chatty town car chauffeur.

«««—»»»

Bing!

Faye stepped off the elevator onto the second floor of St. Matthew's hospital, bouquet in hand. It had been two days since she stepped into the exhibit room at Oman's National Museum and subsequently pitched the golden axe into the Indian Ocean, and she was looking forward to seeing Zachariah, but at the same time dreading the visit.

Faye walked into the sterile white room and saw the Vanguard leader sitting up, eyes wide, reading the *London Times.* "Catching up from your two-week sabbatical?" she quipped.

"Faye! Finally another familiar face," the bald man said with a smile. "If I have to look at Kenji's stone grimace another day, I'm going to scream."

"These are for you," she said, handing over the pink and yellow bundle.

"You're sweet," he said, breathing in the floral bouquet and then setting the bunch on the bedside table.

He picked up and ruffled his paper. "Did you hear," he began, having dispensed with the pleasantries, "Oman reopened the Strait of Hormuz. The global powers are standing down, their fingers coming off the buttons."

"I heard something to that effect."

"And did you hear about the stolen golden axe blade," he said, his eyes sizing up the Vanguard standing at his bedside.

"A robbery?" she said slyly.

"Quite a sophisticated scheme. The thieves used EM—"

"Michael's dead," she blurted, thinking of no way to sugarcoat the tragic news. Zachariah's warmth frosted over at her words.

"It was Death," Faye went on. "The Horseman's treachery was rampant through the Vanguard."

"Eric Stoneridge," Zachariah said.

Faye nodded. "Her mole, and Diana Waterford," she added, remembering the Dragon Lady's bloated corpse. "The Horseman playing dress-up."

Zachariah focused his solemn gaze on Faye. "Michael died a Vanguard, died with courage. He was my apprentice...my friend."

"A lot of Vanguards are dead. Our offices are destroyed, and the Chronicles are gone. What do we do? What will become of the Vanguard?"

"Gone?" Zachariah questioned. "The Chronicles are not gone. They are where they've always been, in the hearts of the Vanguard, a symbol that no mole or Horseman could ever steal." The Vanguard leader propped himself up against his pillow. "The ancient text, Nabugar's writings, is safe. I hid the pages between the bindings of a dozen boring volumes in the library."

"You clever Vanguard," Faye remarked.

"Not clever enough," Zachariah replied, tossing aside the blanket covering his paralyzed legs and directing Faye's attention to the wheel-chair in the corner.

"Zachariah, I—"

"I think it may soon be time for a changing of the guard," he interjected, covering his dead limbs with the blanket. "As for our offices and agents, we will do as we have done for thousands of years, rebuild the brick and mortar and recruit the flesh and blood."

Kenji Watanabe stepped into the hospital room, hands clasped behind his back.

"Did you get it?" Zachariah asked.

The bodyguard brought one hand forward. A brown paper bag swung back and forth in his grip. Kenji handed the parcel to the Vanguard leader.

"Thank goodness," Zachariah exclaimed, tearing into the paper.

Faye stepped up to Kenji, throwing her arms around him. "Thank you," she whispered, her lips close to his ear.

The Japanese netsuke master nodded.

"Finally some real food," Zachariah said, maneuvering the battered fish fillet into his mouth.

The fishy aroma assaulted Faye.

Zachariah looked up from his fish and chips to see Faye's pallid face. "Faye?"

Overcome with nausea, she raced into the bathroom and, kneeling on the tile, threw up.

Faye pulled toilet paper from the roll, wiped her mouth, and flushed it down.

"That makes it official," she whispered, touching her stomach.

"A gift, for your gift," she thought, sitting on the bathroom floor, remembering Paul's face and bright smile as he said, "You'll see."

She'd see her gift, hers and Ben's, in nine months. But a gift for her gift…Faye pondered what the ten-year-old boy had smiled so brightly about. Little did Faye realize that she carried a new keeper of light, the next Reliquary, nor could she fathom the trials her child would face in the years to come.

《《—》》

The scientist sat in the overstuffed chair in a lavish hotel suite. The décor was a blend of old-world charm and opulence, from the Italian frescoes and marble floors to the stained-glass windows and walnut-paneled library.

"Bring me more champagne," Pestilence shouted.

The Horseman relished the sway of his butler's gray morning coat and the click of his well-polished black lace-ups. The servant, wearing white gloves, handed the Horseman the crystal flute, bubbles rising like balloons from the stem.

The servant nodded.

"Oh, and one last thing," the scientist remarked to his servant, "I will have the duck for dinner."

"Very well, sir."

"Thank you, Seth," the Horseman said with a toothy grin.

Pestilence sipped his champagne and basked in the entertainment his clone, the perfect copy his brethren, provided.

"I don't have to rule the world," the mad scientist declared, staring into the bubbles in his glass. "Just my own little world."

Pestilence directed his gaze down to his bare feet. "Rub a little harder, darling," he instructed, staring down at his gothic Horseman facsimile. "That's perfect."

Stacks of comics and episodes of *Star Trek: The Original Series* and *The Twilight Zone* paved the way for Ken's vivid imagination. And while the Avengers, Captain Kirk, and Rod Serling were not ideal role models, his creative writing juices were flowing.

His love of science fiction and fantasy led to a career in the laboratory, where he conducted experiments and published results as a research scientist. After earning a master's degree in business, he racked up thousands of frequent-flyer miles as a marketing executive and did consulting for the biopharmaceutical industry. But amidst the business proposals and annual reports sat *War of the Oaks* and *Symphony of Ages*, among others, nuggets of inspiration and the fodder for fantasy adventures.

Ken lives in the Bay Area with his wife and two children. He enjoys attending sci-fi and fantasy conventions, often in costume, mingling with science fiction and fantasy fans and letting his geek flag fly.